THE REPINGTON CHRONICLES

COMPLETE SIX BOOK BOXED SET

KELLY ANNE BRUCE

COPYRIGHT

Copyright 2018, Kelly Anne Bruce
All rights reserved.
No part of this publication may be reproduced in any form,
electronic or mechanical, without written approval by the author,
except for short excerpts used in a book review.
All characters, places, events, businesses, or references to historical
facts are fictitious and products of the author's imagination. Any
references to actual people, places, or events are purely incidental.

http://www.KellyAnneBruce.com

KELLY ANNE BRUCE'S READERS GROUP

If you want to stay up to date on new releases and get notifications about sales and other fun stuff, join Kelly Anne's Readers Group. You might even get a freebie or two!

http://kellyannebruce.com/join-the-readers-group/

ABOUT THE REPINGTON CHRONICLES SERIES

The Repington family was close, though they did have their disagreements from time to time. Headed by the Duke of Castborough, the family had responsibilities, difficulties, and camaraderie.

The duke and his wife had six children. Headstrong and determined in their own ways, the children were similar but often vastly different. Though they struggled through troubles, they loved each other fiercely.

This series has six parts - one for each of the duke's children. Read about how each one grew to exceed the duke's hopes and how each one found true love.

A BROTHER'S DUTY

JAMES

CHAPTER ONE

James Repington pushed his chair back from the desk with a sigh.

"Where are you off to?"

He looked up to see Matthew leaning lazily at the library door. Matthew was one of his brothers, he had four of them.

"I was going to go round and check on the tenants," James replied as he stood up and pulled on his coat.

"You seem quite unhappy about the prospect," Matthew commented folding his arms over his chest.

James shrugged, as the second son it was not specifically his responsibility to check on the tenants. However, it had fallen to him as his elder brother, Philip was too busy spending the Season in London. Yes, gambling and going to parties with a number of other members of London's social elite seemed to be more important than running the estate. Kicking up larks and spending most of their days half sprung was what the Season was all about for much of the crowd that Philip chose to run with.

Matthew leaned against the doorway and shrugged. "Father usually visits the tenants, does he not?"

"Father is not back from London yet. He has been rather busy tending to Parliament business and it seems that has taken a bit longer than he had anticipated." James moved toward the door pausing to add, "I do not want the tenants to suffer because no one else is here to help them."

"Surely, they could wait a few more days," Matthew suggested.

"If everything is fine, yes. If there have been no problems since last month I would think so. I will not know unless I go check."

Matthew shook his head with a harsh laugh. "And this responsibility falls to you?"

"It is simply something that needs to be done. Since no one else is here to do it, then yes, I suppose it does fall to me." James pushed past him into the hall.

It truly was not his responsibility but with the absence of his father the Duke of Castborough and his older brother someone had to do something. As a member of the Repington family, he could see that the tenants were an important part of their entailed land and James would always step up and do what was needed for the betterment and success of the family.

James continued down the hall with Matthew close behind him. He got as far as the bottom of the stairs before Thomas rushed past them to open the front door.

"Your grace, so good to see you. I hope your journey from London was pleasant," Thomas said as he stepped out the door.

A moment later their father appeared in the doorway looking tired, but still his tall and formidable self. "The journey from London was bloody awful. It began to rain shortly after we left and only stopped in the last few minutes."

"Father, I thought you had been delayed by Parliament business," James said, stepping aside as his father turned down the hall toward the library.

"There were some delays but we finally got Wellington to be quiet long enough to take a vote." His father paused at the library door. "Where is your brother?"

"Which one? There are several of us." Matthew quipped from behind James.

"Philip. Where is he?"

James looked back at Matthew. "Philip?"

"Yes. I saw him at the house in London and told him he needed to return to Castborough immediately." Their father sat down in the chair that James had just vacated. "When did he arrive?"

"He has not arrived, Father. And we have received no word from London that he was on his way home," James said.

"What?" Father roared as he pushed back to his feet. "I told him in no uncertain terms that he was to return here."

"His failure to comply cannot come as much of a surprise to you," James remarked. "This is exactly how he operates."

His brother's irresponsible behaviour had long caused irritation for James. It had started to seem like a cruel joke that his lazy brother was the first son, the heir to the family title. Philip had spent much of his time in London gambling and drinking, leaving James to help their father balance his work with Parliament and to deal with business at their estate in Castborough. James usually handled most of Philips's responsibilities.

"No, I suppose not." Father gave James a steely-eyed look before sitting down again. "Since you seem to know your brother so well, you will go to London to retrieve him."

James scowled. "Why am I to go? If he did not listen to you, he surely will not listen to me."

Father waved his arm in the air dismissing James' complaints before picking up a quill. "You will leave for London in the morning. When you find your brother let him know that he is expected here within a week's time."

Matthew snorted from the doorway. "He will agree to it and then stay in London anyway like he has always done. And you are giving him a week? Mighty generous, I say."

"Yes, a week. And this time he will do as he's told." Their father spoke with such certainty in his voice that James turned back to the desk.

"Why do you think this time will be any different?"

Father held up a folded paper. "Because of this. If Philip has not returned by the date on that note his allowance and all other financial support will be cut off."

Matthew's eyes widened. "Yes, well, that does make a difference. I suppose I would turn up, too, if conditions such as that were set for me."

James was not sure if that made the situation any better as he would still be traveling to London. Although the thought of Philip losing his allowance did make it a little easier on James. He reached out to take the letter from his father. "I will do my best to ensure my brother's return."

Father held the note a moment longer locking eyes with James. "See that you do."

CHAPTER TWO

The carriage slowed and then stopped when James looked out he saw that he had arrived at Repington House, the family residence in London. For the last hour, James had grumbled to himself about having to go after his brother. Father had been in London only the day before having spoken to Philip a week before. Philip had chosen to ignore their father's wishes.

Back in Surrey, the idea of cutting off his allowance had seemed like the best idea but James had begun to think that it would not be enough. In James' mind, Philip had no intention of ever being responsible not when he continually got away with being a gadabout.

"Sir?" The door to the carriage had opened and the footman was standing there looking at him.

"Yes," James said quickly moving to climb out of the carriage. "Thank you."

The front door opened as James approached.

"Good afternoon, sir," the white-haired servant said as he approached. "Welcome to London."

"Thank you, Fletcher." James entered the house stopping at the bottom of the stairs. "Is Philip home?"

"No, sir," Fletcher answered his eyebrows furrowing. "Master Philip has not been here in several days."

"No? You have not seen him in days?" James asked. "Are you aware of where he has gone?"

Fletcher looked circumspect. "He did not say when he left but the footman said that he drove him into Mayfair several days ago."

"Mayfair?" James thought for a moment and then asked, "To Fallbrooke Hall perhaps?"

"Perhaps, sir," Fletcher said a sly smile crossing his face briefly.

Christopher Boswell was the heir to the Marquess of Trisdale. He was known for living extravagantly, gambling, and drinking until all hours of the night. Lord Fallbrooke was too ripe and ready by half and it did not bode well for James to hear that Philip was staying with the young heir. Philip needed no such partner in crime.

An hour later, James was walking up the front steps of Fallbrooke Hall, one of the largest and most elaborate residences in Mayfair. After knocking on the door, James wondered if he should have sent a messenger over to see if Philip was even in keeping here. For all he knew, his brother and Lord Fallbrooke might have hied off to a house party in Kent.

"Good afternoon," a dark-haired man answered the door. "May I help you, sir?"

"Yes, thank you. I am James Repington. From what I understand, my brother is a guest of Lord Fallbrooke. Is Lord Fallbrooke in residence today?"

The servant stepped back. "Yes, sir. Follow me."

He was led to a drawing room and asked to wait. James was not surprised to see that the house was decorated opulently with beautiful fabrics and elegant furniture.

More than ten minutes later James was still waiting and after hearing voices upstairs he moved into the hallway. He was rewarded a moment later to see his older brother as he rushed along the upstairs hallway pulling on his jacket hastily as he moved toward the stairs.

"Going somewhere, are we?" James asked leaning calmly against the ornately carved banister.

Philip froze at the top of the stairs and suddenly looked down with feigned surprise. "James? What are you doing here?"

"I am here to speak with you, of course. I trust you are now available to talk," James told him trying not to smile. He was quite enjoying seeing his brother looking so uncomfortable.

Philip looked around clearly hoping for some sort of escape, finding none readily available he nodded at James looking rather resigned. "Yes, of course. We can go into the drawing room."

James waited at the bottom of the stairs as Philip slowly walked down to join him. It had become quite clear that sending a messenger first would have been a horrible idea. Philip would surely have hopped into a carriage and headed to the next party. Philip led his younger brother into the drawing room before collapsing into a large upholstered chair.

There was a long stretch of silence as James waited patiently knowing that it would further upset his brother.

It did not take long before Philip sighed and turned to James. "Why are you here, dear brother?"

"Do I need a reason to visit London and my elder brother?" James asked with a raised eyebrow.

Philip snorted. "Most definitely. You have not come to London for pleasure all Season. So, do tell. Why are you here?"

James shifted in his seat before saying, "To bring you back to Surrey, of course."

"No, that will not be possible." Philip stood up as he pulled down the sleeves on his high quality jacket. "I am quite happy to spend the rest of the Season here in London."

"Of course, you are." James stood up blocking Philip's path to the door.

"Well, thank you for paying me a visit while you are in London... It was a pleasure to see you, indeed—"

"You should know that Father sent me." James' words hung in the air between them.

Philip gave him a flat smile. "Give him my best."

Trying not to show his annoyance with his lazy brother, James simply said, "Father does not want your best regards. He is awaiting your arrival in Surrey. Immediately."

"Yes," Philip said with a laugh. "I am sure he is."

"What are your plans?"

"My plans? The theater and then drinks and cards at White's." Philip paused looking over at James. "You should come out with us. Perhaps a night out would be good for you."

"Oh, I do not think so."

"Or you could come with us to the house party at the Highsmith's."

"I appreciate the offer," James said straightening his coat. "I am afraid that we will need to get back to Surrey before that."

Philip let out a bark of laughter. "You really think I am going to go back to Surrey with you?"

"The decision is quite up to you, but if I were you I would do as Father asks," James advised.

"Why?" Philip asked his voice mocking. "Father has you to do his bidding. He does not need me there as well."

"If that is how you feel then I will return to Surrey by myself," James turned toward the door.

"Yes, you do that," Philip told him, the smugness evident in his voice.

James suddenly remembered the paper from their father. "I am quite sure that Father will be disappointed, but I imagine it will be easier to take when he speaks to his solicitor. His accounts will be much fuller going forward."

"His accounts? What are you talking about?" Philip asked him with a frown.

"Oh? Did I not mention that part?" James took some time to look like he was thinking about it. "No, it seems I did not."

Philip looked as though he was beginning to understand that something else was going on.

James handed Philip the paper. "According to Father, if you fail to return with me to Surrey your monthly allowance will be stopped."

"What?" Philip nearly shouted. "Please tell me this is some sort of trick."

"I am afraid it is no trick." James nodded at the still folded paper in his brother's hand. "It's all right there. Father was quite clear about his intentions."

James walked out into the hall. "As you said, I will be sure to give Father your best regards, Philip."

Philip swore and there was a loud thud that James assumed was the chair being knocked over. "James! Wait!"

"Yes? Did you have something to add?"

Philip let out a bemoaned sigh. "When do we leave for Surrey?"

CHAPTER THREE

"How much longer is this going to take?" Philip asked.

James tilted his head. "How long has it been since you have been at Castborough?"

They had been in the carriage for less than an hour and Philip had been mostly silent. He was pouting, but trying to hide it most of the time.

"I was home at Christmas." Philip slouched lazily in the corner of his seat. "I came to London after the new year."

"It has not been that long so you should remember the time it takes to travel from London to Surrey." His demeanor was calm but James could hardly stand being in the same carriage as his pompous, selfish brother.

"True, although last time it had been in the snow and we had to stop overnight to wait out the storm," Philip reminded him.

James had forgotten about the snowstorm at the beginning of the year. It had reminded James of a Christmas a long time ago when they were much younger. It had snowed so hard that the road into Castborough had been blocked.

The older siblings had spent Christmas playing games in the great hall. James and Philip had been scolded by both their father and their mother when Matthew, who was barely three years old at the time, had gotten closed up in a pantry. James had been the one to find him asleep in a cupboard full of tablecloths but he had gotten in trouble all the same.

Philip had tried to take the blame but they both had gotten punished. Later that night Matthew had brought them biscuits that he wrapped in a napkin after dinner. They had all been much closer then and James missed the brother who had tried to protect him.

Philip had been happy and honest, someone that James could rely on for help and advice. Philip had gone to Cambridge a year before James was to go off to school. When he came home at the end of the year he had changed.

Philip had no interest in doing anything in or around Castborough, he only wanted to visit his friends in Kent. James had written it off as a reaction to being gone for so long, thinking that he would be back to normal soon. Philip was hardly around and his behaviour had only gotten worse when he was around.

James had attempted to talk to him but Philip had brushed him off. He had been hurt at first and then angry. After that, James had left Philip to his own devices. The distance between them only grew with time.

"This is such a boring waste of my time. I could be doing so many other things," Philip whined.

"Oh? Did you have plans this afternoon?" James asked before adding, "It looked as though you were in bed and planning to sleep a few more hours."

Philip raked a hand through his blond hair, a smile cracking his face. "Well, we did have a late night. I think the dawn was breaking over the horizon as we returned to Fallbrooke Hall. I am not certain, mind you, we were both rather jug bitten by that point."

"Well, at least, you know your way back to Fallbrooke," James muttered as he gazed at the countryside going by his window. He turned to face Philip. "I can certainly see how going back to Castborough would interfere with your important plans. Am I wrong to assume your plans consisted of sleeping most of the day?"

"No, you would not be wrong," Philip answered. "And you can save your disdain. At least, I am doing what I want to do rather than acting as Father's errand boy."

James stiffened, although he should not have been surprised to hear his brother's insults. "Father would not have needed me to go to London if you were not so irresponsible and completely selfish."

"Selfish?" Philip snorted. "Well, that's rich."

"Yes, you are selfish. Mother expected you home and has had the staff waiting for you to arrive. She had planned a special celebratory dinner for you. Although I'm sure the food has been put to other meals by now." James leaned back in his seat "Mother was quite disappointed."

Philip had the grace to look at least a little chagrined. "Well, I am sorry for that, I..."

James held up a hand. "Oh, save it. I care not for your excuses. I suggest you get some sleep. I am sure that father will have much to discuss with you when we arrive. You will need to be alert for that."

James opened a book on his lap hoping that would signal the end of the conversation and Philip would follow his advice. Pretending to read would give him a chance to stew with his own thoughts. Honestly, his own anger.

James had not been lying when he said that he did not care about Philip's excuses. He had had more than enough of his brother's mocking tone and lack of concern over the expectations of their mother and father. For as long as James could remember, he had been told that Philip was important because he was the heir. That Philip was to be the next Duke of Castborough and that he was destined for greatness.

He had believed it when he was younger, but now James knew different. Philip was destined only to find the bottom of the whiskey bottle or a spot at the gambling table. Anything good that happened would be purely an accident.

The weather was favorable so it was not too much longer before the carriage pulled up and stopped in front of the large stone stately home that was Castborough Abbey. James did not bother waking his brother, he simply gathered his coat and alighted from the carriage. He nodded to Thomas as he entered the house and went directly to the library. He was surprised to find it empty and moved back to the hall. He had just made it back to the entry when Philip walked through the door.

"Philip, my boy! Welcome home!" Their father's booming voice filled the room.

"Father," Philip beamed at the older man. "It is good to be home. I apologize for any confusion regarding when you expected me."

Father clapped Philip on the shoulder. "Not at all, not at all." He gestured down the hall toward the library. "Come along, come along. Let us all have a chat. We have a need to catch up on a few family matters."

James gritted his teeth as he followed, annoyed at the picture that was being portrayed in front of him. It was annoying and insulting to see his father welcoming Philip home so profusely. It was clear that Philip was enjoying the enthusiastic response from their father.

James chose to stand near the window that overlooked the garden in hope that the peaceful view would keep him calm. Philip sank unceremoniously into one of the large upholstered chairs that sat in front of their father's desk.

"I am so glad to hear that it has not inconvenienced you." Philip looked at his father earnestly. "I am most happy to stay through the end of the week before I make my return to London. If you need me to do so, that is. Otherwise, I—"

"I am most glad to hear that you are agreeable to staying here but I am afraid that you will not be returning to London for some time."

Philip let out a sigh. "Father, I do not see why—"

"Be quiet," Father barked. "What you want or can see is no longer my concern. You lost any say in the matter when you failed to return home as I asked when we spoke in London over a week ago. I am no longer asking."

Philip opened his mouth to speak again but Father was already talking again. He gestured towards James. "Why can you not be more like your brother? He is responsible and reliable. Any time I ask him to do something I know he will do it without question or quarrel."

James was pleased to hear his father say such nice things about him but knew it would cause more problems for them all. Philip was already annoyed that he had been pulled away from London, their father's comments would only serve to further Philip's displeasure. He was likely to take that displeasure out on James.

"Father, I am not sure what we are discussing here."

"It's time that you settled down, it is past time for you to find a wife."

Philip looked around the room in a mocking manner. "And you expect me to find one here, rather than London?" He leaned back in his chair with a chuckle, shaking his head.

"Yes," Father said with a stern voice. "You will be staying right here. A house party will be held one week hence. The Earl of South-wick will be in attendance with his only daughter. It would be a good time to look toward settling down."

"A house party?" Philip asked, before smiling at his father and saying, "Sounds simply delightful. I look forward to meeting the earl's daughter. Perhaps she will be open to courting a rogue."

The duke did not laugh at his eldest son's joke nor did he give in to his clear distaste about attending a country house party.

James watched his brother's face from his spot near the window. In spite of his jokes and smirks, Philip seemed to want to please their father. He could see through Philip's attempts to mollify their father and it seemed abundantly clear to James that he would need to keep a close eye on his brother.

CHAPTER FOUR

"Elizabeth!"

Elizabeth left her room stopping at the banister to look over to the floor before. Her father stood in the hallway looking up at her.

"Yes, Father?"

He gave her a small smile. "Please come down to the library so that I can speak with you."

"Yes, of course." Elizabeth wondered what her father could want as she calmly moved down the stairs. They had been in London for over a month for her to attend the fanciest balls and parties of the Season. Her father was often busy with his work with Parliament, leaving her Aunt Judith to take care of Elizabeth.

Elizabeth stepped into the library standing behind one of the high-back chairs. "Yes, Father?"

Her father looked up from his desk, his face confused for a moment. "Oh, yes. Elizabeth, I wanted to let you know that we have been invited to a house party in Surrey. We shall be leaving in three days' time."

Of all the things her father could have discussed with her, a house party was not what she expected. "That sounds most interesting. I have found London to be quite tiresome this Season."

Her father was bent over the desk once more. "Yes, it will be good for you, I believe. Miriam will take care of getting you packed and ready to go."

Elizabeth smiled. "Miriam? You mean Marianne, of course."

"What?" He asked looking up. Her father blinked and then said, "Yes, Marianne, is that not what I said? She will take care of everything."

Elizabeth nodded and then left the room quite certain that her father would not notice that she had even left. She continued on to the drawing room as it was almost time for tea. She had barely sat down when Mrs Gibbs came in with a tray with tea and biscuits.

"Good afternoon, Lady Elizabeth," Mrs Gibbs said setting the tray on the small table next to the settee.

"Good afternoon. Those biscuits smell delicious."

Mrs Gibbs smiled. "They just came out of the oven."

"Please tell Annie that I am most grateful that she is such a wonder in the kitchen," Elizabeth said taking a biscuit from the plate.

"I will let her know," Mrs Gibbs smiled and then pointed at the tray. "Make sure to share those, though."

"Share?" Elizabeth looked up at the older woman, her eyebrows furrowed. "With whom?"

"With me!"

Elizabeth looked up to see her cousin and closest friend, Leticia Stewart standing in the drawing room doorway. "Lettie! I did not think I would see you for another few weeks."

"I did not think so either. Joseph was called away unexpectedly and he thought it best if I came back here." Lettie sat down on the settee next to Elizabeth. "He shall meet us at the house party at the Duke of Castborough's in Surrey."

"The Duke of Castborough?" Elizabeth asked.

"Has your father not mentioned it?" Lettie asked as she picked up a biscuit.

"No, he has," Elizabeth said slowly. "He only mentioned that it was a house party not that it was being held by the Duke of Castborough."

Lettie tilted her head as she looked at Elizabeth. "Is that a concern for you?"

Elizabeth looked over to make sure that Mrs Gibbs had closed the drawing room door behind her when she left. Then she put her hand over her mouth and raised her eyebrows. When she lowered her hand, her voice came out in a whisper.

"Not two days ago I overheard my father speaking with someone about Philip Repington, who just happens to be the heir to the Duke of Castborough. I did not hear the entire conversation but from what I gathered my father is in favor of a match between Philip Repington and myself."

"How exciting. Philip will be the duke one day and that means that you will be a duchess." Lettie said clapping her hands in excitement.

"I believe he is currently the Marquess of Holgrave. Perhaps I should meet him before I start planning the wedding, though." Elizabeth bit her bottom lip and tilted her head to the side.

"You do not seem all that pleased," Lettie remarked.

Elizabeth sighed and bit her lip again. "I have not met him but I have heard much about him. It seems that the viscount is known for his gambling and drinking. Behaviour such as that is not the least bit appealing to me."

"Aren't they all, though?"

"I suppose…" Elizabeth agreed. She picked up her teacup and turned to her friend. "Yes, I suppose it would be wise to actually meet the man before I assume that he is shockingly loose in the haft."

Lettie giggled. "Yes, I agree."

CHAPTER FIVE

"There you are!" James turned to see his sister coming into the garden. "I did not realize that you were looking for me, Henrietta."

Henrietta shook her head, her blonde curls bouncing. "Oh, it was not I that was looking for you. Mother was looking for you earlier. She said that she had looked all over the house but you were nowhere to be found."

James squinted back at the house. "Yes, well, I escaped the chaos early. I had planned on having my tea in the drawing room this morning but there was a battalion of servants in there moving furniture and making quite the commotion."

Henrietta nodded. "Mother has planned a large dinner for Philip tonight. Most of the guests will have arrived by either this afternoon or early evening."

"For Philip? Of course," James grumbled under his breath. It should not have been a surprise to him that his family was going to such lengths for Philip, but he was irritated all the same.

"Oh, James, you know how disappointed Mother was when Philip did not come home from London. She has been planning a special dinner for him for weeks."

"Yes, I do know how disappointed she was."

It made James even more vexed that their mother was so eager to see Philip. It seemed no matter his behaviour his older brother would still be indulged and fawned over. Last week, James had comforted his mother as she was near tears that Philip had not come home to Castborough since January. He should have known then that Philip would get an enthusiastic welcome.

James had offered to write to his father to let him know that Mother has been upset. He had posed the idea as being concerned about Philip's safety but his mother had refused. She claimed that she did not want to worry Father during his important time with Parliament. James had suspected it had more to do with coddling Philip and now he was sure.

Before his anger spiraled out of control James turned to Henrietta and smiled but he guessed it looked more like a grimace.

"Please tell Mother that I am on my way to the stables and that I will come back to the house within the hour."

Henrietta stared at him for a few seconds before saying, "I will, dear brother. I will leave you alone now to brood in silence."

James' scowl cracked enough for him to grin briefly. "Well, I thank you for that, you are quite considerate."

"I do understand your annoyance, but I dislike seeing you so affected by it," Henrietta looked up at him concern in her eyes.

"Do not worry about me. Philip will be, well, Philip. He always is and there is no escaping that. And I will be fine, as always."

Henrietta laughed. "You are so serious. Please promise me that you will endeavour to enjoy yourself during the house party.

James found himself smiling at Henrietta, she was his youngest sibling and only sister, and he had always found it hard to say no to her.

"I will do my best." He nodded back to the house. "Now go tell Mother before she tears the house apart looking for me."

Henrietta laughed and began to move away, calling back over her shoulder, "If guests were not expected within the hour she would have already."

Talking to Henrietta had calmed him down some, but only just. He had gone from angry to simply annoyed, although it was not that simple. His eldest brother was a lazy gadabout, time and time again he had acted irresponsibly and disappointed nearly everyone in the family and yet he was continually rewarded for his poor behaviour.

The worst part was that one day Philip would become the Duke of Castborough, their family and tenants would look to him for guidance and assistance. James could honestly say that he did not trust that Philip would ever be someone that any of them could rely on. Most of those who would need him, would not realize they could not trust him until it was too late. That part was a considerable concern for James.

He pushed through the gate into the stable. There on the fence was Philip's saddle all cleaned and shiny just waiting for him to deign to come down there. Without thinking, James pushed it off the fence so that it would land on the ground in the dirt and hay that covered the ground in the stall. He only wished it had been mud instead of dirt and hay.

He had a sudden thought of knocking Philip to the ground, too. It was everything he could do to not stomp on the saddle as he thought about the chance to get back at his brother for his attitude.

Voices coming closer to the stable broke James out of his thoughts. He turned quickly and walked out the far gate not wanting to be seen next to the fallen saddle. He quickly walked over to the fence and leaned against it, his elbows braced at the top as he stared across at the field of mares and new foals.

It was mid-morning and the foals were beginning to skip a little beside the mares, their spindly legs kicking out as they picked up speed. It did not take too long before James could feel the pent-up anger and frustration begin to drain from him. The carefree scene in front of him had given him a new perspective—at least until his next encounter with his brother.

After a bit James decided that it was time to go back to the house and face what was sure to be a trying afternoon and evening.

For his mother, he would put on a happy façade, she deserved to enjoy this one evening before Philip caused more problems. He was almost to the house when he heard a carriage pulling up to the front of the house. James paused at the gate that led back into the garden.

He already knew that several guests were expected to arrive in the morning and afternoon, but something made James continue walking to the front of the house.

Voices reached him from around the corner of the house letting him know that there were several guests arriving. He came around the corner in time to see a young lady alight from the carriage. She turned back toward the carriage laughing at something presumably said by another passenger.

James caught sight of her and nearly lost his breath. She was beautiful, with chestnut brown hair that was shining in the late morning sun. Her smile lit up her face and James fought the urge to approach her. He knew, though, that he would need to go back into the house and wait for an opportunity for an introduction.

Feeling much better about the house party James went back towards the garden to return to the house. Suddenly, it seemed that the special dinner was going to be much more interesting than he had expected.

CHAPTER SIX

"Oh, how lovely," Lettie was standing by the large window. Elizabeth crossed the room to stand with her friend. The window looked over an expansive and beautifully kept garden. "I had no idea. I had not gotten the chance to look out the window as we came through the countryside."

They had only arrived at Castborough a few hours before and Aunt Judith had sent both Elizabeth and Lettie to their rooms to get settled and freshen up.

Down below they could see several guests in the garden, some sitting on stone benches while others wandered and talked as they looked at the flowers and hedges. Elizabeth watched for a moment wishing she could go join them.

"It is quite lovely."

"Perhaps we could go down to the garden for a nice stroll," Lettie suggested.

"I would like that very much but Aunt Judith informed me that she was coming up to talk to me."

"Mother?" Lettie frowned. "What does she want to talk to you about?"

"I suspect she wants to talk to me about the house party. Or more likely regarding the conversation I had overheard concerning Lord Holgrave." Lettie looked confused and Elizabeth added, "The Duke of Castborough's son, Philip."

"You really think your father brought you here to meet the duke's son?" Lettie seemed torn between excitement and concern for Elizabeth.

"Yes, I do," Elizabeth answered with a sigh. It was a difficult situation for her. As the daughter of the Earl of Southwick she has always known she would have to marry well. She would also admit that marrying a gentleman of good standing was important to her as well, but she had also hoped to find love. "I do believe that Father has decided I should marry Lord Holgrave."

"Decided?" Lettie looked dumbfounded. "You have not even met the man. How on Earth are you supposed to marry him? And would he decide this alone? Without consulting either the man or his father first?"

The same thought had crossed Elizabeth's mind as well. It was disconcerting, to say the least, that her father was planning for her to spend the rest of her life with a man she had never met. For Lettie's sake, Elizabeth put on a brave face and said, "I suppose we will simply have to see how things happen. It is entirely possible that I will meet Lord Holgrave and I will be pleasantly surprised. It's also possible that there has been an alliance I am unaware of. Possibly the whole thing will be in my best interest."

Lettie was wide-eyed. "And what if you are not pleasantly surprised? What if it all turns out to be a big mess?"

Elizabeth took a moment to smooth her skirts but finally said, "I am quite confident that I could go to Father with my concerns if I have any. If I were to tell him that I was completely against the marriage and felt that I would be miserable with Lord Holgrave, I believe he would allow me to decline Lord Holgrave's suit."

"In the meantime, though, you must entertain Lord Holgrave's attentions." Lettie sat down on the edge of the bed.

"It is my third Season, after all, I cannot be too choosy about a husband at this point."

Her comment sounded coy but there was more than an ounce of truth to it. In previous Seasons, she had been quite picksome regarding her suitors. They had not been awful—well, not most of them at least. It was just that none of them had caught her eye or made her feel anything more than appreciative of their attentions.

She wanted more than to just be told that she was beautiful or dressed beautifully. Elizabeth longed to be appreciated and needed, and not just for her father's influence. She wanted to be loved and cherished.

Lettie let out a dramatic groan. "I do not care what Season this is. I am much more concerned with your happiness. I care not for what the gossips say."

Just then there was a sharp rap on the door and a moment later a woman came into the room, her dark hair shot with gray.

"Good afternoon, Aunt Judith," Elizabeth said quietly and sat down primly in one of the chairs by the window.

Aunt Judith smiled softly and looked over to her daughter. "Lettie, I think you should go rest in your room for a little while. Your brother should be arriving sometime this afternoon and I know he will be happy to see you. I would hate for you to be too overly tired to see him."

Lettie shook her head. "Mother, I think..."

"Leticia, please do as I ask," her voice brooked no argument.

"Yes, Mother," Lettie said looking taken aback and a little hurt but she soon left the room closing the door softly behind her.

Aunt Judith turned to Elizabeth. "Elizabeth, dear, how are you feeling after our long journey from London?"

"Oh, perfectly fine. Thank you."

"I just wanted to talk to you about the reason we are at this house party," Aunt Judith began.

"Oh, I am perfectly aware of why we are here." Elizabeth glanced out the window. "Father is set to have me marry Lord Holgrave."

Aunt Judith looked surprised but did not deny what Elizabeth had said. She was silent for a moment more and then said, "Your father would like you to meet Lord Holgrave and see if you think you two would make a favorable match."

Elizabeth must have looked skeptical because Aunt Judith patted her hand. "Lord Southwick is one of your father's oldest friends and he believes that you and Lord Holgrave would get on well."

She appreciated her aunt's comfort but Elizabeth was still faced with the fact that if she did not approve of Lord Holgrave she could end up disappointing her father. Even more, she clearly did not want to embarrass her father or insult one of his oldest friends.

Elizabeth let out a long breath and simply nodded, saying, "I will endeavour to make the best decision for all."

CHAPTER SEVEN

Elizabeth looked down at the garden, she could hear the low murmur of voices and the occasional ripple of laughter. She had looked forward to the house party when her father had suggested it back in London. Now there was the added burden of meeting Lord Holgrave that made it more complicated and much less enjoyable.

"Is she gone?" A voice asked quietly.

Startled from her thoughts Elizabeth looked around, only to see Lettie peeking around the door.

"Yes," Elizabeth chuckled. "Come in."

"So have they married you off yet?"

Elizabeth shook her head no and smiled. "No, I am just to meet him. No one is pushing to post the Banns quite yet. At least that's what your mother said."

"Well," Lettie said with a relieved laugh. "Thank Heaven above for that."

"Shall we go down to the garden now?" Elizabeth asked.

They walked down the hall towards the stairs. The Castborough house was beautifully furnished without flaunting what Elizabeth knew must be immense wealth.

To reach the garden they needed to travel through the drawing room. At the end of the hall, doors were held open revealing the largest drawing room Elizabeth had ever seen. The wide doorway sat across from the foot of a beautifully ornate curving staircase.

Lettie was excited and happily led the way through the drawing room. There were several settees and a few small tables with chairs where small groups of people were sitting, talking quietly. There were several glass paned doors that opened to the garden. They walked out onto a stone path that bordered a well-manicured lawn with stone pathways on either side. Tall hedges enclosed the outer edges of the garden while shorter hedges were placed along some of the pathways serving to separate some smaller areas of the garden beyond the expansive lawn.

"How about we go this way?" Lettie pointed toward a path closest to them. "We can promenade around the lawn and see who has arrived. Certainly we will find someone to talk to."

"That sounds perfectly reasonable," Elizabeth answered falling into step beside her.

A few minutes later they were about to cross the lawn after saying hello to several people when Elizabeth heard someone calling her name.

"Elizabeth!" A red-haired girl came rushing towards them. "I did not know that you would be here."

"Beatrice, hello." Beatrice was a nice but often times loud girl that Elizabeth had known for several years. "It was quite a last-minute decision. I only learned of the house party from my father a few days ago."

"I am so glad you are here. We will have to catch up." Beatrice said then added, "I need to get back into the house now, though. My mother will be looking for me before too long."

Elizabeth nodded. "Of course, I will—" She tried to respond but Beatrice had rushed off before she could get the words all out.

Lettie laughed as she shook her head. "It is a wonder that we do not get dizzy when Beatrice is around. She always seems to be moving so fast."

"That, she is," Elizabeth agreed. She thought for a moment and then added. "Everyone loves her, though, and she has always been such a great friend."

"Oh yes, it is amazing how lovely Beatrice is considering that her mother seems somewhat cold, if I may comment on that."

Elizabeth could not help but grimace. "It is certainly not my place to judge, but on more than one occasion I have seen Lady Taltham admonish Beatrice for being too boisterous and unladylike. I believe she is a bit wary of her mother, but that may be an overstatement on my part."

Lettie turned to watched Beatrice go from one group to another greeting each person with a warm smile and a few words of conversation.

Beatrice had almost reached the house when a blonde man strode into the garden. He stopped in front of Beatrice and gave her a dazzling smile when she greeted him with her usual enthusiasm. The man said something next that made Beatrice swat at him with her fan. He ducked comically and then laughed along with Beatrice.

"Who is that?" Elizabeth heard herself ask quietly.

"I do not recognize him. He has not been to any ball or party I have been to this Season." Lettie looked back at Elizabeth and her eyes widened. "Perhaps I should ask some questions and see what I can find out."

Elizabeth shook her head, more to shake the tingly feeling that has started when she saw the man first enter the garden. His hair was nearly golden in the late spring sun in the dark blue jacket just made it seem even more so. His shoulders were broad while his waist was trim, leading her to believe that he was an active man not just a fop who blazed his days away. She automatically thought perhaps he was a horseman or one of the few that still fenced for sports. Either way, she was quite grateful to have an opportunity to look at such a handsome man.

Unable to keep her eyes off him Elizabeth watched him leave Beatrice and then cross the garden to speak with a group of people near one of the hedges across from where she and Lettie stood. Out of the corner of her eyes, she saw Lettie glance back and forth between the man and Elizabeth.

Elizabeth was dying to know the man's name and soon after got her question answered.

"Repington!" someone called out from the gate that presumably led to the stables.

Repington called back, "Lambert, are you ready to see the new horses?"

Lambert, the man at the gate waved him over. "More than ready, I have been waiting for you."

Elizabeth suddenly felt like she knew how Lambert felt. Never had a man affected her so and he had only walked across the garden to greet some people. She had not even been one of them.

"Repington?" Lettie whispered over her shoulder. "That must be the duke's son. It has to be!"

Elizabeth slowly turned to face her friend. "That is the man my father wants to introduce me to?"

Lettie smiled. "I think so."

"Perhaps this will be more enjoyable than I had originally thought," Elizabeth said watching the golden-haired man disappear out the gate.

CHAPTER EIGHT

"Which dress will you wear?"

Elizabeth turned from the wardrobe to look at Lettie. She was not sure how long she had been standing there. Her mind had been on the man in the garden. Presumably, Philip Repington, the Marquess of Holgrave and the eldest son of the Duke of Castborough. Possibly her future husband.

There was something about him that appealed to her. She had never felt like this before. This was her third Season and she had met so many men in that time at various balls and parties. Many of them were quite good looking and very charming, yet, not one of them had caught her eye quite like Philip Repington. Feeling ridiculous she had tried telling herself that she had not met him yet. Elizabeth knew that she must not get ahead of herself.

"Elizabeth? Are you well?"

Elizabeth realized she still had not replied to Lettie's question.

"Oh, yes." Elizabeth reached into the wardrobe to select a light-yellow dress. She turned back to Lettie with the dress in her hand. "I think I will wear this one."

"That is one of my favorites. Lord Holgrave will surely appreciate your choice."

Elizabeth shrugged trying to act nonchalant. She held the dress up in front of her and looked in the mirror. "I do not know if Lord Holgrave will appreciate it or not. Having never met him before I have no idea of what he would or would not appreciate. Nor do I care, really."

"Oh stop," Lettie said sounding a little exasperated. "I saw you in the garden this afternoon. You seemed quite curious about him then. Or am I completely wrong?"

Elizabeth let out a long sigh. "No, you are not wrong. I have to admit that I am somewhat surprised by him."

"How do you mean?" Lettie said down at the vanity began pulling pins from her hair.

"I have heard many things about Lord Holgrave so while I expected him to be well acquainted with most of the guests here, I was surprised that he seemed so warm and welcoming. I honestly had expected him to be more sardonic and lazy. The fact he was greeting guests at all was a surprise."

Lettie frowned. "I have to agree with you. I would have thought the same. I have heard that Lord Holgrave is quite wild at times."

"A rake. Or possibly a rogue." Elizabeth suggested. "What is the difference between the two, anyway?"

Lettie smiled. "I am not sure. I would say they are more than similar. I do not think Lord Holgrave qualifies as a rake or a rogue, but very nearly from what Joseph has said."

"Now I am to trust your brother's assessment of Lord Holgrave's behaviour?" Elizabeth teased.

"Why, of course," Lettie said with mock seriousness. "Joseph is a model of good behaviour, of course."

"Oh, indeed," Elizabeth got out before they both began to laugh. "Perhaps we should make our own determination."

Lettie's face grew serious. "Joseph has changed much since that summer he pushed you into the stream."

"I know," Elizabeth reassured her friend. "I do trust Joseph's judgment, although I hope he is wrong about Lord Holgrave."

"As do I," Lettie agreed.

The two friends began to get ready for dinner. An hour later, Elizabeth and Lettie were following Aunt Judith down the stairs.

"Your father has been quite adamant about you meeting Lord Holgrave." Aunt Judith said spotting Elizabeth's father at the foot of the stairs. "And I must tell you he is counting on your meeting going well. Very well, in fact."

Elizabeth smiled and nodded. "I am hoping it goes well, too."

Her father smiled at her as she reached the bottom of the stairs.

"You look beautiful, just like your mother." Only his voice showed the heavy emotion he was clearly feeling.

She nodded and swallowed trying to keep herself calm. Her mother had died when Elizabeth was young and her father rarely spoke of her, he had been so affected by the loss.

Not wanting to be introduced to the Duke of Castborough and Lord Holgrave with tears in her eyes, Elizabeth blew out a breath and gathered herself.

"We should go thank our hosts," her father finally said.

"This is it," Lettie whispered from behind her.

When they entered the drawing room the Duke of Castborough was standing with Lord Holgrave near the windows to the garden. Her father paused in the doorway and the duke nodded at her father and then moved across the room. At first, Elizabeth thought he was moving to meet them but he stopped next to another blonde man. They exchanged a few words before turning to smile at them.

"Lord Southwick, I am so glad you could make it," The duke said in a loud voice.

"Thank you so much for inviting us." Father turned to the others. "Let me introduce Lady Judith Stewart and her daughter, Leticia."

"Your grace," Aunt Judith said as she dropped to a curtsey. Leticia followed her mother's lead.

"Lady Judith, Leticia, welcome to Castborough."

"Thank you, your grace." Lettie smiled.

"If you will excuse us, I see that the Duchess of Castborough has arrived and we must greet her," Aunt Judith said.

"Yes, of course," the duke replied.

Elizabeth's father waited a moment and raised his chin with a smile of pride. "And this is my daughter, Lady Elizabeth Comerford."

"Lady Elizabeth, it is a joy to meet you." The Duke of Castborough stepped aside. "Allow me to introduce you to my eldest son, Philip Repington, the Marquess of Holgrave."

The duke's son gave her a lazy smile. This was Philip? Elizabeth hoped her smile had not faltered but she was slightly confused.

"It is a pleasure to meet you, Lord Holgrave," Elizabeth found herself saying.

"Good evening, Lady Elizabeth." His gaze traveled down her dress and then back up to her face again. He raised an eyebrow and quickly covered a smirk. "I hope to speak with you more during dinner."

This was not the man from the garden although there were many similarities between he and the man she had seen earlier. Lord Holgrave was exactly what she had expected upon her arrival. He was good-looking in a foppish, dandy sort of way, with an almost mocking and certainly cynical demeanor.

Knowing that her father was in favor of their match Elizabeth simply smiled and said, "Thank you. I look forward to it."

It seemed as though the introductions were finished and Elizabeth was hoping to go find Lettie when to her complete dismay the man from the garden walked up to them.

"Lord Southwick, this is my son, Lord James Repington." The duke smiled broadly. "James, this is Lord Southwick and his daughter, Lady Elizabeth."

"Welcome to Castborough," James said to Lord Southwick. His eyes landed on Elizabeth before moving on to Philip and then back to Elizabeth. A look of disappointment plain on his face. "I hope you enjoy your stay. If you will excuse me I have some guests to greet."

Elizabeth nodded slowly feeling somewhat hurt by his reaction. She was not sure why his dismissal of her had been so acutely painful. It was hard enough to find that Philip was not the man she had seen in the garden or that the man was Philip's brother. His reaction seemed like rubbing salt in the wound.

CHAPTER NINE

"Your mother has offered a lovely dinner tonight."

It took James a moment but he tore his eyes from the other end of the table. "Yes, it is quite nice. I am sure that she would love to know that you are enjoying yourself, Lady Haltham."

The older woman laughed. "I spoke with her earlier and she was so happy that Philip had decided to come home for the house party."

"Philip? Well, yes, of course. We were all quite happy to see him home." James hoped that his true feelings were not evident.

It would not serve him well to appear irritated at about Philip's return home. More importantly, he liked Lady Agatha Haltham. While she was outspoken, she abhorred the gossips that usually plagued the social gatherings of the Season. He gave her a warm smile. "Mother was quite happy that Philip has returned… home."

His eyes strayed back to the other end of the table where Lady Elizabeth was smiling over at Philip. His earlier irritation was nothing compared to the anger he was feeling as he watched Elizabeth and Philip talk quietly.

The scene before dinner had been playing in his mind. When Lady Elizabeth and her father had entered the drawing room,

James had noticed her immediately. It seemed that she had noticed him as well and it was only when his father had ended their conversation to walk over to Philip that James started to wonder if something else was going on.

Watching Elizabeth being introduced to Philip was one of the most difficult moments of his life. He could not believe his luck. The first lady to catch his attention was already destined to marry his brother. While it tore his heart nearly in two, it seemed fitting given how his life had gone thus far. Anything James had ever wanted, Philip had gotten.

It was something he had grown accustomed to when he was young but lately, it had been harder and harder to take.

He stared down at his hands trying to calm himself, getting angry and making a scene would not help him in this situation. He had learned long ago that complaining about Philip only made him look childish and spoiled.

James had originally thought Philip was just playing along with Father's plan in regards to Lady Elizabeth but he was starting to doubt that. He did not quite believe it, but it was clear that Philip was paying quite a lot of attention to Lady Elizabeth.

James looked over at Lady Elizabeth as she laughed at something his mother had said. He could not blame his brother for his interest in the young lady. She was quite beautiful and it was clear from her conversation with his parents that she was well spoken and versed in social graces. Those facts did not surprise him at all. Her interest in Philip was the surprising bit. If she was as well-spoken and intelligent as she seemed, how could she not see that Philip was a lazy and irresponsible fop.

James was only too glad to push away from the table a short time later. Earlier in the day he had been looking forward to the social hour. The time that was to occur after dinner was usually entertaining and quite fun. Now he would be skipping it as she had no desire to see Philip and Elizabeth together anymore that night.

CHAPTER TEN

"Dinner was lovely, was it not?" Lettie asked as they moved into the drawing room.

Elizabeth glanced back at the large dining room that was emptying quickly. "Yes, the food was quite delicious."

Lettie laughed softly. "I was referring to the company, although I have to agree the food was lovely."

"Yes, of course," Elizabeth agreed. "The conversation was enjoyable and not just the civil whiskers."

Suddenly, Lettie groaned dramatically. "That is not the company I was speaking about and I think you know that."

They had found their own corner of the room where they could talk and Elizabeth turned to face her friend. "Lord Holgrave has been very gracious."

"Gracious?" Lettie asked her.

"Yes, gracious." Elizabeth chewed on her bottom lip for a moment. "I cannot help but wonder if he is just being polite due to the friendship between his father and mine."

Lettie seemed to think for a moment. "That is a question to ponder, for sure. More importantly, though, how do you feel about Lord Holgrave?"

Elizabeth paused before she answered. It was a tough question. Lord Holgrave was handsome and dressed in the most fashionable style. He was quite cordial and charming, indeed. Even with all of that, Elizabeth felt that there was something not quite right.

She, herself, could not point to one thing that seemed off and she knew there was no way she could explain it to Lettie. Regardless, whatever it was, she could feel it.

"Elizabeth, dear," her father said joining them in the corner. "Dinner seemed to be a smashing success."

Elizabeth nodded at her father. "Lettie and I were just remarking on the delightful menu."

"And Lord Holgrave?" Her father asked her. "Surely the menu was not the only thing you appreciated in the dining room."

"Yes, of course, Father. I quite enjoyed my conversation with Lord Holgrave, as well as with the Duke and Duchess of Castborough."

Her father nodded at her with a big smile said, "I am glad to hear that. It seems as though Lord Holgrave is enjoying your company, as well. Or, that is the impression I have gotten."

Elizabeth did not know what to say to that so she just looked down. She hoped that if she appeared shy and embarrassed perhaps her father would stop talking about Lord Holgrave.

Her father looked around the large drawing room and she thought perhaps he was looking for someone. If she were lucky if would be someone that he needed to speak to. "The manor here at Castborough is quite magnificent. The Duchess of Castborough was saying earlier that her favorite time to be here is in winter. She said it is rather beautiful in the snow."

"I can imagine it is," Elizabeth said in agreement. She knew that he was hinting that it could very well be her home one day.

Her father looked around the room and then suddenly turned back to her. "Well, I shall leave you young people to enjoy your evening. Good night."

"Thank you, Father. Good night." Elizabeth watched him walk away and caught sight of Lord Holgrave heading their way.

"Lady Elizabeth, I do hope you are enjoying yourself." Lord Holgrave smiled at her as he casually hooked his arm over the back of a high-back chair.

"I am, thank you," Elizabeth said turning to Lettie. "We were just discussing the lovely dinner."

Lord Holgrave eyes barely skimmed over Lettie before going back to set on Elizabeth. "Dinner was in my honour, of course. I have not been back to Castborough since the holidays and my mother wanted to celebrate my return."

"How very thoughtful of your dear mother," Elizabeth remarked.

"Have you been very busy in London, then?" Lettie asked.

"Oh, yes. I have been quite occupied attending the theater as well as many balls and parties," he said with a laugh and a wave of his hand.

It did not escape Elizabeth's attention that Lord Holgrave had answered Lettie's question but still did not design to look at her. Gritting her teeth at the obvious snub to her friend and cousin she simply said, "London is certainly the center of fashion and social activity."

"Do you like the theater?" His question seemed born out of a need to make small talk as opposed to real interest in her likes or dislikes.

Elizabeth nodded. "I have attended a night or two this Season."

"You would like attending the theater with me. I am very well-known and it would serve you well to be seen with me—especially in London. And since I am at the theater so often I would be happy to show you about."

"Of course." Elizabeth was surprised at his words. She, of course, knew he was very active in London's social circles. His demeanor was confusing, though, was she to be impressed that he was well known at the theater?

He bent into a deep bow. "Philip Repington, Marquess of Holgrave, heir to the Duke of Castborough, Earl of Renwood, Viscount Marling and Baron Laskey, at your service."

Elizabeth nearly laughed at his introduction only managing to cover it up by clearing her throat softly. "Oh my! My throat is so dry. Perhaps some lemonade would help."

Lord Holgrave gave her a suddenly disinterested look and waved a hand toward the dining room. "There is lemonade and other refreshments set up in the dining room."

"Oh yes," Elizabeth murmured. "Please excuse us."

She had already known about the refreshments in the dining room as they had announced it after dinner. It had been her thought that he would be the gentleman and leave them to retrieve their drinks. She supposed this was better as she would not need to immediately return to speak with him so soon.

They left the drawing room to cross the hall to the dining room when Elizabeth was suddenly face-to-face with Lord James Repington.

"Oh, my! Pardon me," Elizabeth said taking a step back. She still remembered his look of disappointment when introduced to her before dinner.

Lord James nodded to each of them. "No, not at all. It was I that was not watching where I was going."

"We were going to the dining room for refreshments," Lettie told him.

"Oh? May I get you something?" Lord James offered, smiling at Lettie before looking back to Elizabeth.

To Elizabeth's horror, she felt her cheeks grow red. "Thank you, but no. I shall like to see what has been set up in the dining room." She only wanted to get away from him, inexplicably jealous that he had smiled at Lettie while continuing to nearly scowl at her.

"Then, I will bid you a good night." Lord James gave them each a small bow before he turned to continue down the hall.

Elizabeth and Lettie entered the empty dining room. The long table was filled with small cakes and biscuits as well as large pitchers of lemonade and fruit punch.

Lettie pulled her to the far side of the table. "Now that we are alone I must ask you, were you surprised that Lord Holgrave was not the man from the garden yesterday?"

"It was a little bit of a surprise, yes," Elizabeth admitted to her friend. She pointed to one of the trays. "I think I shall have one of these small cakes. What do you think?"

Elizabeth was hoping to distract Lettie. As she was not ready to admit that she was still thinking about Lord James or that he had hurt her feelings so much.

CHAPTER ELEVEN

The sun was barely shining over the horizon when James stepped into the stable. He had not slept well the night before and thought a vigorous ride would help get his day sorted out properly. Although he knew it would not heal his bitterness it would be a good distraction.

It had been just over a week since the house party had started and he could no longer bear to watch Philip court Elizabeth. The night before he had seen Philip whisper something into Elizabeth's ear and wanted nothing more than to rip his brother's head off. The thought of Elizabeth in his brother's arms was making him miserable. While he could not change it, he would be damned if he was going to stand around and watch it happen.

"You are up a bit early, are you not?" Matthew was saddling up his horse.

"I could not sleep," James told him crossing the stables to pull his saddle from where it was kept. "What brings you out so early?"

"Me? I am here at this time most mornings. Jensen used to insist that I get him up so that he could saddle my horse but I do not mind the routine of it so early in the morning. It gives me time to ruminate."

James nodded. He too appreciated the peaceful moments of a repeated activity in order to let his mind settle. He looked up at his younger brother suddenly. "I pray I am not interrupting your morning routine. I could wait until later if that suits you better."

"No, not at all. I welcome the company this morning perhaps some conversation will do us both some good." Matthew smiled and tilted his head as if about to inquire about his bother's well-being.

"Perhaps," James replied quickly although he was not feeling very conversational at the moment.

They continued in silence until their horses were both saddled. They were mounted and riding away from the stable by the time Matthew spoke. "I was going to ride out towards the river if that is agreeable with you."

"Yes," James answered. "Anywhere is fine, as long as it gets me away from the house."

Matthew glanced over at him. "Are you not enjoying the house party?"

Determined not to discuss his issues regarding their older brother, he simply said, "The house party has been quite enjoyable. It is Father's not-so-subtle interference that has gotten under my skin."

"Ah, yes. That." Matthew said as they rode towards the trees.

They rode on in silence for a moment and James was surprised when Matthew suddenly said, "I am a little concerned about Lady Elizabeth."

"Lady Elizabeth, why?" James asked.

"I know that it is not my place to say anything but I fear that Philip is not as devoted as he would have people think." Matthew kept his eyes forward but James could see that there was true concern on his face.

"I have not been a confidante of Philip's in recent times, so I am unsure of his true intentions. Is there a specific reason that you would doubt him?"

Matthew finally looked over at James. "Yes, I overheard him

talking with Lord Fallbrooke the other night. They were talking about returning to London soon and when Lord Fallbrooke mentioned Lady Elizabeth Philip laughed. I did not hear what he said after but it is my assumption that it was not favorable."

It was not surprising to hear from Philip but since it was regarding Lady Elizabeth James was infuriated by his brother's callousness. Remembering that Matthew was still waiting for his counsel James finally said, "I do not know what our brother is doing. Father has made it clear he expects him to settle down soon and we can only stand by and watch to see what path Philip chooses. It is unfortunate that Lady Elizabeth may be caught in the middle of it. It is my hope that Philip will be responsible for once."

It had been difficult for him to say but he truly did not want Elizabeth to be hurt. He had seen enough of his father and the Earl of Southwick talking to know that the match was favored by the old friends. The courtship between Philip and Lady Elizabeth had been foisted upon them both.

Matthew nodded. "I think I shall keep an eye on Philip, if for nothing than for Lady Elizabeth's sake."

"I think that is wise," James agreed.

They came into a clearing and heard shouting not far away. Without speaking both Matthew and James turned their horses toward the noise. A moment later they rode up to see Philip and Lord Fallbrooke on their horses attempting to jump over hedges and the small creek.

Before either Matthew or James could call out to them Philip was riding swiftly towards the hedge. As his horse left the ground James watched as Philip failed to lean forward. Philip was thrown back off the saddle and disappeared behind the hedge. Lord Fallbrooke was already riding away and did not notice his fallen friend.

"I will catch his horse! You go check on Philip!" Matthew called out before riding after the spooked horse.

Philip was a damn fool. It would serve him right if he broke his bloody neck.

James rode toward where Philip had fallen easily jumping the creek to get to him. By the time James had slid off his horse Lord Fallbrooke had come back to find Philip and join James as he rushed towards him.

Philip sat up slowly looking around confused. "What happened?"

"You fell off your bloody horse," Lord Fallbrooke told him in a loud, slurred voice.

"I fell off?" Philip fell back to the ground laughing hysterically. Fallbrooke falling to the ground next to him.

James groaned. They were both drunk. He had no idea how long they had been out riding in the dark. Quietly James took the reins to Fallbrooke's horse and led it away.

Matthew rode up a moment later with Philip's horse. James took the reins from him. "You stay with them and make sure they do not hurt themselves. They are both well into their cups. I will send the wagon back to get them."

On his way back to the stable James recalled his first thought at seeing Philip fall. It was appalling to him that he had truly hoped that his brother been injured severely. He was so very tired of filling in or fixing mistakes that Philip had made. James had been putting it off because he felt that his father needed him at Castborough but the time had come.

It was time for him to leave Castborough and make a life of his own. Perhaps he would go back to university to finish his law studies. He would not disrupt his mother's house party but he would leave Surrey as soon as he could.

CHAPTER TWELVE

"It is a very lucky thing that you did not break your neck when you fell off that horse, Holgrave," the Earl of Southwick was saying when James walked into the library.

James winced and turned quickly to leave. The last thing he wanted was to relive the incident.

"I am quite lucky. I owe my life to my brother, James. Is that not right?"

James turned to see his brother and Lord Southwick smiling at him. "I would not say that, at all. You were quite all right after the fall."

"My brother, so modest," Philip smirked at him.

"I did not mean to interrupt I was just leaving." James turned to leave but Lord Southwick stopped him with a hand on his shoulder.

"I was just talking to your brother about his plans for the rest of the Season," Southwick gave James a knowing look.

"Oh, I am sure my brother has plenty planned." James smiled when Philip glared at him from over the Earl's shoulder. "Philip is quite popular in London. He gets invited to the most exclusive balls and parties. He's busy every single night."

Southwick laughed, a deep rumbling sound. "Yes, I am quite sure of that. Perhaps as his brother, you can persuade him to make some plans that will affect his future and not just this Season."

James tilted his head to look at Philip. "I do not think that I have much control over the Marquess of Holgrave, but I will be happy to be his counsel if he so desires."

"I suppose I will have to take that then," Southwick said with another laugh and clapped James on the shoulder before leaving the two brothers alone in the library.

"Well, thanks a lot for that," Philip said the exasperation clear in his voice.

"Thanks for what?" James shrugged.

"For what?" Philip repeated. "For telling him that you would talk to me about my future."

"Why would that bother you?"

Philip pointed toward the hallway. "Because he is pushing for a wedding announcement. He wants me to marry his daughter, that is why!"

"I thought you and Lady Elizabeth were getting along quite well," James replied.

"Lady Elizabeth is fine if you like that type." Phillip snorted. "I may just have to marry her to get Father off my back but I am not going to rush into it. There are so many other women in London."

James clenched his fists at his sides if only to keep from slamming them into his brother's heartless, vain face. "You do not want to marry her?"

"Lawks, no," Philip said with disgust. After a moment, he smiled. "She is not totally without her attributes, though. I am quite sure she would make a fine wife and a suitable Duchess of Castborough. I certainly would have no trouble bedding her, that is for sure."

It was James' turn to be disgusted. He turned away from his brother and walked to the window and looked out to the garden. "Perhaps you should just be honest with Lady Elizabeth and end your courtship now."

"What would the fun be in that?" Philip asked with a laugh.

When James turned, he saw that Philip was slouched in one of his father's large upholstered chairs. James was further infuriated to realize that he had been correct in his thoughts that Philip was only having fun at everyone else's expense. "So this is your way of getting back at Father?"

Philip shrugged. "Father forced me to return from London and he and Southwick have pushed Lady Elizabeth in front of me a dozen times a day since the party started."

"So you would punish Lady Elizabeth for what our father and her father have done?"

"You think it is all their doing? You think that Lady Elizabeth has no interest in setting her cap on me?" Philip asked in a mocking tone.

James did not know how it had happened but he had suddenly found himself in the middle of a conversation regarding Lady Elizabeth. Ever since his conversation with Matthew and his errant thoughts regarding his brother's death James had tried to steer clear of Philip. In fact, the only reason he was in the library at all was to write a letter to the University in regard to continuing his law studies. He had decided he would leave for Cambridge at the end of the next week. He was now thinking his departure would happen much sooner.

With a sigh, James held up his hands in front of him. "Philip, really I have no thoughts on the matter. You will do what you want regardless of what anybody says to you."

Philip only chuckled.

James was at the door when he stopped and looked back to say, "I only hope that you figure things out before you do end up getting your neck broken."

CHAPTER THIRTEEN

"What does Lord Holgrave have planned for tonight?" Lettie asked Elizabeth as she finished her hair.

"I do not know," Elizabeth told her pausing as she added one more pin to hold an errant curl in place. "I suppose I will have to go downstairs and see for myself."

Lettie smiled at her through the mirror. She was smoothing down the skirt of her lavender dress adorned with white ribbons and ruffles at the bottom. "I do have to say that I am quite surprised at Lord Holgrave's behaviour."

Elizabeth frowned. "How so?"

"Pleasantly surprised," Lettie said holding up a hand to calm her friend. "He has been so very attentive. I had originally thought that he would be arrogant and dismissive of you. I am quite happy that he seems to appreciate you as he should."

"I had not wanted to admit it but I had thought he would be the same especially given that first night and how he had acted that I should feel lucky to even be in the same room with him." Elizabeth had nearly gone to her father that night to tell him that she could not go through with a marriage with such a selfish and conceited man. The next morning, however, Lord Holgrave had seemed like a new man. He was kind, caring and seemed truly interested in her thoughts on many subjects. "It has been lovely seeing him disprove my early assumptions."

"That sort of thing does not happen often. I am glad of it," Lettie told her and gave her a quick hug.

Elizabeth squeezed Lettie's hand. "As am I."

As they walked to the door to head downstairs Lettie asked, "Where was Lord Holgrave today?"

"I am not sure. I did not see him this morning before Lady Haltham's tour of the rose garden." Elizabeth shrugged. "I suppose he may have gone to the stables with the other gentlemen. I have not seen him since last night at dinner."

Elizabeth frowned remembering she had seen some of the other gentlemen back in the house right after lunch but Lord Holgrave had not been among them. She knew that he was still keeping company with Lord Fallbrooke and that the two of them had a penchant for getting into trouble. Perhaps he and Fallbrooke had gone riding again.

She was not overly concerned about Lord Holgrave as she had not even missed him during their day apart. It was only that there was an odd niggle in the back of her mind that made her feel uneasy as they walked into the drawing room. The room was full of many smaller tables for the card party that Lady Henrietta, the Duke of Castborough's daughter was hosting.

Elizabeth looked around the room and spotted Lord Holgrave across the room at a large table. "Oh, there he is. Do you suppose we should go over and greet him?"

"I do not see why not," Lettie said matter of factly.

Elizabeth's unease grew as they neared the table. Lord Holgrave was sitting with Lord Fallbrooke and several other young ladies. By the time she realized that there were no empty chairs at the table, they were too close to walk by as though they had been heading to another table.

Lord Holgrave looked up at her. "Yes?"

"Good evening, Lord Holgrave," Elizabeth said quietly thankful that she did not stammer or stutter she was suddenly so nervous in front of all the others.

"Good evening," he said but barely looked up from his cards.

Lettie tugged on her sleeve and Elizabeth slowly turned away from the table confused as to Lord Holgrave's strange behaviour. Lord Fallbrooke said something behind them and the ladies at the table all began to laugh. Elizabeth made the mistake of looking back to see several of the women looking at her and whispering to each other.

Lettie hooked her arm through Elizabeth's and said, "Do not listen to them. They are like vultures if you drop a scrap they will swoop in and jump on it. They like nothing better than to gossip about everyone else here."

Elizabeth shook her head slowly. "I do not know what just happened."

"I have no idea why Lord Holgrave was so rude to you, but he certainly was." Lettie squeezed Elizabeth's hand. "Can I get you anything?"

There was more laughter from Lord Holgrave's table. Elizabeth shook her head. "No, I think I just need a few moments. I think I shall go into the garden and get some fresh air."

"Would you like me to come with you?" Lettie asked her.

Elizabeth sighed. "No, thank you, though. I will not be long. I promise."

Elizabeth hurried from the drawing room as she suddenly felt as though she might cry at any moment. She crossed the lawn and ducked into a private spot she had seen earlier that day when Lady Haltham had led them through the gardens. It took some searching but she found it, a single bench hidden behind the hedges.

Dizzy with confusion, Elizabeth sat down covering her face with her hands. She had no idea what had come over Lord Holgrave as he had been so sweet and considerate this past week. Marrying him was still not her first choice but she had begun to hope that it would not be as disastrous as she first thought. Now she did not know what to think. It did not help at all that she was horribly concerned about upsetting her father or insulting his dear old friend, the Duke of Castborough.

Regardless of how much she tried to calm down, she began to cry anyway. She dabbed at her eyes as best she could without a handkerchief. She was about to stand up to figure out a way to quietly get back into the house and up to her room when a pair of shoes came into her view. She looked up to see Lord James standing in front of her.

"Are you well?" He looked at her intently, concern growing on his face.

"Yes," she said her voice cracking with emotion. "It is nothing, please do not mind me."

Lord James seemed to debate his next move for a moment and then he handed her a handkerchief and said, "You seem quite upset and I am afraid I do mind that quite a bit."

"Thank you," she said taking the handkerchief. "I am afraid I am being a silly girl."

"I highly doubt that being silly would cause you to be this upset." Lord James gave her a gentle smile. "Does this have anything to do with my brother?"

Elizabeth nodded. "I am just embarrassed. I clearly misunderstood Lord Holgrave's intentions."

Lord James gestured to the other end of the bench. "Do you mind if I sit down?"

"No, of course not," Elizabeth answered moving over to leave space between them.

"I am quite sure that you misunderstood nothing. My brother can be quite selfish and immature. He oftentimes has little regard for other people's feelings." He shook his head. "I am very sorry that he has hurt you."

Elizabeth dabbed at her eyes again and cleared her throat gently. It was so difficult for her. Lord Holgrave had been so awful to her and here was Lord James being truly sweet and caring. She shook her head. "Please do not feel sorry for me I will be fine."

"I am sorry about his behaviour and I hope I did not upset you further," James said standing up to look at her.

"No, you have been very sweet," Elizabeth said standing up too. "I think I would like to go to my room now."

Lord James took a quick look around the garden. "Yes, we should not linger, lest someone come along and get the wrong idea."

"I had not thought of that," Elizabeth admitted. "I am usually very vigilant about such things. I do not know what came over me."

"Come with me and I will show you the hall door so you can go straight to the stairs and not encounter anyone on your way."

Elizabeth sniffled and nodded trying not to cry again. "Thank you. You have been very kind."

CHAPTER FOURTEEN

Lord James opened the door and pointed down the hallway. "The stairs are right there."

They were on the opposite side of the house from the drawing room and unless someone left the party to retrieve something from their room no one would see her.

"I cannot thank you enough for your assistance," Elizabeth told him. She dabbed at her eyes again and then realized she still held his handkerchief. She held it out to him. "Oh, I almost took this."

He held up a hand and shook his head. "No, please keep it. You are in greater need of it than I and I have more than I will ever need."

Elizabeth nodded and began her walk down the hall because for some reason that final kind gesture had made her cry once more. She went straight to her room, hurrying but not so much as to alert anyone that anything was amiss. A lamp was already lit and Elizabeth thankfully sat down on the edge of the bed.

A moment later her door opened and startling Elizabeth before she saw Aunt Judith appear in the doorway.

"Elizabeth, I am sorry I did not mean to frighten you. I heard your door close. Why have you returned from the card party so early?"

Elizabeth did not want to talk about it. "I have a bad headache and need to lie down for a while."

"Oh goodness," Aunt Judith said and came to sit on the bed beside her. "Oh, but you have been crying. Are you sure nothing happened to upset you?"

Elizabeth shook her head and looked down. Aunt Judith must have done so too.

"Whose handkerchief is that?"

Before she could answer, Aunt Judith said. "That is the Castborough crest. Did Lord Holgrave do something to upset you?"

Elizabeth broke down again. "I do not want to talk about it. Do you think Father would consider leaving the house party and returning to Kent?"

"Why ever for? What about your courtship with Lord Holgrave? The agreement would be in jeopardy."

"I no longer want to think about a courtship with Lord Holgrave." Elizabeth's voice cracking. She added in a whisper. "I am so embarrassed. I just want to go home."

"Shh, now. You get changed and we will talk about this in the morning after you have gotten some sleep."

Elizabeth began to cry again. "Thank you, Aunt Judith."

"It is quite all right, dear," Aunt Judith leaned over and hugged her. "Quite all right."

CHAPTER FIFTEEN

James sat at his father's desk staring at the paper in front of him. He had heard back from Cambridge and would be resuming his law studies as soon as he returned to the institution. His reply was already written the only thing left to add was his date of arrival.

It was a bit of an interesting situation that he found himself in, as he had not told anyone about his plans in case there had been some reason he would not be able to return to the university. Now he would be telling his parents not that he was thinking about going back to university, but that the decision was made and that he was leaving in several days.

Choosing the best day to leave was becoming difficult, as well. He still believed that leaving Castborough was the best thing for him but he kept thinking about Lady Elizabeth. James was worried about leaving her at Castborough.

His brother was not being very nice and he did not believe his father nor her father were paying attention to any of the happenings. They were only interested in the fact that Philip and Elizabeth were courting. He hated that no one was listening to what Lady Elizabeth wanted.

"I want to know why she was so upset," James' father walked into the library with Philip right behind him.

"How am I to know why the chit was upset?" Philip asked his tone clearly annoyed.

James watched as his father rounded on his older brother. "Do not call her that. She is the youngest child and only daughter of one of my closest friends. You will not embarrass me with such disregard for the feelings of my friends."

Philip held up both of his hands and took several steps back away from their father. "Yes, of course, my apologies." He bowed his head and looked away from their father.

James stood up at the desk. He folded the piece of paper in half and made a note to himself to come back to fill in the proper dates that were needed later.

He was almost to the door when his father said, "James, I want you to stay."

James closes arsons were under his breath. "I am not sure I am going to be of much help with this conversation."

"Lord Southwick came to me this morning and said that Lady Elizabeth left the party crying last night. When Lord Southwick tried to speak to her about it she only said that she no longer wanted to be part of a courtship with Lord Holgrave and that she wanted to go back to Kent. She wants to leave immediately."

"Kent?" Philip asked. "Why would she not want to go back to London? That's absurd."

James sighed. "Probably because she was upset and embarrassed. She does not want to see anyone."

Father narrowed his eyes at James. "What do you know about what happened last night?" Before James could say anything, his father added, "You were seen letting Lady Elizabeth in the hall door later in the evening. So, don't try telling me you have no idea. I just hope you have not added more difficulty to the predicament."

"Fine." James shook his head and turned to his father. "I do not know exactly what transpired but I found Lady Elizabeth crying in the garden. She would not tell me what happened only that she was embarrassed. She stated that she must have misunderstood Lord Holgrave's intentions."

Father groaned loudly. "Please tell me nothing untoward happened between the two of you in the garden, James."

"Of course not, Father. I gave her a handkerchief and offered a route to her room to minimize her humiliation. Nothing more than that."

The duke took in a deep, long breath and let it out slowly. "Philip, all I wanted was for you to think about settling down. Is it so difficult for you to act accordingly?"

"Think about settling down?" Philip asked his tone mocking. "That is why you dragged me down from London just to think about settling down? I could have done that from there."

Father pointed a finger at Philip. "None of this would have happened if you had done as I asked when I was in London several weeks ago."

Philip simply shrugged.

"It continues to amaze me how lazy and irresponsible you have become, but I do not know why. I have witnessed your behaviour long enough to be well aware. You need to be more responsible —like James."

"Like James?" Philip snorted. "James is a coward."

"A coward?" Father asked him.

"Yes, James only stays at Castborough because he is too afraid to go make a life of his own. He will always be here and as long as he is here you do not need me."

"Well, I guess you better plan on staying around here for the forseeable future," James said. He held the folded piece of paper in his hand. "This is a letter accepting a position in a course of study at Cambridge to finish my law studies. I will be leaving within a fortnight."

Father was clearly surprised and James felt bad about that but he had had enough of Philip and this conversation. He turned to leave but gave Philip one final comment. "Nice try. You almost got the conversation to focus on me rather than you. You are the heir to the title, as you so often like to remind me. It is past time for you to act like it."

CHAPTER SIXTEEN

Elizabeth looked down at her dress and wanted to cry. It was her most beautiful dress the one that she saved for special occasions. She had thought that the formal ball at the Castborough house party would be one of those occasions but she felt anything but special after this dreadful experience with the Marquess of Holgrave.

Several soft knocks fell against her door and Elizabeth turned away from the mirror. "Yes?"

"It is your Aunt Judith, dear. May I come in?"

"Yes, of course," Elizabeth moved toward the door but Aunt Judith was already coming in. "Well, look at you, you look a sight better than last night."

"Thank you," Elizabeth replied with a weak smile.

Aunt Judith had been so understanding the night before. She had not asked a multitude of questions as her father had this morning.

Once more Elizabeth was so grateful for her aunt, her only connection to her mother. Elizabeth's mother, Mary, had died when Elizabeth with seven years old. Aunt Judith had come to take care of Mary while she was ill, bringing Lettie and her brother, Joseph with her.

She had essentially been raised by Aunt Judith as her father had been quite busy with his work in the Parliament. Although Elizabeth often wondered if he tried to keep busy because of the pain he felt in losing his beloved wife. Either way, her aunt was as dear to her as a mother would be. Elizabeth had always felt loved and she was quite grateful to Aunt Judith that she never felt less important than Lettie or Joseph.

"Now, I understand that you might still be upset about last night." Aunt Judith looked at her with raised eyebrows.

Elizabeth still wanted to go home to Kent but she had been unable to move her father. He'd been adamant that they stay in Castborough.

"Yes. Father spoke to me earlier. He understands my desire to leave, but explained it is impossible to do so. Although, he has assured me that everything is fine… with Lord Holgrave, that is." Elizabeth sighed. "I will go to the dinner tonight as Father has asked."

Aunt Judith fussed with Elizabeth's sleeves puffing them up a little as she said, "It would be good for you to show up. The gossips will have nothing to say when you appear happy and carefree."

Elizabeth could not help but laugh. "That is very true. Gossips being what they are, proving them wrong before they can actually speak their desires is tantamount to stilling their tongues."

She still wanted to go home but proving her steel to the ladies who had laughed at her last night was almost as important to her. Aunt Judith took a step toward the door. "Your father will escort you to the ballroom."

When Elizabeth and her father arrived in the ballroom they were immediately met by Lord Holgrave.

"Good evening, Lord Southwick," Lord Holgrave said before turning to her. "Good evening, Lady Elizabeth. How are you this fine evening? You look quite lovely, indeed."

"Fine, thank you," Elizabeth answered coolly.

"May I speak with you briefly?" Lord Holgrave asked.

Before Elizabeth could answer her father said, "Yes, I think that would be agreeable."

Elizabeth looked back at her father with a mixture of anger and apprehension. While she had agreed to be present tonight, she had not wanted to be forced to be polite to the eldest son of the Duke of Castborough.

"Thank you, sir." Lord Holgrave nodded and offered her his arm to Elizabeth. He led her to the doors up to the garden.

Lord Holgrave walked slowly down one of the paths. "I am truly sorry for upsetting you last night. I had planned on leaving the table where you saw me. By the time the hand was over, you had left and I could not find you to explain."

Elizabeth was not sure if she believed him, so she simply nodded.

He stopped and turned to her. She could see his face in the shadows as he smiled down at her. His smile seemed sincere, though it did not quite reach his eyes.

"Can you ever forgive me? I am truly sorry."

"Yes," Elizabeth said with a smile. "I suppose I could do that."

Lord Holgrave took both of her hands in his and drew her closer to him. She smiled shyly at him expecting him to apologize again. Instead, he pulled her closer and before she knew what was happening he was brushing his lips across hers.

She was stunned at first. It was not her first kiss, there had been a few chaste kisses from nervous young men before, but this was different. There was something more as Lord Holgrave moved his lips over hers, an urgency that she had not encountered before.

A moment later she felt his hand slide up to the nape of her neck and his kisses became more demanding and she put her hands against his chest to push him away.

"No, Lord Holgrave, we must not," she told him.

He stepped away and chuckled. "Yes, that is just what I thought." And with that, he spun on his heel and left her in the garden. Alone.

Elizabeth stood on the garden path in shock. Everyone saw her leave the ballroom with Lord Holgrave. For her to walk back in alone would be quite noticeable. She started back up the path, perhaps she could slip through the hall door that Lord James had shown her the previous night.

Suddenly, she stopped. Not returning to the ballroom could cause as much gossip as returning alone. If Lettie happened to come looking for her they could return together. That thought gave her another idea, she could go to the refreshment room. It was possible that she could slip in unseen then she could act as though she had been there for several minutes.

She had almost reached the house when she saw James enter the garden peering into the darkness as though he was looking for someone. She saw the exact moment that he spotted her, his eyes widened and his shoulders slumped in relief.

"Lady Elizabeth, I am so glad I found you. Are you well?"

"How did you know that I was out here?" Elizabeth was so surprised she almost forgot how upset she was.

"Your friend, Lettie, approached me. She said that you left the ballroom with my brother and that he had returned and that you had not."

Elizabeth nodded and looked away. "Yes, he said that he wanted to talk but then he seemed to get angry and he left me alone in the garden."

"Are you sure that you are well?" Lord James was looking over her as though she had been injured. "Did he hurt you in any way?"

"Hurt me? No, he did not. I do not understand."

James was looking at her strangely.

"I am sorry perhaps I could just go back inside," Elizabeth said and began to walk past him, wanting the night to be over quickly.

Before she can get far, Lord James gently grabbed her arm above her wrist. "I am sorry, Lady Elizabeth, I think you might want to tend to your hair first."

"My hair?" Elizabeth asked suddenly remembering Lord Holgrave's hand at the nape of her neck.

Lord James looked sheepish as he gestured to the back of his own head. "It is a bit mussed."

Elizabeth's cheeks were burning. She turned away from him fearing how he must think her a light skirt.

"It is all right. I will escort you to the library and then enlist help."

Elizabeth wanted to argue with him but she realized that he was right. She followed him into the house and then to the library where she fairly cowered behind a large chair.

"I will be right back," he said and then left her alone. The room was in shadows having only one lamp lit near the desk. If someone happened to come in the room, it was possible they may not see her standing in the corner.

A moment later the door opened and James' sister came in. She looked around and saw Elizabeth behind the chair.

"Lady Elizabeth, my brother said you may need some help."

"Yes, but I thought he would get my cousin, Lettie."

Lady Henrietta nodded. "He had thought the same thing but we thought it would be less obvious if I came instead of Lettie."

Lady Henrietta had already come up behind her and had started removing pins from her hair. "We will get this taken care of straightaway."

"Thank you," Elizabeth said softly. "You must be thinking the worst of me right now."

Lady Henrietta's hand stilled for a moment and then went back to tending to Elizabeth's hair. "Of course not, I think we have all had our share of unwanted advances. I am just glad that you are unhurt."

"I am quite fine, thank you." Elizabeth felt like she was repeating herself but it was getting harder and harder for her to believe it. She was not sure what to say after all Lord Holgrave was Lady Henrietta's brother.

"I have never seen James so furious." Lady Henrietta adjusted some curls over Elizabeth's ears. She moved to face Elizabeth, squeezing her hand briefly. "You look lovely. Shall we get back to the ballroom?"

"Yes, I think so," Elizabeth nodded. She was determined to act naturally. It was Lord Holgrave's behaviour that was suspect, not her own.

CHAPTER SEVENTEEN

"Lady Elizabeth, may I have this dance?" James stood next to her at the edge of the dance floor.

Elizabeth smiled at him calmly. "That sounds lovely. Thank you."

Lord James led her out onto the dance floor just as the music began. She easily fell into step with him and they began to move about the floor.

It had only been a few minutes since she and Lady Henrietta had come back into the ballroom. Lady Henrietta had made a big show of laughing and talking with Elizabeth as they returned. She had been almost immediately surrounded by a small group of people including Lettie, Lettie's brother, Joseph, and Beatrice as well as two of Lady Henrietta's brothers, Lord Matthew and Lord Evan.

Her worries about the Castborough family thinking ill of her had been put to rest quickly, to her relief. Lady Henrietta's reference to unwanted advances put all her worries aside.

Elizabeth had been surrounded so quickly that she had not even known if any of the gossips were doing their usual whispering. As for Lord Holgrave, Elizabeth did not know whether he was on the dance floor or in the ballroom at all.

She dared not look for him, lest someone think she was hoping to catch his eye. Least of all, she did not want him to discover her looking at him and misinterpret her intention.

Feeling a little calmer Elizabeth suddenly was reminded she was dancing with Lord James. She could feel the heat of this hand through her glove.

"Are you feeling well?" James asked her, his eyes narrowed as he looked at her.

Elizabeth looked up at him. "Yes. Why do you ask?"

"You suddenly look a little flushed."

"Oh, I suppose the ballroom is a little warmer than I expected."

"Do you need to rest for a bit?"

"No, I am rather enjoying dancing." She almost added that she felt safer out on the dance floor where she could not see or hear the people talking. There was the added blessing that it was unlikely that Lord Holgrave would approach them.

When the song ended Lord James took her back to where most of her friends were waiting.

"Thank you for the dance, Lady Elizabeth. I hope you will save me another," he said with a deep bow.

"Yes, of course, Lord James." She looked up at him hoping he would understand the full meaning of her next words. "I cannot thank you enough."

"Your smile is thanks enough." He smiled gallantly before walking away.

"Lady Elizabeth, may I have the next dance?" Joseph offered his hand.

"Thank you." Elizabeth had not danced with Joseph since they were fairly young. When they first learned to dance, their teacher would make them all dance with each other. She smiled at the thought of dancing with her cousin again after all this time.

Elizabeth danced with Joseph, followed by Lord Matthew and Lord Evan, and Beatrice's brother, Andrew. It was comforting to know that she had so many old friends and apparently new friends too. She tried to not think about it, though, as it made her a bit emotional.

"I think it is time for a refreshment," Lady Henrietta announced. "Is anyone else interested?"

"I would certainly like a cool drink," Elizabeth agreed.

Lady Henrietta linked her arm through Elizabeth's. "Then we shall investigate what Lucy has prepared for us."

As a group, they left the ballroom and headed across the hall to the dining room where the refreshments had been set up. Several people had just entered the dining room and their small group waited in the hallway.

"I heard she was begging him to marry him and that is why Lord Holgrave left her in the garden," a woman's voice could be heard. "I certainly do not blame him. Such wanton behaviour!"

Elizabeth stared at her hands.

A man laughed. "Judging by how long it took her to get back into the dining room, my guess it was not marriage that she was begging for. That is the wanton behaviour I think you mean."

Lady Henrietta gasped. The man looked through the doorway and blanched. "Lady Henrietta, I did not realize you were there."

"Apparently not, Crawford," Lord James said, his voice like ice. "Perhaps I should have a discussion with your Aunt Agatha."

It seemed not possible but the man's face got even whiter. "No, that is not necessary. My comment was rude and unsavory. I shall watch what I say in the future."

"See that you do," Lord James spat out.

He turned away from the man and looked over at Elizabeth, their eyes meeting briefly before she looked away again. He suddenly turned away and disappeared down the hallway.

She was too mortified to speak. Her reputation was unraveling before her eyes and she had done nothing wrong. If only her father would have agreed to leave for Kent this morning. He had no idea what he had done by making this alliance with the Duke of Castborough.

CHAPTER EIGHTEEN

After an hour of searching, James finally found Philip in the stables.

"What are you doing out here at this hour?" James demanded.

"I have had enough of this place. I am heading to the Tavern in Carelton," Philip told him standing next to his saddle with a bottle of whiskey in his hand.

"Carelton? At this hour? You will be surely robbed by bandits."

Philip shrugged. "It is a risk I will have to take. I will not stay here a minute longer."

"Why? No one else to harass tonight?"

Philip had turned to set the bottle on the ground but stopped to look at him. "What are you talking about?"

"Lady Elizabeth. The entire ballroom is whispering about her. Some loud enough for all to hear."

"Oh that," Philip shook his head. "That is really not my concern."

"Not your concern?" James asked incredulously. "It is your behaviour that has caused the gossips to begin chattering about her in the first place. She is humiliated."

"She is a scrabbling upstart who only came to Castborough because she wants to be a duchess," Philip snarled.

"Did you ever stop to think that as the daughter of an earl she was as pushed into the courtship as you were?"

"I do not know why you are involving yourself in this. Perhaps you should go back to the house and follow Father around. You do it so well, so carry on with it."

"Perhaps I shall go back to the house and tell Father and his friend, Southwick, how you have mistreated Lady Elizabeth." James turned to leave. Then he stopped, but did not turn around. "I doubt seriously either one will be happy with the news—especially Lady Elizabeth's loving father."

"Yes, you do that. Be sure to let them know that the trollop did not act mistreated when we were kissing in the garden."

Slowly, James turned around, rage consuming him to the point he could hardly see straight. Before he could stop himself, he had swung out, his fist smashing into Philip's face.

Philip staggered back. "What is wrong with you?"

James lunged forward again. "I am sick to death of you and your bloody awful behaviour. You are selfish and simply a horrible person. An embarrassment."

Philip stepped aside and they squared off. "At least I am not Father's errand boy," he said reaching over and pulling a leather strap from the rack on the wall.

"I have stayed at Castborough because I am proud of this family and what Father's title means to the family. You have no pride for anything."

"You are nothing but a coward," Philip said whipping the leather strap at James. "You are just hanging on to Father's apron strings. You do not know what else to do."

James turned slightly at the last minute, the strap hitting across his shoulder, his jacket taking most of the sting out of the strike. "And you think your life in London is less cowardly?"

Philip swung the strap at him in several quick motions until James grabbed the strap and lunged at his brother. Knocking Philip off balance they both went to the ground. James quickly gained the upper hand and held Philip down with a forearm to his throat. Philip struggled but James was too strong for him.

"You are a disgrace to the Castborough title!"

"What are you going to do now, brother? Kill me so you can be duke?"

"You think this is what this is about?" James could not believe what Philip was saying. "I do not want to be duke!"

"No?" Philip scowled at him.

"No! This is about you and who you have become. We used to be close but I hate who you are now." James screamed at him.

"Is this where I apologize? I do not think so. Go cry on someone else. You only wish you could live the life I have in London."

"No, I prefer to live my life as a gentleman, which you seem to have completely forgotten how to do. You miss the importance of treating people with respect."

"I have gotten no complaints, save for yours," Philip said with a mocking smile.

"So, you would be fine with Henrietta being treated as you have treated Lady Elizabeth?"

Philip's smile faltered. "That is completely different."

"Is it? Robert Crawford made some very loud and vile comments in the presence of Henrietta just now. His choice of words was more than indecent."

"That goat!"

"And, he has been pushing his suit with Henrietta this Season."

Philip swore again. "He is not fit to stand in the same room with her."

James loosened his hold on Philip. "And yet you treated Elizabeth far worse. You caused the gossips to waggle their tongues. That damage can rarely be undone."

"And you are so perfect that you never make mistakes?"

"No, but at least I accept responsibility and try to do better. I will be leaving Castborough soon." James said. "Father will need you."

Philip let his head fall back onto the ground. "I do not want to be the Duke of Castborough."

"What?" James let him up. "You are the heir. Father has always..."

"No! Father has always looked to you. I have done nothing but disappoint him. I am sick of trying to show him. I have given up."

"Surely, if you would talk to Father," James said to him.

Philip took a step back. "I am truly sorry about Lady Elizabeth. I was wrong and I know that." Philip looked around the stable. "I cannot stay here."

James took a step forward but Philip turned and ran from the stables.

CHAPTER NINETEEN

"Excuse me, Sir."

James looked up to see Thomas standing in the doorway of his room. "Yes, Thomas?"

"Your father would like to see you in the library."

Turning back to the mirror to finish tying his cravat James let out a long sigh before finally saying, "Please let him know that I will be down in a few minutes."

"Yes, sir."

After Thomas had left, James sat down in the chair near the window. His father would certainly be angry with him for fighting with Philip instead of trying to mend the courtship between he and Lady Elizabeth. There was nothing for it, though, there was little chance that James would do anything to encourage that courtship, even if he could go back and do it again.

He walked slowly down the stairs, admitting reluctantly to himself that he should not have resorted to fighting with his brother. With Philip's arrogant attitude it would be difficult to say for sure if he could have avoided it, however.

James took a deep breath and opened the door to the library. He was surprised to see Lord Southwick in the room, as well. James felt his heart drop to his stomach at the quelling look on Southwick's face.

"Good morning." James nodded to the two men and sat down.

"Do you have any idea where your older brother might be?"

James grimaced. "The last I saw him was late last night in the stables. Why? Is there something amiss?"

His father and Southwick exchanged glances before he answered. "Philip, Lord Fallbrooke and several others seem to have left overnight."

"Left?" James asked perplexed.

"Yes, it seems they gathered much of their belongings and departed sometime before dawn," Father explained.

"And you've no idea where they have hied off to?"

"One of the young ladies left a letter to her parents. In the letter, she claimed they were going to Paris. We do not know if it is true, but we have no reason to doubt her, either."

"Paris?" James repeated. "Whatever for?"

"We are not sure," Father answered. "The note mentioned something about being true patrons of the theater."

"Philip did mention frequenting the theater in London."

This time Southwick spoke up. "So, I suppose it is true then." He shook his head. "I do not know what I will say to Elizabeth."

James straightened in his chair. "If you would like, I could talk to her."

Southwick thought for a moment. "Yes, I think that might be agreeable. But please be easy with her, even though she must hear the truth."

He nodded, not sure what he would say to her. James stood up quickly, glad to be leaving this stuffy room.

He left the library and went straight to the drawing room. At this hour of the morning, Elizabeth would either be in the drawing room or the garden.

He had barely walked into the room when he saw her standing near the windows. It seemed the entire room was watching her and there was plenty whispering going on.

Robert Crawford had approached and she had originally tried to step away but he had begun talking to her and she politely stopped moving away. James watched their exchange closely. He could not hear the conversation but even where he was across the room he saw Elizabeth's eyes widened and her cheeks burn with embarrassment.

James crossed the room quickly. "Mr Crawford, it is clear that our discussion last night did not have the effect I expected. Please make sure that you are completely packed and gone from Castborough before nightfall."

"You want me to leave?" Crawford asked loudly. "Because of her?"

James stepped closer until they were nearly chest to chest. His voice never rose but there was a steel edge to it. "You are speaking about Lady Elizabeth Comerford, the only daughter of the Earl of Southwick. You can do as I ask or you can deal with the earl, himself. He is in the library. Would you like me to fetch him for you?"

Crawford shook his head vehemently. "No. No, I will do as you ask. Good day." He nodded at James and then Elisabeth before rushing out of the room.

Before James could turn to Elizabeth she, too, had hurried from the drawing room. James went after her and barely caught her at the bottom of the stairs.

"Lady Elizabeth, may I speak with you for a moment?"

"No, I am sorry. I need to go." Elizabeth looked around frantically.

"It will only be for a moment and we can talk privately in the library," James gestured toward the open door nearby.

People had begun to gather in the hallway and Elizabeth finally relented to keep from making even more of a scene. "Yes, of course. I can speak to you for a moment."

CHAPTER TWENTY

Elizabeth followed Lord James into the library. She wanted nothing more than to leave this horrible house party and return home to Kent. She felt that she owed Lord James these few minutes considering his continued defense of her honour especially following Mr Crawford's coarse mockery.

Just thinking about him and his horrible words made her shudder. She had to steady herself to keep from turning around to run up the stairs and lock herself in her room.

As the daughter of the Earl of Southwick, she had known for a long time that her marriage would be much more complicated than simply finding someone who was like minded. Over the years it had become quite clear that status and family history would take precedence over Elizabeth's affinity for the gentleman in question.

Considering what had transpired at this house party Elizabeth was starting to think that she would rather be a spinster than be married to a spoiled gentleman that is most likely shockingly loose in the haft.

Lord James gestured to the chair but Elizabeth was feeling defiant. "No, thank you. I will stand, after all you said this would not take long."

She spoke sharply, and then immediately regretted her words as a disappointed look came across Lord James' face. He nodded and took a chair looking somewhat defeated.

"Yes, I understand. I shall be leaving Castborough soon, as well, I am going to Cambridge to finish my law studies."

Elizabeth frowned. She was saddened to hear that James would be leaving although she supposed it did not matter as she would be leaving Castborough as well. Perhaps he was as ready for a change as she was. She could easily see him as a barrister addressing the court.

"Lady Elizabeth, I give you my deepest apologies for the troubles you have endured at our house party."

"You do not need to apologize, Lord James. I do not hold the entire Repington family responsible for a few unfortunate moments."

"That is very gracious of you," Lord James said quietly. "I am truly appreciative of your kind nature."

He sat silent for a moment and she wondered if she should go. She suddenly realized that the prospect of leaving Lord James made her sad and anxious. She always felt safe and calm when she was with him. It was a revealing moment for her—wonderful and terrible at the same time.

Somehow as she had been courting Lord Holgrave, she had fallen in love with his brother. The abrupt insight took her completely by surprise.

Her thoughts were interrupted when Lord James let out a long sigh. "I do feel some of the weight falls on me, as I did play a part in what has happened here."

Elizabeth froze. What did he mean? Did he and Lord Holgrave plan this whole ordeal together? Before she could think about it Lord James began to talk again.

"I went in search of Philip last night after I heard the group of idiots gossiping in the refreshment room."

Elizabeth flushed at the memory but urged him to go on. "Yes, I remember you leaving after assuring that Lord Charles would stay with me."

Lord James looked up at her. "I trust he tended to you accordingly?"

"Yes, of course. He was a true gentleman and quite conversational."

"Yes, I can imagine." Lord James smiled for a moment then got serious again. He dropped his head to stare at his hands as he spoke. "After I left the house I found Philip in the stables. I confronted him about his behaviour and I am ashamed to admit that our conversation came to blows."

Elizabeth turned around and moved to sit in the chair across from him. "Are you well? Were you hurt?"

Lord James looked up in surprise. Their eyes met and Elizabeth knew she should look away but she could not.

"I am uninjured. It was Philip that took the brunt of our quarrel. I believe, though, that it was our argument that caused him to leave the house party. I am quite sorry for the gossip his departure may have caused."

Elizabeth shook her head. "It is of no matter. The gossips would be twittering either way. They would say that Lord Holgrave had broken off our courtship in favor of someone else or that he has run off with one of the ladies that left overnight. I have already heard several versions of the story that involves Lord Holgrave racing across Britain to make it to Gretna Green before his new lady love's father can catch them."

Lord James looked confused. "According to your father, the group has gone to Paris."

Elizabeth smiled and nodded. "That very well may be the case but the gossips do not care about truth or fact."

"This is true," he agreed. "I still feel responsible."

Elizabeth was surprised and touched that he would go to such lengths to defend her honour. "I do not know if this is proper and I apologize if this offends you but I am grateful that you confronted your brother. I did not get the opportunity to do so and I am reluctant to admit that I find great pleasure that you did so on my behalf, if only because you felt duty bound."

"I could not stop myself. Philip was acting like a vain and arrogant fool. How he could not see how beautiful and admirable you are, is a mystery to me."

"Lord James, I must confess that your words are the most wondrous that I have ever heard."

Suddenly, Lord James slipped off the chair going to one knee in front of her chair. "Lady Elizabeth, marry me. I will treat you as you deserve and make up for my brother's vile behaviour."

Her next words were the hardest she ever had to utter. "No, Lord James, thank you but I will not force you into a marriage that you are only undertaking out of duty to your family."

He began to speak and she shook her head. "No, it breaks my heart to refuse you because I now know that you are everything that I wanted Philip to be."

Lord James' face fell. "Except I will never be the Duke of Castborough." He began to get up and she reached for his hand.

"I care not if you are the duke or the footman. I only care that the man I marry will love me as I love him." She watched his face hoping he would understand.

He brought her hand to his lips leaving a soft kiss on the back of her hand. "Lady Elizabeth, I have loved you since I saw your family arrive for the house party."

Elizabeth gasped in surprise.

"You were first to alight from the carriage and you were laughing at something someone had said and I thought you were the most beautiful woman I had ever seen."

Elizabeth could not believe what he was saying. "I thought at our first meeting that you did not like me."

"No, I did not like that you had been introduced to Philip and that my father and your father were pushing a courtship between the two of you. To be perfectly honest, I was nearly devastated." He looked away and chuckled.

She looked at him with wide eyes, unable to speak.

He took both of her hands in his. "Please say that you will marry me. I promise that I will love you forever."

Tears sprang to Elizabeth's eyes and she nodded several times. "Yes, I would be so very happy to marry you!"

Lord James stood up and Elizabeth did the same not wanting to let go of his hands. "I would have preferred to court you longer but I think we should announce our engagement as soon as possible to quiet the gossips. If you like, we could have a more lengthy engagement to allow us to court a while longer."

"Lord James..."

"Please, call me James," he said quietly.

She smiled shyly and said, "James, I think that would be agreeable, although, I do not need more time to know that I want to marry you. I think it would be good though for me to spend some time getting acquainted with Cambridge."

He seemed surprised that she remembered. Elizabeth laughed. "If I am to be a barrister's wife, I suppose I should start preparing now."

"Have I mentioned how wonderful you are?" James asked looking down at her.

She tipped her head to the side slightly. "No, but I think I will love hearing it."

Did you enjoy James' story - *A Brother's Duty*, Book One in the Repington Chronicles Series? Want to find out what happens next in the family saga?

Following is a preview of Philip's story – *The Wayward Heir*, Book Two.

Preview of *The Wayward Heir*

"I did not think I would ever say this but I am quite sad to say farewell to France."

Philip grimaced. "I was only too glad to leave Calais far behind."

"That does not surprise me." His friend Christopher Boswell, better known as Lord Fallbrooke, narrowed his eyes at him from across the coach. "You have been in a foul mood for the past week. I cannot think that you have missed England that much."

There had been a moment when Philip had first seen the white cliffs of Dover that he had felt a sudden and deep pang of homesickness. He had not expected it and had immediately pushed the feelings aside as he had so many times before.

He shifted in his seat in an attempt to shake off the heaviness that seemed to settle around him.

"Of course, not. Although I have missed our usual table at White's."

"Quite understandable. The gambling clubs in Paris are just not the same," Fallbrooke lamented. "Although their theater is much more enjoyable, not quite so stiff and compromising."

"I agree wholeheartedly. However, I feel I must point out that I doubt theater patrons in England would consider the performances we viewed in Paris as theater."

Fallbrooke let out a bawdy laugh. "You are quite right, but it does explain why it was so enjoyable for us."

Philip smiled back at his friend, it was more out of habit than any sense of happiness. Fallbrooke had not been exaggerating, Philip had been in a foul mood as of late.

Their visit to France was to be a carefree adventure for them. As they had passed through London, Fallbrooke had had the foresight to stop so that Philip could procure more funds from the Duke of Castborough's solicitor. They were more than a day ahead of Philip's father and they knew there would be no way for him to have notified the solicitor that Philip had been cut off financially.

They had lived extravagantly eating well during the day, drinking and gambling through the night. Often those nights would start out at the theater. That first fortnight in Paris the nights had ended with them getting back as the sun rose over the houses on the banks of the Seine.

Philip had grown tired of it quickly though he had gone along with Fallbrooke's ideas simply because he always had. It was disconcerting enough that he was not enjoying the same activities and lifestyle that he had fought so hard to protect only months before.

His brother's words to him ringing in his ears. "You are a disgrace to the Castborough title! I hate who you have become."

Philip had done his best to forget the argument. James had confronted him in the stable before he and the others had fled his father's house party to run off to Paris. He had not even told Fallbrooke about the argument.

"And really anything was better than that sedate house party with your father and Southwick setting the ever high in the instep, Lady Elizabeth in front of you at every moment."

"Yes, that was most annoying," Philip said dryly and then turned toward the window.

Lady Elizabeth Comerford, the only daughter of the Earl of Southwick. She was a beautiful young lady and quite well-versed in the social graces.

Philip had known that marrying her would not have been so horrible. He had resigned himself to the fate. That was until he had found her talking to his brother. The way she had looked up at James was not something Philip would soon forget. Her green eyes had widened and her smile was as sincere as he had seen since his return to Surrey. Lady Elizabeth had clearly fallen in love with his brother, although Philip had wondered if the girl even realized it.

At the time, Philip had been upset and then later furious. He was the firstborn, the heir of the Duke of Castborough. James was the spare, the unlucky second born son and yet he was always the favorite, always getting what Philip wanted.

In his anger, at James, he had continued to pursue Lady Elizabeth, only to turn his frustrations toward her when he noticed that James had arrived or his father would make another comment. As a result of his anger, Philip had been openly rude to Lady Elizabeth on several occasions and yet she had remained gracious and polite, which had only served to anger him further.

Had she yelled at him, called him a name or slapped him he could have dealt with that but she simply nodded, squared her shoulders and excused herself politely. He felt like the lowest person and he could not help but think that she and James were well suited for each other. They could get married and simply be perfect for the rest of their lives.

Of course, there had been the argument with James. Philip had been aghast when James had landed a facer, that had sent him reeling. He had responded in kind, which had been a stupid mistake. While Philip had been living it up in London, James had been riding horses and tending to the tenants. He was stronger and it had taken almost no effort for him to overpower Philip.

He had expected James to land more blows but instead, he had only held Philip on the ground while he yelled.

"Now that you are free of the chit, you can return to London to finish out the Season." Philip heard Fallbrooke say.

"I am not entirely certain that I will be staying in London long."

"Why ever not?" Fallbrooke asked his dark eyebrows raised. "You are the heir. You can do what you want."

Philip nodded with a conviction that he did not truly feel. "I plan on it."

Find out more about Philip's story, The Wayward Heir.

http://kellyannebruce.com/books/philips-story-the-repington-chronicles/

THE WAYWARD HEIR

PHILIP

CHAPTER ONE

"I did not think I would ever say this but I am quite sad to say farewell to France."

Philip grimaced. "I was only too glad to leave Calais far behind."

"That does not surprise me." His friend Christopher Boswell, better known as Lord Fallbrooke, narrowed his eyes at him from across the coach. "You have been in a foul mood for the past week. I cannot think that you have missed England that much."

There had been a moment when Philip had first seen the white cliffs of Dover that he had felt a sudden and deep pang of homesickness. He had not expected it and had immediately pushed the feelings aside as he had so many times before.

He shifted in his seat in an attempt to shake off the heaviness that seemed to settle around him.

"Of course, not. Although I have missed our usual table at White's."

"Quite understandable. The gambling clubs in Paris are just not the same," Fallbrooke lamented. "Although their theater is much more enjoyable, not quite so stiff and compromising."

"I agree wholeheartedly. However, I feel I must point out that I doubt theater patrons in England would consider the performances we viewed in Paris as theater."

Fallbrooke let out a bawdy laugh. "You are quite right, but it does explain why it was so enjoyable for us."

Philip smiled back at his friend, it was more out of habit than any sense of happiness. Fallbrooke had not been exaggerating, Philip had been in a foul mood as of late.

Their visit to France was to be a carefree adventure for them. As they had passed through London, Fallbrooke had had the foresight to stop so that Philip could procure more funds from the Duke of Castborough's solicitor. They were more than a day ahead of Philip's father and they knew there would be no way for him to have notified the solicitor that Philip had been cut off financially.

They had lived extravagantly eating well during the day, drinking and gambling through the night. Often those nights would start out at the theater. That first fortnight in Paris the nights had ended with them getting back as the sun rose over the houses on the banks of the Seine.

Philip had grown tired of it quickly though he had gone along with Fallbrooke's ideas simply because he always had. It was disconcerting enough that he was not enjoying the same activities and lifestyle that he had fought so hard to protect only months before.

His brother's words to him ringing in his ears. "You are a disgrace to the Castborough title! I hate who you have become."

Philip had done his best to forget the argument. James had confronted him in the stable before he and the others had fled his father's house party to run off to Paris. He had not even told Fallbrooke about the argument.

"And really anything was better than that sedate house party with your father and Southwick setting the ever high in the instep, Lady Elizabeth in front of you at every moment."

"Yes, that was most annoying," Philip said dryly and then turned toward the window.

Lady Elizabeth Comerford, the only daughter of the Earl of

Southwick. She was a beautiful young lady and quite well-versed in the social graces.

Philip had known that marrying her would not have been so horrible. He had resigned himself to the fate. That was until he had found her talking to his brother. The way she had looked up at James was not something Philip would soon forget. Her green eyes had widened and her smile was as sincere as he had seen since his return to Surrey. Lady Elizabeth had clearly fallen in love with his brother, although Philip had wondered if the girl even realized it.

At the time, Philip had been upset and then later furious. He was the firstborn, the heir of the Duke of Castborough. James was the spare, the unlucky second born son and yet he was always the favorite, always getting what Philip wanted.

In his anger, at James, he had continued to pursue Lady Elizabeth, only to turn his frustrations toward her when he noticed that James had arrived or his father would make another comment. As a result of his anger, Philip had been openly rude to Lady Elizabeth on several occasions and yet she had remained gracious and polite, which had only served to anger him further.

Had she yelled at him, called him a name or slapped him he could have dealt with that but she simply nodded, squared her shoulders and excused herself politely. He felt like the lowest person and he could not help but think that she and James were well suited for each other. They could get married and simply be perfect for the rest of their lives.

Of course, there had been the argument with James. Philip had been aghast when James had landed a facer, that had sent him reeling. He had responded in kind, which had been a stupid mistake. While Philip had been living it up in London, James had been riding horses and tending to the tenants. He was stronger and it had taken almost no effort for him to overpower Philip.

He had expected James to land more blows but instead, he had only held Philip on the ground while he yelled.

"Now that you are free of the chit, you can return to London to finish out the Season." Philip heard Fallbrooke say.

"I am not entirely certain that I will be staying in London long."

"Why ever not?" Fallbrooke asked his dark eyebrows raised. "You are the heir. You can do what you want."

Philip nodded with a conviction that he did not truly feel. "I plan on it."

CHAPTER TWO

"Welcome back to Fallbrooke Hall, sir." Jenkins, Fallbrooke's manservant announced as he led them to the drawing room. "How did you enjoy your stay in Paris?"

"It was very enjoyable. I could have stayed for several more weeks." Fallbrooke collapsed elegantly into a large upholstered chair. "Lord Holgrave was apparently not as enamored with Paris, as I was."

Philip grumbled to himself and moved to the window. He did not know why Fallbrooke was still going on about Paris. And that he would bring his servant into the discussion seem distasteful, even for Fallbrooke. In that moment, Philip suddenly wondered if he had grown weary of Fallbrooke and his antics.

The two had known each other since their school days but they had only become close the last two Seasons as they had often been the first to leave the most boring balls and the last to leave the most exclusive clubs. For nearly two years, Philip had spent much of his time in London, a great amount of it at Fallbrooke Hall. Up until a month ago, Philip had no desire to leave the parties and gambling behind but as of late, he was starting to wonder. It was not as enjoyable as it had been.

"I assume you will be visiting White's this evening?" Jenkins surmised.

"No," Philip replied. At the same time, Fallbrooke said, "but of course."

Stanton smiled. "Very good, sirs."

"What is wrong with you, Holgrave?" Fallbrooke asked once Jenkins had left them alone in the drawing room.

"I do not know what you are talking about," Philip replied.

"You have been pacing in front of the window since we arrived. What has you so restless?"

Philip stopped pacing and sat down in a chair, his annoyance with Fallbrooke deepening. Finally, he barked out, "You are talking nonsense."

"Perhaps I should add agitated to the list." Fallbrooke gave him a long look. "Could it be that you are still heartbroken over the fair Juliette?"

Philip swore under his breath and stood up again. "You are a poor excuse for a friend. I believe it is time for me to return to Castborough House."

He was nearly to the door when Fallbrooke said in a sneering voice, "Are you so quick to reconcile with your family? So soon after running off to Paris? My, my, we are suddenly brave."

If there had been any question about Philip's opinion of Fallbrooke it was now very clear. His first urge was to slam his fist into Fallbrooke's smug face the only thing that stopped it was the fact that the arrogant bastard was right.

Having no choice before him, Philip turned slowly with a sheepish look on his face the one he normally reserved for his mother or sister. "Forgive me. I must seem quite ridiculous. I confess that I have not slept well in recent nights."

Fallbrooke nodded as he stood. "I suspected something must be amiss."

"I knew you would understand," Philip told him. He shrugged and motioned towards the stairs. "Perhaps I should go lie down."

"No, my friend you should go with me to White's." Fallbrooke clapped him on the shoulder. "A few games of Whist and a bottle of whiskey will do you some good."

Philip closed his eyes, he did not want to go to White's. His excuse to Fallbrooke held more truth than he had first intended as he realized how tired he really was. In fact, too tired to argue his point. So instead he nodded, saying sagely, "You might have it there. An enjoyable night at our favorite table might be just what I need."

"There you go."

Philip continued to the stairs his only solace in going to White's was that there was little chance he would encounter any of his family at the elite gambling club.

AN HOUR later they were sitting at their familiar table with glasses of whiskey in front of them. Philip was just starting to think that he might finally relax when he heard someone call his name. He turned to see Nigel Coombs waving as he worked his way over to their table. Fallbrooke stood up. "I shall see about getting us another drink."

Philip raised an eyebrow but said nothing as his friend left the table with much haste.

"Holgrave! " Coombs called out once more, a broad smile covering his thin, freckled face. "I did not know that you were back from Paris."

"Well, we have only just returned." Philip began to explain.

"After all of the trouble at Castborough, I thought for sure you would not return until long after the Season had ended."

Philip had hoped to subtly glean some information from other patrons at White's regarding what had happened after they had fled his father's house party. The night was still young and the drinks had not been flowing long enough for him to have asked any of his questions.

His only defense was confusion, he furrowed his eyebrows at the younger man. "Trouble?"

Nigel drew back wearing a similar look of confusion upon his face. "Then you have not heard?"

"I am not sure what you are speaking of so I cannot say whether I have heard or not," Philip said with a raised eyebrow.

"Oh, yes, of course," Coombs replied and swallowed. "Your father and Lord Southwick seemed quite put out that you and the others had left."

Philip shrugged, already turning back to his game of whist. "That was to be expected."

"True. Although it was quite unexpected when James' engagement to Lady Elizabeth was announced." There was a touch of evil glee in Coombs' voice. Philip kept his gaze on his cards until he had schooled his features. He looked wanly up at Coombs before saying, "Was that unexpected?"

Coombs paled, his freckles standing out against his even whiter skin. "But you... We all... " he stammered but then trailed off. "What of...?"

"What of what?" Philip asked nonchalantly, feeling a little twinge of guilt at pushing Coombs. Only a little, though, as Philip was quite sure that their conversation would be repeated as soon as Coombs walked away from the table.

"Holgrave, you must be full into your cups to not realize that everyone at your father's house party watched your courtship of Lady Elizabeth Comerford." This came from Henry Milling, a short man more known for being crass and crude than his true place in society.

Coombs seemed emboldened by Milling's comment, snorting as he added, "And your summary dismissal of the same."

Philip shrugged, a movement nearly imperceptible had Coombs and Millings had not been hovering for gossip tidbits like the gulls on the waterfront.

"It was simply a ruse," Philip said pretending to concentrate on the cards before him.

"A ruse?" Milling repeated, his voice harsh. "What are you talking about? You were to marry Lady Elizabeth and you left her. She had no choice but to marry James."

It was not something that Philip wanted to think about but clearly, the gossips had made their usual assumptions. He pushed the feelings of guilt away, like he always did, and turned to Milling.

"No choice?" He asked in mock dismay. "Have they married?"

"Not yet, no."

"Have they asked for a special license?"

"No, but…"

"So, it seems Lady Elizabeth had some choice in the matter." He stared at Milling waiting for an answer. When one was not forthcoming, Philip remarked, "It appears that our ruse worked."

"What did the ruse entail, pray tell?" Milling asked his black eyes hard.

"The house party, like all events of the Season, was an opportunity for a young lady to find a suitor. Lady Elizabeth and my brother simply wanted a chance to get to know each other without gossip circling them like vultures." Coombs had the sense to realize that Philip was talking about people like himself and Milling.

"You expect us to believe that? Milling asked. "Holgrave, we are all aware of your reputation with the petticoat line."

"I care not whether you believe it or not." Philip pushed his chair back from the table and stood up to tower over the smaller man. "The truth is that my brother, James, is betrothed to Lady Elizabeth Comerford, the only daughter of the Earl of Southwick. They have decided to have a long engagement which could only point to a lasting union."

Milling sputtered for a moment but said nothing.

Philip looked over Milling's head to peer through the club. "Perhaps we should ask Southwick's opinion?"

Milling took a startled step back before looking around quickly. "Southwick? He is here?"

"That is what I heard when we arrived." Philip leaned a hip

against the table. "I am sure we can find him if you would like. What do you think, Coombs?"

The man swallowed before shaking his head vehemently. "No, I find your explanation perfectly acceptable."

Philip turned a hard eye on Milling. "What about you, Henry?" Purposely calling him by his Christian name.

"Yes, quite right." Milling gave them both a curt nod before leaving quickly, disappearing into the crowded cardroom.

It was not much longer before Coombs mumbled an excuse and rushed off as well.

"What was that all about?" Fallbrooke asked returning to the table, a bottle of whiskey in his hand.

Philip waited for the other man to be seated. "Coombs and Milling were here to make sure that I knew that my brother James is now betrothed."

"How interesting. Did they mention who the unfortunate young lady might be."

A strange smile came to Philip's lips at Fallbrooke's question. "Yes, of course. It is Lady Elizabeth Comerford."

"I see." Fallbrooke nodded, his face serious. "Well, that explains a conversation I just had in the other room."

"Oh?"

"I heard that Lady Elizabeth was betrothed but the gentleman seemed to think I would have known already." Fallbrooke pursed his lips before saying, "It seems your complacent brother is quite the romantic. He now frequents London often taking in the opera or ballet with his betrothed."

Of course, Philip thought. He had been unsure about returning to London and this was a sure sign that he was right.

"I wonder now if our return from Paris was a bit premature."

"Not to worry, my friend. We will be leaving London posthaste."

"We are?" Philip asked. "Where might we be going?"

"Brighton. Lord Stratford is having a house party."

Philip groaned. He was not sure another house party was the best idea.

"Not to worry," Fallbrooke was already saying. "It is a small party, not the usual crowd at all. What do you think?"

It seemed his choices were few, he could either stay in London and never leave Fallbrooke Hall or go to another infernal house party. He was trying to reason whether Fallbrooke Hall would be overly horrible when compared to endless garden parties, picnics, and dancing. Although Philip did have good memories visiting Stratford Manor. After a moment, Philip scrubbed his hand across his forehead trying to relieve the throbbing from another blasted headache.

"Fine. We shall go to Brighton."

CHAPTER THREE

Philip closed his eyes sending up a silent prayer that Fallbrooke would eventually stop speaking. It did not seem to be a likely outcome, as the man had been talking since the moment they entered the carriage in London to set out for Brighton. Between Fallbrooke's constant conversation and the jarring movement of the carriage, Philip could barely think.

"Are you even listening to me?"

A long moment of silence stretched out until Philip sighed and opened one eye to look at Fallbrooke. "And what if I say no? Would you stop talking for a longer stretch of time than it takes for you to fill your bloody lungs?"

"I see that you are in a sour mood again."

"I am not a sour mood. My head aches and I simply wish for a few moments of peace and quiet."

"Is it my fault you had too much whiskey last night?"

"Perhaps not but I needn't be subjected to your infernal babbling." Philip did not bother telling the other man that he had hardly drank anything the night before. The pain in his head had started while they were in Paris and he had blamed the drinks at the gambling club. He had hoped the pain would have subsided by now but it only seemed to have increased. He hoped several nights of good sleep in Brighton would help

"Hmmm," Fallbrooke commented. "It sounds like you need a keeper. Too bad you were not able to talk Juliette into returning to London with us."

Philip pinched the bridge of his nose praying that the piercing pain behind his eyes would lessen. Any hope that Fallbrooke would stop talking had already disappeared. He took a calming breath and then speaking slowly and carefully said, "I do not need a keeper. And Juliet did not come to England with us because I did not ask her to do so."

"I bet you are regretting that now," Fallbrooke remarked with a knowing smile.

"No, I do not regret it nor will I ever. Although I have to say I am regretting bringing you back from Paris."

"Holgrave, we have spent much time together and I admit most of it has been enjoyable but you have been nastier than a bawson since we left London for Castborough." Fallbrooke stared at Philip for a moment and then sighed. "There is something wrong but it seems far too much work at the moment to discern the cause."

Silence fell over the carriage as Fallbrooke leaned back into the corner of his seat and turned to look out the window at the slowly passing landscape.

Glad of the silence, Philip closed his eyes once more, holding a distant hope that if he feigned sleep that he might actually gain some rest. It was not long though that he found out that without Fallbrooke's constant conversation that his thoughts returned once more to James and Lady Elizabeth.

Nigel Coombs' revelation the night before had been a surprise to him not because his brother and Lady Elizabeth had decided to marry. He had seen them together, there had been something there that Philip himself had never experienced. They were drawn to each other, somehow connected so it had not caught him as off guard as one would think.

It had taken him merely a moment or two to recover. The news had not been what surprised him. No, it had been his reaction that had been a revelation. He had not expected the embarrassment that he had felt when Milling had mentioned how Philip had left Lady Elizabeth. When they had left Castborough all Philip had thought about was how he hated the disappointment on his father's face. And how James only reminded him of everything Philip had done wrong.

For a very long time, he had little care for what people thought of him. He never really thought about the lasting effects of his leaving would cause Lady Elizabeth. The thought had truly not occurred to him and to be truly honest he had not cared. On occasion during the Paris adventure thoughts of James and Lady Elizabeth had popped into his head and as always, he had pushed them away. He drank more whiskey or followed Fallbrooke to a wilder party, anything to silence the thoughts that seemed to want to gnaw their way to the forefront. It had gotten more and more difficult to push those thoughts away. Hearing Milling's crass comments in White's had made Philip want to cringe.

As much as he tried Philip could not silence the voice in his head, his brother asking, "What if someone had spoken to Henrietta like that?"

Philip had been outraged. Their youngest sibling and only sister deserved nothing but respect and civility. He could not help but feel that Lady Elizabeth deserved no less. While he still did not regret leaving Castborough, it was becoming clear that in doing so he caused great distress to Lady Elizabeth.

The throbbing in his head seem to intensify and he leaned against the back of the seat praying that the pain would subside. Philip closed his eyes knowing that he had some decisions to make.

"CAROLINE!"

Looking up from her book, Caroline let out a sigh before calling out, "Yes, Mother."

A moment later her mother rushed into the room. "There you are." Her voice was exasperated and she looked worried. "Have you seen Simon and Miles?"

"No, I have not. Is there something amiss?"

Mother crossed the room and looked out the window. "It seems that your brothers have disappeared again."

"Would you like me to go find them?" Caroline offered, unable to ignore the distressed look on her mother's face. Her younger brothers were quite adept at getting into mischief.

"Do you mind terribly?" Mother asked. "Since Mrs Addison left I have had the worst time with your brothers. They have been so mischievous."

Caroline looked down at her hands and smiled. The boys had always been mischievous. It was Mrs Addison that had borne the brunt of their antics and her strong hand that had kept the boys in check enough that Mother and Father had not seen the trouble they had caused. Mrs Addison had been gone only a few weeks and without her watchful eye the two boys were more than unruly. They had gone missing more times than Caroline could count. Their mother was surprised and distressed over the boys' behaviour while she also tried to be a gracious hostess for the house party that had started earlier in the week.

"Yes, of course. I am sure that I can round them up in no time. They have probably gone down to the stable to see the new foals." It was more likely that they were watching the gentleman racing their fancy carriages in the lanes beyond the stables. It would do no good for her to tell her mother, though. Not only would she be horrified to hear that the boys were in the middle of that, she would think it too scandalous for Caroline to show her face there as well.

"Thank you, I am supposed to take Lady Halswood and Lady Weston on a tour of the gardens in the next hour."

"You go along," Caroline said while making shooing motions with her hands. "You do not want to keep Lady Halswood waiting."

Mother sighed and raising her eyes to the heavens. "No, I do not. We are all still hearing about the time Lord Cullingham was late for one of her parties."

"That was two years ago, was it not?"

Her mother moved to the door. "Yes, and he was only late because his carriage lost a wheel."

"Surely, he should have run through the streets of London so as not to be late," Caroline said with a smirk following her mother out to the hall.

"Clearly," her mother answered and shook her head. They parted at the end of the hall.

Caroline went into the kitchen to duck out through the east door. She hoped to avoid the guests in the garden particularly Lady Halswood. If she were being completely honest, Caroline had been avoiding the guests since the house party had begun. It was not a very large party so it had not been too great a task. When she did encounter a guest, she was as gracious and accommodating as possible, and if asked she obliged her parents to make an appearance at dinner or a party activity.

A horse whinnied as she passed the stable and Caroline turned toward the stable door muttering, "I might as well check while I am here."

She had barely taken another step when the door open as she collided with someone coming out. Startled, she stepped back and tripped over her skirts. As she began to fall two hands shot out to land on her shoulders, steadying her.

"Caroline?"

She looked up into a pair of very blue eyes. Blue eyes she had not seen in years.

"Philip! I did not know you were coming to the house party."

Apparently assured that she had regained her footing Philip released her shoulders and took a step back. "I had not known myself until a few days ago, Fallbrooke was invited by Lord Stratford's brother."

Caroline smiled thinking of her uncle, Robbie, her father's

youngest brother, a man with a good heart. Her smile faded quickly though, as she recalled Philip's words. "Lord Fallbrooke? Did he accompany you?"

"Did I hear someone say my name in vain?" A tall good-looking man with dark hair asked from the stable door.

Caroline stifled a gasp and took a step back. "No," she said quickly turning back to Philip. "I am looking for my brothers perhaps you saw them in the stable."

Philip looked from her default work before saying, "No, there is no one save the groom in the stables. Have you been looking for them long?"

Caroline shook her head. "This was my first stop." She looked past the stables more to ignore Lord Fallbrooke than anything "I suspect they have gone down to see the buggy races."

Philip followed her gaze. "Surely you are not thinking of walking down to the lanes by yourself?"

Caroline opened her mouth to tell him that she was planning to do just that when Lord Fallbrooke swept over to her. Caroline stiffened seeing the man get closer to her.

"I would be happy to walk you down there." Fallbrooke reached out to take her arm. "I will show you a good time."

"I only want to find my brothers," Caroline retorted pulling her arm away as she stepped back again. "I care not for your good time."

Lord Fallbrooke's face flushed with anger and Caroline expected him to lash out at her.

"Simon and Miles?" Philip interrupted them by asking. "How old are they now? Seven and nine?"

"Miles has just celebrated his twelfth year and Simon his tenth."

Philip shrugged and gave her a crooked grin. "Apparently, it has been longer than I thought." Then to her surprise, he stepped over to the other man. "Fallbrooke, go down to the lanes to retrieve Lady Caroline's adventurous brothers."

Lord Fallbrooke looked to argue but Philip added. "We must be gracious to our hosts. I am sure that Lord Stratford will be quite thankful for keeping his sons out of harm's way."

She thought Lord Fallbrooke's hesitation signaled his dissension but after a moment he nodded his head and turned toward the lanes. Philip called after him, "Two young boys, red hair, much darker than Lady Caroline's."

"I shall return with them posthaste," Lord Fallbrooke said with a flourish of his hand and a deep bow and then disappeared around the stable.

"I must admit I am surprised that he agreed to help." Caroline was more than surprised after all she had first-hand knowledge of Lord Fallbrooke selfishness.

Philip was still looking toward the lanes. "I knew he would not pass up the possible chance to do a favor for your father. He would like nothing more than to impress him. Doing a favor will get him a favor."

"A favor?" Caroline could not fathom what he could mean. "I am afraid I do not understand."

"Of course not, you are a well behaved young lady well instructed in the social graces. Fallbrooke, while certainly well instructed, is not well behaved and often needs a well-placed favor to get him out of scrapes here and there."

"Yes, I can imagine," Caroline told him. She hoped the anger she was feeling was not evident but turned toward the house just in case. "Please tell Lord Fallbrooke to bring the boys to the house."

"I will go down to the lanes now to help him look."

"Thank you for your assistance, Lord Holgrave."

"My pleasure," he nodded at her before walking away.

CHAPTER FOUR

"Holgrave?"

"Yes?" Philip asked looking at the man sitting next to him.

"I was asking if you wanted to play another hand." The man held up his cards as further proof of the question. "You seemed not to hear me."

"Yes, my apologies." Philip shifted in his seat. "It is this blasted pain in my head. Another hand would be a welcome distraction."

The man began the next hand as Fallbrooke added, "You clearly have not had enough to drink, Holgrave."

Fallbrooke thought it a joke but Philip's head had continued to hurt since they had arrived at Stratford. He felt fortunate that he had, for the most part, been able to ignore it.

Instead, he had been thinking about Lady Caroline Hadley. He had known her since she was quite young, quite possibly the same age as one of her brothers. She had been a wisp of a girl with fiery hair.

Philip had been friends with her uncle, Robert. Of course, they had called him Robbie back then, in fact, Philip still did. But even at a young age, Caroline had shown herself to be quite confident and stubborn too.

The memory of his summer at Stratford came to mind. It was a summer day when he and Robbie had decided to explore the countryside in search for the source of their ponds. Caroline had wanted to go but Robbie has said no that it was too far to walk, that she was too small and frail to go. Philip remembered clearly Caroline's disagreement saying that she could walk that far and she had punctuated her argument with a frustrated stamp of her foot.

Robbie had given in and she had been true to her word. She had kept up and never uttered a word of complaint even when it was clear that she was near exhaustion. Her uncle had pulled her up on his back and carried her the last mile or two back home.

Fallbrooke brought Philip back to the present. "I had forgotten that you were acquainted with Lady Caroline."

Philip was about to explain that it had been many years since they had seen one another but Fallbrooke was still speaking. "She is a beauty. You think she will be overly grateful that I directed her brothers from the lane?"

"It is doubtful," Philip answered coolly. The look of anger on Caroline's face suddenly came back to him. "I rather think she was not too glad to see you."

"I am not surprised," the other man at the table spoke up. Philip had nearly forgotten that he was there. "Lady Caroline has not taken part of any activities of the Season thus far."

Philip frowned. "Why not? She is of age, certainly."

"Perhaps she is betrothed?" Fallbrooke asked.

"No," The man shook his head and gave Fallbrooke a pointed look. "She was betrothed last Season to Nathaniel Lymington. I am sure the name is familiar. It all ended quite tragically, though, as you must know."

The name sounded quite familiar. "What happened?" He wanted to know more about Lady Caroline and her recent past.

"Ask your friend," the man said pointing across the room to where Fallbrooke was now speaking to several young ladies.

"Fallbrooke?"

The man nodded as he stood up. "Yes, he was mixed up with the whole affair."

Philip stared at Fallbrooke in surprise, by the time he turned back around the other man had gone. Pausing for a moment, Philip watched his friend across the room. To anyone else, Fallbrooke was quite engaged in the conversation but Philip noticed the furtive glances back to their table. It was rather clear to him at least, that Fallbrooke was attempting to hide something.

It was not all that surprising given the trouble Fallbrooke was prone to get into. Philip joined Fallbrooke, smiling cordially at the ladies before saying, "Fallbrooke, I have a few questions when you have a moment."

"A moment?" Fallbrooke laughed, concentrating his smile on a golden-haired beauty who looked barely old enough to have left the school room. "Currently my moments belong to..." He looked at the girl with raised eyebrows and a smirk.

"Priscilla," the young lady provided.

"Miss Priscilla, yes. Quite right. My moments belong to Miss Priscilla."

Something about Fallbrooke's behaviour irritated Philip causing him to say, "Oh, I am quite sure that Miss Priscilla would be gracious enough to let me steal you away for a few minutes. Yes?" Philip smiled at her and she nodded.

"But, I am quite busy, you see." Fallbrooke protested but Philip was already ushering him from the room.

They had barely walked into the library when Fallbrooke whirled on him. "What is so important that you had to drag me in here now?"

Philip snorted. "As if you were doing anything truly important."

"I was getting acquainted with Miss Penelope."

"Priscilla. She said her name is Priscilla." Philip corrected his friend, shaking his head in disapproval. "You cannot expect me to believe that you are interested in that young lady? You cannot even remember her name."

"You can believe I am interested in some companionship tonight."

Philip stared at the other man. After all, they had been through, it had finally happened, Fallbrooke had truly shocked him. "You cannot be serious." Philip pointed toward the drawing room. "The girl is barely out of the school room."

Oblivious to Philip's irritation, Fallbrooke smiled and nodded. "I have a bet with Bannerman that I can persuade one of the chits into the garden for a late-night interlude."

It took Philip a few moments to realize that Bannerman was the other man at the table playing cards. "I have seen you do a lot of unseemly things but this…" Philip broke off shaking his head.

Fallbrooke stared at him, before laughing. "I do not know what has happened to you. Ever since Paris, you have been different. Surely Juliette—"

"This is not about Juliette!" Philip barked, interrupting. Then suddenly put a hand to his forehead as the pain flared from the normal dull throbbing.

"Then what is it about?" Fallbrooke demanded loudly. "When did you develop a conscience? That is what I would like to know."

Philip had known it had been at the house party at Castborough but he would never admit that to Fallbrooke.

"Does it matter?"

"Yes! You used to be ready for anything, a regular out and outer but lately you have wanted nothing to do with anything remotely enjoyable."

"Oh yes, ruining the reputations of the young ladies at social gatherings has always been high on my list of favorite activities."

"You did not seem to care a bit about that when you were playing with Lady Elizabeth."

"That was different," Philip told him. He was so angry he could barely see straight.

"Why? Because you did not bed her? It was not for lack of

trying I am sure." Fallbrooke stepped toward the door only to turn back. "You should be thanking me, though."

"And why is that?" Philip sneered.

"I was talking to a very lovely young lady at Castborough. I could have had her at any point but I did not."

"Why would I care about that?"

"It was pointed out later that she was your sister."

"Bastard," Philip snarled gripping onto the corner of the desk.

Fallbrooke held up his hands. "I backed off, although I must say it was most difficult. Lady Henrietta has quite the abundance of beauty and shall we say... charm."

Philip was screaming inside his head but only a strangled sound passed his lips. He took a step toward Fallbrooke but his legs felt like lead and his vision blurred. He had the sudden sensation that he was falling. Far away he heard someone call his name and then darkness descended.

CHAPTER FIVE

Caroline backed out of the darkened room shutting the door as quietly as possible. She let out a long sigh and then nearly screamed when someone tapped her on the shoulder.

"Are they all settled for the night?"

Turning slowly, she found her mother standing in the hall. "Goodness, Mother!" Caroline whispered loudly. "You nearly gave me a fright."

"Oh dear, I am quite sorry. I just now came up the stairs and saw you in the hall. I thought you were just checking on the boys."

Caroline shook her head. "No, they have only just fallen asleep. I am glad that I was able to stifle my scream with my hand or they surely would have awakened. That would not have been good for any of us."

Her mother opened the door quietly, smiling sweetly as she looked in and then stepped back. "I think they will sleep quite soundly. They had a rather busy day."

"Yes, yes. They did indeed," Caroline agreed.

"Thank you for finding them and getting them settled. I am sorry that you missed out on the activities tonight. I am told the card party in the drawing room was quite enjoyable." Her mother gave her a sad smile.

"I am sure that it was." Caroline had not wanted to attend the card party but her mother would never understand, so she kept it to herself.

"I suppose you spent the night reading," her mother stopped at the top of the stairs.

"Actually, no, I did not." Caroline frowned remembering that she had left her book next to the chair earlier in the day. "Simon was giving Miles and me a quite detailed account of how he got so muddy. That story took a while to tell."

Mother's eyes widened and she covered her mouth with her hand to suppress her laughter. "That must have been very entertaining. I am somewhat sad that I missed it."

Caroline laughed. "Perhaps if you ask him he will put on a second performance. He seemed to enjoy the attention."

Her mother's soft laughter could be heard as Caroline descended the stairs. She paused at the landing listening for any noise downstairs preferring not to run into any guests. She had done well avoiding most of the activities connected with the house party. She had suspected that her mother had decided to have the party hoping Caroline would want to participate in other events of the Season. Her mother would never understand why Caroline wanted nothing more to do with London society. Although seeing Philip had been a nice surprise, it was people like Lord Fallbrooke that she had wanted nothing to do with.

After listening for a few minutes, Caroline continued down the stairs. The room was shrouded in darkness, which was rather unexpected. She stopped for a quick moment to get her bearings. Father nearly always left the lamp burning in the library.

She heard a noise across the room surmised that her father was still in the drawing room, probably arguing about relations with France or whether the Prince Regent would stay in London through the Season.

Even with the nearly complete darkness, Caroline was able to navigate the room rather easily. She found her book on the table where she had left it earlier. She looked forward to reading for the next hour or so. Sleep still escaped her and reading had been the only way to occupy her mind until she fell asleep. Margaret, her mother's maid had made a habit of stopping at her room to make sure the lamp had been put out.

As with most nights, Caroline held little hope that she would sleep well that night. Lord Fallbrooke's presence had seen to that. It was clear that the vain man had no inkling of how he had affected her life. In that respect, she was pleased he would never understand. She hated the idea of Fallbrooke knowing she had still not gotten over the events that had occurred over a year ago. She shook her head more to dispel the memories that were threatening to surface.

She was almost to the door when she heard another noise. From her vantage point, she could tell it was coming from behind her father's large desk. Her first instinct was to go look behind the desk and then she froze. What if she had interrupted some late-night tryst between party guests? She backed up a step toward the door.

She heard the noise again and for whatever reason, one that she, herself could not explain Caroline decided something was amiss and felt she must investigate. Cautiously, she went to the end of the desk and squinted into the darkness. At first, she saw nothing and gasped as she saw a pair of boots sticking out from behind the desk. They were a man's boots and the man was not moving.

"Oh Lord," she whispered and moved to the other end of the desk to light the lamp. Once lit she held it out and gasped again

"Philip!"

She set the lamp down and rushed to his side. "Philip? What is the matter? Can you hear me?"

At first, there was no response and Caroline feared the worst. Then his eyelids fluttered, not fully opening but surely a response to her questions. She reached down and took his hand in hers. "Philip, it is Caroline. Can you hear me?"

His eyelids fluttered again before opening slowly, his head

falling to the side to look at her. His eyes were glassy she wondered if he could see her at all.

"Philip, I need to go get help. Do not worry. I will be right back." She patted his hand and began to get up.

"No," he said so quietly she almost missed it but his hand grabbed hers again.

"I must go," she told him. His face is pale but his skin glistened. She put a hand on his forehead. "You are burning with a fever."

"No," he said again when she moved to get up.

"Philip, please," she pleaded.

"I do not wish to die alone," he whispered.

"Shh, now. You are not going to die."

"Always alone. Do not want to die."

"Philip, you are delirious." He was still gripping her hand. "I will just go to the door and call to the kitchens. I will not leave you."

"Promise me. I do not want to be alone. Please do not leave me."

"I will stay with you, Philip. I promise."

He released her hand. "Thank you."

As she went to the door she heard him murmur, "Everyone leaves me. Always alone. Do not want to die alone."

CHAPTER SIX

Caroline paced the hallway outside the old nursery. When Caroline had called for help no one quite knew what to do with Philip. After some discussion with several servants, Caroline had directed them to the recently vacated rooms in the old nursery. Miles and Simon had moved to a larger room upstairs the previous fall.

"Any word from the physician?" Caroline's mother asked sitting down in the chair next to her.

"No, he has been in there quite a while. I am becoming concerned."

Her mother patted her arm. "I am sure Mr Notley is doing everything he can to aid Lord Holgrave."

"I hope so." Caroline kept thinking about Philip's words to her. "I wish Mr Notley had let me stay with Lord Holgrave."

"Why ever for?" Mother asked sounding rather shocked.

"Lord Holgrave was upset and had asked me to stay. I promised that I would not leave him, Mother." She looked back to the door wishing the physician would come out soon.

"I am sure he will not remember. Margaret said he seemed

delirious." Her mother sniffed delicately before saying, "Birks thought he was foxed, he is known to dip rather deep."

"No, he was burning up from a terrible fever." Caroline turned back to her mother. "Birks assumed Lord Holgrave was drunk as a wheelbarrow and wanted to carry him outside to sleep it off. That is what he called it, anyway." Her mother shook her head but Caroline went on. "I had to remind Birks that we were speaking about the future Duke of Castborough and depositing him unceremoniously in the garden of Stratford Manor would not be proper."

Her mother's eyes widened. "Yes, not the best way to treat the heir of Castborough and the poor man is ill. Possibly rather ill, considering how much time has passed since the physician arrived."

Caroline opened her mouth to speak but stopped when the door opened and the physician emerged from the room.

"Mr Notley, how is he?" Caroline asked her voice wavering slightly.

"Lord Holgrave is very sick. He is suffering from a horrible fever. The next few days will be very important on whether he will recover."

"Whether he recovers?" Caroline repeated.

"Is it Scarlet Fever?" Mother asked quickly.

"No, Lady Stratford it is not. In my examination of Lord Holgrave, I found no evidence of throat irritation or the rash that is most often found when a patient is suffering from Scarlet Fever." The physician pursed his lips as though he was thinking about his next words carefully. "He is, however, extremely ill."

"Perhaps we should move him to London. Surely his family will want to..." Her voice trailed off as Mr Notley shook his head slowly.

"I apologize but he is much too sick to travel anywhere. I fear he would die before reaching London and I am uncertain if his condition is contagious." He shook his head again. "I am sorry but he must remain here."

Mother nodded, accepting the man's words. "What can be done for him?"

"He will need to be cared for here. Someone will be needed to watch him. Right now, he is asleep, delirious from the fever. While he is currently weakened, I worry that he will hurt himself in his delirium."

Her mother glanced down the stairs. "I suppose I could ask one of the footmen."

"No," Caroline blurted out. Birks had wanted to dump the man outside in the bushes, she could not abide the idea that he would or could care for Philip. "I will do it. I will care for Lord Holgrave."

She had promised to stay with him and after what happened to Nathaniel, Caroline could not walk away.

Her mother turned quickly to her but before she could speak the physician said, "Very well. I will go downstairs to write down instructions for Lord Holgrave's care. I will return in two days' time to check on him. You can, of course, send for me if his condition worsens or if I am needed."

"Thank you, Mr Notley."

"Yes, thank you," mother murmured. She moved to face Caroline after the man disappeared down the hallway. "I must say that I do not think it is proper for you to care for Lord Holgrave."

"Proper or not, I am going to do it." Caroline crossed her arms over her chest and stuck her chin out. She was determined to keep her promise.

"I do not think you have thought about this." Her mother closed her eyes for a moment. "I am sorry but I cannot allow it."

Caroline wanted to shout at her mother but that would do no good. Instead she calmly asked, "And who shall you ask to care for him?"

"Well," her mother looked flummoxed, as though she had not really thought about it. "As I said, I shall ask a footman or one of the grooms."

"Do you think a footman or a groom is competent enough? As

we mentioned before, we are speaking about the heir of Castborough."

"Yes, of course. Mrs Smythe then."

"Mrs Smythe is already too busy running the kitchens and house while we have a house full of guests. Will you be taking over for her then?"

"No," her mother's brow was furrowed. "Margaret could..."

Caroline knew she would not finish because then who would clean the upstairs rooms. "Mother, there is no one else. Lord Holgrave may be contagious. Whoever cares for him cannot also be caring for the horses or moving about the house."

"I am worried, Caroline. I do not want you to become sick as well."

"That is perfectly understandable but Lord Holgrave, Philip, a childhood friend, is in their suffering. I must do what I can to help him."

"Caroline, I do not agree."

"Mother, the physician did not seem overly concerned when I offered to care for Lord Holgrave. Surely if there was any real concern he would have made mention of it."

"I suppose if Mr Notley is coming by often enough that any sign of sickness will be caught early." Mother sank slowly into one of the chairs, her face creased in worry.

"Lord Holgrave is resting in the nursery. I can sleep in the governess' quarters and still be close to him in case I am needed."

"I will have Margaret go in and make up the bed with fresh linens for you," mother said seeming to come around.

"That is fine, and I will need some things brought down from my room as I do not think it wise for me to move about the house once I begin carrying for Lord Holgrave." She gave her mother a weak smile. "I am afraid I will not be able to keep an eye on the boys. I worry that if Lord Holgrave's condition is contagious it is more likely that they could become sick with the fever."

"Yes."

Caroline was sure that her mother had already begun to worry about that very thing.

"Perhaps you could talk to Anna from the kitchens. She has younger siblings. I am sure she would enjoy keeping track of them. Birks or one of the grooms could aid her in keeping them out of trouble."

"That is a very good idea. The boys like Anna very much, she is very sweet but she does not let them get away with anything either."

Caroline smiled as she had seen for herself how Anna dealt with the boys. If they misbehaved and she heard about it then she would not save them any biscuits and cakes. Even when Caroline's father had inquired Anna had told Lord Stratford that the boys had misbehaved and worried Lady Stratford.

"No sweets for either of them," Anna had declared.

Their father had agreed, much to the dismay of Miles and Simon. They had been sure to stay in her good graces for several days after that.

"I believe it is our best solution," Caroline agreed.

"I will go speak to Mr Notley to ensure that he stops by more often to keep an eye on both Lord Holgrave, and you."

"Thank you, Mother." Caroline touched her mother's arm. "I believe I will go look on Lord Holgrave."

"Yes, of course."

Caroline slipped into the room not wanting to disturb Philip. Her worry was for naught though as he was clearly sleeping and could not be awakened. She pulled a wooden chair with a padded upholstered back closer to his bedside.

"Philip, I am here. You are very sick. I promise that I would not leave you. I hope you can hear me."

Philip turned his head and mumbled something she did not understand before falling silent once more.

CHAPTER SEVEN

Philip was awake but he had no idea where he was. His first thought was that he had drunk too much whiskey last night. Too tired to keep his eyes open for long he let them close and tried to remember what had happened the night before.

As much as he thought he had no recollection of what he had been doing. Memories of Paris with Fallbrooke were foremost in his mind but that did not seem right. He vaguely remembered being in a coach with Fallbrooke but somehow, he thought they had been in England. It was possible that he was still in Paris which would explain why he did not recognize the room.

He concentrated on opening his eyes again but the swift glance did not yield enough for him to recognize his surroundings. It seemed to be early in the morning as the light filtering through the windows was dim and it cast shadows all about the room. His vision blurred and then he was not so sure about the time of day. The longer he worried over it, the more confused he became. Drifting away again, he could not control his consciousness.

Some time later, Philip awoke feeling poorly. His mouth was extremely dry and his head pounded. He moved his hand to push up from the bed and came to the sudden realization that he could not move. At first, he thought he was somehow being held down but soon it was clear that he lacked the strength to move. He tried again, his left shoulder lifted briefly before he collapsed back on the bed.

Unable to quell the panic rising inside him, Philip tried to roll over but only managed to rock his shoulders. His breath had started to come in gasps and he closed his eyes trying to calm himself. It was then that he heard someone talking quietly. It took a considerable effort but he turned his head enough to see someone near the window. In the dim light, he could only make out the form of a woman, she looked upon him with the bluest eyes he had ever seen. The last thing he thought before sleep claimed him again was that an angel was watching over him.

Someone was talking, he could hear the voice but he could not understand the words. His body felt heavy and his mind was clouded, flooded with a series of images that made no sense to him.

Opening his eyes took considerable effort he suddenly remembered being in a strange room without the strength to move. Surely it had been a dream, he thought to himself. When he tried a sit up he was unable to and he began to panic once more.

Something must have happened, but what? Maybe he could ask whoever was in the room. The voice sounded familiar and he remembered the angel. It was then that he wondered if he had died. The vague memory of immense pain and then falling to the ground played at the edges of his mind.

He forced his eyes up and tried to talk but his mouth was dry, his voice sounding like the growl of a dog. Frustrated he swallowed and tried to clear his throat. Almost immediately he felt someone beside him. Philip heard the light voice but did not understand. She held his head and put a cup to his lips and he drank feeling the cool liquid soothe his parched throat. After a moment, she took the cup away. He looked up at his helper she was dressed in white and she was flooded in bright light.

"Am I dead?" He heard himself ask his voice still raspy. His eyes were closing but he saw her shake her head and felt her reach for his hand before he drifted off yet again.

When he opened his eyes again he was lying on his back the smell of straw and horses filling his lungs. He looked up to see James standing over him. Philip struggled to get up as James yelled at him.

"You are a disgrace to the Castborough title. I deserve to be the heir."

Philip tried to reach out to him, but James faded into the darkness. The last thing he saw from his brother was a scowl.

Then, he found himself in the ballroom at Castborough. Everyone was talking and laughing as music played in the background. He was leading someone onto the dance floor but when he looked back to see who, she had disappeared. The people in the ballroom had stopped to look at him, the quiet conversation and laughter turned to shouting. People were pointing at him and one by one they turned their back on him and then disappeared.

James and Elizabeth were the only two people who remained in the ballroom. James continued to scowl and shook his head before taking Elizabeth's hand and leading her away.

The room descended into darkness and Philip woke up suddenly gasping, fighting the blanket that covered him. The room was dark and empty. He was now certain he had not died. His dream was surely a sign that he was to die soon though. He must make amends before he left his mortal life behind.

It was quite evident that he could get nothing accomplished whilst lying in a strange bed. He mustered all his strength to roll over. Groaning as he nearly rolled off the bed, one leg slipping to the ground, heavy and weak. He wondered if he would have the strength to stand. Shaking his head, he tried again. It did not matter, he would crawl if he had to, he would not die alone in a strange room with unfinished business weighing on his heart.

Philip held his breath as he pushed himself up into a sitting position. It seemed as though many minutes had passed and the effort had been immense. He was just about to push away from the bed when the door opened. A woman appeared, she gasped and said, "Oh my goodness. What are you doing?"

He could understand her and she spoke English perfectly, perhaps he was back in England and not in Paris as he had originally thought. It was of no matter though, he still needed to get out of there.

As if reading his mind, she said, "You need to get back into bed."

"No," he argued trying to stand up. "I need to go."

"Nonsense!" She put her hands on his shoulders and easily pushed him back onto the bed.

"No," he repeated and struggled to get up but her strength surprised him and he fell back against the pillows exhausted. Finally, frustrated he asked, "Where am I? What am I being kept here?"

"Kept here?" She asked with a frown. "Philip, you are very ill. Do you not remember?"

She had called him by name. Her voice was familiar but she was too far away for him to see her plainly. "Where am I? Who are you?"

"Philip, you are at Stratford Manor in Brighton."

She moved closer laying a wet cloth on his forehead. "It is Caroline. Do you remember me?"

"Caroline," he repeated slowly. She leaned even closer her blue eyes a sudden comfort. It was then that he began to remember a little more. Vague glimpses of being in the coach with Fallbrooke, talking to Caroline at the stables, and the horrible headaches.

"Am I going to die?"

"Of course not," she said her voice clear and definite but she looked away and Philip knew she was lying.

"I need to go, I cannot stay here."

"Of course, you can stay here. In fact, you must. You are still quite ill."

"No," he protested. "There are things I must do before I die."

She began to interrupt him, but he went on. "I need to make amends. Does my family know that I am here?"

"Yes, a message was sent and they are very worried."

"I pray someone arrives in time."

"Philip, I have told you that you will live. The physician has assured us that you will only improve."

Philip shook his head. "Please do not feel that you need to lie to me, dear Caroline."

Caroline let out a sigh. "Perhaps I could write down a letter for you to send to your family. Would that allay your concerns?"

"Yes, it would. Thank you."

CHAPTER EIGHT

"It is good to see that you have improved so much," Caroline said as she came into the room. Her mood seemed as bright as the lemon-yellow dress she wore. "It makes me happy."

Philip scowled at her. "Improved? I do not think you know of what you speak. As for happy, I cannot say that I feel the same."

"Oh hush," she told him sitting down in the chair next to the bed. "I have been by your side since you fell ill. I most definitely know what I am talking about."

Philip wanted to scream at her but for some reason, he stopped and took a deep breath. "I do not feel improved at all. I will agree that I am better than when I did nothing but sleep, but here I am too weak to move about like a normal man."

"You must give yourself time. It has been nearly three weeks since you collapsed in the library and only two days since you awakened from your fever. It will take some time for you to heal and regain your strength."

He knew she was right. It did not seem to matter though as anger and frustration seemed to be all he could manage. He was no longer delirious but he barely possessed the strength to sit up in the bed.

"I do not want to wait. I see no improvement as I cannot move from this bed. I am useless."

"Oh nonsense," Caroline dismissed him with a wave of her hand. "You are much improved. I was there when you could not even swallow clear broth. I had to spoon it into your mouth half a spoonful at a time. You should be very thankful."

Thankful? He would never be thankful. He hated being weak, it was quite distressing to him that Caroline has seen him in such a weakened state. He did not like that she did not see him as strong and capable. The mere thought of it made him angry.

"I shall make arrangements to leave for London as soon as possible." He folded his arms and smiled smugly at her.

She furrowed her eyebrows and nodded. "Yes, quite right. You need to go make amends."

"Amends? What the devil are you talking about?" He demanded his voice gruff with exasperation.

Her blue eyes fairly glittered as she said, "When you were sick with a fever you feared you would die before you were able to make amends to your family and others. When you did speak, you uttered nothing but those words."

"I certainly did not," he retorted and she laughed. Laughed. She was teasing him, that was for sure, but he had a vague recollection of worrying about not seeing his family and dying alone. He tried to remember but his memory was hazy. Uncertain as to how to respond he simply said, "I was delirious with a fever I could have made any number of nonsensical claims. Anyone who believes the ramblings of a feverish man should rethink their opinion."

"Quite true," she agreed thoroughly. "You were quite relieved when I agreed to write down a letter from you to send to your family."

Philip froze. While she had been teasing him before he was certain that she was rather serious about the letter. Had she really sent a letter to his family? He had no idea what it might have said. His distress turned to anger the more he thought about it.

"A letter seems to have made no difference."

She had just opened the large book on her lap and she looked up from the book to his face. "What do you mean?"

"I mean that my family has abandoned me." Philip tried to sit higher up in the bed but could not move, finally giving up with a frustrated groan. "They did not see fit to come see me when they found out I have fallen ill. That proves sending a letter made no difference at all."

"Philip, your family has not abandoned you." She said quietly closing the book.

"How can you say that?" He raised a hand when she started to speak. "No, Caroline, I do not want your pity."

"It was not pity I was about to offer." She stopped and frowned. "While there is a part of me that wants to let you stew over this I must tell you that your family did come to see you while you were delirious."

"I do not believe you," he said staring out the window.

"Whether you believe me or not it is no consequence to me. It certainly does not change the fact that two of your siblings visited Stratford. They stayed here for nearly a week."

Philip grunted in reply, his throat thick with emotion that he dared not reveal to Caroline.

She turned in her chair gesturing to the door. "Shall I go collect Birks from the stable to tell you I am being truthful?"

"No," Philip answered.

"No?"

"No, I would not believe him, either." Philip gave her a haughty look, trying to hide the grin that threatened to come out. "He would surely lie for you."

Caroline let out a bark of laughter. "You clearly have not met Birks then."

Philip shook his head. "I suppose I shall be forced to believe you."

"Well, if you must," she said with a dramatic side. "Your parents were unable to come. Your father was in London dealing with Parliament business and your mother had been sick with a cough. Matthew and Henrietta came to Stratford, although only Matthew was allowed to see you. He sat by your side nearly constantly."

Philip scowled again. "Why not Henrietta as well?"

"She had been tending to your mother before she left Castborough and the doctor was concerned about her getting sick herself. It was decided she would not be allowed to see you, for her own health."

"Is she well?" He asked. "And my mother?"

"In the last letter that I received from Henrietta, she said that she was well and that your mother had recovered fully."

"I am glad to hear it."

"I was as well. Mr Notley has said that it is possible that the fever affected you alone, as no one else has come down with it."

"That is good. I would not want anyone else to be sick. It had occurred to me last night that your young brothers might come down with it."

"It was a concern but much was done to keep them separated. Especially after you had rescued them from the lanes."

"That was more Fallbrooke than I," Philip said and then paused suddenly realizing the absence of his friend. "What happened to Fallbrooke?"

Caroline grimaced. "He left the night you collapsed in the library. In fact, we believe he may have been in the library when you fell ill. Several people saw him leave the darkened room during the card party."

"I cannot believe it," Philip muttered.

"I do not know how that could surprise you. That man is reprehensible."

Philip turned back to face her. "What is it about Fallbrooke that you dislike so much?"

"He is a rake and a coward."

Philip shook his head in confusion. Then he remembered what Bannerman had said at the card party. "What has he done to you?"

"He killed the man I was to marry."

CHAPTER NINE

"He what?"

"He killed Nathaniel Lymington, the man I was going to marry."

"I have known Fallbrooke since I was a boy and I have never known him to be violent. In fact, he goes out of his way to avoid any conflict at all."

Caroline had no doubt that Philip was telling the truth. "It was not violence committed by Lord Fallbrooke but his lack of action that killed Nathaniel."

"I am truly sorry for your loss. I had heard a tragedy had occurred but knew nothing of what had happened."

"Nathaniel had only just asked for my hand a month before. We were waiting for the Christmas holiday to have passed before the Banns were posted." Caroline looked away from Philip not wanting to see the pity in his eyes. "Nathaniel and Lord Fallbrooke had become recent friends. Nathaniel was still expected to attend the parties and balls but only did so to be gracious. He would often leave the party early."

"Which Fallbrooke does as well," Philip finished.

"Yes, quite right. Fallbrooke invited him to White's one night and they began to escape the parties together."

"One night in late January, Nathaniel must have been quite pickled because they left White's and proceeded to walk to Mayfair rather than take the coach that was waiting for them. Nobody knows for sure what happened but Nathaniel was found the next day face down in the snow, not a scratch on him but cold as ice."

"I am truly sorry."

Caroline shook her head wanting to finish before he interrupted again. "Weeks later I learned that Fallbrooke was heard talking about that night. He said that Nathaniel had tripped and fallen into the snow. Lord Fallbrooke kept going knowing that Nathaniel had passed out in the snow. He assumed that Nathaniel would wake up soon and make it to his house in Mayfair on his own."

Caroline was still so angry at Lord Fallbrooke for not caring. For being so apathetic that he would let someone die in the snow. She had confronted him once and he had said nothing shrugging off her questions and outrage. He had acted as though he had no idea of what she was speaking.

"I am quite sure that Fallbrooke—"

"Abandoned Nathaniel just as he did you in the library? Yes, I am quite sure of that, as well."

Philip pressed lips together and turned to look out the window. Caroline felt bad for pointing out that Fallbrooke had left him sick and helpless after he had collapsed. It must be a great disappointment to find out your friend abandoned you in your moment of need.

She was about to say something when a knock sounded on the door. Caroline opened the door to see one of the servants from the kitchen standing with a tray of food. "Oh, Rosemary, I can take that."

"Can I bring you anything else?" Rosemary asked with a shy smile.

"No. This is perfect. Thank you." Caroline took the tray and set it on the table next to the bed.

"Lovely. Another bowl of broth and one more boiled egg," Philip complained his voice dripping with disdain.

Caroline paused before picking up the tray to take back to the door. "I offer my apologies. I thought you were growing tired of broth and boiled eggs. It had the cook make a beef stew with potatoes." Philip started to respond but she shook her head sternly. "I will send this tray back and have them bring more broth then another egg straight away."

She had almost gotten to the door when Philip finally said, "Do not dare do that."

Slowly, Caroline stopped in the middle of the room. "Oh? You have changed your mind about the luncheon fare?"

Philip let out a long-suffering sigh. "Just bring the blasted tray over here."

"Oh, yes. Of course," she said in a mocking tone, caring not what he thought. She well understood his frustration with being sick but she could not abide by his continual whining and complaining."

Philip ate several bites of the stew and then leaned back against the pillows. "What I would give for a thick slab of beef and a glass of whiskey."

Caroline and frowned. "Is there something amiss with the stew?"

"No," Philip replied mirroring her look of confusion. "It is quite delicious."

"Then, why, may I ask, are you complaining about wanting something different?"

Philip looked even more confused opening his mouth only to close it again having said nothing.

"Philip, be grateful for what you have in front of you. Always looking for something better is a fool's errand and eventually you will find that nothing or no one is good enough."

He harrumphed.

"That would be a very lonely life indeed."

Philip placed the barely eaten bowl back on the tray. "I am no longer hungry."

"You are acting like a child."

"I am the heir to the Duke of Castborough. You cannot speak to me in that manner."

Caroline stood up and pointed at him. "I do not care if you are Prince Regent himself. Be quiet and eat your stew." She nearly screamed at him. Philip looked shocked but he picked up the bowl and began to eat.

She blew out a slow breath before saying, "You cannot continue to always be so angry. So difficult in everything."

"How do you mean?"

"Stop complaining about what you cannot change and look to what you can change. You waste so much time trying to find someone to blame, for every little injustice. All while ignoring the moments that you should be so thankful for." She did not want to lecture him like a governess but she truly wanted him to understand. "Philip, you should be thankful that you are alive."

Nathaniel is not, is what she thought, but did not say knowing that might have been a step too far. She looked up to find Philip's eyes upon her. Their eyes met and it was clear he had understood without her having to speak the words.

CHAPTER TEN

"Mr Notley, how lovely to see you." Caroline set down her needlework as the tall man crossed the room. She had only picked up the fabric to busy herself while the physician was in with Lord Holgrave.

"Good morning, Lady Caroline. I have just been in to look at your charge." He smiled as he spoke.

"How is he?" Caroline asked as calmly as possible. "He seems to have improved much over the last week."

Mr Notley nodded. "Yes, he has. Thanks in no small part to you. Your constant attention and care have surely resulted in his recovery."

"Then you feel he is recovered?" Caroline had told herself not to ask but she was so hopeful for him that she could not stop herself.

"Yes, Lord Holgrave has recovered from the fever, he will only improve," Mr Notley explained. "However, he is still very weak. It may take him some time to regain his strength."

"I understand." Caroline was so relieved that tears sprang to her eyes.

"Perhaps we should take him to London or to Castborough to recover," her mother suggested.

Caroline's stomach dropped. The thought of Philip leaving made her feel empty and bereft. She had known that her attachment to Philip had grown but she had not realized the extent of it until that moment.

The physician shook his head. "I would not recommend that. A trip like that would be too taxing. No, he needs to rest. Unless, of course, his staying here has become a burden on you. I could look into other arrangements for Lord Holgrave."

Caroline's mother spoke up quickly. "No, no. He is welcome to stay as long as is necessary. I only thought he would be more comfortable in his own home or with family."

"Yes, of course, Mother," Caroline reassured her. "It would be difficult for you if one of us was ill and you could not tend to us."

"Lord Holgrave will regain his strength slowly but you should encourage him to leave his bed to sit in a chair and to walk a little each day." The physician smiled again. "I have spoken to him about this already."

From Mr Notley's expression, Caroline could imagine how Philip had responded. She laughed and said, "I will see that he follows your instructions."

"Send for me if he proves to be difficult," Mr Notley nodded at her moved to leave the room.

"Thank you, Mr Notley. I will."

A few hours later she had convinced Philip to join her in the drawing room for their midday meal. Rosemary and one of the grooms had moved a table near the open doors to the garden.

"It is a beautiful day," Caroline said trying to breach the silence that had fallen since they sat down.

Philip did not say anything for a moment. "Quite. It reminds me of the summer that I visited with Robbie."

Caroline nodded hoping her cheeks had not reddened at the memory. She had been rather taken with Philip when he had come home from school with her Uncle Robbie. He was several years older than her but had been very kind to her, not treating her like a child.

Her infatuation was only reinforced when he included her in some jokes he had played on Robbie. It had been so nice to be included and when Philip had turned to her with a smile at their shared joke her heart nearly burst.

"That was one of my favorite summers," he said his voice wistful.

"It was?" Caroline was surprised she had assumed he only remembered because he was back at Stratford. When Philip nodded, she admitted, "It was one of mine as well."

He turned and smiled at her and just like that she felt like the young girl from that summer. Caroline wondered if Philip had known how she had felt and then cringed inwardly hoping he did not.

When he spoke next, she was surprised. "I remember Robbie had been worried about your parents. Particularly your mother that summer."

Caroline had not thought about that in a long time. "My mother had fallen ill the winter before, Simon had just been born. She was quite ill. Scarlet Fever."

"Oh Lord," Philip breathed.

"We were all very worried about Miles and Simon but neither of them ever got sick." Caroline stared down at her hands. "No, it was Catherine and Oliver that came down with it."

"Your sister and brother?"

"Yes, Oliver was nine and Catherine six. Mother was heartbroken, we all were of course, but Mother took at the hardest. She was so worried about Simon and Miles that she slept in the nursery for months."

Philip looked quite distressed. "My apologies for bringing such dreadful memories to your attention."

He looked so overwrought the Caroline felt bad.

"It is not your fault, you had no way to know. I am sure that Robbie did not share that with you. It was a sad time but it was a reminder that we must be thankful for what God has given us.

Mother is alive and well, as are my two brothers. I feel blessed that they were spared."

CHAPTER ELEVEN

Philip stared out into the garden unable to speak. He was full of awe at Caroline's grace and fortitude in the face of such obstacles. She had endured pain and sorrow in the loss of not only a brother and sister but the man she was betrothed to. And yet she continued to display an amazing depth of happiness and patience.

He turned back to look at her. "Scarlet Fever is a horrible illness. Although I have never had to suffer its effects, I have seen the damage it has wreaked on other families. Your mother's sorrow must have been great, as well as the blame that she surely laid upon her own shoulders."

Philip could not even begin to understand the abject misery a parent must endure after the death of a child. Surely that of a mother must be that much greater. He thought about James and Henrietta, and his other siblings and how much his life would be altered if one of them had died.

"I cannot imagine losing any of my siblings."

Caroline surprised them with a smile. "I remember when James and... Charlie, was it?"

Philip smirked thinking of what his rather serious brother

would say. "Err, yes. Although I believe he prefers Charles these days."

"I suppose you are correct," Caroline said with a knowing grin. "I do remember them visiting that summer and how much fun you all had. You are still quite close then?"

Philip was too embarrassed to say that before the house party it had been months since he had seen his siblings. At the request of his mother, he had left London to spend several weeks at Castborough in the weeks around Christmas. They had not been good weeks, although he would have to admit that he was mostly to blame.

The tension between him, James, and their father had caused him to be defensive and almost immediately he had begun to grow restless. He was so impatient to return to London that he had spent much of his days complaining and planning what he would do when he was able to leave.

"We were very close when we were young," Philip told her. "In recent years, though that has not been so, I am afraid."

Just remembering how he acted back at the house party appalled him. He had barely spoken to Hugh or Henrietta. His argument with James had actually been the longest conversation he had had with anyone in his family in a very long while.

There was a moment that Philip began to get angry. If he had not felt the need to prove himself to his father, prove that he was better than James then he would still be close to his family. Just as quickly though Philip remembered Caroline's words. It was difficult to tamp down his anger but he knew that she had spoken the truth finding someone to blame was a waste of time and it would bring him no closer to his siblings.

It had done him no good to be angry with James or their father. It only made it easier to run away to London. The more he stayed away the more he resented James for driving him away. He was still angry but at least now he understood how it would not help him.

Even more upsetting was the look of sadness on Caroline's face.

It was like a physical blow to think she was somehow disappointed in him. More than anything, he wanted her to understand but it was difficult for him to explain. "Please understand that I am not happy about it and I do not want that to continue."

He hoped that she believed that he was being sincere. Since his return from Paris, Philip had been thinking about his family. He did not know how but he would make it right. It was very important to him that she understood that.

"I am glad that you want to be close to your family." Caroline was facing the garden but he could see that her eyes were shining with unshed tears.

His first reaction was to go on as though he had not noticed but he looked over at her again. It was beyond his capability to leave her upset. He knew not what to say. Naturally, he thought she was upset about the loss of her siblings so long ago and Nathaniel more recently. As well as being rather disappointed with him for rejecting his own family.

She must give thanks every day that her mischievous brothers were so healthy. And that is when he realized Caroline's depth of character.

"Caroline," his voice quiet so much so that he swallowed before going on. "I cannot thank you enough for caring for me while I was ill. It was an enormous sacrifice that you undertook. I can only imagine the concern you must have felt regarding Miles and Simon. I will be forever grateful."

Caroline only nodded seeming to understand that Philip had taken a rather big step.

He wondered if he should say something more when she pointed at his plate.

"You better finish eating before it gets cold. I will have to call the footman if you do not." She tried to be serious but could not hide her smile.

"We cannot have that." Philip picked up a fork thinking he would eat all his food ice cold if it would make her smile.

CHAPTER TWELVE

Philip groaned as he pushed himself out of the chair. He had improved much over the last few weeks but he still encountered weakness and he tired easily. It was a matter of time, Philip knew but patience had never been a virtue that he had held dear. He despised having to rely on other people.

Bored and frustrated Philip tossed the book he had been reading into a chair only to have the book bounce off and land on the floor near the desk. Philip closed his eyes to calm himself before stretching to retrieve the book.

"Blasted book," Philip muttered and then stood up. The room seemed to tip and he staggered sideways as he fought to stay on his feet. He clutched at the desk and only barely saved himself from falling to the floor.

There, his arms braced on the desk Philip suddenly remembered that last night with Fallbrooke. It had not occurred to him until that moment that he had not been in the library since he had fallen ill. The word fallen seemed far more than appropriate as he remembered the events that had occurred.

He remembered arguing with Fallbrooke and the piercing pain in his head that had been bothering him for weeks. Another thought struck him and he worried that this dizzy spell would mean that the headaches were returning. He took several deep breaths before lowering himself into the chair behind the desk.

During his illness, Philip had been lying to himself thinking that Fallbrooke would not have left him incapacitated in the library. Surely, Philip had thought, he had collapsed after Fallbrook had left the room.

The truth of it though was quite the opposite. It was a fact that Philip had not wanted to believe but if he were being honest it was not that surprising, Fallbrooke had long been known for being a selfish cad. Philip, himself, had seen it a hundred times over. Fallbrooke's selfishness had always been harmless. Until now. Or if Caroline was indeed correct, until Nathaniel Lymington.

Anger seem to give him strength and he pushed himself from the chair. He walked around to the front of the desk thinking about confronting Fallbrooke. It was only a matter time before he would regain his strength. It gave him pause, though, as once he was fully recovered he would be leaving Stratford to return to London.

The thought did not elicit the feelings of joy that he had anticipated. He had rather enjoyed being at Stratford. It had been a welcome distraction upon his return from Paris and he had been well cared for during his illness. He was not sure that he was ready to leave the relative comfort and safety of Stratford.

And what of Caroline? A voice in his head asked. He could no longer lie to himself. He did not want to leave Caroline. As true as the sentiments were, it was not something he was ready to think about.

"What are you doing in here?" Caroline asked standing at the door.

"I was reading." Philip picked up the book from where he had left it on the desk.

"It is much too beautiful a day for you to be sitting in this dark stuffy library."

"Is it?" Philip looked out the window. He had been so preoccupied with his own frustrations and concerns that he had not even looked to the windows.

"Is it?" She repeated shaking her head in mock disgust. "Yes, it is. Now enough of this."

Caroline pulled back one of the curtains revealing a door. "It is past time for some fresh air. Come, Lord Holgrave let us take a stroll in the garden."

Before he knew it, Caroline had linked her arm through his and began to lead him to the door.

The door opened out to the garden but a secluded corner that Philip had not seen during the house party. It was separated from the main garden by the usual hedges seen in most of the more fashionable gardens. Philip stopped next to one of the ornate urns that held greenery. It seemed to be made of stone or possibly marble with intricate carvings around the top and the pedestal.

Caroline noticed his interest. "My mother's father brought them over from France. According to the story, my grandfather saw similar ones at Versailles and had to have one."

"These are from Versailles?" Given the ongoing hostilities between Britain and France, he could see why the impressive urns were hidden away.

"My grandfather would never say for sure. They were often admired by my mother and my grandfather gave them to her after my parents were married."

"They are magnificent. I can only imagine how pleased your father must have been."

Caroline chuckled. "Yes, well, he was not actually pleased at all. He did not want to upset my mother so he placed the urns here so that she could enjoy them and he would not incur the wrath of owning French artifacts."

"Your father is a smart man, indeed," Philip replied.

They continued down the path that led to a carved wooden gate. Caroline opened the gate and they entered the main part of the garden. He spotted a bench and proceeded to sit down while Caroline kept walking.

"Caroline come sit," Philip called out to her.

"No, we should walk some more."

"But I am tired." Philip sat down on the bench and smiled up at her, confident that she would join him.

Caroline stood fast on the path. "The physician said you needed to walk to build up your strength."

"But I..."

"We need to walk and that is what you are going to do. Now come along."

To his complete surprise, she turned away and continued down the path.

It was astonishing to him that Caroline continued to quarrel with him. It all came down to caring for him, he reminded himself. What was even more astonishing was the fact that while it was clear that she cared for him she would not coddle him. It was undoubtedly something he was not accustomed to at all.

He stood up staring at her figure as she continued down the path, her red hair shining in the summer sun. No one had ever cared enough to tell him no when he needed to hear it, at least not since his childhood.

It was a revelation that seemed to change everything for him.

"Caroline! Wait, I want to walk with you."

CHAPTER THIRTEEN

Caroline had not gone far when Philip had called out to her. Truth be told she had been about to turn back. She knew that she was being tough on Philip, but Mr Notley had said that Philip needed to build up his strength.

She felt even worse knowing that Philip was not accustomed to being challenged. He was the heir to Castborough, after all. People did what he asked without a second glance, not the other way around.

"Are you sure you are well enough?" Caroline asked him as he joined her on the path.

"Yes." He smiled down at her his blue eyes looking as bright and clear as they had that summer so many years before.

Her breath caught and she fought to hide her reaction as she spoke again. "You said before that you were tired. I do not want you to grow too weary."

"I will be fine," he said turning down the path. "You are quite right. A nice walk on a beautiful day is precisely what I need."

Caroline wondered if he was merely humouring her but she quickly decided the reason did not matter. She only cared that Philip was following the advice of the physician.

"It is a beautiful day. I am quite sure that you will enjoy it and the fresh air and sun could only be a benefit. It is important that you tell me immediately though if you grow tired and need a rest."

"I will be happy to do so," Philip dissented. "I had not fully grasped how much I have improved."

"It has been truly wonderful to see." Caroline did not think she would ever forget how frail he had looked those first few days. She had prayed for him every day and every night since finding him motionless in the library. "It will not be long before Mr Notley declares that you are fully recovered."

Philip nodded. "It is just a matter of time."

Caroline could not see his face but he sounded somewhat sad. She had barely finished that thought before admonishing herself. It was merely her own feelings on the matter crowding her perception of Philip's response.

As cheerily as she could she said, "You must be looking forward to getting back to your life in London."

Philip was quiet for so long she wondered if he had not heard or perhaps she had said something wrong.

Finally, he said, "I have not really thought about going back to London. I suppose it is rather inevitable that I return though."

His head was down, looking at the path before glancing over at her briefly. "Perhaps you will come to London and let me take you to the opera."

"I do not know," Caroline told him nervously.

"It would only be right since you have done so much for me."

"Philip, you do not need to feel beholden to me. I am only happy that I was here to help you." Caroline continued on when he wanted to interrupt. "I do not like going to London. It is doubtful that I will participate in any other events of the Season."

He set his jaw. "Yes, of course. I did not mean to be a sod. After what happened to Nathaniel it is quite understandable that you do not want to be part of the festivities."

Caroline was not sure what to say. She had cared for Nathaniel and she had believed that he would make a good and responsible husband. She did not like to speak ill of the dead but she had often questioned Nathaniel's involvement with Lord Fallbrook. In her opinion, it had not spoken well of his sense of decorum and responsibility. Nathaniel had been good to her and he did not deserve to die alone in the snow, but the truth of it was she had never loved him.

"It is true that Nathaniel's death precipitated my decision. My choice to distance myself from London society was due more to the apathy of those that participate rather than because of unpleasant memories."

"Well in that case, I will do my best to convince you that I am much different than other members of London society." He raised his hand and a fist over his head. "It is a challenge I will rise to, I assure you."

"I can hardly wait," Caroline said with a laugh.

She was surprised to realize she meant it, too. As much as Caroline disliked London, she might relent if it meant that she could spend more time with Philip.

CHAPTER FOURTEEN

"I heard that Mr Notley has arrived," Caroline's mother said suddenly breaking the silence in the drawing room.

"Oh? I did not realize." Caroline hated not being completely honest with her mother but it was clear that Philip had made a complete recovery. She was very thankful that he was doing so well but the news also made her quite sad. She was sure that it would not be long before he would be leaving Stratford.

Dreading the day that he would leave Stratford, she had already started to prepare herself. She had spent less time with Philip over the last several days, telling him that she needed to check on her brothers or speak with her mother about some important topic.

It had only made her sadder, that she was missing even more time with Philip. Stratford would be much different after Philip had gone. It was her own fault, though, she had let herself fall back into acting like a foolish girl. Caroline would pay for it with a broken heart as she would surely feel Philip's absence like an open wound.

"Caroline, dear, are you well?"

"Yes, of course, Mother. Why do you ask?" Caroline's looked up from her embroidery.

Her mother tilted her head and finally said, "I was watching you just now and you looked rather in pain. Are you sure you are well?"

Caroline held up her finger. "My thimble slipped off and I pricked my finger. It is nothing to worry over." She turned her head back to her embroidery, an activity that she normally enjoyed quite a bit. At the moment though, it was nothing more than a distraction. It was simply something to keep her busy so she would not think about what Mr Notley was telling Philip.

It seemed like a cruel joke since she had done little else than think about him. Her mother's questions had certainly not helped. Her last answer seemed to have appeased her mother and silence fell over them again. Caroline looked up as voices could be heard outside in the garden. It must have been some time later as the flowers she was embroidering were beginning to take shape.

"I wondered what your brothers had gotten up to," Mother said quietly.

"Have they gotten away from Anna?" Caroline asked looking toward the windows. "I thought they were behaving much more since Anna and Birks were looking after them."

"Oh yes, Birks has promised to teach them how to jump their horses."

"Jump the horses?" Caroline could not believe it. "Are you sure that would be safe?"

Mother laughed. "I am certain that Birks knows that it will be a long time until the boys exhibit the type of responsibility required to start training. In fact, Birks has assured me that even if their training began today it would be nearly a year until either of them would be actually jumping."

"Well, that is a relief," Caroline admitted. "Pretty clever too."

"It was your clever idea to have Birks and Anna look after the boys."

"Miles and Simon are not mischievous because their hooligans. They simply lack for something to do. Birks has clearly given them a purpose for behaving."

"Given the noise in the garden, it is unclear if that purpose is currently working," her mother said with a sly smile. Before Caroline could reply the door burst open, Simon and Miles nearly fell down in front of them.

"I found her!" Miles hollered behind him.

"What? Oh, splendid," Philip said looking surprised and delighted.

"Good morning," Caroline said as calmly as possible. She hated that she was so happy to see him.

"We have a surprise for you," Simon blurted out.

"Shh," Miles said loudly and pushed him on the shoulder. "We are not supposed to tell."

"Tell what?" Caroline asked Simon leaning forward to look at him.

His eyes shot over to Philip and he shook his head. "Oh, no. I promised Lord Holgrave that I would not tell."

"And I thank you both for your magnificent discretion." Philip bent into a deep bow in front of her brothers. "You are fine gentleman that I now count among my most valued friends."

Caroline watched her two brothers stand up taller and tried to act as though they were not pleased as punch by Philip's comments. "We were rather happy to help," Miles said returning Philip's bow.

Caroline's heart warmed at the sight of Philip with her brothers. Their admiration for him was clear and she felt that Philip was equally pleased with them. She could not help but think of what a wonderful father he would be someday. Almost immediately the joyful thought plunged her heart into sadness.

Philip turned to her then and she hoped her smile did not reveal her melancholy. "Lady Caroline, would you honour me with your company on a walk through the gardens?"

Caroline looked to her mother, unsure if she was looking for permission or a reprieve.

Her mother nodded. "Go on. I believe the peonies have come into bloom. Quite the beautiful display."

Philip waited for her to set her embroidery aside and stand up before he moved closer to offer his arm.

"Thank you, Lord Holgrave," Caroline told him not daring to look at his face.

He led her out to the garden and then along one of the paths.

"Where are we going?"

"In time," was all he said.

He stopped at the tall wooden gate in the hedge. He opened it and stepped back. She looked in to see a table set up next to her grandfather's beautiful earns.

"What is this? She asked.

"I thought it would be nice to take our midday meal here."

It was such a beautiful thought, and Caroline tried to ignore the tears that were gathering behind her eyes. She only managed to say, "Thank you. It is lovely."

CHAPTER FIFTEEN

"This was a very nice surprise. Thank you," Caroline said after Rosemarie had taken their plates away.

"I am so glad that you enjoyed it." It had taken some work to surprise her. Philip had enlisted the help of Caroline's brothers to talk to Rosemary and get the table moved into the small area by the urns.

"I simply wanted to thank you for everything you have done for me. I cannot ever repay you for the care and kindness you have shown me." He hoped she truly understood how thankful he was.

"Philip, you did not have to do all of this. Anyone would have done the same in my place."

"That is not true," he argued. "Fallbrooke left me in the library after he collapsed and if it was not for you one of your servants would have dumped me in the bushes."

The most darling look of horror crossed Caroline's face. "Oh! Lord Holgrave, I do apologize. I have no idea what he was thinking."

Philip held up a hand to stop her. "He was thinking I was a drunk, which nearly any other night I very well could have been."

"Still I am rather dismayed that you learned that one of our servants very nearly contributed to your death."

Philip laughed, he could not help it. "Caroline, please do not give it another thought," he told her taking her hand.

"But," she said beginning to protest again.

He told himself he did it to silence her protests but it was something he had wanted to do for many days. Leaning forward, he pressed his lips to hers, marveling at the softness he found there.

Caroline was startled at first and he expected her to pull away. Instead, she surprised him by leaned into him for a long moment before ultimately pulling away. The kiss had been everything that he had hoped it would be and more, it took everything he had not to lean forward once more. Her face was flushed and she quickly averted her eyes and stepped away.

"I apologize. You must think me a rake. You were most distressed, and oh, I was not thinking." Philip had not wanted to scare her or upset her.

Caroline was clearly flustered. She walked toward the gate. "I promised Mother I would look at the peonies."

Yes, of course," he said taking her arm again.

"Have you written to your sister yet?" Caroline asked once they were back in the main garden.

"No," Philip answered. He did not want to talk about his sister, as he was quite distracted thinking about Caroline and their shared kiss.

"She has written several times asking about you. Your family is quite looking forward to seeing you."

"Yes, I have been meaning to write," he said distractedly. He had long suspected that Caroline cared for him and her reaction to his kiss seemed to confirm his suspicions. He could think of nothing else but what he should do to keep Caroline in his life.

Caroline dropped his arm to leave the path saying quietly, "The peonies are over here."

Philip wondered if he had imagined the sadness in Caroline's voice and tried to catch up with her.

"Mother said that Mr Notley came to see you today."

Philip had thought it odd that Caroline had not been around when the physician had arrived but he understood now that she had done so with purpose.

"Your mother was quite right. Mr Notley was indeed here. He has determined that I am fully recovered and fit to travel."

"Are you to return to London then?" Caroline had managed to stay ahead of him. "Or perhaps to Castborough?"

"I have not decided, as of yet. I have discovered that I like Brighton very much." Philip could not bear the thought of leaving Stratford.

"I am afraid I do not understand."

She had paused in front of a large raise bed of flowers. Her copper hair and blue gown bright and alive against the mass of white petals.

He fell silent and he was sure her confusion was growing but he was thinking about what he was about to do.

"Marry me," he blurted out.

"What?" She said her eyes wide.

"I should apologize for being so impetuous but I do not feel like I can wait another minute to tell you how I feel."

Philip knew it would be more proper for him to have spoken to Caroline's father first but somehow this seemed right. She had endured the loss of Nathaniel not so long ago but Philip knew that she cared for him. It was his belief that they would be happy together.

Caroline said nothing so he rushed on. "You are wonderful, caring and kind. Beautiful beyond any words that I could utter. I want to look upon you always." He took her hands in his. "Please say you will marry me. Be mine for the rest of our days."

Caroline looked up with him tears shining in her eyes. "Philip. Dear, Philip. I care about you far more than I ever imagined that I could care for anyone. Marrying you would make me the happiest of women."

Philip's heart soared. "Then you will marry me?"

"I am sorry, Philip. On this day, I cannot. As much as it hurts my heart, I must refuse you." Tears streamed down her face as she spoke.

Philip wanted to brush them away but he found that he could not move. She had refused him. He could not believe it.

"I do not understand. You say you care about me and yet you say you cannot marry me." He had a sudden thought. "I know I did not speak to your father first. I will do so once if it pleases you."

"It is not my father that I wish you to speak to but your own. You have responsibilities there that you must attend to. You cannot continue to run from them. I will not be another excuse for you to run away."

"You believe that is why I asked you to marry?"

"I do not know." The misery in Caroline's eyes nearly broke him. "The only way for me to know for certain is for you to make amends with your family and assume your responsibilities."

He could bear to look at her no longer for fear that he would break down. His heart rent in two, he left her in the garden. The sound of her weeping stayed with him well after he reached the house.

CHAPTER SIXTEEN

"I did not think I would ever see this."

He looked up to see James standing in front of him.

"And what is that, or should I even ask?"

"You," he said and sat down in one of the chairs. "Here at Father's desk."

Philip had been back at Castborough for nearly a month's time. He was fortunate that his father had not made him grovel or lecture him about his irresponsible actions. Father had simply asked him if he was feeling well again. Philip had answered that he was quite recovered and looking forward to assuming his duties at Castborough. His father had happily clapped him on the shoulder and taken him around to show him all of the recent changes to their entailed land.

Philip had not seen James since their fight in the stables months before and he had been dreading their first meeting. Philip looked around the desk. "I am sure it is odd for you to see me here, rather than you."

"New, perhaps, but not odd. You are well suited for it and I have already heard good things," James told him and laughed. "Showing me up already, as usual."

James' reaction was not at all what Philip had expected. Normally, he would have responded with a snide remark. He did not want to argue with James. Philip looked down at the paper in front of him.

"I doubt that is possible. Father has always been proud of the assistance that you gave him in my stead." Philip looked up again to lock eyes with James. "And I am immensely thankful that you were able to step in when I was unable."

James seem surprised by the change in Philip but only said, "I am thankful as well, I have finished my studies at the Inns of Court and will very likely become a barrister in the next year."

Philip nodded. "It is more than simply likely. I have heard your name mentioned several times in regard to some appointments at Parliament."

It was clear that James had not heard the same rumblings. Not long ago, James had been unsure of his future but now he had a profession and a bride to marry. At the thought of James' betrothal Philip realized that he had more to say.

He stood up from the desk to face his brother. "I find that I cannot speak another word until I make this right. James, brother, I apologize for my wretched behaviour and how I treated Lady Elizabeth. I was blinded by jealousy and misery. My actions were inexcusable. I hope that one day you and Lady Elizabeth will be able to forgive me."

James held up a hand. "You need not say another word. You are already forgiven."

"You are too kind," Philip said, relieved by his brother's words. He gave James a hopeful look. "And Lady Elizabeth?"

James laughed. "She tells me often about how thankful she is of you."

"Surely, as a joke." Philip could not see any reason for him to have gained Lady Elizabeth's good favor.

"Lady Elizabeth and I owe you are most humble thanks." James smirked. "If you had not misbehaved to the point that forced

Father's hand. There may have never been a house party. I might have never met my betrothed."

"That certainly would have been a tragedy." James raised an eyebrow at that. "You and Lady Elizabeth had a connection that even I could see."

James relaxed. "I knew how I felt but I was uncertain as to what Elizabeth was feeling. Thankfully she was much smarter than I."

"Well, I am glad that I have been able to help someone achieve their happiness," Philip said with a wry smile.

James gave him a curious look. "You sound as though you are unhappy yourself. Is life here at Castborough so bad?"

"No," Philip assured him swiftly. "I am happy to be home." And he was not lying, coming back to Castborough had been beneficial for him. He was miserable though, he missed Lady Caroline more than he thought possible. Her refusal had hurt him far more than any physical blow had.

"Is it Lady Caroline?" James asked.

Philip's head snapped up to look at his brother. "How would you know that? I have not said a word to anyone."

"You did not have to say anything." James turned in his seat. "It was Matthew and Henrietta. When they returned from Stratford. Henrietta told Mother to prepare for your upcoming nuptials."

"I do not understand."

"Henrietta spent quite a lot of time at Stratford Manor. It was clear, at least to our dear sister, that Lady Caroline cared deeply for you and that she possessed a brightness in spirit that you needed." James went on to explain, "And according to Matthew that even in the delirium of sickness you spoke of almost nothing but Lady Caroline. It was as if you thought of nothing else."

"I would be lying if I said that fact had changed." Philip led out a long sigh before dropping into the chair next to James. "My wretched behaviour may have cost me dearly. I am uncertain as to whether I will ever be able to prove myself worthy."

"I wish I could give you some sound advice." James reached

over to put a hand on his shoulder. "All I know is that if Lady Caroline is as important as you say, you will find a way to change her mind."

Philip stood up to shake his brother's hand. "Thank you, James. I aim to do so."

CHAPTER SEVENTEEN

Caroline turned the page of her book and stared at the words. A moment later turning the same page back to read once more as she could not remember what she had just read.

Her eyes skimmed over a few sentences before she gave up and stared out the window. She was restless and there seem to be nothing that could distract her.

"Are you well?" Caroline's mother asked.

Caroline had nearly forgotten that she was even in the room. It would be impossible for her to explain how she was feeling since she barely understood it herself. She merely said, "Yes, Mother."

"Are you certain? You do not have the fever do you?"

"No, Mother. I promise I am quite fine." Caroline had answered that question twice daily since Philip had left. She felt fine, except for how completely horrible she felt.

Philip had been gone for over a month and while she did not regret her decision, she did regret hurting him. She had not thought he would leave so swiftly. Then, after he had left she had thought perhaps he would write to her but she had not received anything from him.

It had taken her nearly two weeks for her to realize the truth of it. Philip had come to rely on her while he was ill. He had been weak and away from home, his proposal has simply been born of his gratitude and nothing more. It had broken her heart but she knew that she must face the truth.

"I am glad to hear that you are feeling well." Mother thought for a moment and then said, "I have to wonder though if your melancholy mood has anything to do with Lord Holgrave's departure from Stratford."

"I suppose I grew accustomed to his presence." Caroline shrugged as if she had not thought about it. "I am sure it will pass soon enough."

"Missing someone you care about is not something that will merely pass." Caroline thought to protest but mother raised her chin and went on. "I have dealt with missing your father often when he has been called to appear at Parliament. Keeping busy was the only way to get through the day. It is something that I understand well."

Caroline appreciated that her mother wanted to help. "I have tried occupying my time doing things that I enjoy. But I have found that reading and working on my embroidery has not helped."

"Perhaps you should try something different. Perhaps a new activity that will force you to concentrate."

"Yes, something new would truly occupy my mind." Caroline wondered what activities she could pursue.

"Caroline!" Simon called running into the drawing room. "We just came from the stables. Birks is teaching us to jump horses."

"Goodness, how much have you learned?"

Miles walked in behind him. "We have a lot to learn still but we learned how to exercise the horses today."

Caroline and mother exchanged a look before Caroline said, "Oh, that is very important. Birks must trust you very much."

Simon nodded with a large grin. "He does. Birks even wants us to come back tomorrow."

"That is wonderful news," Caroline told him with her own smile.

"I do believe that Anna might want to see you if only I could remember why." Mother tapped a finger to her chin. "I think it was something about extra cakes."

The boys nearly fell over themselves on their way to the kitchen.

Spending time with her brothers always managed to make Caroline smile and had been the best part of her days since Philip had left. She was grateful for them once more as they had reminded her that she had not gone riding in weeks.

The next morning Caroline arrived at the stables before breakfast. Birks was not in the stable yet but one of the younger grooms saddled her horse for her.

She started out at a slow pace as she left the stables and passed the lanes. It was not long before her horse was galloping along, following the winding path of the creek. The cool air was blowing against her face and for the first time since Philip left that she felt unfettered by worry and despair.

Rushing along on her beautiful horse she let everything else fall away. For so long she had been worrying about everything and everyone else. She worried about her mother and her brothers when Father was away in London.

She had dealt with the loss of Nathaniel and then seeing Philip again and his illness. The absence of Philip had been the hardest, she missed him immensely. Caroline often reminded herself to be thankful for the time they spent together.

If nothing else Caroline hoped that she had helped him make amends with his family. He was the first born and he was honour bound to tend to his duties. As much as he tried, he could not run from that.

It suddenly occurred to her that she was no better. The depth of her ignorance was sobering. She had refused him, sent him away, accused him of running instead of facing his responsibilities. All the while she had been doing the same. She had been avoiding London and the events of the Season. She had been running as much as Philip had, if not more. If she ever saw him again, Caroline promised herself that she would beg his forgiveness.

She had been so deep in thought that when her horse moved around the stand of trees she was barely able to duck her head in time to avoid a low hanging branch. A moment later her horse came to a sudden halt. Before Caroline could readjust her weight in the saddle, she felt herself tipping back. Caroline scrambled to hang on to the saddle but she was already falling. The next thing she knew she was on the ground with her arm pinned beneath her.

At first, she did not think she could move. She tried to calm her breathing, knowing that panicking would do nothing to help her. Quietly she said to herself, "Stay calm, Caroline. You can figure this out."

As carefully as she could, she rolled over onto her back and stared at the sky. After several deep breaths Caroline pushed herself into a sitting position. Not too far from her she could see that a tree had fallen across the creek. It was clearly what had spooked the horse. Caroline looked over her shoulder and saw that her horse had run farther into the meadow.

She took a quick inventory and found that both of her legs were uninjured. Next, she bent and twisted one arm and then the other crying out as pain radiated up her arm from her wrist.

"Oh, Caroline, now you have done it." It was evident that she would need to begin walking back to the house. She was deciding how to maneuver herself to stand when she heard a horse in the distance.

CHAPTER EIGHTEEN

Philip spurred his horse across the meadow. He could not believe that the groom had let Caroline ride by herself. He was sure she was a competent rider but there was no telling where she had gone. He wanted to see her now.

It had been thirty-six days since he had seen her. In his opinion that was far too many days. He only hoped that she felt the same way.

Birks had taken two other grooms out to help look for Caroline and Philip wondered if they had found her yet. He was contemplating going back to the stables to check when he spotted a riderless horse near the creek. Trying not to panic he turned toward the creek A figure in dark blue could be seen on the ground not far away. Philip pushed the horse faster as he crossed the meadow. Not waiting for the horse to stop completely Philip jumped down to rush to her side.

"Caroline!"

"Philip?"

"Caroline, are you injured? I was so worried." He crouched down next to her.

Caroline seemed to be in shock. "You came back."

Philip brushed a wayward hair from her cheek. "I could not stay away."

"I am so glad to see you," Caroline told him.

He looked around where she was sitting on the ground. "Caroline what happened? Are you hurt?"

She seemed to suddenly remember where she was. "My horse stopped suddenly I slipped from the saddle."

"Infernal side saddles," Philip grumbled and swore under his breath. Then he noticed that Caroline was holding her left arm with her right hand. "Did you hurt your arm, sweetheart?"

"Yes, I landed on my side. I think it is my wrist."

"It is no wonder that you did not hit your head," Philip said pointing to the rocks at the creek's edge. "I will take you back up to the house and have someone send for Mr Notley."

"I do not want to be a bother."

"Caroline, dear, you are not a bother." Philip set back on his haunches. "Do you think you can stand?"

"Yes, if you will help me. This riding habit is a bit cumbersome."

"Of course," Philip stood up and pulled Caroline to her feet taking special care with her left arm.

"I will put you on my horse and walk you back to the house." Her only response was to shake her head no.

"Is something amiss?"

"I am sorry, Philip. I just cannot believe that you are here."

"Hope your disbelief is born of surprise and not displeasure upon seeing me."

"No!" She replied quickly and loudly. "Please do not say that, Philip. I am so very happy to see you."

"I cannot tell you how relieved I am to hear you say that. I have missed you in a way that I cannot explain."

"It is like trying to breathe underwater," she said quietly.

"Yes, it is very much like that." Philip hoped that meant that she was willing to hear him out. "I had to come back to Stratford to see you. To prove to you that I am worthy."

"Oh, Philip you have always been worthy. I am so very sorry that I made you feel that you were not."

"No. You only showed me that I can be better." There was so much he wanted to say to her. So many things he needed to say. It would have to wait though, her injuries needed to be attended to first. "I am sorry. I need to get you back to the house."

They had taken a few steps and Caroline stopped and turned to him. "Oh, I am so sorry that I sent you away. I accused you of running from your responsibilities fully unaware that I was no different. Avoiding the events of the Season did not aid me in my sadness after Nathaniel died. It was simply easier for me to avoid all of it. It only proved to prolong my sadness and upset my family. I hope you can forgive me."

"There is nothing to forgive. You were right. I returned to Castborough and assumed my duties as heir to Castborough." He touched her cheek. "I am so glad that you believed in me. It feels right being there."

"That is wonderful, Philip."

"I am glad to be at Castborough but I am miserable without you. Please say that you will reconsider my proposal." He put a hand to his chest. "You make me want to be better, to do better."

"It's because I care so deeply for you. I want all the best for you."

"I want that for you as well." He dropped to one knee right there in the meadow, afraid of her answer but knowing that he had to ask. "Lady Caroline, will you marry me?"

"Yes!"

"Yes? You said yes?" He asked, not sure if he had her correctly.

Caroline pointed across the meadow. "Shall I call Birks to tell you the truth?"

"No." Philip shook his head, unable to stop smiling. "He would surely lie for you."

Caroline laughed as he stood up. "Thank you for being the bright spot in all of my days." He tipped her chin up and brushed his lips against hers. There was a loud whoop from behind them.

Philip stepped back startled and Birks rode up with the two grooms.

"I hope this means you are going to marry this jug bitten young blood," Birks said to Caroline, a broad smile across the man's worn face.

"Yes!" She turned to Philip, "Did you hear me that time, Lord Holgrave."

"Yes, I did." He said and then bent to pick her up. "This time I get to take care of you."

A HERO RETURNS

CHARLES

CHAPTER ONE

The coach rambled over a rough spot in the road pulling Charles Repington from his thoughts. He had hoped to rest during his journey back home but that was not meant to be. It had been a long time since he had been back, more months than the young man wanted to count.

Charles shook his head to try to dispel the thoughts that were coming to mind. He had many adventures and had learned many things and met many people. Most did not get that sort of opportunity. However, there was much about his time on the Peninsula that he did not care to remember.

When it had come time for him to return to England, he had first thought to visit London for a time before heading to Castborough to see his family. A few weeks of gambling and drinking were sure to make his return easier. It was not to be though, as his mother had discovered that he was to return from the Peninsula. Days before he left he had received a strongly worded letter from his father suggesting that his presence at home would be much appreciated sooner, rather than later

So, here he was almost to Castborough, happy but also quite apprehensive. With a sigh, he looked out to see that the coach had made the final turn on the road, the large stone manor loomed large sitting atop a hill overlooking Surrey. It was good seeing the familiar home, he had not expected that. For the first time, Charles thought coming home may not have been such a poor idea.

It was not too long before the coach was pulling up in front of the house. He had not even alighted from the coach when the front door flew open.

"Charles!" His youngest sibling and only sister dashed down the steps.

"Henrietta!" He called back laughing and then grunted as she flung herself at him hugging him tight.

"I did not believe Mother and Father when they told me you were coming home."

"Why not?" He tilted his head to the side and grinned.

"I have been so worried over you that I would not have believed anyone until I look upon you with my very own eyes."

Charles stood back spreading out his arms. "Here I am. Safe and well… mostly sound," he quipped with another grin.

"Hear, hear! The hero has returned."

Charles turned to see Matthew, the youngest of his brothers, walking slowly down the steps. His words struck a nerve with Charles, he was no hero. He thought to say something but soon saw that it his brother was smiling and had intended no ill will.

Charles turned to look behind him. "Hero? Me? No. I am just a soldier like everyone else."

"That is not what we heard from Major Stewart," Matthew said clapping Charles on the shoulder.

"Ah, I see." Charles shook his head. "Major Stewart is known for his over exaggeration. It is the best to ignore his nonsense."

Matthew looked to protest but Charles cut him off. "I have traveled all the way from Spain. Is it possible that I may actually go inside? Or am I to stay in this coach for the entirety of my visit?"

"No, sir," Thomas answered, picking up Charles' valise. "Your rooms have been cleaned and are waiting for you."

"Thank you, Thomas." Charles walked to the bottom of the steps.

It was an odd feeling looking up at the house, so much that had stayed the same but it felt quite different for him. It made him wonder how much his time away had changed him. He was not the only one who had changed though, he thought, looking at Henrietta. She had moved to stand next to him and he linked his arm through hers.

"Sister, dear. What has happened in my absence? Other than you growing up to become a lovely young woman?"

Henrietta's eyes widened then she smiled. "Oh, so much! I do not know where to start."

"He does not care about your Season?" Matthew scoffed. "Charles, tell us about what it was like on the Peninsula."

Charles frowned. He was happy to see Matthew but he did not want to talk about the Peninsula and certainly not in front of Henrietta. Instead of saying so he turned to Henrietta and whispered loudly, "I take it Matthew's Season has not gone as well."

Henrietta let out a whoop of laughter and then covered her mouth. Charles laughed as she tried to compose herself.

First, she glanced over to Matthew and then leaned conspiratorially against Charles' shoulder. "Truth be told, it has not. Abigail Underwood has caused him great distress."

"She has not," Matthew retorted.

Charles nodded with a serious look on his face. "I cannot say for sure, but you seem rather distressed. What do you think, Henrietta?"

"Oh yes, quite right," Henrietta agreed. "Distressed indeed."

"No, I am not distressed. She... Well, I really am not distressed," Matthew stammered and quickly went up the steps to the house.

After a moment, Henrietta chuckled before resting her head against Charles the shoulder. "I'm so glad you are home."

Charles smiled down at her. "As am I."

CHAPTER TWO

Beatrice looked up from her book, she thought she had heard voices in the hall. The door to the drawing room remained closed and after a moment she shrugged and turned her gaze back to the pages.

She had still not gotten used to the activity at Castborough. The noise still disturbed her concentration when she was reading. Her family home was much quieter as it was only she and her mother much of the time.

Thinking of her mother she looked down at the book on her lap and laughed. Beatrice was quite sure that her mother would be rather angry that not only was she reading, but that she was also reading an adventure tale.

It made little sense to her that she would find so much enjoyment in doing something that would anger her mother. Beatrice Taltham had always been careful to follow her mother's instructions to the letter. It had been harder as of late since it seemed no matter what Beatrice did her mother had been upset with her anyway. Perhaps that was why she found such great amusement in her harmless but wayward pursuit.

It had been a stroke of good luck for Beatrice that prompted her stay at Castborough. Martha Taltham had needed to go back to their country home but did not want Beatrice to miss social events in the middle of the Season. Henrietta had spoken to Lady Castborough about Beatrice staying with them. Her mother had been quite happy to allow it if only to brag that her daughter had been personally invited to stay at Castborough. The woman had been doing everything she could to make Beatrice more popular with the social elite, much to Beatrice's chagrin.

Thinking about her mother made her suddenly feel restless. She set the book on the settee beside her before getting up to walk to the windows. She had barely reached the window when the door to the drawing room opened and the room seemed filled with people.

Beatrice smiled at the few people she recognized. Henrietta came in next, her arm linked through the arm of a man Beatrice had never seen before. It was clear that he was related to Henrietta's brother, Matthew, but that is where the resemblance ended. He was much taller than Matthew and where Henrietta's eldest brothers had blonde hair this man had darker hair. It was a bit longer that what was fashionable but Beatrice thought it suited him. She wondered if perhaps he was an uncle or a cousin.

Henrietta led the man straight to Beatrice. "Beatrice, you will never guess who has arrived," Henrietta said.

Beatrice shook her head smiling at her friend. "I could not even begin to guess."

Henrietta laughed. "This is my brother, Charles Repington."

"Oh!" Beatrice exclaimed remembering Henrietta talking about how worried she had been while he was fighting the war on the Peninsula. It seemed to explain a lot to her as well as he had the appearance of a young man but his demeanor was much more mature. "It is a pleasure to meet you, Lieutenant. Henrietta has spoken of you often."

Charles grimaced and then glanced over at Henrietta. "I am unsure if I should be flattered or not."

Henrietta gasped in mock horror. "I have no idea of what you are speaking."

"I assure you," Beatrice spoke up quickly. "Your sister has spoken quite highly of you."

"That is a relief. I would hate to think that you thought ill of me upon our first meeting."

He was smiling down at her and Beatrice had to collect herself in order to reply. "Of course not, Lieutenant. Welcome home."

"Thank you," he said with a slight nod. "That is quite kind of you, um, Miss..."

"Where are my manners?" Henrietta gasped, her hand flying to cover her mouth. "Charles, this is my dear friend, Beatrice Taltham. She has been staying with us while her mother has gone to tend to their home in London."

Charles raised an eyebrow and smiled. "Miss Beatrice Taltham, it is indeed a pleasure to make your acquaintance."

Beatrice was trying to think of something else to say that did not sound silly when a deep voice interrupted her thoughts. "Charles!"

They all turned to see that Lord and Lady Castborough had joined them in the drawing room.

"Mother, you look as lovely as ever." Charles crossed the room and embraced his mother.

His mother dabbed at her eyes with her handkerchief. "Charles dear, you are being too kind. I am merely happy that you are here."

"Of course, Mother where else would I be?"

"Yes, indeed," his father said with a raised eyebrow. He smiled quickly, though. "Welcome home, Charles, my boy."

Beatrice watched as several emotions seemed to flicker across Charles' face. He shook Lord Castborough's hand and appeared most sincere when he said, "I am quite happy to be back. Thank you."

Beatrice could almost appreciate Charles' conflicting emotions. While watching Henrietta and her family she was happy but also rather envious of their large family and how close they were. She, herself, had two older brothers that she hardly knew, born to her father's first wife.

She rarely saw her father and when she did it was awkward and uncomfortable. He and Mother no longer got along and much of their time together was spent arguing. She had long wished for a family like Henrietta had and regretted, even more, the fact that soon she will be forced to return to London and face her mother once more.

CHAPTER THREE

"I cannot tell you how glad I will be when this is over," Charles said straightening his cravat.

Matthew stood in the hall waiting for Charles to join him. He laughed out loud at his brother's words.

Charles fell into step next to him. "Did Mother send you to check on me?"

"Yes, she certainly did," Matthew admitted. "She was somewhat concerned that you would disappear again."

"Again?" Charles asked. Although he knew exactly what she was talking about. Over the last week, he had taken to slipping out one of the many doors and to go on long walks in and around Castborough. He then continued, not wanting to hear any sort of explanation from Matthew. "I told Mother that I would be here. She has no need to worry."

"I know, and I am sure that she knows too," Matthew told him. "She is extremely pleased you are here and wants everything to go well tonight."

Charles nodded knowing that his brother was correct. "I tried to tell her that a party was not necessary, but she told me to be quiet."

Matthew laughed and then paused turning to face Charles.

"Mother has been talking about throwing a ball in your honour since you left for the Peninsula. I think it may have been what kept her from worrying over you too much while you were gone."

Charles had not thought his family would be distressed by his time away. When he had acquired his commission, they had been quite proud.

"I will endeavour to not disappoint her," Charles said continuing down the hall once more.

Charles had spent most of the last hour with his parents greeting guests that had arrived for the ball. It had been fairly tiring and he highly doubted that he would remember many of the names of the people who had been presented to him.

The room was filled with people and music had already filled the ballroom when he entered. He was glad of it too. It gave him the opportunity to move about the room and observe everyone without really being seen. He had just found a good spot at the far end of the ballroom when he spotted one of his elder brothers entering the ballroom with a lovely woman on his arm. She could only be James' new bride. Charles had gotten word that James was to marry but the letter had been delayed by several weeks.

Charles had been somewhat surprised by the news as James had never been much interested in participating in the events of the Season. The last time Charles had seen James, he had been much too busy here at Castborough. He had actually thought he had misread the letter and that it was Philip, their eldest brother, who was planning to marry.

"Charles," James said reaching up to shake his hand. "Glad to see you survived your time on the Peninsula."

"Thank you," Charles replied. He looked from James to the woman on his arm. "And it looks as though you survived the Season rather well."

A wide smile broke out on James' face. "Yes, absolutely. Please meet Elizabeth, my wife."

Charles took her hand and bowed slightly. "I am honoured to meet you."

"Thank you," she said. "I am pleased to meet you as well."

"And congratulations on your recent nuptials. My deepest apologies that I was unable to attend."

"Please do not worry over that," Elizabeth said quickly. "While it is true that your presence was desired and missed, we understand your duties as an officer were far more pressing."

"Thank you." He smiled broadly at her and then turned to James with a smirk." She is quite understanding, am I to understand that this is one of the reasons that she agreed to marry you?"

James looked over fondly at his new wife who had laughed at Charles' question. "Yes, I believe it did. Why else would she agree to marry such a stuffy codger?"

Before Charles could come comment further Elizabeth spoke up. "I suppose that is a weakness of mine, being so very kind to the less fortunate."

Charles marveled at the serious face she was able to keep.

"Charity? That is what it has come down to?" James shook his head sadly before smiling once more as he turned to Elizabeth. "And I will ever be grateful for your kindness," James told her dropping a sweet kiss at her temple.

"Yes, of course," Elizabeth said with a sweet smile. "Dear Charles, we must leave you. Lady Haddington is beckoning us over."

James began to protest and Elizabeth patted his hand effectively quieting him. "You can stand beside me and say nothing, dear."

They had barely walked away when Charles saw an old schoolmate walking towards him. It suddenly occurred to him that he had not seen Peter Humphries in over five years.

"Repington, good to see you. Glad to be back, I imagine." The shorter man said to him as they shook hands.

"Yes, it is always good to come home to Castborough," Charles agreed. "How are you, Humphries?"

It was then that he noticed the women waiting patiently behind his old friend. A young raven haired woman and an older woman he assumed to be her mother. Charles smiled at them cordially.

Humphries stepped aside. "Lieutenant Charles Repington, let me introduce Lady Taltham and her daughter Lady Judith."

"I am very pleased to meet you," Charles said nodding at them both. "I hope that you are enjoying yourselves."

"Oh yes," Lady Judith said with a smile looking out over at the dance floor. "The music is quite nice."

It was then that Charles remembered his manners. "Yes, it is. Would you honour me with the next dance?"

"Why yes," Lady Judith replied her smile triumphant.

Charles had thought her extremely beautiful but he was quickly reminded of how calculating some of the young ladies could be during the Season. He wondered again if being home from the Peninsula was a good thing or not.

CHAPTER FOUR

"Beatrice, are you ill?" Henrietta asked.

"No, why do you ask?" Beatrice shook her head feeling her blonde curls brush against her neck.

"You had a most pained expression upon your face."

Beatrice had not realized that her feelings had shown so plainly on her face. "It is nothing. My mind has been wandering, that is all."

"Are you not enjoying the ball?" Henrietta asked with furrowed eyebrows.

"Oh, goodness. Of course, I am," Beatrice assured her. "It is magnificent."

"Then what is bothering you?" Henrietta asked again.

Beatrice had not intended to upset her friend with her troubles. She began to shake her head, but Henrietta grabbed her hand and led her from the ballroom.

"Come with me. We will get something to drink and you can tell me all about it."

Henrietta took her out the side door and into the dining room where the dining table had been set up against the wall. Trays of cakes and other sweets covered the long table, while a second smaller table had been placed in the corner with pitchers of lemonade and punch.

Henrietta handed Beatrice a cup of punch. "Now tell me what you were worrying over so much."

As much as Beatrice wanted to keep her problems to herself she wondered if talking to Henrietta may help her feel better.

"I received a letter today," Beatrice began. "It was not unexpected and it should not have upset me, but I find myself quite preoccupied."

"Who was the letter from?" Henrietta waited until the room was empty to ask, "What did it say?"

"It was from my mother telling me that I am to return to London in two weeks' time."

"Oh," Henrietta said quietly. "I will miss having you here. I will be coming to London in the next few weeks as well, I hope we will see each other often while I am there."

"That is good. It will be nice to see a friendly face at Almack's." Of course, that all depended on whether her mother could acquire the necessary vouchers. As the daughter of the Duke of Castborough, Henrietta needn't worry about acquiring vouchers. The patronesses of Almack's were quite excited about the sons and daughters of the peerage attending every Wednesday night.

"Has your mother been... well, less distressed about those other matters?" Henrietta asked, clearly hesitant about upsetting Beatrice.

It was an understandable question as Henrietta had accidentally walked in on a conversation between Beatrice and her mother. It had been a very awkward moment.

Her mother had been most upset and had said some rather wretched things to Beatrice. Henrietta had been so gracious, she apologized for the intrusion and had left at once. Unfortunately, her mother had not been so understanding and had admonished her for embarrassing her in front of the Duke of Castborough's daughter.

Beatrice could have pointed out that it was not she who had been yelling. Or that Mother had been upset about something

Father had done, but she knew it would do no good. Beatrice had learned long ago that nothing was ever her mother's fault.

Beatrice nodded. "Yes. She is quite happy we are to return to London."

At the time of the misunderstanding, Beatrice had explained her mother's behaviour away as being upset about being called back to Kent. Henrietta had been understanding as was her kind nature. Beatrice was sure that Henrietta's mother did not get angry with her over matters that Henrietta had nothing to do with. For a moment, she had to push her jealousy aside over that detail.

Henrietta stared into her glass of punch for a moment. "I understand it may not be my place to say anything, but if you ever need someone to talk to I am here."

Beatrice began to shake her head.

Henrietta covered Beatrice's hand with her own. "My family has seen its share of troubles. My brothers have not always gotten along with each other or with my father."

She doubted that Henrietta's family had seen the kind of troubles that Beatrice's had but she appreciated Henrietta trying to comfort her.

Before she could say anything in response, they were joined in the refreshment room by two other guests.

"Lady Henrietta!" a beautiful girl with dark hair gushed. "I am having the most wonderful time."

Henrietta smiled. "I am so glad to hear it, Lady Judith. Beatrice and I were just taking a moment for a refreshment."

Lady Judith's eyes passed over Beatrice with of the look of disdain before turning back to Henrietta without acknowledging the young woman at all.

"I have just met your brother," Lady Judith said her eyes widening.

"Oh," Henrietta responded. "Which one?"

Beatrice tried not to laugh. Henrietta had five brothers and was most likely quite used to other young ladies coming to her to talk about them.

"Charles, of course. He is rather charming." Lady Judith told her. "I cannot believe that I have not seen him all Season. Where has he been hiding?"

"On the Peninsula," Henrietta said dryly. "He has only just gotten back."

"An officer? Goodness, I had no idea all that charm came from a man who was also a hero." Lady Judith glanced back toward the ballroom. "Perhaps I should be going back."

"Yes, of course. We would not want to keep you," Henrietta replied her turning cold.

Henrietta let out an exaggerated sigh. "I cannot abide by Lady Judith's rude behaviour. Her superiority complex is too much for me to bear."

"Well, she did seem rather abrupt," Beatrice agreed unsure what to say.

Henrietta started back to the ballroom. "Beatrice, you are much more gracious than I."

They had barely returned to the ballroom when Henrietta groaned.

"What is it?" Beatrice asked looking past her.

"Lady Judith is dancing with Charles again. I am quite annoyed that he is seeming to enjoy her company."

"It is not surprising. She is rather beautiful. She is the daughter of a viscount after all. It would be a very favorable match."

Henrietta turned to her horrified look on her face. "I cannot imagine a more horrible fate for Charles."

"That seems to be a great exaggeration," Beatrice remarked.

"Exaggeration or not. I will have to speak with Charles immediately." Henrietta stepped away to look around the ballroom. "Ah, there he is. The dance is over and he seems to be alone for the moment. I will be back directly."

Henrietta had barely been gone when Lady Judith walked by sneering at Beatrice. Then she stopped and stood squarely in front of Beatrice blocking her way. "How on Earth did you get invited to a ball at Castborough? Surely your father..."

"Lady Judith, surely you know that Beatrice and I have been friends for years."

Lady Judith was so startled that she very nearly jumped. "Oh, yes, of course. How silly of me," she said quickly before she and her friend, Lady Sarah Mockersly, moved away.

"She is a vile creature," Henrietta muttered through gritted teeth.

"I'm feeling much less gracious," Beatrice admitted following Henrietta as they walked along the edge of the ballroom.

Beatrice had no idea what she would have done if Lady Judith had finished the sentence about her father. Hopefully, she would never have to know.

CHAPTER FIVE

Beatrice stood in her room at Castborough staring at her reflection in the large mirror. She could not help smiling as she looked at her favorite dress, mint green with white lace on the sleeves and hem. Originally, she had planned to wear her yellow dress but it was to be her last event before her return to London and she wanted it to be special. She had to look her best.

Looking at herself in the mirror Beatrice watched as her smile faded. She truly did not know what to feel, she missed her mother terribly. For a long time, it had been just the two of them, as her father spent much of his time in London.

Her mother had not always been awful, everything had changed when Beatrice had begun her first Season. Mother had become increasingly angered and annoyed, blaming Beatrice for silly things and for the most ridiculous reasons.

First, it was that Beatrice was too quiet and timid. Then she angrily claimed that Beatrice had become overly loud and boisterous. It had upset Beatrice so much that she had missed several parties at the end of the previous Season claiming she was ill. It was not a complete lie either as each time her mother had begun to lecture her about how important it was to find a good match, Beatrice had felt a certain sickness in her stomach.

It was not the fact that she needed to marry well, everyone wanted that. No, it was the fervor in which her mother would talk to her about it. Her intensity on the subject was unnerving.

Her mother had been obsessed in her desire for Beatrice to marry well. Like most girls Beatrice had always known that she would need to marry a man well placed in society. If not a peer, then an older son from a respected and revered family.

While she was prepared to marry well she also hoped to find a good match that would yield a companionable relationship. After watching her parents, Beatrice had long given up on the idea of love. Friendship would be a worthy goal.

Beatrice sat down with a sigh. A soft knock sounded on the door just before it opened slowly.

"Beatrice?" Henrietta peeked around the door.

"Yes, Henrietta, please come in," Beatrice stood smiling at her friend.

"Oh, I do adore that dress on you and the lace on the hem is a very special touch," Henrietta said taking Beatrice's hand.

"Thank you, Henrietta. It is my favorite." Beatrice looked at herself in the mirror.

Beatrice noticed the look on her friend's face. "Is everything all right? You do not look happy."

Henrietta sank down into one of the high-back chairs that were positioned under the window. "I cannot believe that we must endure another party with Lady Judith." She grimaced. "And in her own home as well. I anticipate she will be even more disagreeable than usual with people there adoring her estate and her family's wealth. I almost do not want to go."

"Surely that cannot be the case. Every party I have been to the hosts have been most gracious. I am sure it will be fine." Beatrice looked at her friend with curiosity at her opinion.

"That is what I have encountered as well, but I am afraid that Lady Judith will not be so gracious." Henrietta went on to explain,

"She has been coddled horribly by her parents. They have given her anything she has ever asked for and more. Therefore, she believes that the rest of us are rather beneath her touch."

Beatrice could not help but agree with Henrietta but dared not speak her mind on the matter. Instead, she patted Henrietta's hand and said, "I suppose then it will be up to us to be polite."

"Yes, of course." Henrietta nodded several times. "We shall be courteous to a fault, all while ignoring and avoiding Lady Judith and Lady Sarah whenever possible."

"I think that is an ingenious idea," Beatrice agreed. "We shall have a grand time in spite of them."

"Undoubtedly," Henrietta agreed with a laugh. "I suppose we should go downstairs. The carriage should arrive at any moment."

CHAPTER SIX

The carriage ride to Colchester had been short and it was not long before the carriage pulled up and stopped in front of a magnificent home. The door to the carriage opened. "Good evening, Lady Henrietta. We have arrived at Colchester Manor."

"Thank you, Porter," Henrietta told him before stepping down from the carriage. Beatrice followed close behind.

Lord and Lady Castborough were led into the ballroom with Henrietta and Beatrice not far behind. As discreetly as possible, Beatrice took in her surroundings she had been surprised when the carriage had stopped in front of the grand house. It was nearly as large as Castborough she had expected a more modest country home. It was a ridiculous thought on her part as Lady Judith's father was the Viscount of Colchester and clearly held a great deal of entailed land. It was no surprise that the inside of the house was decorated lavishly.

Henrietta turned to Beatrice suddenly with a tight smile. "It seems as though we will be tested from the start."

Beatrice had no idea what her friend meant and was about to ask when Henrietta squeezed her hand and smiled brightly and said, "Lady Judith, what a lovely party."

Beatrice turned just in time to see Lady Judith along with Lady Sarah walk up to them.

"Oh, thank you, Lady Henrietta. It was a last-minute decision but I told Mother that we just needed to have another gathering before we returned to London."

"We are so glad to be here, are we not, Beatrice?"

"Yes, thank you. It is quite wonderful." Beatrice smiled.

"I heard you shall be returning to London, as well," Lady Judith replied making a quiet sniffing sound. Then smirked before saying, "Perhaps I will see you at Almack's."

Beatrice ignored the smirk and nodded. "Yes, of course. I look forward to it."

Lady Judith's eyes widened. "Yes, I am sure you are." Then she turned to Henrietta. "I must admit much of my excitement is due to the arrival of your brother."

"My brother?" Henrietta repeated looking about the room. "Philip? I believe he and Caroline arrived in the coach before us."

"Oh, Lady Henrietta, you are so very amusing." Lady Judith giggled behind her fan. "Although I am always glad to see Lord Holgrave, it is Lieutenant Remington, I am excited to see tonight."

"Charles?" Henrietta's hand went to her chest. "Please forgive me, Lady Judith. I had no idea you had become acquainted with Charles. He is quite popular though, of course, so I imagine it is possible that your paths have crossed."

Lady Judith flushed at Henrietta's implication and quickly said, "Lieutenant Repington asked me to dance several times at the ball held at Castborough."

"Did he?" Henrietta asked. "Well as I said he is quite popular, so it makes sense he would dance the night away with anyone willing."

Beatrice was surprised by Henrietta's bold comments, although she understood Henrietta's reasoning, she was filled with a mix of gratitude and apprehension.

Lady Judith narrowed her eyes at Henrietta and huffed. "I do not..." She trailed off abruptly as Charles and Matthew approached them.

Charles smiled at Beatrice and his sister. "Here you two are. I had wondered where you had gone off to."

"Lieutenant Repington, how lovely to see you again." Lady Judith stepped up before Henrietta could respond, pushing her way in front of Beatrice.

Charles glanced over at Beatrice before replying. "Good evening, Lady Judith."

"I was just telling Lady Henrietta how honoured we are to have you at our party."

"Honoured?" Charles repeated. "Really?"

"Of course, you are a hero."

"Not I," Charles began to disagree.

"Oh goodness, I have embarrassed you," Lady Judith said opening her fan hiding her face behind it only her eyes were visible over the top. "My apologies, Lieut."

"Nothing of it," Charles replied politely. "And just to show my good nature please promise me the next dance."

Lady Judith fluttered her eyelashes at him. "I would love to." The music quieted signaling the next dance and Charles offered Lady Judith his arm.

Beatrice watched as they began to move around the ballroom. She tried to ignore her growing irritation. It made no sense for her to be jealous. Clearly, she was letting her personal feelings for Lady Judith affect her. The other girl's blatant rudeness and obvious disdain had upset both Henrietta and Beatrice.

"I think I shall look for a cup of punch."

She took one last look at the ballroom just as Charles expertly navigated Lady Judith through a turn. Charles took that moment to look up, locking eyes with Beatrice. Her breath caught and suddenly her stomach seemed to flutter out of control. Startled, Beatrice nearly ran from the ballroom.

CHAPTER SEVEN

Charles watched as Miss Beatrice rushed from the room. He glanced back to where Henrietta still stood wondering what had upset her friend. His sister was frowning at him but she stood by herself, he had no inkling of what could have caused the young woman to flee the ballroom.

"Is something amiss, Lieutenant Repington?"

"Not at all." Charles smiled down at Lady Judith. "I was merely thinking how fortunate I am."

"How so?" She looked up at him demurely, clearly expecting a compliment.

"I am here at this wonderful party, enjoying some wonderful company. How could I not be happy?"

"You are too kind, Lieutenant Repington, but I expect that you would have no trouble finding a party or dance partners here in Surrey, or London for that matter." She looked away with a laugh.

Charles shrugged elegantly. "While that may be true, after my time on the Peninsula, I have found that even the little things make me rather grateful."

"I am not sure how I feel about being included in that list," she told him a skeptical look on her face. "I would rather that you were enamored or fascinated by me, rather than simply grateful for my company."

Charles laughed jovially. "I am quite sure that you have many admirers that are both enamored and fascinated by you."

She was quite beautiful, tall and slender, her hair so dark it was nearly black. Charles had been away for some time but even he could see that she was in the latest fashion. It was no surprise that she was well-versed in the social graces as her father was the Viscount of Colchester, a revered member of the peerage.

Charles appreciated the irony, Lady Judith would be a good match, if he were actually looking for a wife. It is not as though he had not thought about marriage. Indeed, someday he would need to think about looking for a wife. But not for a while. For now, he appreciated the attention and that was that.

Lady Judith was not the only young Lady that had expressed interest in him, even Lady Sarah, Lady Judith's closest friend had cornered him in the refreshment room during the ball at Castborough. He had become more acquainted with Lady Judith only because they had crossed paths quite often. It was most likely by Lady Judith's doing but Charles did not mind at all. It was flattering to be sought out and the attention provided a much-needed distraction.

The dance ended and Charles led Lady Judith back to where his sister and Lady Sarah still stood.

"Lieutenant Repington!" A booming voice called out. Charles turned to see a robust man with a rather magnificent mustache walking toward him.

"Major Stewart, hello." Charles had not seen the man in several months and he was glad to see him looking so well.

The two men shook hands and Charles realized that Lady Judith still stood at his elbow.

"Major Stewart, may I introduce Lady Judith Powell."

"Lady Judith, this is Major Stewart. An old friend of my father's," Charles explained. When Major Stewart grumbled Charles added, "Oh, and we were on the Peninsula together as well."

"Oh," Lady Judith said with a sparkling smile for the older man. "You must tell me all about Lieutenant Repington."

Charles rolled his eyes dramatically. "That would be a waste of breath. There is nothing interesting to tell."

"I beg to differ." Major Stewart moved to face Lady Judith. "The lieutenant here is being quite modest. He served his commission quite well and is a hero to King and country."

Charles shook his head. "Do not believe a word he says. He is prone to exaggeration."

"Balderdash!" Major Stewart exclaimed his voice allowed us to start out others around them. Major Stewart continued on. "Lieutenant Repington's leadership and courage saved my life and other soldier several times over."

"A true hero," Lady Judith said breathlessly looking adoringly at Charles. "Is there anything you cannot do?"

"Yes, there is a very long list," Charles said with a sardonic grin. "It would bore you to tears though. At the top of the list, is the fact that I was unable to stop this conversation before it started."

Major Stewart laughed and clapped him on the back. "You are too modest, my good man. I am more than indebted to you and you know it."

Lady Judith smiled up at Charles looking as though she wanted to say something, though she was a bit hesitant. He was relieved when they were interrupted before she could speak.

"Major Stewart! It is so good to see you here." Matthew stepped forward and reached out to take the older man's hand, chuckling deeply. "I see you have managed to corner my brother. War talk?"

"Well, Matthew, my boy. It is good to be here. And to see you and your family. And only a little war talk since tonight is a festive occasion." He grinned and then looked at the ladies with Matthew and smiled. "Lady Henrietta. I am more than pleased to see you."

"Oh, Major Stewart, it has been far too long since you have visited." Henrietta beamed her brightest smile at the man as he kissed both her cheeks. "And this is a friend of our family, Miss Beatrice Taltham."

The older man bowed slightly as he turned to Beatrice. "I am pleased to meet you, Miss Taltham."

"And I you, Major Stewart." Beatrice smiled and nodded her head.

Charles noted the look of disdain on Lady Judith's face as she looked upon Miss Beatrice. He suddenly wondered if her look had anything to do with Miss Beatrice's hurried departure earlier.

Matthew had begun to ask Major Stewart about the Peninsula. Rather than stay for the stories to be dredged up again, Charles turned to Lady Judith who was now standing with Lady Sarah. "Please excuse me. I must say hello to a few people."

"Yes, of course," Lady Judith graciously agreed.

Charles had no intention of saying hello to anyone but realized that with Lady Judith's attention he should at least talk to one or two people as he moved through the ballroom. Pausing to look around he saw his mother speaking to an old friend and decided to join them.

"Good evening, Charles"

"Good evening, Mother," he said leaning in to kiss her cheek. "Good evening, Lady Ramsbury."

"Lieutenant Repington, so good to see that you are back safe," the older woman answered.

"As am I. It is good to see you as well, is Lord Ramsbury here?" Charles turned slightly to look across the ballroom.

"He is. I just saw that he was walking toward the refreshment room. He will surely eat every cake in the place if left to his own devices."

Charles chuckled. "Well, please do walk slowly, then. Let him enjoy at least some of them."

"Of course, dear," she said with a gravelly chuckle. "It would be unseemly for me to rush."

Lady Ramsbury had barely left when his mother said, "Charles, your father wanted to talk to you. Did he find you?"

"No, I have not seen him since the party began." Charles eyed the door not looking forward to a conversation with his father. "I will go see if I can find him."

"See that you do." His mother gave him a pointed look and then smiled. "I would hate for him to think I had failed to deliver his message."

Charles chuckled in spite of his suddenly anxious mood and nodded at her. He turned and made his way to the door. If he was lucky he could avoid being seen and duck out to the garden. He walked to the end of the hall and breathed a sigh of relief as he turned the corner. Stopping abruptly as he came face-to-face with his father.

"Charles, just who I wanted to see."

Charles pointed back to the ballroom. "Oh, well, I really need to..."

"It can wait, whatever it is." His father put a strong hand on Charles' shoulder steering him through the open door of the library.

His father sat down in one of the large chairs that had been placed in front of the desk. "I wanted to talk to you about your courtship of Lady Judith."

"My what?" Charles asked utterly confused.

"Your courtship. I understand that she is quite beautiful and from a well-placed family. Honestly, it is a match we would approve of under normal conditions. I feel I should remind you that you have only just returned from the Peninsula, though, and I think you should wait before you do anything rash. A marriage is a life-long commitment, after all."

Charles knew it was useless to explain so he simply said, "I agree completely. I will put off any decisions for the time being."

His father nodded sagely. "I believe that is best."

CHAPTER EIGHT

"Would you like to dance again?"

Beatrice looked up into Mr Townsend's hopeful face. "Thank you, but I think I would like to rest a little."

"You like dancing, do you not?" Mr Townsend cocked his head to the side with a questioning grin.

"Yes, of course," Beatrice replied hoping her smile did not falter. She found herself to make her next point. "I have been dancing quite a bit. I believe I will get some punch and sit down for a few minutes."

Beatrice had barely taken two steps when someone took her by the elbow. "What?" She asked turning around to see who had taken her arm.

"You sit down here," Mr Townsend was saying as he directed her to a line of chairs sat against the wall. "I will bring you a refreshment."

"But, I can get it."

"You said you needed to rest," he reminded her.

"Yes, thank you," she finally told him simply hoping that he would leave her alone.

She sat down on one of the chairs only to stand back up as soon as Mr Townsend disappeared through the door. Before she could change her mind, Beatrice left the ballroom through a door at the other end of the room. She stepped out into a hall which must have been used by the servants. Off to the left, she could hear noise coming from what must have been the kitchen.

Walking calmly as though she was supposed to be alone in that very hallway, Beatrice continued in the other direction until she came to a door. Turning the knob as quietly as possible she carefully opened the door and saw that it opened into the garden. Looking behind her first she slipped quickly quietly out the door and shut it behind her.

The area was well lit by lanterns and Beatrice soon realized that she was just outside the garden. A break in a low stone wall revealed and ornate iron gate. The latch was easily found and she let herself into the garden moving towards the closest pool of light.

As much as she wanted to escape Mr Townsend's attentions, it would not be wise for her to be found lurking in the darkness. Alone or not it would be fairly easy for someone to accuse her of meeting someone for a romantic interlude. Her reputation would be ruined for no reason at all.

Careful to stay clear of the windows just in case Mr Townsend was already looking for her, she moved closer to the house. She stopped in front of a pillar that was well lit and in plain sight of anyone coming in or out of the house. She fanned herself and nodded at two girls that passed by going back into the house.

It was silly that she was going to such lengths to get a few minutes away from Mr Townsend. He was from a well-established family, he was very nice and extremely attentive. So attentive, in fact, that she was beginning to feel somewhat distressed. Smothered, even. He would ask her something and get his feelings hurt if she did not answer breathlessly.

He ran hither and yon to attend to her, much like his quest to bring her a refreshment. On the surface, it seemed as though he was being sweet by getting her the punch. To Beatrice, though, it felt as though he was trying to keep her from getting away from him. To make her beholden to him. That made her want to get away from him even more.

"Have you seen Miss Beatrice?" Someone asked from near the door. Without thinking she move quickly to the other side of the pillar.

"I have not seen her. Perhaps she has gone to the refreshment room."

She could not hear the reply but apparently, it appeased Mr Townsend because it sounded as though both people had gone back into the house.

"I am not sure I like that you are spending so much time with Charles Repington."

Beatrice froze behind the pillar.

"Why ever not, Mother?" Lady Judith asked.

"You were destined to marry a peer, not a third son."

"That is ridiculous. Lieutenant Repington is the son of the Duke of Castborough," Lady Judith reminded her mother.

"I know who he is," Lady Colchester retorted, her voice sharp.

Lady Judith made a frustrated sound before saying, "His father is very important."

"Of course, I am just not sure that your father would approve the match. He has been speaking with the Marquess of Reigate. His heir is unmarried."

"Yes, and he spends most of his time visiting the establishments on the waterfront."

"Judith!"

"It is merely what I have heard. I cannot believe that Father would want that for me. It is a sordid situation, to be sure."

"Not if it is untrue," Mother said slowly.

"More importantly, I like Lieutenant Repington. He is a hero and a gentleman."

"Yes, I understand that, but—"

"He will make me look good, marrying an officer, and all. Do not forget he is a hero." There was a pause. "Mother, it is he that I want. Talk to Father for me."

There was a sigh and then Lady Colchester said, "I suppose if that is who you want I will do what I can to aid you."

"Thank you!"

"I suggest you snag him quickly. He is only just back. Get him before the other girls learn that he is back and looking for a wife."

"Do not worry I have a plan."

"If that takes too long then I shall do something drastic."

"Drastic? Judith, what are you speaking about?"

"I could get caught alone with him in the garden."

"Judith! I forbid you to do such a thing!" Lady Colchester exclaimed.

The voices were getting quieter and Beatrice could tell that they were going back to the house. Any further protestation was lost as the door closed behind them.

Beatrice had not been happy at the thought of Lieutenant Repington with Lady Judith but now she was thoroughly upset by the prospect and what might happen to force such a match.

She gathered up her skirts and rushed toward the house. Any worry over Mr Townsend completely forgotten, she needed to find Henrietta and share what she had overheard about Lieutenant Repington.

CHAPTER NINE

"Yes. I had planned to return to London, but I was persuaded to stay in Surrey."

"Persuaded?" Charles chuckled. "I hope it was for a good reason."

Humphries nodded. "It was. I was able to complete some business for my father."

"Oh yes, how is he doing?"

"He is a stubborn old goat," Humphries replied. "But he is improving now that the doctor is keeping an eye on him."

"I am glad to hear that."

"Peter! Hello!" Lady Sarah said suddenly appearing with Lady Judith at her side.

"Good evening, Lady Sarah," Humphries replied. His face lighting up as he looked at the blue-eyed girl. "I am surprised you are not on the dance floor."

"I danced earlier but Lady Judith and I decided to rest for a bit."

"I am feeling much better," Lady Judith added with a smile for Charles. "I should think I am ready for another dance."

"There you are!" Charles recognized Henrietta's voice.

"Yes, here I am." He turned to her with a raised eyebrow.

"Should I be somewhere else?"

Henrietta rolled her eyes at him making him laugh. "No, I suppose not," she said with a sigh. " But, I have been looking for you."

"Oh? Whatever for?"

"I..." Henrietta trailed off as another young man joined them.

"Miss Beatrice, what happened?"

Beatrice looked surprised and slightly dismayed. "Mr Townsend, I do apologize. I stepped out into the garden for some fresh air."

"I looked in the garden. You were not there." Mr Townsend scowled at her.

Beatrice blinked at him. "Again, I am sorry for the misunderstanding."

Henrietta spoke up then. "I am afraid that is my fault. Miss Beatrice came back into the house and I asked that she help me find Charles."

Mr Townsend looked at Henrietta with a frown. "I was bringing her refreshment, she said she wanted to rest."

"Mr Townsend," Beatrice started. "As I said before, I am quite sorry that I inconvenienced you."

"Miss Beatrice, you said that you needed to rest." He repeated again looking thoroughly confused.

Lady Judith sniffed and turned to Charles. "This is my last party before I return to London. Perhaps we should leave them to their conversation. I am bored with it and it has only just begun."

"Lady Judith, you are not the only one returning to London," Mr Townsend said. He then turned to Miss Beatrice. "Will you be attending Almack's on Wednesdays?"

Miss Beatrice froze for a moment and then smiled. "Of course, I will. Does not everyone go to Almack's on Wednesday's?"

Lady Judith made what sounded like a snort although she covered it up with a delicate cough. "That reminds me, Miss Beatrice. I would be happy to give you the name of my modiste. That way you can arrive at Almack's in the very latest fashion."

Even if Charles had not seen the look of anger pass over his sister's face he would have realized that Lady Judith's comment was meant to be insulting rather than helpful.

To her credit, Miss Beatrice simply smiled and said, "Why thank you that is quite kind of you."

Lady Judith gave Beatrice an icy smile and then put a hand on Charles' arm. "Lieutenant Repington, I think I would like a refreshment."

Henrietta stepped in front of her brother. "Charles, I really need to speak with you. It cannot wait."

Charles frowned at Mr Townsend briefly before saying, "Mr Townsend, since you seem to be concerned about the welfare of the young ladies, would you please take Lady Judith to get some lemonade? I believe there is sufficient supply in the refreshment room."

"Of course," Mr Townsend agreed, looking back at Beatrice still scowling.

"Thank you," Charles replied.

"Oh, well, that is not necessary," Lady Judith protested stepping closer to Charles.

"Please excuse me." Charles stepped away from Lady Judith and paused at the shocked look on her face. Turning back to her, he cocked his head to the side. "Surely you were not suggesting that I ignore my sister?"

Lady Judith suddenly remembered to be gracious. "Of course not. Mr Townsend, I would be happy to accompany you to the refreshment room."

Henrietta took Charles by the arm dragging him out to the hallway.

"What is so important, dear sister, that you have interrupted the festivities? And brought us to the servant's hallway, as well?"

"It is about Lady Judith."

Charles groaned inwardly thinking not Henrietta as well. "I have already talked to Father about that."

Henrietta and Beatrice looked at each other in confusion.

"Father? How could he know?"

"It does not matter. Do not worry yourselves, I am not planning on starting a courtship with Lady Judith, or anyone."

"That is a relief to hear but that is not our concern."

"Our?"

"Miss Beatrice and mine." Henrietta decided and rushed on. "Miss Beatrice overheard Lady Judith and her mother discussing you. Particularly Lady Judith's interest and her hope to trap you in marriage."

"Trap me?" Harris chuckled. "Not likely."

"Yes," Miss Beatrice looked embarrassed. "She told her mother that if you proved reluctant to court her that she would not hesitate to get caught alone with you."

"She would compromise her reputation?" Charles asked not quite believing what he was hearing.

Beatrice nodded. "Henrietta and I were concerned that since you have been showing Lady Judith some attention as of late that it would be believable. I had hoped that her mother would discourage her but while she sounded shocked she did not dissuade her."

"That is a problem," Charles admitted. He thought for a moment and then let out a long sigh. "I suppose, it is time I went to London."

"But Lady Judith will be arriving there soon." Henrietta reminded him. "She will surely try to corner you no matter where you get off to."

"I will be quite busy in London. There are many more parties held in London. Hopefully, once I am seen paying attention to other young ladies, Lady Judith will lose her interest."

Henrietta seemed skeptical. "I do not think she will lose interest. I hate that you will be leaving early for London, but it probably is what needs to be done."

Charles looked across the ballroom to where his mother and father were standing, his father's words suddenly coming to mind. "Yes, I believe it is for the best."

CHAPTER TEN

The door slammed upstairs and Beatrice started. Her mother was up and apparently angry about something already. "So early in the day?" She groaned under her breath and sighed.

It would only be a matter of time before she came into the drawing room to talk to Beatrice. Every day since Beatrice had returned to London had gone the same way. Her mother would go out or receive guests and then she would find Beatrice and complain.

It made Beatrice sad, not only because her mother was being awful but also because they never spent any pleasant time together. When she had been younger, Beatrice would sit with her mother while they embroidered or her mother would read to her. They would talk often about the new fashions and about father's business in London and when he would return.

Many evenings had been spent in the drawing room, her mother playing the pianoforte and Beatrice singing along. Those were among Beatrice's favorite memories. But when they returned to London last Season, the pianoforte was gone from the drawing room. When Beatrice had asked where it had gone her mother said she had grown tired of playing it and had it removed from the house. Beatrice had wanted to ask more questions, but her mother had clearly not wanted to talk about it because she gathered her needlework and left the room.

Knowing her mother was already upset and on her way to the drawing room, Beatrice decided that she would give her mother some extra time. Her first thought was to escape to her room but there was little chance she would be able to make her way there without meeting up with her mother on the stairs. Her only chance of avoiding her mother would be to slip into the library until her mother had gone into the drawing room. With that thought still in her mind, Beatrice closed up her book and moved quickly across the hall it into the library. She stood in front of the bookcase near the door listening for her mother to pass into the drawing room.

When the door opened a moment later Beatrice barely was able to compose herself.

"Beatrice, what are you doing in here?" Mother asked a frown creasing her brow.

Holding up her book Beatrice said, "I was choosing a new book."

"Nonsense, you only started that book yesterday."

"Yes, but I..." Beatrice started.

"I care not for your excuses. I know you are trying to avoid me. I had no idea I had raised such a selfish daughter." Her mother stepped out to the hallway waving her hand for her to follow. "I realize I should not be surprised, you were bound to pick up some of your father's more unsatisfactory traits."

"Mother, I do apologize I only—"

"Beatrice, there are more important matters at hand," her mother interrupted. She pointed at the settee. "Please sit down."

Beatrice did as her mother asked, but furrowed her brow at the unexpected request. "Is something amiss?"

"It has become abundantly clear to me that you will never find a husband without my assistance."

Beatrice felt as though she had been slapped. "I have been doing everything you have asked of me."

"And yet you still have not gained the favor of any suitable gentlemen." Mother stopped pacing to look at her. "You are too quiet and when I pointed that out to you, you proceeded to bellow like a goose!"

In a moment of anger, Beatrice retorted, "I do not bellow like a goose."

"It is of no matter." Mother waved her hand. "I have acquired vouchers for you to attend Almack's this week. I expect you to act appropriately."

"Yes, Mother," Beatrice said quietly.

"You must try to look happier. Be more cheerful. You look weak, no man is going to want to be shackled to you when you look like that."

Beatrice pursed her lips, refusing to answer angrily again. It was better to not address her mother's comments as they seemed to lead to more anger and insults. She was not up to an argument, anyway.

"I want you to wear your mint green dress." Mother set down seemingly calmed by Beatrice is subdued demeanor.

Beatrice remembered Lady Judith's comments at the party held by Lord and Lady Colchester. She had been wearing the very dress her mother had just suggested.

"I am wondering if my dresses are fashionable enough. Should we perhaps visit the modiste soon?"

"You are an ungrateful child!" Mother pointed her finger at her again and jumped to her feet. "We will visit the modiste when you have entered into a courtship."

Beatrice could not believe her mother's reaction. "I was only trying to help my chances of procuring a husband. As you have said, I shall need all the assistance that I can gather."

"You are being purposely difficult and I will not listen to you when you are being so rude." Mother walked away closing the drawing room door behind her.

Beatrice let out a long sigh. Partially from relief that her mother had left her alone but also because she was being so awful. Mother was blaming Beatrice for not finding a husband. Everyone, including her mother, knew where the blame should lie. Right at the feet of Baron Taltham, Beatrice's father. There was little Beatrice could do but cry.

CHAPTER ELEVEN

"Excuse me, Lieutenant Repington," Fletcher asked. "Will you be staying in tonight?"

Charles looked up from the paperwork he had been reading. He had been in London for nearly a fortnight and every night the manservant had asked the same question, and each night Charles had told him that he would indeed be staying in.

"No," Charles answered, surprising even himself. "I believe I shall go to White's tonight."

"If I may, sir, it is Wednesday. I believe Almack's will be in fine fashion."

"Yes, right you are. I had not thought of that." Charles nodded. "Thank you for the suggestion."

He had been avoiding much of the events of the Season but it was time that he did something different. Most of his days had been spent in the house alone with Fletcher, save one day when he met with James at a club near Parliament.

The silence was beginning to distress him. He had far too much time to think, and memories of his time on the Peninsula were foremost on his mind. Everyone thought he had been on a great adventure but it had been quite the opposite. While Charles had learned much and had done great things, it was outweighed by the many awful experiences. Memories of the horrific death and destruction of war haunted his thoughts and dreams.

With a shake of his head, Charles pushed back from the desk. "I suppose I shall get ready."

Later that night, Charles found himself standing in the corner of Almack's ballroom. As expected it was a rout, there were so many people in the ballroom it was nearly impossible to move about. Charles was glad of it though. Lady Amelia had stopped to say hello and he had seen the moment that Lady Judith had seen him from across the ballroom. The crowd in the ballroom afforded him a great amount of time to make his escape.

Charles nodded at Lady Agatha Radcliffe and Lady Matilda Watson both dowagers chaperoning their young nieces, as he moved slowly through the crowd. He looked back in an effort to see where Lady Judith had gone and when he turned around he ran headlong into a young lady with blonde hair who had also been glancing behind her. She let out a rather loud squeal as they collided and then stepped back quickly.

"Miss Beatrice, are you all right?" Charles exclaimed. "My apologies, I was not paying attention to where I was walking."

"Oh no, Lieutenant Repington, it was I that was not looking. Please forgive me."

He turned as she moved past him. "Please think nothing of it."

She gave him a weak smile and he wondered if she was all right. Then over her shoulder, he saw that Lady Judith had worked through the crowd much quicker than he had anticipated. He turned back to Beatrice praying that she would take mercy on him. "To show you I shared no ill will, please have this next dance with me."

Miss Beatrice glanced back the way she came before nodding. "Yes, thank you. I would like that."

Charles led her into the middle of the ballroom. They took their positions as the music started Charles looked up to see Mr

Townsend and scowling at them. Clearly, Miss Beatrice had been avoiding Mr Townsend's attention.

"It seems that we have a similar problem."

"Oh?" Miss Beatrice asked her blue eyes wide.

He smiled at her and could not help himself. "Yes, it seems we are both dealing with unwanted attention."

"Unwanted attention?" Miss Beatrice repeated, seemingly confused at first. "Oh, yes. Mr Townsend has been quite persistent."

"I do not doubt that. I recall his behaviour at the Colchester party."

"He means well, but I…" Miss Beatrice's voice trailed off.

Charles steps nearly faltered as he watched emotions flit across her beautiful face. It was fear that had caused him to pause mid turn.

"Has he done anything untoward?"

Miss Beatrice shook her head quickly. "No, he has acted the gentleman. It is just that he is so very imperious. He expects me to do everything he asks regardless if I want to do so or not."

Charles looked over to where the other man stood. "That does not seem very gentlemanly at all."

"I see that Lady Judith's interest in you has not waned." Miss Beatrice looked up at him briefly "I hope her intentions have improved though."

The change in conversation almost caught him up but Charles simply smiled. "I do not want to seem ungracious but, yes, after you and Henrietta warned me I have done my best to stay far away from her."

Miss Beatrice nodded. "How are you enjoying London?"

Charles did not answer right away concentrating on the dance and enjoying having Miss Beatrice so close to him. "I have only been back a short time but I suppose I have little to complain about. And you, Miss Beatrice, how are you finding London?"

"London is wonderful but it can take me several days to get adjusted." Miss Beatrice paused as if thinking of her next words carefully. "I can imagine that you may experience the same feelings of unease after being gone so long. It must be difficult to adjust."

"Yes," Charles agreed, appreciating that she understood his plight. Not a single person, including his family, had given a thought as to how he was doing being home. Certainly, he was immensely thankful to be back in England, but he still found it a difficult transition.

When the music changed Charles led Miss Beatrice back to the edge of the ballroom. They had barely stopped when Mr Townsend appeared at their side.

"Here you are, Miss Beatrice. I have brought you a refreshment," Mr Townsend said handing her cup of lemonade.

"Mr Townsend, thank you," Miss Beatrice said rather stiffly.

"Good evening, Townsend," Charles said by way of greeting.

Townsend nodded. "Repington."

"Miss Beatrice, good evening," Lady Judith said as she and Lady Sarah joined them.

Lady Sarah adding, "It is so good to see you here tonight."

"Good evening, thank you." Miss Beatrice smiled but to Charles, she looked rather uncomfortable.

Lady Judith quickly turned to him and said, "Good evening Lieutenant Repington. I am quite thrilled to see you here in London."

"Thank you." Charles reverted back to his standard answer. "It is rather nice to be back."

"You must be looking forward to attending so many of the parties and balls, now that you are back."

Charles was deciding how to answer when Townsend suddenly asked, "Miss Beatrice, would you like to dance?"

"Oh," Miss Beatrice replied clearly wanting to decline his invitation. "I need a moment..."

"You have had a moment to rest and I brought you a refreshment," he said with a satisfied smile. "I wanted to make sure that you would be able to dance. It appears you have had respite enough."

"Oh," she repeated clearly surprised by his response. Charles wanted to intervene on Miss Beatrice's behalf but was unsure how to do so. Lady Agatha and Lady Matilda were sitting nearby watching their small group. It was a well known fact that the two women were the biggest gossips in London.

After a slight pause, Miss Beatrice smiled weakly at Townsend. "Yes, thank you."

As Townsend led Miss Beatrice to the middle of the ballroom Charles found himself getting far more irritated than he had been in weeks.

Lady Judith seemed not to notice his irritation. "Lieutenant Repington, will you be attending the opera next week?"

Charles had no interest in discussing social events with Lady Judith. "I am unsure if I will be there. I have much business to attend to and I may not be in London for long."

"Not in London for long? Wherever are you going?" Lady Judith asked a look of astonishment on her face.

Charles had not meant to say the last part but realized that he was ready to tell her anything if it meant she would leave him alone. To further that he pulled a watch from his pocket and said, "I had not realized it was so late. I must be going."

"Leaving? Now?" Lady Judith said her voice panicked.

Charles nodded at her stiffly. "Good evening Lady Judith, Lady Sarah."

He turned on his heel and left the ballroom. He was still quite irritated, unsure if he was unhappier with Townsend for conniving to get Miss Beatrice to dance with him, Miss Beatrice for accepting his invitation or at Lady Judith's utter selfishness. Standing outside of Almack's, Charles decided that he needed a drink. Perhaps he would go to White's after all.

CHAPTER TWELVE

"Good evening, sir."

Charles nodded curtly at the man that opened the door and walked into the club. He was still fuming about Townsend. During the walk to White's, Charles had realized that Miss Beatrice had had little choice when Townsend had asked her to dance. Surely Lady Agatha and Lady Matilda would have felt obligated to pass on the gossip if Miss Beatrice had refused Townsend's invitation. There was really no choice for her but to accept.

Townsend, though, knew what he was doing and had effectively forced Miss Beatrice to dance with him regardless of what she wanted. Charles had seen her level of discomfort and now regretted leaving when he did. Debating on whether he should go back to Almack's, Charles paused. If he went back, the risk of running into Lady Judith would be quite high.

He was still debating when someone called his name.

"Repington!"

He turned to see a well-dressed man with blonde hair standing just inside White's cardroom. Charles stopped in the hall, momentarily disconcerted at seeing Captain Patrick Wainwright in London.

"Wainwright?" Charles exclaimed. "When did you arrive in London? I did not realize you had left your commission on the Peninsula."

"I have only been in London a week." Wainwright gestured toward an empty table. "Come have a drink with me. We can play some cards if you would like."

Charles hesitated, unsure if he was up for company. The thought of going back to the empty house alone made him want to scream. He realized he was tired of the solitude. Finally, Charles nodded. "Lead the way."

"How long have you been back?" Wainwright asked once they each had a glass of whiskey in front of them.

"I have been in London for nearly two weeks but returned from the Peninsula several weeks before that."

Wainwright seemed to think about that before asking, "How has it been?"

"I want to say that it has gone well, but it has not been so."

"It has been the same for me. I was so looking forward to coming back, and leaving all of that behind me." Wainwright shook his head in disbelief. "I lie down at night and I cannot sleep."

"I have been doing the same," Charles admitted. "I close my eyes and it is like I am back there. It is hard for me to admit it, but it is quite true."

"Yes, I know what you mean. I do not like to admit it, even to myself. But the truth is that some nights, I swear that I can still hear the cannons," Wainwright said staring down at his hands.

Charles took a long drink of his whiskey. "I have been drinking far more than I should be, just so I can sleep."

Wainwright nodded. "I have as well."

Charles drained his glass and set it down. The glass made a sharp, hollow sound as it hit the table.

"You seem quite angry. Is there something that has upset you?"

Charles had not intended to talk about his night at Almack's but the whiskey seemed to have relaxed him a bit. He quickly told

Wainwright about the interaction with Townsend and Miss Beatrice at Almack's.

Wainwright listened to him and almost immediately said, "I am not surprised. Townsend was a schoolmate of mine. He was odd even back then, he was smaller than most of the other boys and he kept to himself mostly. Older boys can be rough with each other though."

Charles smiled wryly thinking about the trouble he and his brothers got into. "Yes, I have a few scars to attest to that."

"Well, Townsend was quite particular about his clothing. One night one of the boys thought it would be amusing to take all of Townsend's clothing outside and lay it all out in the snow."

"I think everyone dealt with behaviour like that."

Wainwright let out a chuckle. "Yes, with me someone filled my shoes with frogs."

"Always with the frogs." Charles laughed too. "What happened with Townsend?"

"The schoolmate who was thought to have stolen Townsend's clothes was found the next day."

"Found?"

"Someone, had beaten the boy until he was bloody. We all knew it with Townsend but we had no proof. "

Charles remembered Townsend's insistence that Miss Beatrice dance with him and how at the previous party he had kept repeating that she had said that she wanted to rest.

"Do you think that he is dangerous?" Charles asked looking at Wainwright sharply.

Wainwright paused as he took a sip of his whiskey. "I think he could be if he was pushed."

"I worry about Miss Beatrice. If Townsend would react violently regarding his clothing I can only imagine his reaction if he felt he had been snubbed by Miss Beatrice."

Wainwright stared down into his glass. "It is unfortunate that he has set his attention upon Miss Beatrice. She has already dealt with enough. Although perhaps that is part of why he has focused on her."

Charles frowned. "What do you mean?"

"I would hate to spread gossip," Wainwright said hesitantly.

"I'll not say a word," Charles told him leaning towards the table. "My only concern is Miss Beatrice's well-being."

"Her father, Baron Taltham, spends much of his time gambling in the clubs. He seems rather flush these days but in the past, he has been in quite deep. He has taken in several loans in the past the covers losses."

"I see." Charles trying to imagine what it would be like to have a father who was so ridiculously irresponsible. His own father was completely the opposite, responsible and trustworthy to a fault. Even pushing his children to be the same.

"Unfortunately, Miss Beatrice's mother is not any better."

"No?"

"No, she is overbearing and blames Miss Beatrice for many things that are not her fault. From what my sister has said, Lady Taltham has been rather horrible to miss Beatrice, criticizing her for not snagging a husband. Apparently, Lady Taltham thinks her daughter will save them from their plight."

The irritation that Charles felt earlier was being replaced by concern. "Perhaps Miss Beatrice is wanting the same."

Wainwright shook his head. "Normally, I might think so but no, not in this instance. I do not envy you, my friend."

"I suppose we will have to keep an eye on Mr Townsend."

"I will do what I can before I leave England."

Charles raised an eyebrow. "Back to the Peninsula?"

"No. India."

"India?" He had not expected that answer. He raised an eyebrow and tilted his head to the side. "What takes you there?"

"I will be working forward the East India Company, training soldiers for the army there."

Charles knew that Wainwright did not get along with his older brother or his father. It was not surprising that he was seeking a position elsewhere. "I hope it is a good position for you to go so far from home."

"By the time I am done, I will be swimming in large," Wainwright said with a big smile.

Charles smiled. "Sounds wonderful. Hopefully, I will find something as good."

Wainwright refilled their whiskey glasses. "Why not India? There are more positions open that you are more than qualified for."

Charles thought about his father and replied, "Maybe I will."

CHAPTER THIRTEEN

"Oh, good you are up already," Lady Taltham said happily.
"Good morning, Mother," Beatrice said.
"Good morning, Lady Taltham, can I get you anything?"
"Some tea and biscuits, please," her mother said evenly.
"Yes, ma'am," Ruth nodded and left the dining room.

Beatrice had already eaten her breakfast and was just finishing her second cup of tea.

"Beatrice, I must say that I am very pleased that your evening at Almack's went so well."

"Thank you, Mother." She was not sure why her mother was pleased but Beatrice was happy her mother was not yelling or scowling or complaining.

"It seems that Andrew Townsend is quite enamored with you." The older woman smiled and blinked slowly.

Beatrice's heart sank. "I do not know about that, Mother. I think I am merely a friendly face."

"No, it is more than that."

"Besides I danced with several other gentlemen at Almack's, as well." Lieutenant Repington came immediately to mind, she could still feel the warmth of his hands as she had the night before.

"Yes, you did," Mother agreed. "Mr Townsend is a good match, though. He is the second son of the Earl of Marlsfeld."

Beatrice only nodded. There was nothing she could say to deter her mother, though the thought of having to marry Mr Townsend made her mouth go suddenly dry.

Mother went on. "Lord Marlsfeld holds an immense piece of entailed land and is quite influential in Parliament."

Beatrice frowned. "Mr Townsend is the second son though. Surely he will be pursuing a gentleman's profession and that was not to your liking if I recall."

"Yes, he would be, but the earl's heir has fallen deathly ill."

"Oh, how horrible," Beatrice gasped.

"It really is," Mother agreed. "He is not likely to survive and that means your Mr Townsend will be the earl one day."

Beatrice was horrified by her mother's excitement over the possible death of the elder son of the Lord Marlsfeld.

Before Beatrice could say anything her mother suddenly announced, "We will be going for a carriage ride this afternoon. Please wear your best dress!"

"I will." Beatrice said, simply happy that her mother had planned something for them to do together.

"We will be going to Hyde Park for the fashionable hour. I am hoping you can hold on to whatever magic you had from last night. We must capitalize on anything positive, you know."

Beatrice immediately admonished herself for thinking her mother had any good intentions. Their carriage ride was all part of the quest for a husband, not because her mother wanted to spend time with her.

Beatrice finished her tea and then excused herself, wanting nothing more than to get away from her mother and be alone again.

CHAPTER FOURTEEN

"You look very nice," Lady Taltham noted when Beatrice came downstairs.

"Thank you," Beatrice replied in a flat, uninspired tone.

As they went out the front door to get into the waiting carriage her mother said, "Now remember to be jovial. Not too quiet, but not too loud."

"Yes, Mother." Beatrice stepped into the carriage turning to the footman. "Thank you, O'Brien."

"You are welcome, miss," the older man nodded with a smile lighting up his blue eyes.

"Thank you," Mother said curtly, dismissing the footman.

He nodded at Beatrice and then pulled himself up into the driver's seat.

"Now when you see Mr Townsend make sure to show your interest, but please try to be demure."

"Yes, Mother," Beatrice said automatically them paused as her mother's words soaked in. "What do you mean, when I see Mr Townsend?"

The carriage had already pulled into Hyde Park when her mother finally answered. "Yes. Mr Townsend sent a note to the house this morning. It was an invitation to take a ride during the fashionable hour."

Beatrice was furious. "You accepted the invitation without asking me and also did not tell me that you had done so?"

"There was no need to," her mother said smoothing back a strand of hair. "Do not be disrespectful. As I told you yesterday we have been brought to this point by your lack of action in the matter. I am doing what needs to be done."

Beatrice stayed silent, seething. She was far too angry to speak without causing a public argument.

She could not believe her mother had accepted the invitation and the realization that she had done so before even speaking to Beatrice this morning in the dining room. It was one more way that her mother had hurt her. One more reason for Beatrice to not trust her mother. She was certain she could not trust her father, either. It was clear that there was no one that cared about how Beatrice felt or what she needed. The sense of betrayal weighed heavily on her.

"Mr Townsend, hello," her mother said suddenly. Mr Townsend had pulled his carriage alongside their own.

"Good afternoon, Lady Taltham," he said quite cheerily. "Hello, Miss Beatrice."

"Good afternoon, Mr Townsend," she greeted him politely, but did not meet his eyes.

"You two have a nice afternoon," her mother said prompting the footman to come help Beatrice from her carriage to sit with Mr Townsend in his more fashionable curricle.

Mr Townsend smiled at her briefly as he guided the horses back onto the path. "I was very pleased to get your reply this morning."

"Thank you for the invitation." Beatrice had wanted to tell him to thank her mother, but she held her tongue.

"We had such an enjoyable evening last night at Almack's that I wanted to make sure we were able to see each other again soon."

Beatrice looked away feeling more miserable than she could remember. "That was very considerate of you."

"Lord and Lady Alderside are having a party at their London

residence next week. A recital for Lady Sarah and her sisters." He looked over at her waiting for her reply.

"How nice," she replied thinking it actually sounded rather awful. Beatrice had been to a number of recitals that had all been awkward afternoons listening to girl sing in wretchedly high voices or plinking what seemed like random keys on the pianoforte.

"I thought you would enjoy it." His smile was smug when he turned to her and said, "That is why I told Lady Alderside that you would be attending with me."

Beatrice could not believe what she had just heard. "Thank you, that was very… kind of you. I will have to check with my mother to be sure that we do not have another engagement."

A frown formed on his face. "Surely, your mother would understand."

Beatrice could see that Mr Townsend was getting frustrated which made her even more uncomfortable. Nervous, even. That is when she realized he had driven the carriage off the main path onto a path that would go deeper into the park.

"Mr Townsend, could you please stop the carriage? I think I shall like to walk for a bit."

"No, we are here at the park for a carriage ride."

"I apologize but I am not feeling very well at all. Please stop the carriage."

He took some time to think about it but finally, Mr Townsend pulled the curricle to a stop. In most circumstances, social propriety demanded that she wait for him to help her down from her seat. However, the thought of him touching her made Beatrice want to be ill so she jumped down before he could get around the carriage to help her.

"You really should have waited for me to assist you," he told her sternly.

"As I told you I do not feel well," she reminded him. "I simply wanted to walk."

"Well, it is the fact that you are ill that indicates even more that you should have waited."

"Mr Townsend," Beatrice stopped to look at him. "It has already been done. I cannot go back and change it now."

"That is true, but I think it is important that you understand what you have done wrong. I cannot expect you to learn if I do not correct you."

Beatrice let out a frustrated cry and before she knew it she had turned back down the path heading back to the busier part of the park.

"Miss Beatrice, where are you going?"

Beatrice did not stop. She simply called back over her shoulder, "Home, Mr Townsend. I am going home."

"But you cannot. We are taking a carriage ride."

She had reached the main path and continued walking toward the path to Grosvenor Gate. Suddenly, Mr Townsend was right in front of her.

"You must go back to the carriage," he commanded.

"No, Mr Townsend. Thank you but no."

"Miss Beatrice, you must listen." He took her by the elbow and began to turn her around.

"No! Let go!" She protested his grip on her arm tight. "You are hurting me."

"You need to listen. You will not learn unless you do as I say." Dragging her back toward the carriage.

"Let me go," she cried out again.

"Excuse me, Townsend. I believe Miss Beatrice has asked you to release her."

Beatrice nearly cried with relief when she recognized Lieutenant Repington's voice.

"Repington! This does not concern you," Mr Townsend said continuing to pull her down the path.

Beatrice held her breath praying that the lieutenant did not listen to Mr Townsend Then, suddenly Lieutenant Repington was standing on the path in front of them.

"I beg to differ. I could hear the young lady calling out from a good distance. I would hate for it to get out that you were attacking ladies in the Park.

Mr Townsend blanched and then a look of fury passed over his face. He let go of Beatrice's arm so fast she almost fell down.

"Yes, of course. Forgive me."

Beatrice stepped away from him afraid that he would change his mind and grab for her again.

"Miss Beatrice, I look forward to seeing you soon. Good afternoon." He bowed curtly before shooting a glare at Lieutenant Repington and walking away.

"Are you all right?" Lieutenant Repington asked coming to stand next to her.

"Yes," she answered quickly. "I am shaken but I am unharmed."

"I have my carriage parked over there or I can walk you home."

"Do you mind walking?" Beatrice did not think she could bear to get in another carriage.

"Not at all." He gestured towards the path.

They walked in silence for a minute or so.

"Thank you," she said quietly. "I am not sure what I would have done had you not shown up."

"You are quite welcome. I only wish I had gotten here sooner." He shook his head.

"Please do not be upset," she started, her voice cracked and to her horror, she began to cry.

"Oh, Beatrice, do not cry," Lieutenant Repington said quickly turning to face her.

"I am so sorry." Beatrice said trying to compose herself.

They had stopped right behind a large oak tree. Beatrice was trying to calm herself, but she was much more shaken by Mr Townsend that she admitted.

"Oh, you are shaking," Lieutenant Repington said. In the next instant, she found herself enveloped by his strong arms. Beatrice knew that she should step back, if anyone saw them they would be in trouble, her reputation ruined but she could not. It had been the first moment of kindness she had felt since she had left Castborough. And she began to cry again.

"Shush, now. You are safe now," he said soothingly.

They stood there like that for a moment until she finally stepped away.

"Thank you," she whispered and began to walk down the path again.

"You are most welcome." He fell into step beside her and then handed her a handkerchief.

"Oh," she said. "I must look a fright."

He looked over at her and shook his head. "Not at all, you look beautiful, as always."

Beatrice nodded and swallowed, and tried not to cry again.

CHAPTER FIFTEEN

"Remember to smile."

"Yes, Mother," Beatrice answered for what must have been the twentieth time that day. "Please remember that Lady Alderside sent you a personal invitation at Mr Townsend's request."

"Yes, Mother." It was bad enough that Beatrice was being forced to attend Lady Sarah's recital, she would not only see Mr Townsend also it would be necessary to be polite and gracious to him.

She was grateful for her long gloves, as they covered the yellowing bruises that still lingered above her elbow. Feigning a headache Beatrice had been able to bow out of any social events, over the last week. While it was true that she did not want anyone to see the discoloured spots on her arm she was more concerned about seeing Mr Townsend again. His behaviour at the park had been extremely upsetting.

In their earlier conversations, Mr Townsend had seemed nice except for his peculiar habit of telling her how she should act and feel. Beatrice had thought perhaps it was nervousness on his part. After witnessing his reaction when she chose to disagree with him, she knew it was much more than that.

The door to the Alderside house opened and Beatrice steeled

herself to deal with Lady Sarah, and Lady Judith surely would be there as well.

"Miss Beatrice!"

Being looked up quickly not expecting anyone to be overly excited to see her. She was even more surprised to see Henrietta hurry across the room.

"Lady Henrietta!" Beatrice exclaimed. "I cannot believe you are here."

"Oh, Miss Beatrice, I am so glad you're here. I thought it was going have to endure this all on my own."

"I was fearing the same," Beatrice admitted. "When did you arrive in London?"

"At the beginning of the week," Henrietta exclaimed. "I had hoped to see you at Almack's on Wednesday."

"I was feeling ill and missed most of my social engagements." Beatrice looked around to make sure her mother was not listening before she said, "We need to find a quiet place so we can talk."

They were all led out to the garden where many stone benches and several ornately decorated wooden chairs had been set up. Henrietta quickly guided them to a bench in the corner of the garden half hidden by a trellis of climbing flowers.

"Beatrice, what has happened?"

"There is so much to tell I am unsure where I am to begin."

"You left Castborough less than a month ago. I cannot believe so much has happened."

Beatrice knew that her friend was not doubting her, she was truly confused and upset for her.

"Must you sit over here in the corner?" Lady Taltham spat at her. "You will never get a husband sitting off by yourself."

"Good afternoon, Lady Taltham," Henrietta said leaning forward to be seen around the trellis.

Beatrice his mother looked horrified for a moment before her face adopted a serene look once more. "Good afternoon, Lady Henrietta. I did not realize you were back in London."

"We just arrived from Castborough a few days ago. We were all invited to see Lady Sarah's recital."

"Oh, are Lord and Lady Castborough here as well?"

Henrietta smiled. "Yes, I believe they are speaking with Lord and Lady Alderside."

Beatrice's mother began to look back toward the house. "I should go speak with them."

"Yes, of course," Henrietta replied.

Beatrice stared down at her hands. "I apologize for my mother. She..."

"Beatrice, there is no need to apologize. The words were not yours," Henrietta assured her. "I know that there have been difficulties in recent months."

"No," Beatrice said. She had not planned on saying anything but her mother's embarrassing words were too much. "My mother is awful. I can do nothing right. She is critical of everything that I do."

"Beatrice, you do not—"

Beatrice shook her head and held up a hand to stop her friend. "She thinks I am incapable of finding a husband. She complains that I am too quiet, and when I tried to be more gregarious she said I was bellowing like a goose."

"Oh goodness," Henrietta said covering her mouth with her hand and the nervous giggle that she could not stop. "Oh, Beatrice, I am so sorry."

"It is so ridiculous as to be amusing." Beatrice let out a chuckle of her own, then she felt her smile falter. "Except she is extremely upset all of the time. I spend much of my time trying to avoid her."

"I am so sorry. Do not blame yourself. My father can be completely awful with my brothers. He interferes in nearly every aspect of their lives and can be very critical. I truly believe he is trying to help them but he can be quite horrible. And of course, they hate the intrusion."

"I am rather sorry for your brothers then. This Season has been miserable save for the week I spent with you at Castborough."

"Not entirely miserable," Henrietta teased her. "It seems Mr

Townsend is still pursuing his suit. Surely your mother is happy about that."

"Unfortunately, she is more happy about Mr Townsend's interest, than I."

"Unfortunately?" Henrietta asked her quickly.

Beatrice looked around the garden to make sure that their conversation was still going unnoticed. Lord and Lady Alderside were still speaking with Lord and Lady Castborough while Beatrice's mother looked on. Only Mr Townsend glanced over at them.

"Mr Townsend appears nice in most conversations but as I continue to speak to him I find that he is fairly presumptuous. He has no qualms about making decisions when we are together regardless of my feelings on any manner."

Henrietta frowned. "I feel as though I have missed something. Are you and he officially courting?"

"No, we are not. He sent an invitation to take a ride in the park last week, which my mother accepted without my knowledge. I only found out once we were at the park."

"She accepted? Without speaking to you?"

"It was horrible." Beatrice quickly told her what had happened.

"He was dragging you back to his carriage?" Henrietta asked, her eyes wide with worry. "What did you do?"

"Someone came upon us and Mr Townsend released me. I went straight home." Beatrice was not sure why she did not mention that it was Henrietta's own brother that had come to her rescue. She had been so scared, then so happy and relieved when Lieutenant Repington had arrived. Her feelings were all mixed up and she was not ready to share them.

"Thank goodness," Henrietta said with relief. "Is that why you were not at Almack's this week?"

Beatrice nodded. "I have tried to avoid seeing Mr Townsend. Of course, my mother has other ideas."

"Your mother is still encouraging a match with Mr Townsend?" Henrietta glanced across the garden at Beatrice's mother.

"She says that I must be wrong. That I had gotten upset over nothing."

"You must have told her what happened. She must have wondered when you came home alone."

Beatrice let out a long sigh. "She was furious that I acted so rashly. It was unladylike of me to have left Mr Townsend in the park." Beatrice noticed more people were moving about the garden and she rushed to finish before they were interrupted. "She forced me to come today since Mr Townsend had procured me an invitation."

Henrietta looked horrified for a moment and then reached over to pat Beatrice's hand. "Do not worry. I will make sure that you are never alone with that horrid Mr Townsend."

"Thank you, Henrietta." Beatrice blew out a sigh, "I suppose we should appear to be more social. I do not want you to suffer consequences because of my plight."

Beatrice stood up and straightened her skirts. When she looked up she saw that Lieutenant Repington had arrived. As soon as she laid eyes on him she felt her heart warmed and she turned away before everyone saw her smile. Her reaction was a surprise to her as well, although she had been thinking about him ever since they had danced at Almack's the previous week. His appearance in the park had just furthered her feelings for him. His embrace being foremost in her thoughts, a memory she would not soon forget.

Henrietta turned to her and excited smile upon her face. "Charles is here. Come with me to talk to him."

"Of course," Beatrice answered, happy to go along but hoping she did not look too eager.

Her worry was for naught as Henrietta rushed across the garden to greet her brother boisterously. "Charles! I did not know you would be here today."

"Hello, Henrietta!" Lieutenant Repington grinned down at his sister.

Beatrice's heart fluttered, she told herself that it was natural to react to him. He was a very handsome man. He wore a navy coat that fit his broad shoulders impeccably and she was sure matched the blue of his eyes. It was simply a reaction to seeing any handsome man. A little voice inside her head laughed but she ignored it.

"I expected to see you at the house but Fletcher said you were staying at the Wainwright house."

"And Fletcher was right. Patrick Wainwright was on the Peninsula at the same time I was. He just got back and going mad alone in the large house by himself. He asked if I wanted to stay with him since he knew you would be coming up from Castborough." Lieutenant Repington explained." At least until he leaves London."

"Where's he going?" Henrietta asked looking over at a nice-looking gentleman standing near the trellis where they had been sitting. "Not back to the Peninsula?"

Lieutenant Repington seemed surprised by her question but easily said, "No, to India."

"India? But it is so hot there." Henrietta turned to Beatrice. "Can you imagine?"

Beatrice thought for a moment. "I do not know. It sounds rather fascinating to me." Lieutenant Repington smiled at her and then looked away quickly as though he wished he had not.

Beatrice his cheeks burned at his reaction. She looked down as though to fix her gloves. Suddenly, she was embarrassed about her emotional behaviour in the park. Mr Townsend's actions had upset her so much that she had forgotten herself. Lieutenant Repington had been so gracious, she hoped that he would forgive her melodrama. To make matters worse, Lady Judith had arrived and came straight to their group.

"Good afternoon, Lieutenant Repington," Lady Judith said looking up at him through her lashes.

"Good afternoon, Lady Judith."

"Good afternoon, Miss Beatrice," Mr Townsend said from just behind her.

Henrietta turned around before Beatrice could and said brightly, "Hello, Mr Townsend, I have not seen you since the party given by Lord and Lady Colchester. Are you enjoying this Season?"

Mr Townsend blinked seemingly confused by her many questions. "Yes, I have very much. Thank you. How have you enjoyed the Season?"

He looked back at Beatrice as he spoke, but Henrietta went on as though she had not noticed. "It has been very good. Thank you. It is so wonderful to be back in London."

"Miss Beatrice," Matthew Repington had moved to stand next to her. "I believe everyone is moving into the drawing room to begin the recital."

"Thank you, Matthew."

He held out his arm. "May I show you in?"

"Yes, that would be lovely," Beatrice answered with a smile and took his arm.

"Oh look," Beatrice heard Henrietta say as she and Matthew moved towards the house. "Everyone is going into the drawing room."

The last thing that Beatrice saw as she and Matthew left the garden was Henrietta looping her arm through Mr Townsend's. "Lead the way, Mr Townsend."

CHAPTER SIXTEEN

Charles stood in the garden watching first Matthew lead Miss Beatrice into the drawing room followed by Mr Townsend and his sister. He was glad that Miss Beatrice had been spared Townsend's attention although Charles was not so sure he liked his sister dealing with the man.

"You orchestrated that nicely," Wainwright said from where he was standing off to the side.

Charles shrugged. "I was able to tell Matthew to keep Townsend away from Miss Beatrice."

"He was quick to follow your instructions," Wainwright noted watching the others walk into the house.

"He accepted that it was for a good reason and did what I asked. I will tell him about the incident in the Park later." Charles had been relieved that Matthew had not asked questions but simply nodded and moved away to keep an eye on Townsend.

Wainwright nodded. "I still cannot believe that Miss Beatrice's mother is not more concerned about Townsend."

"It baffles me as well," Charles said shaking his head. "As I told you the other day. I waited by the carriage when Miss Beatrice entered the house. Her mother was furious, I could hear her all the way out on the street. She thought that Beatrice should not have come home on her own. Even after Miss Beatrice explained that Mr Townsend had upset her and mistreated her."

Wainwright shook his head. "It should not be a surprise. As I told you, Lady Taltham has long treated Miss Beatrice poorly."

Charles stared at the ground for a moment as anger flared through him. It was unfathomable to him that a mother could be so dreadful to her daughter. His own father could be hard on him, demanding respect and responsibility. They all knew, though, that their father would always aid them and certainly protect them if needed. His father's good intentions were never in question.

He tried to imagine Henrietta having to deal with someone like Townsend, knowing that would not end well for such a terrible man. Then forced himself to stop. If you he kept thinking about it, he would have to go into the drawing room and drawn Townsend's cork.

"You coming?" Wainwright asked from the door.

Charles blew out a breath. "Yes, I cannot wait."

Wainwright chuckled and followed him into the house. "Do not fret. I am sure my cousin will keep you quite entertained."

"Yes, I am sure Lady Sarah will do her best. Although I do not know if entertained is the best way to describe what will happen next."

"No, probably not," Wainwright admitted quietly as they entered the room. Before Charles even realized anyone had approached him, he heard Wainwright offer with a slight bow, "Lady Judith, allow me to show you to your seat."

Charles sent his friend a silent thank you before finding his own seat. He was so very glad in that moment that Henrietta and Miss Beatrice were friends. It made sense that he would sit with his family, which meant he could be near Miss Beatrice.

When she and Henrietta had come over after he had arrived in the garden he had wanted to say hello and ask Miss Beatrice how she was feeling but Townsend was standing not far away scowling at anyone that spoke to the young woman. Charles decided that provoking Townsend would not help Miss Beatrice, so he had been reserved in his greeting to her.

Charles took a seat with his family and he was pleased that he had a good vantage point to see Miss Beatrice quite clearly as she carried on a quiet but lively conversation with his sister. When he had walked out into the garden he had noticed Miss Beatrice right away. She was wearing a yellow dress that seemed to match her usual sunny disposition.

Which only served to remind him of how upset and shaken she had been when he had intervened at Hyde Park. It had truly been fortuitous that he was even in the park that day, as he had never even looked at the park since his return to London. He had been agitated and restless alone in the house and Fletcher had suggested that he take a walk, even reminding him that Hyde Park was not too far away.

After taking Miss Beatrice back to her home where she insisted on entering alone, Charles had immediately gone to Wainwright's to tell him what had happened. The other man had shared Charles' worries and they had stayed up rather late discussing what could be done. Wainwright had suggested Charles stay in one of the many rooms at Wainwright House instead of taking the carriage back in the early hours of the morning. He had not liked the silence any more than Charles and after some discussion decided that he would stay until Wainwright left London for his post in India. It had been an easy decision for Charles, as much as he hated the silence in their large London residence trading it for the noise and well-meaning intrusion of his family was not something he wanted to do.

Lady Sarah walked up to the pianoforte signaling the beginning of the recital. Her sister, Helena, stood next to the pianoforte looking fairly nervous. Charles sat up attentively trying his best not to react when Lady Sarah hit the wrong piano key or Helena's voice missed a high note. He looked over at Miss Beatrice at one point, she cringed turning her head toward him. She caught him looking and smiled sheepishly. He smiled back and then grimaced comically as Helena's singing turned into a drawn-out screech.

Miss Beatrice's eyes widened and he saw the smile on her face briefly before she covered her mouth with a gloved hand. Her shoulders shook briefly and he realized he had made her laugh. He immediately wanted to do something else to make her laugh again.

After the recital, Lord and Lady Alderside invited everyone to enjoy refreshments served in the dining room. Miss Beatrice held back, presumably trying to avoid Townsend who Henrietta and Matthew managed to herd out of the drawing room.

He waited for her at the door. "Miss Beatrice, I hope you are faring well after that fine musical performance."

She nodded, a serious look on her face. "Of course. It was quite lovely."

"Lovely," he repeated slowly, nodding. "You, Miss Beatrice, are far more gracious than I."

"You can learn to be just as gracious, with a little practice," she said serenely.

His eyebrows furrowed in concentration. "Are you suggesting that I attend a multitude of recitals in order to learn to be more gracious? Your estimation of my abilities may be somewhat exaggerated."

She laughed. "Clearly, you need to work harder."

"Perhaps you could teach me," he said plaintively.

"Oh," she replied seemingly surprised. Then she pursed her lips. "Perhaps."

"If you are up for returning to the park, I shall be there Tuesday afternoon."

"I think a walk in the park would be lovely," she said quietly.

"I look forward to it," he said taking her gloved hand in his before bowing to drop a light kiss on the back of her hand.

CHAPTER SEVENTEEN

"I am glad you are feeling better." Beatrice's mother sat down in the chair next to the settee.

"Thank you, Mother," Beatrice replied focusing on her own needlework and never looking up at her mother.

In the days since the recital, Beatrice had spent most of the day in her room reading. She had been happy to avoid her mother's complaints and as she had no other social events there had been no way to meet with Mr Townsend either.

"I was worried I would need to call the physician."

"I do apologize for worrying you. Although I did tell you that I felt better after the recital."

Beatrice knew better than to believe that her mother's worry had anything to do with her. She was quite sure that her mother was far more concerned about the hunt for a husband than any real concern over Beatrice's health.

"I had hoped that you would have been able to talk to Mr Townsend at Lady Sarah's recital, but it seemed that every time he tried to talk to you there was some sort of interruption."

"Oh?" Beatrice pulled the needle through the fabric before finally looking up at her mother. "There were so many people there

I had not noticed. It was a very nice to see Lord and Lady Castborough again. Was it not?"

"Yes, of course, it was," her mother replied.

Beatrice counted on that to keep her mother from further complaining about Beatrice not talking to Mr Townsend. It had been Henrietta that had caused most of the interruption that her mother had mentioned.

"Now that you are feeling better you will be able to attend the upcoming parties."

"Yes, Mother."

"I think you should attend Almack's tomorrow night. Although that would involve paying a visit in order to get the vouchers."

Beatrice put down her embroidery. "No, Mother. I would rather not."

"Beatrice, you must go. You will never find a husband staying here all day, every day."

"Yes, Mother," Beatrice said stifling a groan. "I was not saying that I wanted to stay home. It is just that I would rather miss Almack's and go to Lady Westerton's ball at the end of the week."

"Oh!" Her mother exclaimed in surprise. "Lady Westerton's ball?"

"Yes, I received the invitation this morning," Beatrice nodded to the small table near the door. She was sure that her friendship with Henrietta had precipitated the invitation but she did not care. Lady Westerton's ball was one of the greatest events of the Season.

"Yes, you may stay home from Almack's. Lady Westerton's ball will be a great opportunity for you and Mr Townsend to talk. I expect you will be very happy."

"Mother, I do not want to speak with Mr Townsend."

"Now, Beatrice," her mother started.

"There is something not right with him, Mother. He scares me."

"I do not want to hear another word about that," her mother commanded in a shrill voice. "Mr Townsend is a great match for you and you will talk to him at Lady Westerton's party."

"Yes, Mother," Beatrice gave her standard reply. Her mother was not listening to her anyway.

"Lady Alderside told me at the recital that Mr Townsend's brother still has not improved." Her mother looked across the room they breathe this hint of a smile crossed her face. "There is no telling if he will recover."

Her mother was as bad as Mr Townsend, wishing for the air of Marlsfeld to die. It was so horrible.

The door to the drawing room opened. "Lady Henrietta is here to see Miss Beatrice."

"Thank you, Porter," Beatrice got up from the settee and put her embroidery in a basket.

Henrietta walked in a moment later. "Good afternoon, Lady Taltham."

"Good afternoon, Lady Henrietta."

"Beatrice, my carriage is waiting to take us to Hyde Park."

"The park?" Beatrice feigned surprise.

"Yes, you need to get some fresh air," Henrietta told her. Then turned to Beatrice's mother. "She has been inside all week. It will be good for her to get some exercise. Do you not agree?"

Beatrice tried not to laugh. Her mother clearly did not want her to go to the park but she did not want to contradict Lady Henrietta either.

"It will be good for you to be seen, too," Henrietta added. "You know everyone will be there this afternoon, especially the night before Almack's."

"Well, yes. Of course," Lady Taltham said slowly. "You ladies have a good time."

"Thank you, Lady Taltham," Henrietta said dutifully and then sent a bright smile to be Beatrice.

"Thank you, Mother," Beatrice said and they left the drawing room.

The carriage ride to the park was short. They had barely left the house when the carriage began to slow down.

"I hope you do not mind but I asked the driver to drop us off at Cumberland Gate."

"No, I would rather walk." Beatrice had so much nervous energy she could have walked to Surrey and back.

As soon as they entered the park, Beatrice could not help looking around hoping to spot Charles. She worried that his plans may have changed.

"Beatrice, are you sure you are well?"

"Yes, why do you ask?"

"You seem very nervous," Henrietta stopped, looking back to Cumberland Gate. "Are you worried Mr Townsend will be here? Should we go back to the carriage?"

"Oh, no." Beatrice suddenly felt guilty for not letting her friend in on her secret—her true reason for coming to the park. "I am not worried about Mr Townsend."

She started walking once more and Henrietta asked, "Then what is bothering you?"

"Henrietta, I should have told you this before, but I can hardly believe it myself." Beatrice took a deep breath and looked at her friend.

"Please tell me. I cannot stand another minute not knowing." Henrietta reached out for Beatrice's hand.

"It was Charles that saved me from Mr Townsend last week." Henrietta's mouth opened but Beatrice went on wanting to tell her everything as soon as she could. "I did not say anything before because I feel like a silly schoolgirl. I kept telling myself that it was just hero worship because he helped me."

"He saved you," Henrietta corrected her. "Yes, I believe that, too."

Beatrice shrugged. "I hope this is not awkward, but I fear that I have feelings for your brother."

Henrietta stopped and turned to face her friend. "Awkward? No! This is wonderful!"

"Are you sure?" Beatrice asked her not quite believing her.

"Of course. You are my closest friend." Henrietta clapped her hands in glee. "If you marry Charles you would be my sister! How exciting!"

"I agree, that would be wonderful," Beatrice said quietly and swallowed. "But I cannot even think of that, I have only just realized how I feel. I do not know how your brother feels. He probably does not think of me in that way at all."

"Do not worry about that," Henrietta said with a wave her hand. "I will do whatever I can to help."

"Thank you, Henrietta. I am so glad that I confided in you."

"As am I," Henrietta agreed, her face so serious that Beatrice knew she was thinking. "Now we just have to see about when you can see him again."

"Well, actually that is why I wanted to come to the park today."

"Because of Charles?"

"Yes," Beatrice nodded feeling fairly silly once more. "At Sarah's recital, your brother said that he would be at the park today and that he hoped to see me if I was comfortable returning to the park so soon."

"Charles is here?" Henrietta did not wait for Beatrice's answer and was already looking about the park.

"I am not sure, but possibly."

"We will keep walking towards the ring. It is the most likely place for him to go, especially if he is looking for you."

"I do not know if I would say that he is looking for me."

"Hush," Henrietta told her. "Charles is the one that suggested it, yes?"

"Yes, he said he would like to see me again."

Henrietta started walking faster. "And you have nothing to worry over."

Beatrice looked down the path and realized that Henrietta had already seen her brother and Captain Wainwright walking down another path that would soon cross their own. Beatrice could suddenly feel her heart beat more rapidly, she was happy to see him but also extremely nervous.

"Charles is my brother and I could just call to him, but I would rather make it seem as though we just happened upon them."

"I like that idea, too," Beatrice told her sounding odd even to herself.

"You do not need to be nervous," Henrietta smiled at her. "Charles is very sweet, except when he is being a bossy older brother."

Beatrice laughed. "Thank you, I feel so much better now."

They were nearing the other path when Henrietta gave a conspiratorial smile.

"He will surely be glad to see you at Lady Westerton's ball. Was it not your lavender dress that he commented on?"

At first, Beatrice did not know what Henrietta was saying but she was talking louder the necessary and it occurred to Beatrice that it was meant for Lieutenant Repington and Captain Wainwright to hear.

"Yes, it was my lavender dress. I do not think I shall wear it to Lady Westerton's ball though."

"No? But he liked it so," Henrietta said.

"I shall wear my white, or perhaps something new. I have not decided."

They turned down the other path heading away from Lieutenant Repington and Captain Wainwright.

"Henrietta?" Henrietta turned around wide-eyed with surprise. "Charles? What are you doing here?"

He looked over at Beatrice and smiled. "It is just too lovely to stay at home."

CHAPTER EIGHTEEN

"It is a lovely day, Lieutenant Repington," Beatrice agreed with a shy smile.

"Good afternoon, Miss Beatrice. It is so very nice to see you," Charles said cringing at how banal he must sound. Against his better judgement, he added more dullness. "It is a lovely day, indeed."

"Good afternoon, Lieutenant Repington," she replied. Then smiled at Wainwright. "Good afternoon, Captain Wainwright."

Wainwright, the rake, actually bowed. "Good afternoon, Miss Beatrice and to you as well, Lady Henrietta."

Henrietta stepped toward him. "Major Wainwright, am so glad that you are here."

"You are?" Wainwright sounded suspicious rather than surprised.

"Why, yes, I am." She fell into step next to him on the path. "I want to hear all about Charles and the mischief he got into. I am more than sure you were at his side the entire time."

"Mischief, eh?" Wainwright asked with a raised eyebrow. "I suppose there are a few tales to tell."

"Oi!" Charles protested but it lost its power when he laughed. It did not really matter as they had already continued walking along the path. Although Henrietta could be heard saying, "All right then. Do tell me about India."

"I suppose we should follow them," Beatrice suggested.

"I suppose so. Seems as though they will leave us behind otherwise."

They started down the path slowly.

Charles felt so happy that Beatrice had shown up. She had seemed agreeable about visiting the park when they spoke at the recital, but he had worried in the days since that she had changed her mind. He also worried that perhaps her mother had intervened. He had all but convinced himself that there was no need to come to the park. If not for Wainwright, Charles may have spent the day in the stuffy library.

"I am glad to see that you survived Lady Sarah's recital unscathed," Charles joked.

Miss Beatrice laughed jovially, making his heart warm.

"Yes, well, I did have a little bit of a headache the next day," she quipped. "Honestly, it was not that bad."

"Not that bad?" He asked incredulously, remembering Helena's awful singing.

"I am being quite truthful." She nodded sagely before adding, "I have attended far worse recitals."

"Is that possible?"

"It is," she assured him. "I will not reveal the names of the performers, but the hunting dogs started to howl every time one singer opened her mouth."

"You are making that up," he said to her with a laugh.

"I am not," she said primly.

"I'll not believe you," he replied.

"Whether you believe it will not make it any less true," then she laughed. "You can ask anyone at Almack's and they will tell you that I am being more than truthful."

"Speaking of Almack's," he said suddenly. He wanted to know

when he could see her again. "Will you be attending tomorrow night?"

"No," she told him quietly.

Charles immediately regretted his words. Wainwright had mentioned that it may be difficult for her to obtain the much sought after vouchers. Charles had not wanted to embarrass her. He sought for something to say that might lessen the impact of his words.

"My mother wanted me to go but I told her I would rather not."

"I see."

"She had wanted me to be ladylike and social toward Mr Townsend." Miss Beatrice let out a sigh. "Staying home seemed much easier."

Charles gritted his teeth and clenched his fists. He could not believe Lady Taltham was still encouraging a courtship between Miss Beatrice and the horrible Townsend.

"Yes," he said calmly. "Almack's has been quite the crush. I do not blame you for not wanting to attend. I, myself, have only gone twice since I returned to London."

He had gone the previous week hoping to see Beatrice but had heard that she was suffering from a headache and left soon after he had found she would not be there.

"And other than the spectacle that is Almack's and attending shrill recitals, how have you enjoyed your return to London?"

"It has been fine. Thank you."

"I heard you tell Henrietta that you are staying with Captain Wainwright. Has that made your time in London easier?"

Charles appreciated that she cared to ask. "I suppose it could have."

"I would imagine it would be easier spending time with someone who understands your experience on the Peninsula."

Charles was once again surprised by her insight and compassion. She was quite right. Staying with Wainwright had made it somewhat easier. If he was up in the middle of the night, he did not have to explain himself as he had found necessary when he stayed at Castborough.

"Miss Beatrice, you are a wonder. Were you aware of that fact?"

"Certainly not I." She blushed heavily and looked away.

"Yes, you," he assured her. "How is it that you are the only person to realize that coming home might not be as easy as simply coming back to my home."

Miss Beatrice shrugged. "I do not know. It may be the stories my grandfather told me as a child. He had been in the British Navy and always said that he felt extreme guilt for not simply being happy when he got home. It was difficult he said, being in charge of so many men and then coming home to a nice quiet house."

"Well, I, for one am glad that you took the time to listen to your grandfather."

Miss Beatrice nodded a sweet smile on her face. "Me, too."

"I thought I heard Henrietta make mention of the Westerton's ball. Will you be attending?"

"Yes. Being friends with your sister has been most helpful."

Charles wanted to protest but he knew she would not believe him. So he joked, "I hope it is more than just invitations that you find as a benefit for being friends with my sister."

Beatrice flushed and turn to him quickly. "Yes, of course! Henrietta is my closest friend and I do not know what I would do without her. Please forgive me as I misspoke."

Charles groaned inwardly. He had been speaking about himself when he made the comment and had not meant to insult her or upset her.

"Miss Beatrice, I was being facetious," he said calmly. "I had only meant to imply that had you not been friends with Henrietta that you and I might not have ever met." He watched her closely waiting for her reaction.

"As I said Henrietta and her friendship means a great deal to me and I am very thankful for everything that she has done for me," she said with a slight smile playing at her lips before turning back towards the path.

It was not a declaration of her undying love, but Charles was happy to take it.

Their wanderings brought them to the end of the footpath and they found Wainwright and Henrietta waiting for them.

"Well, dear sister, did Captain Wainwright tell you all of my secrets?"

"Not all of your secrets, dear brother, " Henrietta mocked him playfully.

Wainwright shook his head. "I have told her next to nothing. She has been mostly asking about my position in India."

"I think it is quite interesting, but I just cannot imagine having to live there."

Wainwright had a very serious look on his face. "She seems quite concerned about the weather and my wardrobe."

"Well it is very hot there and I just wonder how do you dress for that," Henrietta blustered.

Charles tipped his head back and laughed. "Henrietta, only you would be concerned about what to wear in exotic place such as India."

"You tease her but she has a point, " Miss Beatrice interjected. "I think her questions are valid. How would you prepare for a trip to India if you had no idea with the proper attire would be?"

Wainwright nodded his approval and turned to Henrietta. "She is quite right. My apologies, Lady Henrietta. Are you planning a trip to India?"

Henrietta flushed surprising Charles. "No," she said hesitantly. "And as I said I find the whole idea fascinating and just wanted to know more about it. I do fear that it is much too far away."

Charles had never seen his sister flustered and he was quite enjoying it.

"And you, Miss Beatrice, " Wainwright asked. "What are your thoughts on the matter?"

"I rather like the idea. As much as I enjoy London and living in England, the thought of leaving it all behind sounds most wonderful to me."

"It does?" Henrietta asked. "Wouldn't you miss everything? The conveniences?"

"No, I do not think I would," Miss Beatrice said almost immediately. "I would miss you, of course."

Charles watched his sister react to her friend's words and the understanding dawn on her face. He thought about her words himself and made a promise to himself that he would do what he could to make Miss Beatrice's life different, better.

"Well, while you two were discussing the mysteries of India, Miss Beatrice and I were discussing Lady Westerton's ball."

At the mention the elaborate event Henrietta began to speak rapidly which gave Charles a chance to think about what he wanted to do. He knew that he needed to make some decisions and he had the distinct feeling that he was running out of time.

CHAPTER NINETEEN

"Are you enjoying yourself?" Charles asked. Miss Beatrice looked beautiful in a light blue dress with white ribbons on the sleeves and neckline. He did not normally notice details like that but when it came to Beatrice he could not help but notice.

"Yes, thank you," Beatrice told him her cheeks flushed from the most recent dance in the ballroom. She opened her fan and waved it in front of her face. "I have never danced so much."

Charles had danced with her nearly every dance although both Wainwright, Matthew and another of Charles' brother, Hugh, had danced with Beatrice as well.

"Would you like to get some fresh air?"

"Oh, yes. That would be lovely," Beatrice agreed happily. "It has become a bit stuffy in here."

Charles offered her his arm. "We can go out onto the terrace that overlooks the garden."

Charles led Beatrice from the ballroom and out to the broad terrace where a number of people were looking at the garden.

Beatrice gasped. "How beautiful."

Charles watched as Beatrice looked around at the large terrace.

An ornate stone banister ran along the edge of the terrace. A wide staircase led down to a lush jungle of plants and trees that filled the garden.

"This is the most magnificent garden I have ever seen." Beatrice leaned over the wide railing peering into the darkness at the plants below.

"They are all tropical varieties brought back by Lord Westerton after his travels to Africa and India."

"And they grow here in London?" She asked, her eyes still on the plants.

Charles was so glad that he had suggested they get some air. He had forgotten about Lord Westerton's tropical garden. "In the summer, yes, with great care, I am sure."

"And in the winter?" She looked back at him. "I would think it would be much too cold in London."

"I do not know for sure but I believe they are moved into a greenhouse to protect them from the cold in winter."

She shook her head in wonder. "It is a truly amazing sight to see."

Charles marveled at her joy and enthusiasm. Looking at her when he said, "Yes. Yes, it is."

Beatrice looked away shyly, taking a step back toward the house.

Not wanting their quiet moment to end he asked, "Would you like to look at the plants closer?"

She took several steps toward the stairs and then halted. "Should we? I mean, would be proper?"

"I believe so. There are a great number of people walking the grounds. There will be little chance that we would be caught alone," Charles explained trying to assure her. As though to prove his point, several people walked past them to go down the stairs and into the garden.

She seemed to debate silently over what to do. "I would rather enjoy looking at the garden. Do you mind very much?"

"Not at all. I find the garden quite interesting."

They walked into the garden following the same path the others had taken. Stopping here and there to study and comment on the large broadleaf plants that seemed so foreign to them.

"Oh look!" Beatrice exclaimed pointing to a small pond ringed with stonework similar to that on the terrace. There were large flowers with white and pink petals floating on the water's surface.

"What beautiful flowers," she said walking around the pond. "I wonder what they are."

"I believe they are lotus flowers from India where they grow in large masses."

She stared at the flower for a moment, reaching out to touch one only to have it float away, the moonlight reflecting on the rippling water.

"What it must be like to go to a place like India and see flowers like this. It must be stunning."

"You are stunning," he told her suddenly.

"Lieutenant Repington..."

"Charles," he corrected. "Please call me Charles."

"No, it would be improper to call you by your Christian name."

"I do not care about improprieties. It is just a name, my name. I want to hear my name spoken in your voice."

She seemed to struggle for a few moments before saying, "You are absolutely right… Charles."

He had to stop himself from asking her to say it again. Instead, he said, "I am so glad that you liked the garden."

"I am so happy you brought me to see it. Thank you for that."

Charles wanted to tell her how he felt but he worried about scaring her. "I very much like spending time with you."

Beatrice stared into the water. "I have enjoyed our time together, as well."

"I would like to court you. If you are agreeable." He held his breath waiting for her response.

She nodded slowly as if she had not quite heard him. "I am most agreeable."

"Yes?"

She turned to him. "Yes. Although I do not know what my mother will say."

He stepped closer to her. "Hopefully she will be happy for you. For us. I know that I am happier than I have ever been since I have been spending time with you."

"I share in that." She said looking up at him. "What if she is not agreeable?"

"Do not worry, my sweet Beatrice," he said looking down into her beautiful face. He was in love with her, he could admit it now. Nothing would keep them apart. "I will not let anyone come between us."

"Oh, Charles, I so want to believe you."

She was so close that he could control himself no longer. He leaned down toward her pausing briefly expecting her to stop him, but she did not. He continued with his intent and pressed his lips to hers. Her lips were soft and inviting, and he forced himself to pull back. She sighed into his mouth and he kissed her again, a long lingering kiss that left him breathless.

Voices in the garden caused him to remember where they were and he stepped away from her.

"Propriety says I should apologize," he told her.

"But you do not care much about impropriety," she said repeating his words with a smile.

"Exactly," he said and then waved a hand toward the path that led back to the terrace. "We should go back before the gossips wonder where we have gone."

"Yes, I suppose we should."

They had only just walked back into the ballroom when Charles was almost immediately beset by Lord Castborough.

"Good evening, Father."

"Good evening, Miss Beatrice," his father said cordially. "Charles, I would like to speak to you for a moment."

"Of course, Father," Charles answered. He nodded at Beatrice to let her know he would be back momentarily.

His father left the ballroom and Charles followed him into the Westerton's library.

Charles waited for his father to speak. His father paced behind the desk for a moment and then finally said, "I was wondering about your courtship with Lady Judith."

"There is no courtship with Lady Judith," Charles told him trying to hold his temper. "Nothing has changed since the last time that you spoke to me about it."

His father nodded with a grumble. "I am sorry that I discouraged the match, I should not have interfered the last time."

"It is fine. I have no interest in courting Lady Judith." Charles hoped that this would be the end of it.

"No?" His father asked was a raised eyebrow.

"No, I do not." Charles had no idea why his father did not believe him.

"Lady Judith would be a very favorable match, perhaps you should reconsider."

"There is nothing to reconsider, Father. I have no interest in courting Lady Judith."

His father began pacing again. "I have just been talking to Lord Colchester and we believe..."

Charles interrupted his father. "It is of no matter what you and Lord Colchester have discussed. I still have no interest in courting Lady Judith."

"Charles, now that you are back from your adventures on the Peninsula. I think it is time for you to think about your future. You must be responsible, I will not let you gad about like a dandy. I already made that mistake with Philip, I will not let it happen again."

Charles wanted to lash out at his father, but he held his tongue. "I have already begun making plans for my future."

"Have you?" His father asked his skepticism clear on his face.

"Yes, and you are right."

"Good, good." His father's face was smug. "So then, you will consider a courtship with Lady Judith."

Charles was already moving toward the door. "No, I will not. You need not have interfered as I have the matter in hand."

Furious, Charles left the library and went in search of Major Stewart.

CHAPTER TWENTY

After Charles had left the brief meeting with his father, Beatrice stood in the corner of the ballroom not sure what she should do. She still felt a bit warm, but she was sure it had more to do with Charles' kiss rather than overexertion from dancing. Her cheeks burned thinking about it. It had been wrong of her to not push him away, but she had felt cared for and safe. It had been exciting and comforting at the same time.

Looking around the ballroom she saw that Henrietta was dancing with Captain Wainwright. Mr Townsend was thankfully across the room and she decided to go get a drink of punch from the refreshment room before he saw that she had returned to the ballroom. Beatrice smiled at Lady Agatha and Lady Matilda on her way out of the ballroom.

She had just picked up her glass of punch when Lady Judith and Lady Sarah walked into the room. Lady Judith immediately locked eyes on Beatrice and walked over to her.

"I saw you dancing with Henrietta's brother," Lady Judith said to her.

"Matthew?" Beatrice asked knowing that Lady Judith was actually talking about Charles but not wanting to talk to her about it.

"No," she said with the sniff. "I am talking about Lieutenant Repington. I am quite certain you are aware of the brother I meant."

"Oh?" Beatrice nodded. "Yes, I have danced with the Lieutenant."

"I just wanted you to know that he is just biding his time."

"All right," Beatrice said calmly taking a sip of her punch. "If you say so, it must be true."

"Until he marries me that is. He is merely having some fun while he can. Because very soon he will be announcing our courtship and I am sure that our engagement is not far behind."

Beatrice knew that Lady Judith was lying, that she was only trying to upset her. Still, though, Beatrice could not help but wonder about Charles' interest in her. She refused to let Lady Judith see her upset and so she said, "Lieutenant Repington can do whatever he likes. It is of no matter to me."

Lady Judith looked taken by surprise. It was as if she expected an argument or at least some sort of disappointed reaction.

Beatrice walked to the door but stopped and turned. "Congratulations to you both. I wish you the best."

"Thank you, Miss Beatrice," Lady Judith said magnanimously.

Beatrice left the room and went out to the hall thoroughly annoyed and upset. not only about Lady Judith's words but that she let the spoiled girl upset her. When she looked up Beatrice realized that she had gone the wrong way and found herself in the conservatory. It was quite beautiful, paned windows covered one entire wall. An exquisitely ornate pianoforte stood in the middle of the room. Distracted, Beatrice walked into the room walking towards the paned windows.

"There you are," a man's voice said from the door.

Beatrice felt a twinge of dread go up her spine. She looked up to see Mr Townsend standing in the doorway. "Mr Townsend, I just stepped in to look at the room. I should be getting back now."

"Please do not leave on my account," he said to her.

"Oh of course not," Beatrice laughed nervously and tried to move past him. "I do not want to Henrietta to worry."

"Henrietta will not have even known that you are gone. She is dancing with that Wainwright fellow." He moved to the side blocking her even further.

Beatrice backed away and tried to stay calm. "Still I should get back it would be unseemly if we were to be caught here alone even though we are doing nothing untoward."

"Aren't we though?" He gave her a sly smile and again she felt the dismay overtake her otherwise good mood.

Beatrice took another step back. "Well, I am certainly not doing anything untoward. I would like to go back now. Please move."

"No." Mr Townsend folded his arms are crossed his chest. "I have told you before that you must learn how to behave and I am afraid this may be the only way to teach you that lesson."

"I do not understand what you were talking about, nor do I care." Beatrice did not trust Mr Townsend at all and the thought of being trapped in the conservatory with him only caused her to panic more. Acting much braver than she felt, Beatrice, squared her shoulders and moved toward the door. "I am going back to the ballroom. So move out of my way now."

Mr Townsend reached out to grab her but she was ready for him and she ducked out of the way. She moved around the pianoforte and as she expected, he pursued her.

"You stupid chit," he spat at her. His hands were on the pianoforte. "I would think you would be happy to receive my attentions. You could be the Countess of Marlsfeld."

"I would not. You are speaking in untruths," she said trying to distract him. "You are not the heir."

He let out an exasperated cry. "I will be once that useless fop dies. It has already taken him too long to die. Even after I replaced his medicine with water and syrup, he is slipping away much too slowly."

Beatrice stifled the gasp that had come in response to his evil admission. It had seemed as though he did not realize what he had said and she did not want to give him another reason to detain her.

"I do not want to be a countess."

He began to move around the pianoforte after her but moving away from the door. It was still a fair distance and she knew that he would catch her before she could get out the door.

"I do not care. Once Lady Judith discovers us in a heated embrace your reputation will be ruined and you will be forced to marry me." He slapped a hand onto the pianoforte. "This would have been done with over a week ago if Repington had not intervened in Hyde Park. Lady Judith was waiting with some others to catch us alone."

"You are horrible. I cannot believe you would do such a thing." She looked around frantically for anything she could grab to hit him with.

"Do not worry about Repington, I will take care of him, too," the man's face twisted in an ugly snarl. "I did not tell Lady Judith about that part."

Spurred into action by his statement, Beatrice suddenly grabbed the large silver candelabra that had been standing on the pianoforte and threw it at Mr Townsend. She did not wait to see if he had been injured but simply ran from the room as fast as she could.

CHAPTER TWENTY-ONE

Beatrice ran down the hallway not looking back when Mr Townsend called after her. Relieved to find Henrietta and Captain Wainwright in the hall outside of the ballroom.

"Beatrice! What has happened?" Henrietta asked.

"It is Mr Townsend," Beatrice said trying to catch her breath. "I just escaped him, he had me trapped in the conservatory."

Captain Wainwright quietly asked, "Are you harmed?"

Beatrice swallowed. "No. I was able to keep away from him. I threw a candelabra at him and managed to run away."

"Thank the Heavens, " Henrietta breathed.

"It was awful. He said that Lady Judith would find us in a heated embrace and I would have to marry him."

Major Wainwright swore under his breath. "That man this vile."

"He was telling me that could not believe that I did not want to be a countess."

Henrietta confused. "The countess? But he is not the heir."

"No, he is not," Captain Wainwright answered. "Although elder brother is very sick and may not survive."

"But it is Mr Townsend's fault." Beatrice was nearly in tears. "He has been tampering with his brother's treatment. He is trying to kill his brother by seeing to it that he does not get the medicine he needs. He is waiting for his brother to die."

Henrietta gasped. "No! Even he is not that reprehensible. A murderer?"

"Yes, it is true. He admitted it to me. He has been replacing the medicine with sugar and syrup."

Captain Wainwright turned around looking into the ballroom and motioned for someone to come out.

A moment later Matthew appeared. "Is something amiss?"

Major Wainwright and Matthew stepped away and spoke for several moments. Beatrice heard him say, "I need to go speak with Lord Marlsfeld immediately."

Matthew nodded and stepped back into the ballroom.

"How did you get separated from Charles?" Henrietta asked.

"Your father needed to speak with him and they left the ballroom. I went to the refreshment room for some punch and Lady Judith came in after me."

"Lady Judith, of course. What a horrible creature."

Beatrice sighed. "Yes, she is. She told me that Charles was only spending time with me so that he could have a last bit of fun before he married her."

Matthew snorted. "She is lying. Charles wants no more to do with her than he wants to go back to the Peninsula."

"I knew she was trying to upset me and the worst part is that it worked. I ended up going the wrong way when I left the refreshment room and that is how I ended up in the conservatory."

Before she could say anything else, Mr Townsend walked up to them. He smiled slightly at Beatrice and said, "Oh, this is where you have gotten to, my dear."

"Mr Townsend, we do not wish to speak to you," Henrietta told him, stepping between him and Beatrice.

He looked down at Henrietta his smile turned menacing. "Go away, Lady Henrietta, lest you cause a scene that Miss Beatrice would not appreciate."

"Oh?" Henrietta asked loudly. "And where have you and Lady Judith been? I have not seen either of you in quite a while."

"What?" he asked her surprised. Suddenly, people began to gather in the hallway.

"You and Miss Judith both went toward the refreshment room but neither of you was there a few minutes ago." Henrietta turned to a young lady. "Miss Thea, you were there. Did you see Lady Judith or Mr Townsend?"

Lady Thea shook her head, her eyes wide. "No, I was in there with two other girls and the only other person that we saw was you, Lady Henrietta."

"No, I... I," Mr Townsend stammered. "I have not seen Lady Judith all night."

Just then, Lady Judith came around the corner and stopped suddenly seeing the crowd gathered. Her eyes cut to Mr Townsend's, guilt playing across her face. A murmur went through the crowd.

Only snippets of conversation could be heard. *Lady Judith was alone with Mr Townsend... Her reputation... ruined... they will surely be wed soon...*

Lady Judith looked horrified for a moment and then her face was suddenly a mask of serenity. "Mr Townsend, there you are."

"Were you looking for Mr Townsend?" Matthew asked sounding quite helpful.

Mr Townsend shook his head trying to get her to be quiet.

Lady Judith beamed at Matthew, she seemed quite overjoyed that he was coming to her rescue and did not comprehend her mistake.

"Yes. Mr Townsend asked for my help." She turned her smile on Mr Townsend who looked positively sick. "I am sorry that I was not able to help you find Miss Beatrice."

"They lie," Lady Agatha said.

Lady Matilda replied, "It must be true."

Lady Judith's smile faded as she tried to figure out what had happened.

A woman pushed her way through the crowd. "Judith, what is going on here?"

"Mother! I..."

Lady Agatha spoke up. "Your daughter has been missing for some time as has Mr Townsend. They were both caught sneaking back into the ballroom when they were discovered."

"Discovered?" Lady Colchester asked looking between Lady Judith and the dowager. "What do you mean?"

"They have been caught lying." Lady Matilda threw up her hands. "Mr Townsend claims to have not seen Lady Judith all night and yet Lady Judith has just said that she had been helping Mr Townsend find Miss Beatrice."

All eyes turned to Beatrice and Lady Agatha asked, "Do you know anything about this?"

Beatrice looked straight at Mr Townsend and said, "No, I do not know what either of them is talking about."

Lady Agatha turned to Lady Colchester. "Perhaps you should take Lady Judith and Mr Townsend into the library to make arrangements."

"Arrangements?" Lady Colchester asked.

"Yes, for the Banns."

"The Banns..." And Lady Colchester fainted.

"Wait!" A woman's voice called out as Beatrice his mother pushed through the crowd. She pointed at Beatrice and said loudly, "No, it was Beatrice. She was with Mr Townsend."

CHAPTER TWENTY-TWO

The crowd gasped. Charles, who had been standing in the open door to the library, stepped out into the hallway.

He could see Beatrice, her mouth open but unable to speak. The hurt of her mother's raw betrayal unmistakable on her face.

His anger spiked again. His voice edged with steel he asked, "Lady Taltham, surely you are not trying to compromise your own daughter's reputation?"

Her mother began to sputter. "No, I... She and..."

"I cannot imagine a mother who would try to ruin her daughter's life."

"Why do you care?" Her mother seemed to have found her voice again.

He stopped in front of Lady Taltham. "Why do I care about what happens to Miss Beatrice?"

"Yes." She looked over at Beatrice. "She has been a thorough disappointment."

Charles shrugged. "Because I love her. She is far from a disappointment to me."

The crowd gasped again.

Her mother whirled on her. "Beatrice!"

Beatrice was staring at Charles with surprise and hope.

"Charles!" A deep voiced bellowed.

Charles rolled his eyes at Beatrice and then grinned. "Yes, Father."

Lord Castborough folded his arms. "Your Mother and I do not approve of this."

"Thank you for your opinion, Father," Charles said, not taking his eyes off of Beatrice. "I do not care."

"What?" his father bellowed.

Charles finally turned to face him. "You said that I needed to plan for the future and being responsible. That is exactly what I am doing."

"I suggest you..."

Charles stopped him with a raised hand. His anger was gone and all that was left was determination, no one was going to stop him. "Father, I have been to war. I have watched men I called friends be killed and I have spilled blood, too. I have no need for your suggestions."

He expected his father to grumble and grouse but instead, his father seemed to reassess Charles. "Is this what you truly want?"

Charles smiled at his father. "Yes, it most assuredly is."

"Then I will not oppose you," he said. "I will not aid you either."

"Thank you, Father," Charles said again. "Your aid is not necessary."

Beatrice's mother grabbed Beatrice by the wrist. "He may not oppose you, but I will."

"Mother, stop!" Beatrice pulled away from her mother. "I have had enough of your insults and mistreatment."

Lady Taltham looked at the crowd that had gathered. "You are an ungrateful child," she spat before walking away.

Charles crossed the small space to stand in front of Beatrice. "Are you all right?"

She nodded looking sad but relieved. "Yes. Much better now."

Before he could think about it, he kissed her in the hallway in front of everyone.

She looked up at him in surprise. "You will have to marry me now."

"I know, it is all part of my plan," he said and took both of her hands in his. "Beatrice, will you marry me?"

"Yes, Charles," she said her voice soft and her eyes shining with unshed tears.

There were murmurs from the crowd.

"We will be leaving for India as soon as we are married," he announced.

"We are?"

"You are?" his father echoed.

"I have accepted a job with the East India Company."

Henrietta rushed forward and hugged Beatrice while Matthew stepped toward him. "I suppose congratulations are in order."

"Thank you," Charles said shaking his hand.

They headed back towards the ballroom as Lady Judith and Mr Townsend were shown into the library by a sorrowful looking Lord and Lady Colchester and an incensed Lord Marlsfeld.

"I suppose the constable will need to be called. Unless Lord Marlsfeld can find a way to stave them off." Charles looked over his shoulder, shaking his head. "What a horrible thing to do. Try to kill your sick brother."

"He might prefer a dirty dungeon to being married to Lady Judith." Beatrice could not help but smile at her own sad joke.

"I do not blame the old sod. Either way, his future is not bright." Charles held his crooked arm out for Beatrice and she tucked her hand in with a smile.

"Are we really going to India?" Beatrice asked him once they had a quiet moment to themselves.

"Yes," he told Beatrice. Hoping that she would be as excited as he was about it. "You said you looked forward to leaving London behind you. "

"I did say that," she admitted, though her voice sounded small and far away.

He was starting to wonder if he had made the right decision when she turned to him. "Thank you."

"For what?"

"For listening and remembering what I said." Beatrice's smile was bigger and brighter than he had ever seen. "I never thought I would feel this way. Lieutenant Repington, I love you."

He reached down to touch her cheek. "And I love you, Miss Beatrice. I cannot wait to start this adventure with you."

THE BARRISTER'S CHOICE

HUGH

CHAPTER ONE

Hugh Repington opened the door and was suddenly agape at seeing his brother, James standing on his doorstep.

"Hugh!" James greeted him smiling, his voice jovial.

It took him a moment but Hugh finally stepped aside saying, "James, hello. Come in, please."

"Very good." James looked around briefly nodding and then frowned. "Do you always answer your own door? Is there not a servant here?"

It was then that Hugh realized that this was James' first visit to his house. It was a small house by London standards, with only a few rooms and decorated modestly, but it suited Hugh's needs while studying at the Inns of Court. There was room enough for him to sleep upstairs and a large desk downstairs for him to tend to his studies. He led James into the small drawing room indicating one of the upholstered chairs as he sat down in the other.

Shrugging, Hugh replied, "I do not get many visitors. So, yes, I often tend to my own door. There is a woman that comes in once a day to cook and clean for me, but I seldom see her as I am either out or studying in the library."

James seemed to take a moment and process information before giving Hugh a pointed look. "Speaking of your studies, I happened to see Mr Wright today, on my way back from Parliament."

"Oh?" Hugh asked when James paused.

"He saw fit to tell me that you had finished your studies at the Inns of Court," James said clearly waiting for a response.

Hugh nodded. He had been informed thusly only a few days before and had planned to notify his family by letter, but had not taken the time to do so. "It was only decided in recent days," he explained.

"And are you to be a barrister?" James asked cautiously, his face hopeful.

Stifling a sigh, Hugh answered, "Yes, Mr Wright—"

His words were cut off by a joyous whoop from James. "Congratulations! Hugh, I am immensely proud of you."

"It is nothing," Hugh told him shaking his head.

"Nothing," James repeated, exasperation in his voice. "I know more than anyone that it is not nothing. You have been studying for nearly four years for this."

Hugh was quite aware that James knew exactly what Hugh had accomplished. James had finished his own studies and had been chosen as a barrister only the year before. It had been a bit of a surprise for all of them as James had taken a break from his studies in order to help their father with affairs at Castborough.

James, upon being chosen as a barrister, had been given a position with Parliament almost immediately, to the delight of their father, the Duke of Castborough. Hugh appreciated James' understanding but had hoped to keep the news to himself for a little while longer.

"Thank you, James. I have only just gotten the news and still have much to think about."

"Surely you plan on begging Father's counsel," James replied a frown forming on his brow.

"Perhaps, once I have had the opportunity to investigate my options further."

The thought of speaking with their father had not crossed

Hugh's mind at all. It had been a point of pride for Hugh that he had been able to avoid the attention and interference of his family, particularly their father.

The Duke of Castborough was a well-respected man, responsible and successful. He expected no less from his children. Hugh had watched as his father had interfered and tried to control Hugh's three eldest brothers. It had caused an innumerable amount of fights, not only between father and son but among the brothers as well. One such fight resulted in his eldest brother, Philip, hieing off to Paris for what he called an adventure. It caused quite a stir in their family for a time.

Hugh was proud that his father had left him to do things on his own. The house Hugh was currently living in was the only help he had accepted from his father. The duke, of course, already held a London residence but Hugh had put forth a strong argument that there would be too many distractions for him to study properly. The Duke could hardly argue, Hugh's five siblings along with the duke and duchess made for quite a disturbance when they arrived in London.

James was speaking again and Hugh's attention shifted back to his brother. "Quite right," James agreed. "You should come with me to White's. We shall raise a glass to your success."

Hugh hesitated, thinking of the things he still needed to do.

James went on quickly. "Brother, you are too serious by half, come have some fun."

With a refusal on his lips, Hugh halted. If he declined James' invitation he would be proving his brother right, a result he cared not to accept. Although Hugh had long admired his older brother, he had recently begun to resent him as well. His return to his studies at the Inns of Court and his much sought-after position with Parliament had caused Hugh some consternation. Letting James win now seemed quite unsettling.

"Why not?" Hugh stood up and reached for his coat. "I have spent enough time at my desk. A night at the club seems appropriate."

"I have my carriage ready if you would like to leave now."

"We might as well," Hugh said, trying to sound more positive than he felt.

"How is Elizabeth?" He asked once they were in the carriage. James and Elizabeth had married several months ago and lived in a fairly large house on Castborough land in Surrey.

"She is quite well. Thank you for asking." James sat back in his seat. "Elizabeth will be disappointed that she did not get to see you. I am only due to be in London for a few days and she elected to stay behind."

"I am sorry that I missed her. Please send along my best wishes. Hopefully, we will have the opportunity to see each other again soon."

James admission regarding Elizabeth's absence explained a lot. Hugh had thought it somewhat odd that James was wanting to visit White's and had invited Hugh to join him. It was common knowledge that James was quite enamored with his new wife and spent much of his time with her.

Hugh could hardly blame him, Elizabeth was both beautiful and charming. Most importantly she kept James from working all hours of the day and night. An annoying virtue brought on by their father's constant interference, James had developed an overly strong sense of responsibility. He was still immensely responsible, but Elizabeth simply reminded him what was truly important.

"You should visit Castborough," James suggested after they had climbed down from the carriage. "It would give you some time to think."

More like time for the family to interfere, Hugh thought to himself. "That is a thought," he agreed not wanting to argue.

"Father would be happy to help you get established in London," James suggested as they entered the club.

Hugh had figured that that was what James had in mind. He did not answer, instead acting as though he was searching out a table for them. Not surprisingly, he found one almost immediately, it was still rather early in the night and they were served their celebratory drinks not long after.

James raised his glass. "To your success!"

Hugh raised his glass and nodded at James and they both drank.

"You really should think about coming home to Castborough. Father and I will be able to aid you in your decision making."

He was already trying to think of how to tell James that he did not want his help, or their father's when their conversation was interrupted.

"Repington!" The man looked surprised when they both turned. "And Repington!" He added with a hearty laugh.

Hugh recognized the man as Timothy Sedgwick.

"Sedgwick, how are you?" James said standing up to shake hands with the younger man.

"Good! Not as good as you, though," Sedgwick told him. "Congratulations on your recent marriage."

James laughed. "Thank you. I am quite lucky."

"I would say so. Never thought you would find a lady that would actually want to put up with your sullen disposition for evermore," Sedgwick teased, elbowing Hugh.

"Yes, it was a surprise to us all," Hugh agreed dryly.

"Elizabeth is a saint and I am eternally grateful for her enduring patience and kindness," James said, a slight smile showing his amusement.

"You look well, James," Sedgwick noted. "What brings you to White's?"

Hugh spoke up suddenly. "Oh, just two brothers taking in a drink." He then added, "James was lonely all by himself at the Repington residence, as his new bride remains in Surrey."

His intention to change the subject so that their true purpose there was not revealed.

James, however, had no such qualms. "My brother is too modest. We are here to celebrate. He just finished his studies at the Inns of Court, and has been chosen to be a barrister."

"Congratulations!" Sedgwick told them.

Hugh nodded. "Thank you."

"Have you acquired a position yet?" Sedgwick's eyes shifted to James. "Perhaps a position with the government like your brother."

Hugh stiffened and fought the scowl from forming on his face. "I have not made any decisions regarding my profession. I have only learned the news in recent days. Now that my studies are finished, I will be able to devote some time into making a decision."

"Quite right," the man said nodding. "Very wise of you. In the meantime, you will have to come to our house party. Eastbridge will be brimming with London's finest."

Hugh's first thought, as always, was to decline the man's invitation. But as he himself had said, his studies were complete. For the first time in a long while, he would have time for a party.

Hugh also recognized it as a fortuitous opportunity for him too. Not only would he be seen by London society, the very people that would be his potential business associates. Most of all, it was the perfect excuse for him to avoid going home to Castborough.

"Wonderful idea," Hugh said trying not to laugh at the total shock on James' face. "When shall I plan to arrive?"

"The party starts the day after tomorrow," said Sedgwick explained. "I believe my parents are expecting guests over the next two weeks."

"Fantastic. I shall make arrangements to leave as soon as possible." Hugh raised his glass. "To Eastbridge!"

CHAPTER TWO

Julianna Merchant looked up as the door to her room opened, her mother bustling through a moment later.

"Julianna, dear, may I come in?"

"Yes, of course," Julianna answered although it seemed unnecessary as her mother had already entered the room and stood right in the middle of it at that very moment.

Her mother looked around the room nodding several times. "It looks as though you have settled in. Perhaps we should go downstairs."

"I am in favour that. Anything is better than sitting up here in this stuffy room."

"Now, Julianna, you must be polite. This room is perfectly fine, rather nice actually. Lord and Lady Eastbridge have a lovely home and we should be thankful that we have been invited to their house party."

"Oh, mother, you are being silly." Julianna shook her head causing her mother to reach over to fix the pins in her hair. "Father is a Peer. We always get invited to the parties."

Her mother sighed and Julianna knew what was coming next.

"No, that is not quite true. Last season we were not invited to Lady Dalverton's party."

"Yes, Mother," Julianna said trying to keep the annoyance out of her voice. "Lady Dalverton did explain that she had thought we were still traveling and would not have arrived back in London in time to attend her party."

"Yes," her mother agreed. "Although I am quite sure the gossips are saying that we were snubbed by Lady Dalverton. Oh how I hate being talked about behind my back!"

"Oh, Mother, the gossips will say all sorts of nonsense. It is always best to ignore them and get on as though nothing untoward has happened, especially when nothing has actually occurred," Julianna told her pausing at the top of the stairs.

"If only that was... Goodness! Is that what you were wearing?"

Julianna looked down at the pale pink dress she was wearing. "Yes, Mother. I am wearing this dress."

"What if we happen upon Lord Norsely?"

"Then I suppose he will see me in this dress," Julianna remarked with a smirk. "Perhaps we shall say hello."

"Oh, Julianna," her mother sighed. "Perhaps you should go back and change into your yellow gown."

Julianna closed her eyes briefly hoping to summon some patience to deal with her mother and her constant fussing.

"Lady Alverston, hello."

Both Julianna and her mother turned to see Lady Amelia Sedgwick walking toward them. "I am so glad that you have arrived. I hope your travels were pleasant."

"Yes, thank you. We are so very pleased to be here," Julianna's mother fairly gushed.

Lady Amelia smiled at her mother and then looked to Julianna. "Lady Julianna, I was wondering if you would like to accompany me on a tour of the house and grounds?"

"Yes," Julianna said quickly. She was so very relieved to be given the opportunity to escape the good intentions of her mother. "That sounds lovely."

THE BARRISTER'S CHOICE

Lady Amelia gave Julianna a quick nod and then turned back to Julianna's mother. "I believe my parents are in the garden, I am sure they will be quite pleased to see you."

"Thank you, Lady Amelia, I will do just that."

Julianna watched as her mother hurried down the stairs and tried not to roll her eyes. She would never understand her mother's worry over what other people thought. One would think they were hangers-on and not actually part of London society. It was as though Mother forgot that Father was the Marquess of Alverston. He was well respected in Parliament and among those in London society.

Alverston was in the north, far from London and her mother worried about missing out on events and being forgotten. Julianna tried to remind her that everyone did not live in Kent or Surrey. Her mother so worried over the issue. She was sure that everyone would forget about them.

"Did you find your room satisfactory?" Lady Amelia asked.

"Oh yes," Julianna said quickly feeling badly about disparaging the room. It had been fine she was only tired of waiting in the room for her mother to collect her. "The room is more than satisfactory, quite lovely, in fact. Thank you."

Lady Amelia smiled and gestured towards the stairs. "I am glad that you are all settled. Your mother seemed distressed."

Julianna rolled her eyes and smiled. "Yes, well, to be truly honest that seems to be a permanent state for my mother as of late."

Lady Amelia's eyes widened briefly as though gleefully surprised. "Mine does, as well, you should have seen her these last two weeks." She paused on the stairs and grimaced. "No, I take that back. I am extremely glad that you did not see her like that."

Julianna laughed and followed Lady Amelia down the stairs.

"This is the library," Lady Amelia told her, stopping at an open door. "Please feel free to visit anytime you would like. My father takes care of Eastbridge business in a smaller room at the end of the hall. We have many books including many of the new adventure novels."

"Oh?" Julianna asked looking in the room.

"Is that bad?" Lady Amelia asked, looking a little stricken.

Julianna shook her head. "Goodness, no! I am quite looking forward to choosing a title to read this evening."

"The newest books are there." Lady Amelia walked into the room and pointed to a shelf in the corner near two large windows.

Julianna nodded and walked over to one of the windows.

Lady Amelia continued walking around the room. "The drawing room is across the hall. You can take your book in there to read if you would like."

Julianna was only half listening as she was looking out the large windows behind the desk. Far back from the main house was a building with a large fenced in area, several horses moved beyond the fence.

As though reading Julianna's mind Lady Amelia began to explain, "From this window, you can see part of the garden and of course, the stables. I might see if anyone wants to tour the stables I know that we have several foals that were born in the spring. They are quite sweet."

"Really?" Julianna asked hardly able to conceal the excitement in her voice.

"Yes, do you like horses?" Lady Amelia asked turning to face her.

Julianna smiled. "I do. I like them very much."

"Oh good! As do I," Lady Amelia said with a big smile and then sighed. "Please pardon my delight, it is not often that I find another young lady with an affinity for horses."

"No, I understand completely. Ladies our age are more interested in new dresses and attending parties."

Lady Amelia looked out at the window at the horses. "Perhaps you would like to see the stables while you are here."

"Thank you," Julianna nodded. "I do look forward to it."

CHAPTER THREE

"Repington!" Hugh had barely stepped out into the garden when he heard his name called. Across the garden, he saw Timothy Sedgwick wave as he moved to meet him.

"Hello, Sedgwick."

"Glad to see you, I had not heard that you had arrived. Actually thought perhaps you changed your mind."

"No, not at all. There were a few arrangements that needed to be made before I could leave London." Hugh grinned at the thought of being out of the city and on holiday for a while.

Hugh had notified his father that he had finished his studies and would be leaving London for several weeks. He also spoke with Mrs Bennett letting her know of his intended absence while assuring her she would still be paid to keep the house.

"I hope your trip was without issue. Are you all settled?"

"Yes. I arrived this morning and I am already enjoying myself immensely."

"Good, good!" His friend laughed and slapped him on the back good naturedly.

It was a bit of a surprise but he was very pleased that he had come to the party. Hugh had to admit that James had been right about him being too serious and having spent far too much time on the studies. He needed a holiday. Yes, indeed.

Although it was the fact that it had been James to point it out that was almost too much for Hugh. James had always been the most serious one of the brothers. For him to have noticed meant that Hugh had an even larger problem to solve.

Lord and Lady Eastbridge paused in their tour of the garden to speak to Sedgwick.

"Hello there, Timothy," Lord Eastbridge said.

While Lady Eastbridge asked, "Mr Repington are you enjoying yourself?"

"Most definitely. What a wonderful party you are throwing," Hugh replied.

"Thank you," Lady Eastbridge said with a smile. "Is your betrothed with you?" She looked around him. Hugh was puzzled for a moment and then realized the confusion. "I believe you are thinking of my brother, Charles. He has just recently become betrothed to Miss Beatrice Clarke."

"Oh, my apologies!" Lady Eastbridge looked so troubled that Hugh quickly spoke in order to calm her nerves.

"Not to worry. It was an easy mistake," Hugh reassured her. "It is not the first time that I have been confused with one of my brothers."

"Well, there are five of you," Sedgwick reminded him.

"Quite right," Lord Eastbridge said with a low rumbling chuckle. "You have been studying at the Inns of Court, have you not?"

"Yes, I have actually finished my studies quite recently."

Sedgwick broke in, "He has been chosen as a barrister. Wonderful news, that."

"Congratulations, Repington," Lord Eastbridge replied and clapped him on the shoulder.

Hugh staggered slightly under the unexpected weight of the

older man's hand. "Thank you. I am looking forward to working in London."

"Of course, well if you are anything like your brother, James, I have no doubt that you will be quite successful."

Hugh fought the urge to reply abruptly but he knew that Lord Eastbridge had meant it as a compliment. It was not the man's fault and it had not been his intention to rankle Hugh. It was a fortuitous moment as Hugh looked across the garden and saw the solution to his current predicament. "Thank you, Lord Eastbridge. If you will excuse me, I see that Lady Ramsbury is beckoning me," he said with a chuckle of his own.

"Oh, by all means," Lord Eastbridge said quickly.

Lady Eastbridge glanced across the garden. "Please give her our regards."

Hugh had counted on Lady Ramsbury's reputation of being overly fussy and vocal in order for him to get out of the conversation. Of course, now it would be necessary for him to speak with Lady Ramsbury. He had known both Lord and Lady Ramsbury since he was quite young, and although Lady Ramsbury could be rather opinionated, Hugh had discovered that she was exceedingly sweet and caretaking in spite of the fact. Lord Ramsbury could be a little mischievous but Lady Ramsbury kept her eye on him.

"Good evening, Lady Ramsbury," Hugh said with a bow.

"Good evening, Mr Repington," she said with an approving smile.

"Lord Ramsbury, you are looking well."

"Thank you, Mr Repington," the older man told him straightening his coat, the buttons straining over his considerable girth. "I hear you have been chosen as a barrister."

"Yes, your grace," Hugh answered.

"Have you received an appointment yet?"

"Not yet, no," Hugh answered. "It has only been a few days and I have not yet decided on the course of my profession. I am using my time at this house party to make those decisions."

"A sound plan, indeed," Lord Ramsbury paused as he looked longingly toward the house. Patting his round belly, he made a point to not look at his wife. "I wonder if they will have dessert later."

Hugh covered his smile by looking down to straighten his coat. Lord Ramsbury's fondness for sweets was well known. As well as Lady Ramsbury's efforts to keep him from growing even more rotund.

"Whether they have dessert or not is none of your concern," Lady Ramsbury told him and then turned to Hugh. "I heard that your brother, Lieutenant Repington has become betrothed to the Clarke girl."

"Yes, ma'am," Hugh replied. "They seem quite happy."

"So, what about you?"

Hugh was not sure what she meant he thought for a moment but finally said, "I am rather happy for them as well."

Lady Ramsbury huffed again and gave him a sharp smack on the upper arm with her fan. "Do not be insolent. I am asking about your plans for marriage, of course."

"I apologize, Lady Ramsbury, I had not realized that was your meaning." Hugh rubbed his arm. "I have no plans at this time to acquire a wife."

"Why ever not?" She asked sharply tipping the fan into her hand.

Hugh stepped back clearly hoping he had moved out of her reach. He opened his mouth to reply but found he had no answer for her.

Fearing that she might think him insolent for not answering Hugh swiftly replied, "I have not attended many events this Season and I fear that I have missed out on many introductions."

"I suppose you should be speaking to the young ladies instead of standing here with me, eh?" she gave him a pointed look when he looked to protest. "Mr Repington, far be it for me to tell you what you should be doing with your time."

Hugh stifled the snort that very nearly came out. Lady Ramsbury enjoyed nothing more than telling other people how they should be living their lives. The unfortunate part is that she was very often correct so he was unable to ignore her advice out of hand.

"I would be honoured to garner your wisdom on the matter," he said with a smart bow.

She narrowed her eyes slightly and he was sure he would pay for the gesture with another blow to his arm but instead, she smiled slightly.

"It would do you well, Mr Repington, to find a young lady of good standing with the social graces that would be required of a barrister's wife."

Hugh nodded slowly. He had meant it to appease the whims of the older woman but the more he thought about it, he realized that she was correct, as usual.

"Thank you, Lady Ramsbury. I do believe you are right, once again. I will have to remember you the next time I have a dilemma." Hugh gave her another lower bow. "I believe you would have made an excellent barrister. You seem to always have the best counsel."

Lady Ramsbury seemed surprised by his reply. "Yes, well. My father was a barrister. He was a very wise man and I suppose I learned much from him. Thank you for your observation."

"The gratitude is all mine. I suppose I shall follow your advice." Hugh smiled broadly at her. "Good evening, Lady Ramsbury."

"Good evening, Mr Repington. Do have a pleasant time."

Hugh walked farther into the garden finally stopping next to one of the many stone pillars. Lady Ramsbury's advice still in his head. He had not been lying to her when he said that he had not attended many events during the Season. In fact, he had only been to the ones that his family had forced him into attending.

"What are you doing in here?"

Hugh turned to see Sedgwick standing at the door.

"It has come to my attention that as a barrister I need to find a reputable wife that will help further my status in London society."

"Hmmm," Sedgwick seemed to mull the idea over. "I am not

sure if it is entirely necessary but I cannot see how acquiring a wife would hurt your reputation."

"Finding a suitable young lady may prove difficult as I have not been to many events this Season," Hugh confessed.

Sedgwick waved his hand. "That is no worry. I have been to nearly every event, party, and ball, as well as several nights at Almack's. Maybe I can be of assistance."

"Very good for you, then. As for me, I suppose the young lady I find will need to be from a respectable family that is well versed in social graces." Hugh then added, "I suppose she should be pleasant to look upon as well."

"I suppose so," Sedgwick repeated, a slight frown forming on his brow. "That is all you require? Good manners and a pleasant visage?"

"Yes," Hugh answered with a sigh. "Although I suppose if she had a sizable inheritance that would be helpful as well."

He knew he must sound odd but he had no need of a love match. Furthering his career as a barrister was his only goal. If finding a bride would help that then he would look for a wife.

"Well, if that is the case then I think Lady Priscilla Munro might fit the bill."

"Oh really?" Hugh asked somewhat surprised that Sedgwick would think of someone that quickly.

"Yes, her father is the Earl of Ridgewood. She is, of course, very well versed in the social graces and is well received in London." Sedgwick shrugged. "Her name came to mind as it has just recently been discovered that she will receive a rather large inheritance from a distant relative. I do not know much more than that, I am afraid."

"No, that is quite useful information." Hugh tapped his chin thoughtfully. "Is she to be at this party?"

"Yes. Lady Priscilla and her family arrived last night." Sedgwick looked around the garden. "I would be happy to introduce you."

"I would like that," Hugh replied feeling good that he was making decisions that would help him further his profession as a barrister.

"She is there by the hedge with her mother," Sedgwick gestured slightly across the garden. "The young lady in the light green dress."

Hugh nodded. She was quite beautiful, her honey colored hair was swept back from her face save for a few curls as was the fashion. He watched her as she waited patiently with her mother while the older woman conversed with several other guests, smiling and answering questions politely. "Yes, I think she will do."

Sedgwick looked at him for a moment as though he wanted to say something but eventually just shook his head. "I will go talk to Lady Ridgewood. I will return in a moment."

Hugh watched as Sedgwick moved across the garden speaking to people briefly as he went. He stopped at the group where Lady Priscilla stood speaking to everyone for a moment before turning to Lady Ridgewood. They spoke for a moment before Hugh saw him gesture towards where he was standing and Hugh stood up a little straighter and smiled at the people that stood near him hoping he would look more social.

It was not too long before Sedgwick returned with Lady Ridgewood and Lady Priscilla following along.

"Mr Repington, allow me to introduce Lady Ridgewood and her daughter, Lady Priscilla Munro."

"It is lovely to meet both of you. I hope you are enjoying the party." Hugh tried to speak as graciously as possible since this meeting might be very important to his future.

"Yes, it has been wonderful, has it not, Priscilla?"

"Oh yes," Lady Priscilla replied. "The garden is so beautiful."

"It is a lovely night out." Lady Ridgewood opened her fan. "A little warmer than I had anticipated."

"Oh? Can I get you some lemonade?" Sedgwick offered.

"I would be happy if you would direct me to the refreshments," Lady Ridgewood said amiably.

"Yes, of course," Sedgwick offered his arm. He smiled at Hugh as they walked away leaving him alone with Lady Priscilla.

Lady Priscilla looked at him expectantly.

Hugh nearly panicked but his training as a barrister helped him to stay calm and think of something to say. "How have you enjoyed the Season thus far?"

She smiled broadly at him. "It has been quite enjoyable. I have been to a number of parties and balls, and Almack's of course."

"Of course." He had not expected such an enthusiastic reply from the young lady.

She looked at him and almost frowned. "I do not believe I have seen you at Almack's this Season, though."

"You are quite right. I have been rather occupied, actually. I have been finishing my studies at the Inns of Court."

"Congratulations, Mr Repington," Lady Priscilla said demurely. "Does this mean that I will see more of you at social events in London?"

Hugh smiled down at her. "Yes, I believe it does."

CHAPTER FOUR

"I was thinking tomorrow morning I could take you down to the stables."

Julianna turned to Lady Amelia. "That sounds wonderful."

"What are you two whispering about?" Miss Diana asked, her blonde hair looking almost white against her yellow dress.

"Oh, pardon us, Miss Diana. Lady Julianna had asked to see the stables—" Lady Amelia began to say.

"Why ever for?" Miss Diana asked a look of shock on her face.

For a moment, Julianna worried that Lady Amelia would be offended but she only laughed. "I am quite lucky to have found a friend who shares my fondness of horses."

"Horses are very beautiful but the stables are always so dirty," Miss Diana said wrinkling her nose. "I do not enjoy being there."

"Yes, all of that hay and dirt can be rather dusty," Julianna replied with a wry chuckle.

Miss Diana laughed. "I must sound rather silly but my riding habit is always so dusty when I have come back from riding. Mother is always lecturing me about how unladylike it is to be dirty."

"Well, that certainly is not your fault," Lady Amelia told her.

"How are you to enjoy your ride when you are worried about getting dirty?" Julianna did not wait for her to answer. "That is just silly. Riding should be fun and carefree."

"I think so, too," Lady Amelia agreed.

"My mother is like that, as well. Every time I laugh in public she reminds me that ladies do not laugh loudly, they giggle softly." Julianna shook her head in dismay.

Miss Diana shook her head. "What if something particularly humorous occurs? What do you do then?"

"Like when Horace Scriven tripped over Lady Esther's dress and landed in Lady Agatha Radcliffe's lap?" Lady Amelia began to laugh and covered her mouth before she got too loud.

"Oh my! What did Horace do?" Miss Diana gasped.

Lady Amelia composed herself long enough to say, "Why Horace simply stood up and asked Lady Agatha if she would like to dance."

"No!" Miss Diana exclaimed.

"He did," Lady Amelia confirmed before beginning to laugh again.

"What did Lady Agatha do?" Miss Diana asked her eyes wide.

"She accepted, of course," Julianna told her collapsing into a fit of giggles.

"She did not!"

"She did!" Lady Amelia assured her. "I have never seen Horace so red."

"I so wish I had seen it," Miss Diana lamented. "I was at a house party in Surrey."

"Oh, watching Horace was quite amusing but be glad you were at the house party." Lady Amelia replied her face growing serious.

"Why do you say that?"

Julianna remembered that night at Almack's and she answered before Lady Amelia. "Many of the girls were being quite mean to Miss Francis."

"Why ever for?"

"I am not sure. It started early in the night when she was dancing with Mr Townsend."

"Oh, yes. I remember," Julianna said. "Almack's was tremendously crowded that night. It was rather a crush. Right in the middle of the dance, Mr Townsend left the dance floor."

"He left her in the middle of the dance floor?" Miss Diana repeated. "Why?"

Miss Amelia nodded soberly. "No one knows. He simply stopped dancing and left Miss Francis alone in the middle of the room."

"How horrible." Miss Diana shook her head in disbelief.

"It was horrible. Then Lady Judith and Lady Sarah and the others begin to make comments and giggle at her."

"Oh," Miss Diana looked away.

Julianna understood why. Each of them had encountered the perniciousness of Lady Judith and Lady Sarah. They thought it quite entertaining to upset the other young ladies.

It made no sense to Julianna why anyone would purposefully be mean to other people. She was not so naïve to think that everyone was perfectly nice all of the time and she was well aware that there were undesirable people in the world. She just hated that some of those people were mean to her friends.

"We did our best to talk to Miss Francis but she was quite distressed," Lady Amelia added.

"I can only imagine how upsetting it had been to have that awful Mr Townsend leave her alone in the middle of the dance floor. It had to have been humiliating." Julianna was getting angry. "And then she had to endure gossips like Lady Judith and Lady Sarah."

"I have not seen Lady Judith at many events recently," Miss Diana commented.

"Yes, well," Lady Amelia said slowly. "That is a completely different story."

Just then they heard a twitter of laughter across the way. Julianna saw Lady Sarah and several other ladies gathered across the garden. Lady Sarah said something prompting them all to look over at someone that Julianna could not see. A moment later, Lady Eleanor made a comment that caused the ladies to laugh again.

"They are most unpleasant," Miss Diana said quietly.

"You are being rather kind, I think," Julianna told her. "I cannot abide their cruel remarks and their malicious behaviour."

"I always try to stay away from them. Lady Judith was the worst out of all of them. I had hoped Lady Sarah would have learned from recent events and make a few changes," Lady Amelia noted sadly. "Clearly not."

"Lady Sarah would have to actually think about someone other than herself to have learned anything at all," Julianna said with a snort.

Before either Lady Amelia or Miss Diana could respond, Julianna's mother gasped "Julianna, please remember yourself! You are a lady and should act like one. At all times, my daughter."

Julianna rolled her eyes at her friends while her mother looked at them apologetically and said, "If you will excuse us ladies there is something we need to tend to."

Miss Diana tried to hide her smile behind her fan only managing to nod at her.

"Yes, of course," Lady Amelia said pleasantly.

"Thank you." Lady Alverston said primly before addressing Julianna, "Come along, dear."

Julianna gave her friends a puzzled look. She had no idea what matters her mother would want her to attend.

"Mother, may I enquire as to where we are going?"

"We are going into the drawing room. It is the time to meet Lord Norsely." Her mother stopped behind one of the hedges and began to fret. She looked at Julianna and frowned, tucking a stray hair behind her ear and retying the ribbons on her dress.

After a moment Julianna stepped back. "Mother, it is fine. We should be going, we do not want to keep Lord Norsely waiting."

Her mother's head snapped up. "Of course, you are quite right."

Lady Alverston straightened and smoothed her own dress before she began stepping into the garden once more.

They strolled into the drawing room where they were swiftly joined by Julianna's father.

"Julianna, you look beautiful today."

She nodded self-consciously. "Thank you, Father." Julianna and her father did not speak often given he was gone quite regularly to London to deal with Parliament business. They had many spirited discussions over various books but it was rare indeed that he would comment on her appearance.

He and her mother looked at each other for a moment and nodded. "Let us get this done."

Julianna followed behind her parents feeling increasingly nervous after their odd display.

Across the drawing room, Julianna saw a man who looked somewhat familiar standing with an older man and woman. Given the resemblance, Julianna could only assume that they were his parents.

"Good afternoon, Lord Marsfeld, Lady Marsfeld," her father greeted them. "I would like to introduce my daughter, Lady Julianna."

"Good afternoon," Lord Marsfeld said smiling at Julianna. "It is a pleasure finally meeting you. This is my wife, Lady Marsfeld and our son, Lord Norsely."

"Good afternoon. It is an honour to meet you." Julianna had been introduced to many people and had never felt so apprehensive.

Lord Norsely stepped forward to give her a quick bow. "Lady Julianna, good afternoon. Would you like to take a stroll in the garden?"

"Yes, that sounds lovely," she told him taking the arm he offered.

He nodded at his parents while Julianna gave her parents a polite smile and they left the drawing room. "I apologize for the high theater," he said once they had reached the garden. "My father can be rather dramatic."

Julianna laughed. "It was not only your parents, Lord Norsely. My parents have been acting strangely as well."

"I feel as though I should offer an apology for that, but honestly I am much relieved that I am not alone in this."

"Yes, indeed. I feel the same."

Julianna was surprised Lord Norsely was much more charming than she had anticipated. Since her parents had first discussed the idea for her introduction to Lord Norsely she had been expecting the worst. Perhaps this party would be more enjoyable than the awkward exchange she had expected.

They walked along one side of the garden and then he turned leading her into the main part of the garden smiling and nodding at people as they passed.

"It is always good to be seen," he said lightly. He made a point of looking at her hair and dress and added, "I am pleased that you are as interested in the latest fashion as I am."

Julianna glanced down at her dress and shrugged inwardly. She had chosen that dress at the modiste merely because she had liked how the white dress looked with the blue ribbons adorning the sleeves and neckline. She had not given much thought to whether or not it met the current fashion trends in London.

Julianna started to suspect that Lord Norsely was more interested in parading around in front of the other guests as the pinkest of the pink. It was disappointing to think that his charm may be for appearances only. Her hopes for a more interesting party began to fade quickly.

CHAPTER FIVE

Julianna stopped at the bottom of the stairs when she heard a rustling noise behind her.

"Good morning," Lady Amelia whispered from the hall.

"Good morning," Julianna whispered back, relieved that she had not been caught sneaking through the house.

She had awakened early, almost at first light excited about going down to the stables to see the new foals. Julianna hoped that could dispel some of the worry she was feeling about her first meeting of Lord Norsely. She had not slept well as she had continued to think about the man she had met the day before.

Had she been giddy, or nervously excited she would not have minded losing those hours of sleep but it was quite the opposite. Julianna had tossed and turned with apprehension and an unease that she could not quite name.

"Come with me to the dining room." Lady Amelia opened a door across from the drawing room.

An older woman was just setting a tray on the table.

"Thank you, Martha." Lady Amelia gave her a warm smile. "Hope it was not too much trouble."

"Oh no! It is a pleasure," she said with a Scottish accent and nodded at Julianna. "Are ye going down to the stables to see the wee foals again?"

"Of course," Lady Amelia said with a laugh. "I am lucky enough to have found a friend to go with me today, though."

"Ye like horses, too, do ye?" Martha asked Julianna.

"Oh yes, I cannot wait to see the foals," Julianna replied not able to keep from smiling.

"They are very sweet," Lady Amelia said. "Are they not?" She asked turning to Martha.

"Aye, they are at that." The older woman nodded her head in agreement, pouring tea into two cups. "Sit down and have yer tea and biscuits. Kirk will have only just let the wee foals and their mams out of the stable. Ye have plenty of time."

"Thank you," Lady Amelia told her.

"There is fresh jam for the biscuits, too."

"Thank you," Julianna said. "It looks perfect."

Martha gave them an appreciative smile and left the room.

Julianna took a biscuit and began to spread jam on it.

"I saw that you met Lord Norsely yesterday afternoon," Lady Amelia said quietly.

"Yes." Julianna sat for a moment before letting out a sigh. "My parents think we will make a good match. Lord and Lady Marsfeld apparently approve as well. Our introduction was quite formal."

"I do not doubt that," Lady Amelia commented as she raised her cup to her lips.

Julianna wondered if she meant something by that. Then she remembered her thought when she first saw him standing in the drawing room. "I could not get the idea out of my head that Lord Norsely looks quite familiar but I am certain I have not met him before. It is so strange I cannot explain it."

"I can." Lady Amelia set her cup down and leaned forward. "Lord Norsely is Andrew Townsend's older brother."

"Oh!" Julianna shook her head in disbelief. "I cannot believe that I did not know that."

"I am quite sure that there will be no mention of Mr Townsend."

Julianna frowned. "I would imagine not."

"I do not like to speak ill of people but I must admit that I feel that both Mr Townsend and Lady Judith are well deserving of their fate."

Julianna nodded slowly thinking about her first meeting with Lord Norsely. "Yes, I would have to agree with you on that."

Lady Amelia tilted her head. "You still seem troubled."

"I keep thinking about Lord Norsely. He was very polite, of course."

"I am sure that he was, but there is something else bothering you, is there not?"

"Yes, it is difficult to explain but he seemed more interested in parading around in front of the other guests than with speaking to me." Julianna looked at Lady Amelia and said, "He spoke very little to me, instead saving much of his conversation for the many people we encountered on the walk through the garden."

"That is rather odd," Lady Amelia thought for a moment. "Although I cannot remember seeing Lord Norsely at any social function since the incident at the Dalverton's ball. It is quite possible that this is the first time Lord Norsely has attended an event since his recovery."

"Oh, I had not thought of that. I would have preferred to speak with him more but I understand that simply attending the party might have been difficult for him." Julianna could not imagine what the man had endured over the last several weeks. "Perhaps we will have more time to talk and get to know each other on another occasion."

"It most likely explains the formality of your introduction as well." Lady Amelia set her cup down and sat back in her chair. "It would not be presumptuous to think that Lord and Lady Marsfeld are hoping to smooth over any gossip that may be lingering from before."

"I believe that you are quite right. I suppose I will have to wait and see what happens next." Julianna pushed back from the table not wanting to think about Lord Norsely or Mr Townsend anymore. "Shall we go see the foals now?"

"Yes, of course." Lady Amelia stood up quickly, a warm smile on her face. "I am so glad you were able to come to the house party. I am quite enjoying having you here."

She nodded and smiled back at Lady Amelia. "I am glad as well."

Julianna followed her new friend down the hallway to a door that opened out to the garden. They followed a low stone wall along one side until Lady Amelia stopped at an iron gate nearly hidden by a tall hedge and left the garden.

"Oh look!" Julianna pointed toward the stables as a foal galloped around, gangly legs seeming to fly every which way.

Lady Amelia laughed. "Martha was right. Kirk let them out at just the right time."

Julianna was puzzled. She had not heard the name Kirk before Martha had mentioned it in the dining room but given the conversation, she assumed that he was one of the grooms that worked in the stables. "How would Martha know though?"

Lady Amelia continued walking towards the stables. "Kirk is the head groom in the stables and Martha knows everything that goes on around here. Oh, and she is Kirk's wife."

"Oh!" Julianna said. "That makes such perfect sense now."

They stopped at the fence watching as the foals ran around while the mares grazed lazily in the morning sun. "Aye, Lady Amelia, are ye here again?" An older man with bright blue eyes asked from the nearby doorway.

"Is that surprising for you, Kirk?"

"It would be more surprising if ye were not down here," he said with a gruff laugh. "And did ye drag another lass with ye?"

"Oh yes," Lady Amelia replied slipping her arm through Julianna's. "My friend admires horses as much as I do."

He crossed his arms and nodded at Julianna. "And ye came to see the wee foals, too?"

"I did. They are rather darling."

"Aye, that they are, but full of spirit, too." He pointed across the pen. "The red one nearly fell in the watering trough this morning."

"Oh!" Julianna exclaimed and as though the foal knew they were talking about her suddenly twitched her ears and took off running across the pen startling two of the other foals into the running as well.

"I do not believe Crawford's mount is anything to worry over," a voice came from behind them.

Julianna turned to see two men on horseback presumably returning to the stable.

"Amelia, are you down here bothering Kirk again?" a blonde man asked her.

"No, dear brother, I am not," Lady Amelia said rolling her eyes at Julianna. Of course, she caught the slight smile on her friend's face as well. "I brought Lady Julianna down to see the foals."

"Oh, so you were bothering Lady Julianna, then?" Amelia's brother asked, a sly grin crossing his face.

Julianna spoke up. "No, not at all. I asked Lady Amelia to bring me here to the stables." Lady Amelia gave her hand a quick squeeze.

Lady Amelia's brother slid off his horse. "I do not think we have been introduced."

"Timothy, this is Lady Julianna Merchant. Lady Julianna, this is my brother, Mr Timothy Sedgwick."

"It is a pleasure to meet you, Mr Sedgwick" Julianna said.

"I hope you are enjoying the party." Timothy gave her a warm smile before leaning closer to whisper loudly, "Thank you for befriending my sister, she is so in need of new friends."

Julianna ignored Lady Amelia's shocked gasp to ask. "She is? What happened to her old friends?"

Mr Sedgwick seemed surprised that she was playing along. The second man had gotten off his horse and joined them at the fence. Mr Sedgwick then said, "Her old friends? I am not sure there were many to begin with but I assume they grew tired of her silliness."

Lady Amelia stamped her foot but Julianna was ready with a

retort of her own. "Oh? I was sure it must be because you had scared them all off."

Mr Sedgwick's mouth dropped open as Lady Amelia clapped her hands in delight. "Oh, too right!"

Julianna hid her smile as she turned to her friend and patted her hand sympathetically. "Do not worry I promise to stand by you no matter how mortifying your brother may become."

"Do you hear her, Repington?" Mr Sedgwick asked the other man. "She does not even know me, yet she mocks me."

His friend looked at Julianna for a moment before saying, "It seems as though she is a good judge of character."

Timothy looked up at the sky as if looking for strength from the divine muttering, "Attacks from every quarter." He turned to the man he called Repington. "You wound me, my good man."

"Dear brother, it seems as though you have been thoroughly found out."

"Yes, it appears so." Mr Sedgwick agreed with a smile and then suddenly seemed to remember his manners. "My apologies, Amelia, Lady Julianna, this is Mr Hugh Repington."

"Good morning," Lady Amelia said readily.

"I am pleased to meet you," Julianna replied and then looked behind him at the beautiful black horse he had been riding.

"Good morning," Mr Repington nodded at them both.

From the front of the house there was a loud cracking sound and suddenly Mr Repington's horse reared back, his front legs flailing in the air.

"Watch out!" Mr Repington cried out.

CHAPTER SIX

Hugh watched in horror as his horse reared back, its hooves slashing at the air above where they stood. Before he could even act, Lady Julianna had turned toward the horse, whether it was out of shock or fear he could not say.

He wanted to cry out for her to stay away but he dared not upset the horse further. Moving slowly, he hoped to pull the young lady away swiftly and carefully before she got hurt. As he got closer though he realized that she was talking softly to the horse. Just at the point that he was sure she would be injured the horse's front legs settled back to the ground. Its ears still flicked back with its eyes wide.

"Shush, now. All right now, there you go," she was saying in a soft, soothing voice.

Hugh stopped dead in his tracks as he saw her pluck the reins deftly from where they hung across the saddle and gently tie them to a cross piece on the fence.

"There now. All better," she stroked the beast on the shoulder the tension visibly leaving it until eventually the horse calmly stood looking down at its dark-haired tamer.

"Well, that was exciting." She turned around and said with a smile.

"Exciting?" he asked, much too loudly. Hugh had no idea why but he was suddenly furious with her. "What do you think you were doing? You could have been killed!"

Unbelievably, she shrugged her shoulders and said, "Perhaps, but the horse was scared and my only thought was to calm him down. I suppose I acted out of instinct."

"Your only thought was to calm the horse," he repeated, not quite believing what she was saying. "You should have been scared to death. Why were you not scared?"

"Oh, horses do not scare me," she said easily turning back to the large horse. "I ride nearly every morning when I am home at Alverston."

"You enjoy riding horses?" Hugh realized that he must sound like a complete idiot as he seemed to be repeating everything that she said. It was not often that he met a young lady that was not either scared of horses or thought they were much too untidy, or more so, enjoyed riding beyond the occasional outing at house parties and the like.

"Goodness, Repington, is there something wrong with your hearing?" Sedgwick was leaning against the fence looking delighted at Hugh's discomfiture.

"Nonsense," Hugh very nearly shouted. "I was only distracted by the horse being startled."

"And look at Lady Julianna, she does not look distracted or concerned, does she, Timothy?" Lady Amelia asked, clearly teasing Hugh even though the question was directed at her brother.

"It is all right, Mr Repington," Julianna remarked. He was about to thank her when she went on. "Not every person can be as comfortable around horses, as I am. It is a gift."

Sedgwick began to howl with laughter.

"Are ye lads ever going to bring the horses back in or are ye going to let them suffer at the fence all day?"

Sedgwick and Hugh turned away from the fence.

"My apologies, Kirk. It is all my sister's fault."

"It is not!" Lady Amelia exclaimed, sounding so like Hugh's only sister, Henrietta, that he could not help but laugh.

"Oh right, it was Lady Amelia who neglected her horse and then stood there doing nothing as it reared up and try to stomp us all to death," and Lady Julianna said to him lightly. Then turned to him. "Oh, Heavens, I am all mixed up. That was you, was it not, Mr Repington?"

"Yes, I believe it was Mr Repington," Lady Amelia agreed.

Once again, Sedgwick began to laugh and Hugh felt himself begin to scowl again.

"Oh, Mr Repington, do not be so sour," Lady Amelia told him. "We are only teasing you."

"What is the lass talkin' about, Master Timothy?"

Sedgwick grimaced at his sister before turning back to the man standing in the stable door. "Kirk, it was nothing. Juno was startled and when up on his back legs for a moment."

Lady Amelia sniffed at Sedgwick's explanation but said nothing. Kirk, however, was not to be deceived.

"Are ye tellin' me the truth, lad? Yer sister and the lass seem to think it was more than nothin'."

Sedgwick shot his sister a frown, but Hugh had heard enough. "It was indeed my fault. My apologies, Kirk. I left Juno unattended near the fence and when he was startled I was not close enough to settle him."

Kirk made a tsking sound which made the others chuckle and Hugh hoped that his face was not turning red as it often did when he was embarrassed.

"It is not yer fault, Mr Repington. Juno has been known to be nervous and Master Timothy knows that very well." The older man turned to Sedgwick. "Ye should have kept a closer eye on the horse."

"Aw, Kirk, do not be angry with me." Sedgwick began leading his horse into the stable. Hugh nodded at the two ladies before leading a much more placid Juno into the stable.

Sedgwick and Kirk were arguing amiably, something that they did often. Hugh stood in the stable trying not to think about Lady Julianna. While he wanted to be annoyed with her for being so outspoken upon just meeting, he could not help but appreciate her apparent interest and knowledge of horses, as well as her loyalty to Lady Amelia.

The house party was his first event of the Season but he had been quickly reminded that most of the young ladies were interested in little but fashion and the next ball or party. As much as he found Lady Julianna exasperating he was somewhat intrigued by her.

"Repington, I did not get a chance to ask you about it during our ride, but how was your evening with Lady Priscilla?" Sedgwick asked when they had left the stable.

Hugh thought about the young lady with whom he had spent most of his previous evening. "It went rather well. She is quite beautiful and as you might expect, extremely gracious and perfectly comfortable at social events."

"And yet you do not look happy. I thought that Lady Priscilla would be exactly what you were looking for, is she not?"

Hugh knew that Sedgwick was right, he did not feel happy. He was not sure what the problem was, although his relaxing morning ride had done nothing more than cause him to be more anxious. He shook his head. "No, Lady Priscilla is perfect. I believe the problem lies with me."

"With you? Whatever do you mean?"

"I have been locked up by myself for far too long. It seems I have forgotten the normal conventions of today's society."

"Oh?" Sedgwick replied.

"I have been around no one but academics. I was not prepared for the long discussion regarding the latest fashions in London."

"Oh, of course," Sedgwick said giving him a knowing look then stopped to look Hugh over. "Hmmm. Perhaps she was trying to tell you something."

"Perhaps," he answered not really listening until suddenly the other man's word sank in. "Wait. What do you mean by that?"

The other man grimaced slightly. "When we return to London I believe we should visit my tailor."

He looked down at his breeches, he had not followed the current trend of men wearing pantaloons. If he were to court Lady Priscilla and become a fixture in London society he should be dressed for it.

With a sigh, he said, "Yes, I suppose that I should."

CHAPTER SEVEN

"She is rather beautiful, is she not?"

Hugh turned to see Nigel Coombs standing at his elbow staring across the room at Lady Priscilla where she stood with several other ladies. He would have liked to ignore the man but he dared not. Coombs was not a very influential man in London but he was notorious for passing on tidbits of information whether it be true or not.

It was more than likely that if Hugh snubbed the man, news of it, in some highly exaggerated form, would have spread through London in a matter of days. He had heard stories from his eldest brother, Philip, about Coombs and his less than exemplary history.

After a moment, Hugh nodded at the man. "Good evening, Coombs."

Coombs looked at him for a while before saying, "Good evening, yourself, Repington."

"You seem puzzled. Is there something amiss?" Hugh looked around as though he were trying to ascertain the problem.

"I am simply wondering if your reticence in answering the question means that you do not agree with me."

Hugh furrowed his eyebrows in confusion. "And what question was that?"

"I made the comment that Lady Priscilla is quite beautiful and asked your opinion."

"And you were waiting for an answer?" Hugh asked giving the other man a long look.

Coombs looked mildly uncomfortable but pushed on. "Well, yes."

Hugh had hoped to avoid answering but there seemed nothing for it. "Hmm. I thought your question was rather rhetorical. I suppose one would have to be blind not to see that she is beautiful." Hugh waited, assuming Coombs would have more to say on the subject.

"I noticed that you and the lady were introduced the other night."

Hugh only nodded in response.

Coombs smiled conspiratorially. "I expect you will be pursuing a courtship."

"Perhaps," Hugh told him. "We shall see what happens when I return to London."

"Perhaps?" Coombs looked skeptical. "Surely you do not expect me to believe that you will not be pursuing Lady Priscilla."

Just then Lady Priscilla glanced across the room at Hugh and smiled shyly. Hugh turned to Coombs. "I care not what you believe. If you will excuse me."

Coombs opened his mouth to speak but Hugh was already walking away. He crossed the room and stopped near the group of young ladies that included Lady Priscilla.

"Good evening, Lady Priscilla."

"Good evening, Mr Repington."

"Are you enjoying the party?"

"Yes, it is quite lovely." Lady Priscilla looked toward the dance floor. "The music is especially enjoyable tonight."

Hugh smiled at her. The music began to swell signaling the next dance. "Yes, it is indeed. Would you like to dance?"

THE BARRISTER'S CHOICE

"Oh," Lady Priscilla sounded surprised. Not that Hugh believed it but he appreciated her attempt. "Yes, of course. Thank you."

Lady Priscilla primly took his arm as he led her to the middle of the ballroom. She smiled up at him and he sought for something to say. "You look rather lovely tonight."

She looked away shyly and murmured, "Why thank you, Mr Repington."

He wondered if he should say more but she turned back at him to say, "I am so glad my mother insisted that we pay a visit to the modiste before we left London."

Hugh had no idea how to reply so he simply said, "I can imagine."

She looked confused for a moment but continued on. "I saw this dress and just loved it, but my mother did not think it was fashionable."

Lady Priscilla paused and Hugh knew from conversations with Henrietta that it was best to wait. Lady Priscilla said nothing, he sighed and led them through the next turn hoping that the subject would soon change.

"Fortunately, Corrine, that is the modiste," she looked at him to make sure he was paying attention. "She is French and is well acquainted with all of the latest fashions. She assured mother she could make the dress more fashionable and added the extra ruffles at the bottom and on the sleeves. It is simply perfect now."

He continued to move them around the ballroom, suddenly noticing that Lady Priscilla had fallen silent. He looked down to see that she was pouting. She looked so much like Henrietta when she was younger that he almost laughed. Lady Priscilla surely would have been insulted if he laughed at her.

"Have I said something wrong?"

"No, it is that you have said nothing at all," she said with a shake of her head.

Without thinking, Hugh said, "About what?"

Lady Priscilla let out an exasperated huff. "Mr Repington, have you not been listening?"

The dance had ended and they moved to the edge of the ballroom. "Oh." Hugh stopped and turned to face her. "My apologies. You are quite right. Your dress is perfect indeed. And although I am far from an expert, I believe your dress is the top of fashion."

"Why thank you for noticing, Mr Repington," Lady Priscilla simpered, looking up at him adoringly.

"Would you like a refreshment? I believe Lady Eastbridge has set up the dining room with punch and cakes."

"Yes, that would be lovely," Lady Priscilla agreed.

Hugh led her from the ballroom and into the dining room where he handed her glass of punch. They moved aside as another group of people entered the dining room. Lady Julianna smiled as she waited for another gentleman to hand her a glass of punch.

"Good evening, Lady Julianna," he said and nodded to the gentleman.

"Good evening, Mr Repington," she said. "Lady Priscilla."

"Good evening," Lady Priscilla said with a small amount of disdain. Her eyes narrowing as she looked past her at the gentleman beside her.

The gentleman turned and smiled at them, Hugh felt himself bristle and sought to appear normal. The man's smile seemed too practiced and Hugh recognized the man as Lord Norsely. It was not surprising as he looked much different than the last time Hugh had seen him. He should have expected that though and the other man had been quite ill only a few months ago.

Lady Julianna and Lord Norsely had barely left the room by Lady Priscilla turned to him.

"Do you know who that was?"

"Yes, I met Lady Julianna the other—" he began but Lady Priscilla interrupted him.

"No, it is Lord Norsely." Lady Priscilla looked rather gleeful before her face grew serious. "I do not know if you have heard the latest news. Lord Norsely was recently involved in quite a messy scandal."

He smiled at her, sure that she was trying to be humorous. She apparently did not notice his reaction as she went on almost enthusiastically. She was clearly enjoying a moment of gossip and did not care to detect his reluctance to participate in such ill words.

"As you know, Lord Norsely is the heir to the Earl of Marsfeld. He currently holds the title of Viscount of Norsely." She looked at him with a knowing smirk. "A few months ago, he fell ill, the physician was called. The family was told that the viscount was afflicted with a fever and that he would improve with care and medicine. Only he did not improve and seemed to worsen under the physician's supervision."

Lady Priscilla paused for a moment and Hugh thought he would comment but she continued on before he could speak.

"Lord Norsely has a younger brother, Andrew Townsend. You probably know him as he is usually at every social event in London. It turns out that Mr Townsend was pouring out his brother's medicine and replacing it with a mixture of water and whiskey. Lord Norsely nearly died."

Finding an opportunity to try to stop the awkward conversation, Hugh simply nodded, "Terrible. Shall we return to the ballroom?"

"Yes, thank you. I thought the sordid event was terrible, as well," she replied with a bright smile and took his arm. "Mr Townsend was in the midst of courting that strange girl, what was her name?"

Lady Priscilla's voice trailed off and Hugh scowled at her.

She did not bother to notice his reaction and suddenly smiled again. "Oh, yes. Her name was Miss Beatrice Clarke. Mr Townsend was nearly caught alone with her but there was some confusion. As it was then discovered that Mr Townsend was thought to have compromised Lady Judith Powell."

Hugh paused at the door to the ballroom, sure that Lady

Priscilla would halt her story now that they were joining other people.

"Yes, it turns out that Lady Judith and Mr Townsend were forced to marry and have been fairly banished to a family home in Cumbria." Lady Priscilla sniffed. "And Miss Beatrice's reputation would have suffered if not for some officer just home from the war. I heard that he gallantly stepped in to ask for her hand, though why a man would do such a thing is beyond me. It was a rather fortuitous turn of events for Miss Beatrice if I am being completely honest. She likely did not deserve such graciousness. It all caused quite a scene at Lord and Lady Dalverton's ball."

"Yes, I did hear about the situation." Hugh was in such shock at her telling of the story that he could not manage to say more.

It amazed him that she did not know that he would have already heard the story. His elder brother, Charles, was the gallant officer that Lady Priscilla had mentioned. Charles and Miss Beatrice had formed a friendship during the beginning of the Season and he had already planned on proposing to her before the trouble with Mr Townsend had begun at the Dalverton's party. It was the misbehaviour of Mr Townsend and then actions by Lady Taltham, Miss Beatrice's mother, that had caused Charles to act publicly.

While Hugh understood that Lady Priscilla had most likely not known that Charles was his brother, he could not mistake the glee in which she shared the horrible details with yet another person. Hugh rather liked Miss Beatrice, and Lady Priscilla's characterization of her and the events was not to his liking at all.

Hugh walked Lady Priscilla over to the other young ladies that she had been talking with earlier. He bowed slightly. "Thank you, Lady Priscilla."

"Thank you, Mr Repington," she replied demurely.

"Good evening," he said to her and nodded to the other ladies, ignoring the pout that was forming on her pretty face. He smiled again and then walked away wondering whether Lady Priscilla was as perfect as he had originally thought.

CHAPTER EIGHT

"Lady Julianna, are you enjoying yourself?"

"Yes, very much."

Lady Amelia stepped closer. "I felt I must ask, as you appear to be somewhat disconcerted."

"I cannot believe this is the last night of the house party," Julianna lamented.

"Neither can I," Lady Amelia shook her head. "It is going to seem very quiet after everyone is gone."

"I would imagine so." Julianna looked around the ballroom try to envision it empty, all the people having gone home. She could picture it but it did not seem right.

"It will be strange to return to London."

"I shall be returning in another week as well." Lady Amelia told her. "I hope to see you at Almack's and the other parties."

Julianna smiled. "I hope so too. Perhaps we could go riding at Hyde Park as well."

"Yes, that is a wonderful idea," Lady Amelia agreed happily, clapping her hands together.

"I saw that you were dancing with Lord Norsely earlier." Lady

Amelia looked across the dance floor where Lord Norsely stood talking to two other gentlemen. "You do make a striking pair."

"Thank you," Julianna said with a smile, though she was only trying to be polite.

Lord Norsely had proven to be every bit of the perfect gentleman he had been rumoured to be. He was charming, handsome, fashionable, popular, and responsible. He came from a highly revered family, as his father, the Earl of Marlsfeld, was well respected in London society and in Parliament. As she had been advised on many occasions, a match between them would be quite favourable.

Julianna knew all of this and yet she still found herself uncertain about Lord Norsely. There had, as of yet, been no mention of a courtship and for that Julianna was immensely grateful. She was very unsure of her feelings toward him which made her feel like a silly schoolgirl as there was no real reason for her hesitance. Lord Norsely had been very nice and solicitous toward her at every meeting since their introduction at the beginning of the house party. But the niggling worry about him remained.

Julianna sighed. "Yes, we have danced twice tonight."

"And yet you look distressed," Lady Amelia commented.

With a practiced smile, Julianna turned to her friend. "No, I have much enjoyed it..." She trailed off when Lady Amelia gave her a knowing look. "Now, now. I am not distressed."

"Has Lord Norsely done anything untoward?" Lady Amelia's voice became sharp as she glanced across the room at him again.

Julianna was sure that Lady Amelia was recalling the distressing behaviour of Mr Townsend, Lord Norsely's brother. "Goodness, no. He has been very gracious and kind."

"Then what is wrong?" She tilted her head and knitted her brow. "Tell me."

"I really do not know. He is very nice but our time together is fraught with awkward silences. And to be perfectly honest I do not find myself looking forward to seeing him again when we part."

"Hmm, that does not sound very promising." Lady Amelia

opened her fan and fluttered it as she thought. "Perhaps if you could find some common interest with him."

"That would be extremely nice although he seems to only talk about parties and the latest whims of London society. I like pretty dresses but I am not so concerned with the latest fashions as to speak of nothing else."

Lady Amelia nodded and then snapped her fan closed. "I heard Timothy speaking to Father last night about Lord Norsely's carriage."

"His carriage?"

"Yes, he just recently acquired a new curricle. Timothy said that he is rather proud of it and his new horses."

"Perhaps," Julianna said slowly. "I rather like the idea of having something to speak about."

She looked across the room just as Lord Norsely looked up. He smiled at her and she smiled only to look away soon after.

"I believe he is coming over to speak with you," Lady Amelia said quietly. "We shall act as though we have not noticed."

Julianne opened her fan and fluttered it in front of her face. "I do not know what you are talking about."

Lady Amelia laughed softly next to her.

"Good evening, Lady Julianna," Lord Norsely said coming up to her. "Good evening, Lady Amelia."

"Good evening, Lord Norsely."

"Would you like to get a refreshment and take a walk in the garden with me?"

Julianna could feel Lady Amelia next to her urging her to accept his invitation. After letting him wait a short little while, Julianna deigned to reply. "Yes, that would be rather nice."

"Thank you," he said and offered her his arm. "Please excuse us, Lady Amelia."

"Yes, of course," she replied, giving Julianna an encouraging smile.

Lord Norsely led her from the ballroom smiling and nodding at others as they passed and Lady Julianna began reminding herself of his many good points.

The dining room was rather crowded so Lord Norsely left her near the door with the promise to return shortly with a glass of punch.

She saw Lady Priscilla come out of the dining room with Lady Sarah and several other ladies. Lady Priscilla caught sight of Julianna and whispered something to Lady Sarah. They both looked back over to her and then laughed. Annoyed with their behaviour, Julianna started laughing and then covered her mouth as if trying to hide the fact that she was laughing from them. Lady Priscilla's brow furrowed in confusion and the smile left her face. She quickly looked down at her dress and then suddenly hurried down the hallway with Lady Sarah and the others following quickly behind.

Julianna chuckled to herself and then remembered seeing Mr Repington with Lady Priscilla earlier. He had not looked very happy and as she heard Lord Norsely talking in the dining room she realized that she felt the same way.

Lord Norsely brought her a cup of punch. "There you go."

"Thank you, "

They stood silently for a moment and Julianna let out a long breath searching for a way to start a conversation. "Will you be traveling back to London with Lord and Lady Marsfeld in the next few days?"

"We are all leaving tomorrow afternoon, but my parents will be traveling in their coach. I will be returning in my curricle."

"You have a curricle? Oh, how wonderful," Julianna said trying not to cringe at how she sounded.

"Yes, it is a rather new acquisition," Lord Norsely said proudly.

Pleased that they were finally conversing added, "Oh yes, I did hear about that in the garden earlier this week."

"Oh? You heard?" He raised an eyebrow and turned his head to look at her.

"Yes, I heard that your new curricle is all the crack."

Lord Norsely puffed up at the compliment. "That is quite true. It is the newest and latest design and my new horses are a prime bit of blood."

"Do you ride often?"

"No, I do not," he said dismissively and then seemed to realize how he sounded. He hurried on to explain his reasoning. "While I appreciate the majesty of the horses that pull my curricle, I've no desire to spend time in a dirty stable or dealing with commanding such unexceptional creatures."

Julianna immediately thought of the young foals that lived with the mares in the stable. She yearned to stomp on his foot and retreat from the dining room. How dare he say that those sweet creatures were unexceptional!

"Lady Julianna, are you well?"

"Yes, why do you ask?" She said looking away, her voice cool.

"You just had the most peculiar look on your face. Are you sure that you are well?"

Given a second opportunity to answer the question Julianna shook her head. "I am afraid that I have come down with a headache. If you will excuse me, I believe I shall go for a rest."

"Yes, of course," he replied. "Are you sure you will be all right on your own?"

"Yes, thank you, Lord Norsely," Julianna set the glass of punch on the table. "Good evening."

She left the dining room and instead of turning down the hall that would take her up the stairs to her room, Julianna went the other way and made her way out into the garden.

Realizing that she might be discovered by Lord Norsely if he happened to continue with his plan to walk in the garden, she slipped into one of the smaller side gardens, stopping suddenly when she saw that she was not alone. Mr Repington was standing near a stone pillar. A lantern hung from near the top illuminating the small area of the garden.

"Oh, pardon me," she muttered and turned back toward the gate.

He turned as if noticing her for the first time. "Do not leave on my account. I only stepped out to enjoy some fresh air. And a sliver of silence."

"That is my aim as well."

"I invite you to join me," he said.

She paused looking back toward the house. They were fairly out in the open but she still wondered about anyone discovering them alone in the garden.

He pointed to a bench on the other side of a large stone planter. "Perhaps you could sit there and I will sit on the bench over there. If anyone were to come upon us there would no reason for them to think anything untoward."

She contemplated his idea briefly before deciding that some peace and quiet was worth the risk. "Yes, I believe that would be agreeable." Julianna moved to the bench and sat down.

They sat there in silence for a few minutes until Julianna spoke up. "It is quite lovely out."

"It is, indeed," Mr Repington agreed. "I only wish that we had a closer view of the stables."

Julianna laughed softly. "Oh, Mr Repington, I was wishing the very same thing."

CHAPTER NINE

Hugh sat at the large desk in his residence in London wishing he was back at Eastbridge. It had been nearly a week since he had left the house party and had done little in regards to the next step in his profession as a barrister.

He had gone to Eastbridge hoping to take some time to contemplate what he wanted to do upon his return to London. Unfortunately, he had spent far too much time enjoying the house party and too little time thinking about being a barrister. All Hugh knew was that he would be much happier if he were back riding a horse through the trees and meadows near Eastbridge. Or at least out in the countryside somewhere.

When he had returned to from the house party, Hugh had found that he had received several letters in his absence regarding his selection as a barrister. He only needed to decide whether he wanted to accept a government appointment or present cases brought to him by solicitors. It should not have been a difficult decision.

Hugh suspected that his hesitance was borne of the knowledge that his father and brother would be involved, no matter which direction he chose. However, he did not want to spite himself in his attempt to distance himself from the interference of his family.

Hugh picked up one of the letters. Lord Fairburn had written to make him aware that a government position was available. Fairburn had requested that Hugh pay him a visit at Parliament by the end of the week. It was already Wednesday, so he would need to arrange a visit the next day as he did not want to offend Lord Fairburn. Surely, it would do no harm to talk to the man.

Hugh's thoughts were interrupted by the sound of knocking on his door. He had no idea who could be calling as he did not get many visitors. From the insistent knocking. Hugh discerned that it was most likely the delivery of another letter.

Hugh opened the door.

"Good afternoon, Hugh."

Hugh stood stock still for several moments somewhat shocked to find not the delivery boy that he had expected, but his father, the Duke of Castborough, standing tall at his doorstep. "Good afternoon, Father. Please come in."

"I apologize for not letting you know that I would be arriving." The duke smiled, though Hugh could tell he was not really sorry for dropping in unannounced. Hugh knew that his father wanted to catch him unawares. While Hugh knew to be wary, he did not know what his father was about quite yet.

Hugh followed his father into the small drawing room.

"I had forgotten how small this house is." Looking around with amusement, the duke steepled his fingers together and then took a seat near the window. Clearly, he was biding his time with small talk until he was ready to share his reason for being there.

Hugh smiled. "It is not that small. It certainly serves its purpose. I am very thankful for it."

"Yes, yes. Of course, you are." His father leaned back in the chair setting his hands on the arms of the chair, looking regal and stately. "I am glad that it served you well, and I am sure that you are looking forward to moving back into Repington House."

"Moving back?" Hugh repeated.

"Well, yes. You cannot be thinking of staying here when you could be living at Grosvenor Square," his father looked at him as though Hugh had clearly not thought the idea completely through. "If you are to be a barrister you should not be living in such a small house on the outskirts of London. Living in Mayfair will certainly play to your favour."

Hugh knew that he was right but hated that he had to concede to his father's interference.

"Yes, of course, Father. I had not thought of it that way. Once I have my affairs in order here, I will consider moving back. Thank you."

"Do not thank me yet. I have much to tell you." Hugh realized that they were about to get to the true reason for his visit.

"Oh?" Hugh asked calmly.

"Yes, while you were gone at your little house party," the duke paused and Hugh endeavoured to ignore his father's clear disdain for his sojourn. "I had some nice conversations with some other members of Parliament."

Hugh closed his eyes briefly, hoping he was wrong about what his father meant. He nodded and said, "That is good. Have you and Wellington finally come to an agreement?"

"No, that old goat is the most stubborn man in all of England," his father grumbled. He looked to go on but suddenly stopped, giving Hugh a sharp look. " But as I was saying, in your absence, I spoke with many in Parliament. Lord Fairburn was rather forthright. There is a government position open and Fairburn is very interested in speaking with you about it."

Hugh wanted to yell at his father but he tempered his words. "Father, thank you but I assure you it was unnecessary of you to talk to anyone on my behalf."

"But—" The duke continued his thought, but Hugh would not allow him to go on.

"I have not made any decisions regarding my profession," Hugh told him. "As soon as I do though, I will be most happy to let you know."

His father sat stoic and quiet for what seemed an interminable length of time but most likely only truly amounted to a few moments. Finally, he looked up. "There is one other matter that I came to discuss, namely your courtship with Lady Priscilla."

"There is no courtship, not with Lady Priscilla nor any other young lady." Hugh smiled wanly. "There is much time left in the Season for that."

"I understand that you have only just been introduced but I believe that you and she would make a favourable match."

Hugh took a deep breath set on arguing with his father but it became quite clear he did not trust himself to stay civil. Instead, he stood up looking at his watch. "My word! I did not realize that it was so late. Thank you so much for stopping by to deliver the news."

His father did not move although he did appear somewhat confused. It was likely the fact that he was not used to being dismissed.

Hugh tried to look as apologetic as possible. "My apologies but I must get ready for my evening out."

"Are you attending Almack's this evening?"

Hugh had not thought about what night it was but his father was quite correct Almack's would be in full swing. "Yes, now that I am back in London and my studies are complete, it is time for me to enjoy the social events of the Season."

His father finally stood up and began to follow Hugh out. "I am glad you will be there. Your sister and brother will be there, as well."

"How fortuitous," Hugh said with a smile. "I am looking forward to seeing them."

Hugh ushered his father out the front door, groaning as he did so. He had had no intention of going to Almack's but would now have to attend. Henrietta would surely tell their mother and father that he was not in attendance.

"Lawks!" He kicked a table leg that was the closest to him and stalked out of the room to get dressed.

CHAPTER TEN

Julianna let out an exasperated sigh. "Mother, if you do not stop fussing, those gossips you are so concerned about will surely notice and begin to fabricate a story to explain your nervousness."

Her mother's hands immediately dropped to her sides. "You are right. I am just so nervous about tonight."

"I do not understand what has made you so uneasy." Julianna stood quietly next to her mother. "We have been to Almack's several times already this Season."

"Yes, but we have been away from London for a time and you never know when a new scandal has appeared, fabricated or not."

Julianna tilted her head slightly, amazed her mother would worry over events that had not even happened. Indeed, events that would probably never happen. "While it is true that one can never tell when the gossips will be talking, I am not sure I understand why that makes you anxious."

Her mother began to wring her hands again. "I worry over what the gossips may have said in our absence. I would hate for Lord Norsely to believe something that is not true."

"Do not be concerned about Lord Norsely. Anything the gossips may have said in our absence he would know to be a lie as he was at the same house party that we were."

Her mother nodded. "Of course, you are right but still it has been a week since we have returned to London and you have heard nothing from Lord Norsley." Her mother began to glance nervously around the large ballroom.

Julianna sighed. "It is true that we have not heard from Lord Norsley but that means nothing."

Her mother turned back to her with a shake of her head.

Julianna held up a gloved hand. "We do not even know whether he has arrived back in London. There are other house parties being held. We were invited to the party held by Lord Cullingham and while we declined the invitation in order to come back to London, it is entirely possible that Lord Norsley did go to the party."

Julianna was not concerned about Lord Norsley, after all, they had only returned to London a week ago. Perhaps if they had been back for a longer period of time she would have been worried although that was unlikely as well. Not that she did not want to see Lord Norsley again. She only hoped their meetings would be less uncomfortable now that they had returned to London.

"Oh look! It is Lady Eastbridge. Perhaps I shall go speak to her," her mother said sounding hopeful.

"Yes, that would be wonderful," Julianna replied glad that her mother was starting to calm herself.

"I can ask Lady Eastbridge if she has heard anything."

Julianna stifled the urge to roll her eyes, but better Lady Eastbridge abide her mother. "Perhaps some conversation will help to ease your mind."

Her mother nodded and they began to move through the crowd. As they grew closer to Lady Eastbridge, Julianna saw that Lady Amelia was nearby speaking with Lady Henrietta. Before Julianna could even react to seeing her friend, Lady Amelia was beckoning her to join them.

"Lady Julianna! I am so glad you are here. I was hoping to see you." Lady Amelia smiled. "Have you met Lady Henrietta?"

Julianna smiled at the other girl. "Yes, although we have only spoken a few times."

Lady Henrietta nodded. "Lady Julianna had the pleasure of being at Lady Sarah's recital a few weeks ago."

Julianna's eyes widened briefly as she recalled the horrible screeching and equally abysmal piano forte music that accompanied it. "I will admit to being at the recital, and I could say many things but as I endeavour to be polite, I will only say that it was not very pleasing at all."

Lady Amelia began to laugh and covered her mouth as her mother turned quickly with a stern look. "You are teasing me. Surely it was not as bad as that." She glanced at Lady Henrietta. "Was it?"

Lady Henrietta grimaced. "Honestly, Lady Julianna was being rather kind. I think my brother described it as sounding as though a half-foxed parrot was playing the pianoforte while several cats fought over a bucket of fish."

Julianna nodded in agreement as Lady Amelia said, "Oh goodness, that is terrible."

"Yes, it truly was," Lady Henrietta agreed.

"And completely accurate," Julianna said and they all laughed.

"Oh Heavens!" Lady Henrietta suddenly exclaimed.

"Lady Henrietta, are you all right?"

"Oh! Yes, my apologies. I just saw my brother walk in. I had no idea that he planned on attending." She looked rather astonished. "I do not think he has been to more than a few events all Season."

"Really?"

"Yes, he has been studying with the Inns of Court. He has recently been chosen to be a barrister."

"That is wonderful," Lady Amelia said.

Julianna nodded, suddenly distracted as she saw Mr Repington moving through the people gathered around the ballroom. While she had thought of him often since leaving Eastbridge Julianna had not thought that she would see him in London. She turned back to the others not wanting to get caught staring but found herself checking his progress as he walked through the ballroom.

She was quite surprised when he stopped at their small group and even more so when Lady Henrietta threw her arms around his neck.

"Hugh! I did not know that you would be here. I simply cannot believe you are here!"

Mr Repington grinned down at her and Julianna ignored the emotions that suddenly welled within her.

"It was a last-minute decision. Father told me you would be here."

"Father?" Lady Henrietta asked clearly confused.

He shifted on his feet slightly. "Yes, he stopped by my residence late this afternoon."

"Oh, I am sorry, dear brother." She patted his arm sympathetically.

Julianna feeling suddenly silly that she had not known that Mr Repington and Lady Henrietta were siblings.

Mr Repington laughed. "It was not all bad. I am seeing you, now that I am here."

"Yes, you are," Lady Henrietta said with a laugh of her own. He glanced over at Lady Amelia and Lady Julianna. "Good evening ladies," Mr Repington said.

"Good evening," Lady Amelia replied first.

"Good evening, are you enjoying being back in London?"

"Yes," he said and then paused as if he had spoken too soon. "Although I do miss the morning rides at Eastbridge."

"As do I," Lady Julianna agreed happily.

Lady Henrietta looked from one to another confused again. "You know each other? How? When did you meet?"

Mr Repington patted his sister's hand. "Lady Julianna and I were introduced by Lady Amelia at the Eastbridge House party. We saw each other in passing most mornings at the stables."

Lady Henrietta nodded looking at her brother oddly. "I heard

James saying that you had gone to a house party but thought he was being humorous. I am glad that you are enjoying yourself."

"Repington! I wondered if you would be here this evening." Mr Sedgwick appeared from the crowd. "It seems you have found everyone as well."

"Timothy, how do you always end up getting here so much later when our carriages left the house at the same time?" Lady Amelia asked shaking her head sadly.

"Dear sister, it is not that I got here later," Mr Sedgwick said with a mischievous grin. "I simply had more people to say hello to as I moved through the room."

Lady Amelia rolled her eyes at her brother. "Yes, I am quite sure that the dowagers were more than happy to see you."

Lady Julianna laughed as Mr Sedgwick gasped in mock surprise, then nearly jumped as someone spoke beside her.

"Good evening."

It was Jonathan Webb, he had been so quiet that Julianna had not even known that he had walked up. "Good evening, Mr Webb."

He nodded but he was looking beyond her. "Good evening, Lady Amelia."

"Good evening," she replied her face flushing slightly.

The music began to play once more. "Would you like to dance?"

"Yes, thank you." She took his arm and they moved to the center of the room.

Then Lady Henrietta looked surprised as Mr Sedgwick stopped in front of her and gave her a little bow and said, "Lady Henrietta, may I have this dance?"

Julianna stifled a laugh as Lady Henrietta looked very caught off guard by Mr Sedgwick but she recovered quickly saying, "Thank you, Mr Sedgwick. That sounds lovely."

Julianna found yourself standing alone with Mr Repington and did not know quite what to do with herself.

He stood still there in silence for a moment and then Julianna heard a sharp cracking sound. Mr Repington turned away quickly and Julianna suddenly remembered that she had seen Lady Ramsbury sitting close by.

Lady Ramsbury was pointing her fan at Mr Repington. "I thought you were raised to be a gentleman."

Mr Repington rubbed his arm but seemed at ease with talking to the older woman. "I certainly was raised to be a gentleman."

Lady Ramsbury pointed her fan at Julianna. "Then why have you not asked the young lady to dance?"

Julianna panic. "Oh, no, I am fine. I... will just go over there and..." Julianna pointed off behind Lady Ramsbury vaguely and took a step away.

He grabbed her gloved hand gently as she turned to leave. "Lady Julianna, please wait."

"Pardon me, Lady Ramsbury, but I was about to do just that when you interrupted."

Lady Ramsbury huffed at him but said no more.

Mr Repington turned back to Julianna. "Would you please honour me with this dance?"

Julianna shook her head. "You do not need to do that." She stepped away clasping her hands in front of her trying to make the tingling where he had touched her hand lessen.

"You are quite right. I do not have to ask you to dance. I want to." Mr Repington took a step forward. "Lady Ramsbury may have spoken first but I truly was going to ask you to dance."

Julianna hesitated, she wanted to walk away fearing that he was being forced into dancing with her. The thought of dancing with him thrilled her but the thought that he was only doing so because of Lady Ramsbury's interference was most distressful. She looked up to tell him no and he looked so earnest that she found herself nodding.

He offered her his arm and she took it without saying a word. Julianna tried to focus on dancing and not on how she was feeling. The hand he had held so gently before still tingled beneath her glove, her stomach fluttered and her heart was beating faster.

Before she knew it, the dance was over and they were leaving the center of the ballroom. Julianna hoped that her feelings had not been evident during the dance. Once they had stopped on the edge of the ballroom she turned to Mr Repington.

"Thank you, I—" She broke off when she saw his face. He seemed as affected as she was and as shocked by it as well.

He bowed. "Thank you. Good evening," he said and swiftly walked away.

Julianna stood there for a moment and watched him disappear into the crowd. She finally shifted glancing around in hopes of seeing Lady Amelia or Lady Henrietta. Her eyes landed on Lady Ramsbury who sat smiling at her as though she had known what would happen all the time.

Thoroughly shocked she spun on her heel wanting nothing than to be out of the crowded ballroom. She had barely taken two steps when she ran headlong into someone that had stepped into her path.

"Lady Julianna, good evening."

Lady Julianna looked up to see Lord Norsely standing before her.

"Good evening," she said hoping her smile appeared bright and not panicked as she well and truly felt. "I was not aware you were here, Lord Norsely."

"I was hoping to see you here tonight," he told her. "Would honour me with the next dance."

"Oh, I…" Julianna began to decline but saw her mother standing not far away with an excited smile on her face. Julianna sighed inwardly. "Yes, thank you."

He led her to join the other couples. Lord Norsely was a fine dancer and she followed him through the dance easily. She should have been happy but all she could think of was that she felt nothing like what she felt dancing with Hugh Repington.

"Are you all right, Lady Julianna?" Lord Norsely asked her, his face concerned.

"I think I would like to sit down for a few moments," she told him already turning toward one of the doors out of the ballroom.

"Certainly," Lord Norsely took her arm and guided her through the great number of people that had come to Almack's.

Across the room, she watched as Mr Repington led Lady Priscilla out for the next dance. She felt a sadness she did not expect. Not wanting to dwell on her sadness, Julianna she looked to Lord Norsely.

"Thank you. I think some fresh air would help me immensely."

CHAPTER ELEVEN

"Good morning," Julianna's mother fairly sang as she breezed into the drawing room.

"Good morning, Mother."

Julianna knew her mother was about to cut up her peace when sat down on the settee instead of taking her usual chair. Julianna kept her eyes on her needlework hoping that her mother would leave her in silence. From the look on her mother's face when she first came into the room, Julianna suspected that it was not to be.

Her mother had done nothing but talk about Julianna's night at Almack's and how happy she was that the night had gone so well. Julianna, on the other hand, had done everything she could to keep busy and not think about her night at Almack's. In the few days since, she had read two books and spent many hours working on her embroidery.

While her mother was overjoyed that Lord Norsely had paid Julianna so much attention she could not stop thinking about Hugh Repington. Her reaction to him during their dance was so unexpected and foreign that she had no idea what to do with herself.

In her two Seasons, she had been to a multitude of parties and balls. She had danced with many different gentlemen and had never felt anything other than the exhilaration of dancing around the ballroom. Dancing with Mr Repington had been so different, every time she thought about their dance she felt the same flutter in her stomach.

Her mother sat quietly for a few minutes and when Julianna did not say anything she sighed and said, "You must be so looking forward to going to Almack's again."

Julianna leaned forward as if she were intent on her needlework, slowly guiding the needle through and pulling the thread taut until it laid straight. She could feel her mother looking at her, clearly waiting for her response.

"Yes, it is always good to be at Almack's," she said still not looking from her embroidery.

"I am sure you will have another wonderful night."

Julianna was saved from having to respond when the door to the drawing room opened.

"Excuse me, Lady Alverston, Lady Julianna, this letter was just delivered." Bernard came into the room holding an envelope.

"Thank you, Bernard," her mother said taking the envelope. "Oh, it is for you, Julianna."

Bernard nodded at them and left the drawing room.

Instead of handing the envelope to Julianna her mother turned it over. "I wonder who it is from."

"Perhaps if I could read it we would find out," Julianna suggested.

To her utter surprise, her mother opened the envelope and took out a folded sheet of paper.

"It is from Lord Norsely. He has invited you to attend the opera with him and both his parents this evening. How wonderful!" Her mother stood up from the settee, in excitement.

"This evening?" Julianna turned back to her needlework. "That is certainly short notice. I am sure they will understand that I must decline the invitation."

"Decline?" Her mother asked, her face a mask of confusion in horror. "You cannot decline such a generous invitation. What in the world would Lady Marsfeld think?"

"Is it possible that she would think that I had a prior engagement," Julianna posed. She should not have been surprised that her mother was being unreasonable.

"That may well be but you will be accepting the invitation. Your father has made it very clear that a match with Lord Norsely would be quite favourable for both families." Her mother took the envelope and opened the door to the drawing room calling out, "Bernard, I need to send a letter."

CHAPTER TWELVE

Many hours and many conversations with her mother later, Julianna looked out the window of the carriage as it pulled up in front of the London opera house. After waiting in a long carriage line filled with London's social elite, the carriage door opened and the footman helped her down from the carriage.

"Thank you," Julianna said to him. The man smiled briefly and then looked away before moving on to help the others step out.

Lord Norsely moved up beside her and took her arm. "You do not need to thank him. He is only a servant."

Julianna looked up at Lord Norsely surprised and ready to comment but he failed to notice as he was already looking at the other people waiting to get into the opera house.

As she and Lord Norsely entered the opera house, Julianna looked around, not only at the many people there but at the lobby of the opera house itself. It was beautifully decorated with ornate carvings and lush fabrics. She had been to many performances at the opera house and always admired the opulence of the lobby and gallery.

"The opera house is rather beautiful. I am so glad that you accepted my invitation so you could see it."

As politely as possible Julianna said, "I am very appreciative that you invited me tonight, but I have been to several operas here."

"Then why are you looking around as though you are a simpleton?" His voice was sharp as he smiled at another couple in the lobby.

Julianna sucked in a breath, shocked at his bold, rude rebuke. She longed to comment on his behaviour, but she attempted to be gracious as she reminded herself that Lord Norsely's family had just rid themselves of a family scandal. Lord Norsely knew that the gossips were watching, ready to jump on any misstep, it was understandable that he would be somewhat anxious for everything to go well.

Playing her part, she smiled and greeted people graciously as she and Lord Norsely followed Lord and Lady Marsfeld to their seats. She attempted to hide her surprise when they stopped at one of the private boxes.

Lord Norsely smiled. "This is our box. My father rented it for the entirety of the Season."

It had not been unknown to Julianna as she had seen Lord and Lady Marsfeld in attendance on the nights she had attended previously. She simply had not realized that she and Lord Norsely would be sitting with them. Her only reply was to simply nod as all previous attempts at conversation had been met with what seemed like disdain.

If she were entirely honest she was not pleased that he was bragging to her about having a private box. Her father was the Marquis of Alverson. Her parents had a private box for the theater and had done so for several seasons. If her father had liked opera she was more than sure that they would have had a private box for the opera as well. There was certainly enough money in the coffers to cover both.

Julianna and her father had discussed the merits of opera several times. While her father enjoyed the music and songs of the performance he did not appreciate the exaggerated expressions and movements of the actors. He felt it too comical and took much away from the story.

If Lord Norsely noticed Julianna's silence he did not let on and seemed content to converse with Lord and Lady Marsfeld while she sat quietly next to him. She began counting the candles in the elaborate chandeliers that hung over the many seats below to pass the time. Julianna was much relieved when the music began to play signaling the beginning of the performance.

She was happy to ignore Lord Norsely and watch the actors on stage.

"Are you enjoying yourself?" Lord Norsely had deemed to talk to her between the first and second acts.

"Yes. It is quite magnificent."

"And you are able to follow what the actors are saying and doing?"

Julianna hoped he was attempting to be humorous but from the look on his face, he was rather serious. "Yes, thank you." The opera was being performed in English and while her father would complain about the actors, following the songs or the story had not been difficult.

"Ah, good. I was worried that you had gotten lost a bit in the middle there."

Julianna stifled a groan, smiled sweetly and went back to counting candles until the next act began.

When the fifth and final act began Julianna sighed in relief. Sitting quietly in the private box was starting to make her feel annoyed and skittish. She sought to keep herself busy by paying specific attention to the actors on the stage. Making a game of it, she began to watch only a single actor as he moved about the stage. The act was nearly over and as the actor sang, a second actor walked slowly and hunched over behind him to slay him with a sword.

The stabbed actor continued to sing as he made the most awful faces and as the music raised to its crescendo the actor fell to the ground rolling and writhing in the most ridiculously exaggerated death portrayal imaginable. Before she could stop herself, a laugh escaped her mouth just as the music came to a sudden stop. Her laughter rang through the opera house and every head turned to look to see who had made the disturbance.

CHAPTER THIRTEEN

"Your father spoke to Fairburn?" Sedgwick asked leaning back in his chair.

"Yes, he had his conversations while I was gone to my house party as though I had gone to the house party on a lark."

He shook his head and took a sip of his port. They were at a dinner party hosted by Lord and Lady Alderside for Lady Sarah. The dining completed, he and Sedgwick were enjoying a glass of port in the dining room with the other gentlemen.

It had ended up being a larger crowd than the usual numbers for a dinner party but it had gone well. Lady Priscilla was also in attendance but had been seated with Lady Sarah and another friend, Miss Danielle Something-or-other at the other end of the table. Several times Lady Priscilla had smiled at him shyly and then turned to her friends with giddy laughter. Hugh was flattered by the attention but still somewhat grateful that she was sitting at the other end of the table.

"Did you still pay a visit to Fairburn?" Sedgwick put his empty glass onto the table.

"Yes, it was not as though I had another option. I cannot afford to offend Fairburn."

"I am in complete agreement. It does you no good to spite yourself because of the actions of your father." Sedgwick then asked, "What did Fairburn have to say?"

Hugh sighed and glanced behind him to make sure that the other gentlemen in the room were paying no attention to them or their conversation. "There is a position for which Fairburn will appoint. The barrister chosen would be working with a certain member of Parliament that has little understanding of law and procedure. The chosen barrister would provide assistance to the Peer in subject matters that will be discussed in Parliament."

"How odd," Sedgwick commented. "Depending on the Peer, it could be a favourable appointment or…"

"Or complete Fustian nonsense." Hugh finished the sentence for him with a deep frown. "Regardless of the work I would be doing, it would be wise for me to take the appointment. I would not be tethered to that position forever."

"True, true," Sedgwick agreed. "You are leaning toward taking it then?"

"No. I am no closer to making a decision." Hugh blew out a long breath. "Although I have little desire to take a position that was offered to me only because my father interfered."

"If you did not take the position what would be the alternative?"

"I would present cases brought to me by solicitors but—"

He was interrupted when the door opened and a servant appeared to announce, "Excuse me, gentlemen, tea is being served in the drawing room."

Hugh, Sedgwick and the other men left the dining room to walk down the hall and join the ladies for tea and polite conversation.

Sedgwick chose a large upholstered chair close to the settee and Hugh gladly took the chair next to his. It was only after he was seated that he realized that Lady Priscilla and her friends were missing from the drawing room. A short time later they returned and took their seats on the settee.

THE BARRISTER'S CHOICE

The ladies had already been speaking when they sat down. Hugh and Lady Priscilla shared a smile while Lady Sarah continued with her story.

"I would not have believed it myself but I heard it straight from Miss Louisa."

Hugh turned to engage Sedgwick but Webb had pulled him into a conversation across the room.

"Well, do tell what happened." Miss Priscilla leaned forward excitedly.

"It seems that Lady Esther encountered Mr Russell and Miss Clara alone speaking in one of the back hallways," Lady Sarah told them.

Miss Danielle leaned toward Lady Sarah to say, "Miss Clara is thoroughly compromised. Mr Russell will have no choice but to marry her."

"From what I understand Miss Clara has argued that she had gotten lost and Mr Russell had come upon her and was only helping her find her way back to the ballroom." Lady Sarah raised an eyebrow and continued. "My mother said that if the Banns are not posted in the next two weeks then it is likely that Mr Russell has refused to marry Miss Clara."

"Oh my," Lady Priscilla gasped. "She shall never recover."

Lady Sarah smiled. "It is not as though she would have done any better than that dull Mr Russell. Her dresses this Season are abominable."

Hugh tried to think of something to say to the young ladies that might change the subject, before he could say anything though Lady Priscilla suddenly blurted out, "Oh! I cannot believe that I almost forgot to tell you."

She paused dramatically as she was assured that everyone within earshot was listening. "As you both know, my parents have rented a private box for the Opera for the entirety of the Season."

Lady Sarah nodded. "Yes, of course. Your father always ensures you are in the highest of fashion."

Lady Priscilla glanced over at Hugh making sure to catch his eye seemingly to make sure that he was listening. "Well their last performance of the Season was just last week and I was there of course."

"Of course," Miss Danielle said dutifully.

"But you would not believe what happened at the end of the performance," Lady Priscilla said and then paused again waiting for a reaction.

Lady Sarah leaned forward apparently waiting to hear the juicy tidbits of Lady Priscilla's story.

Hugh wished that Webb would go away so that he could speak with Sedgwick and not have to listen to more silly gossip.

"The performance was quite wonderful as you may imagine. But for some reason as the final scene played out someone in the opera house was laughing. Out loud. Everyone could hear it."

Missed Danielle frowned. "Laughing? Why ever for?"

"Clearly some uncultured heathen had gotten into the opera house," Lady Sarah said with a very unladylike snort.

"It was quite the upset. Everyone could see that Lord Norsely, as well as Lord and Lady Marsfeld, were quite upset by the incident."

Lady Sarah put a hand to her chest. "Certainly, the person laughing was not laughing at Lord Norsely or Lord and Lady Marsfeld."

"Oh no. It was Lord Norsely's companion, that impertinent Lady Julianna Merchant."

"Oh goodness," Miss Danielle said.

Lady Sarah sniffed. "Well, I for one am not surprised. She has always seemed somewhat beneath our touch."

"Yes, as have I." Lady Priscilla shifted into her seat. "And I have even heard that she spends most of her days out in the stables with the horses."

Hugh had known that Miss Priscilla enjoyed gossiping and while it was annoying and disappointing when she had discussed his brother and Miss Beatrice he found himself rather angered that she would be talking about Lady Julianna. Suddenly he could take it no more, Hugh stood up causing both Sedgwick and Lady Priscilla to look over at him.

He bowed slightly towards the settee and said, "If you will excuse me."

Hugh nodded to Sedgwick and left the drawing room.

CHAPTER FOURTEEN

Hugh stared out the window feeling restless. He had gotten up early that morning intent on visiting the mews so that he could take an early morning ride in Hyde Park. He had awoken to gray skies and the sound of rain on the rooftop, causing him to forego the idea. If they had been at Eastbridge he would not have minded the rain but riding through the dirty streets of London even the short distance from the mews to Hyde Park was not something that he wanted to do.

The weather was not the only thing weighing on his mind that morning though. Hugh was highly annoyed that he allowed himself to react so poorly to Lady Priscilla's gossiping the night before. While he abhorred the tendency of London's social elite to delight in the misfortune of others, he well knew that it was normal behaviour all year but especially during the Season. It had been rude of him to stand up and leave so abruptly and he hoped he had not offended Lord and Lady Alderside.

Lady Priscilla had seemed quite astonished when he stood up to leave and he felt a pang of remorse for that. He had been angered and acted upon it but she most likely had no idea why he had left. It would be ridiculous of him to ruin his chances of a courtship with Lady Priscilla all because she was doing something everyone around was doing.

That thought suddenly causing him to sit up in his chair. Perhaps if he could spend some time with her without her companions he would be able to learn more about her. He selected a new piece of paper from his desk to write a note inviting Lady Priscilla to go riding with him in Hyde Park. Once he was done he put on his coat and left the house. He went directly to the family residence off Grosvenor Square directed Fletcher to deliver the invitation to Ridgewood Hall and then sought out his sister to ask for a favour.

"Henrietta, I cannot thank you enough for agreeing to come with me," Hugh was saying several hours later.

Henrietta shook her head and laughed. "I am glad that you asked me. I have not gone riding in weeks. I am rather looking forward to it."

"Are you not going to thank me profusely as well?" Matthew asked.

"No, not at all," Hugh told him. "I did not ask you to come, you invited yourself."

"And it was a good thing too," Matthew assured him. "Now we have an even number. Henrietta and I will be talking to each other which will make it much easier for you to talk to Lady Priscilla."

"I suppose you are correct," Hugh admitted, although begrudgingly.

"You suppose? You will not be alone with her but she will be forced to endure your sparkling personality." Matthew bowed theatrically. "You can thank me at the wedding."

Henrietta giggled while Hugh rolled his eyes and then turned around as they heard someone approaching.

Hugh was surprised to see a carriage appear around the corner. He thought his note had been rather clear that he wanted to ride horses even going insofar to direct her to indicate in her reply if she needed a horse to ride.

Before he could discuss it with either Henrietta or Matthew the carriage door was opened by one of the footmen and Lady Priscilla emerged looking beautiful and somewhat out of place on the riding trails of Hyde Park. She was wearing the most magnificent and elaborate riding habit he had ever seen. While the question of if she had understood his invitation had been cleared up he wondered if she would actually be able to alight a horse in the habit.

Behind him, he heard Matthew say quietly, "What on Earth is she wearing?"

Henrietta had hushed him whispering loudly, "I do not know but be quiet."

"Good afternoon, Mr Repington."

Hugh was about to ask about the carriage when one of the footmen led a chestnut horse out from behind the carriage. A second footman hurried out with a large wooden box setting it down next to the box. "Lady Priscilla, we are ready."

"Good," she said and moved toward them her riding habit fluttering behind her. The pricked its ears back briefly as she passed but the footman calmed the horse while the other footman helped Lady Priscilla to mount the horse. After several minutes of arranging and rearranging, Lady Priscilla was seated in her saddle and they set off with Matthew and Henrietta in the lead.

"Oh no," Lady Priscilla suddenly gasped.

"What is wrong?" Hugh asked looking over. As far he could see there was nothing amiss, both horses were moving along at the same pace and Lady Priscilla looked well seated in her saddle.

"Water is being splashed upon my riding habit," Lady Priscilla said as though her predicament was the same as rotten tomatoes being thrown at her.

"It is merely water, I..."

"No! Stop it!" She cried out and leaned over as if to brush something off of her skirt.

One of the fluttery pieces on her sleeve floated out over the horse's head which caused the horse to come to a sudden and complete stop. It happened so fast that Hugh could only watch as Lady Priscilla tried to sit up in time to grasp at the pommel but she had already left her seat when she stretched out her arm. A second later she landed flat on her back in a mud puddle that the horse had managed to avoid on the side of the trail.

Hugh scrambled off his horse amid screams from Lady Priscilla. "No! My riding habit!"

By the time Hugh got around his horse and hers she was sitting up and looked horrified. "I am covered in mud! What am I going to do?"

A moment later Henrietta hurried up beside him. "Oh dear, Lady Priscilla, are you unhurt?"

Henrietta was being very kind and caring but Hugh could tell she was trying not to smirk. He could not blame her. Lady Priscilla was quite the sight still sitting in the puddle of mud.

"Perhaps we could get you up out of the mud," Henrietta suggested, holding out her hand to help the other young lady up.

"No, do not touch me. I want to go home."

"I understand," Henrietta her voice soothing. "We will get you back on your horse and we will set off right..."

"No," Lady Priscilla said again. "I want to go home, now."

Henrietta stood up and stepped away, irritation showing clearly on her face.

"You..."

"Someone needs to fetch my carriage straight away." Lady Priscilla gave a stern look from her place on the ground.

"I would be happy to," Matthew offered, the only one among them still seated on a horse.

For a moment, Hugh wanted to say he would go but he realized it had more to do with not wanting to wait with Lady Priscilla for the carriage. He only wanted to be away from her.

"Are you sure you do not want me to help you out of the mud? There is a tree stump right here that you could sit on to wait," Hugh offered.

"No. Please just leave me alone."

Hugh did as she asked stepping back across the trail where Henrietta had tied up the horses.

"Well, this went rather well," Henrietta told him.

"Is it quite unladylike to be sarcastic," Hugh said lightly.

"Did you really expect it to go better?"

"I had hoped so, yes." He shook his head and then smiled. "At least I know this will not be spread about London." It was unlikely that she would spread gossip about herself.

"Oh, I am sure some version of it will be spread about," Henrietta looked across the trail at the petulant young lady in the mud. "Only the version that you will hear about will be quite different. Unfortunately, Lady Priscilla will the only person that will not be blamed for her predicament."

"Yes, you are most likely in the right." Hugh nodded and sighed.

CHAPTER FIFTEEN

"It is your move, Lady Julianna," Miss Diana said.

Julianna looked up to see you both miss Diana and Lady Amelia looking at her. "I am sorry I cannot seem to concentrate."

She had accepted the invitation to the card party hoping to have an enjoyable evening. It had not occurred to her that Lord Norsely might be in attendance. Since the incident at the opera, she had not exactly been avoiding him but she had not sought him out either. She felt fortunate that she had not seen him at any of the social events she had attended in the last week. He had already been involved in a card game when she entered the room so she was unsure if he even knew that she had arrived. Of course, she had taken care to bring as little notice to herself as possible.

"Are you all right?" Lady Amelia asked.

"Yes, "Julianna said with a sigh.

"Are you upset because Lord Norsely has not said hello?"

Julianna shook her head. "No, that is fine."

Julianna sincerely did not mind that Lord Norsely had not come over to greet to her.

It had been hard for her to not think about what it happened at the opera. Lord Norsely had been so upset with her that evening.

She had not meant to make him angry and she had not meant to laugh at all, for that matter. He had immediately been offended and told her and no uncertain terms that she had embarrassed him. He had curtly added that it was not likely that he would take her to the opera again anytime soon.

Of course, her thought had been that it was unlikely she would want to attend the opera with him anytime soon, but she decided it would be improper to share that thought with him. He had been so angry with her that he had left her to ride in the carriage back with his parents.

Julianna had not minded that so much as his mother was quite tickled, she had also found the death of the main character quite amusing at the end of the fifth act.

And while she did not care to actively search out Lord Norsely or have him search her out, she knew her parents were still expecting her to be gracious. That is if they did meet again. It was that meeting that was making her so distracted.

Lord Norsely was sitting at a table across the room playing Vingt-et-un with several other gentlemen which she was grateful for, as it prolonged their eventual meeting.

"Oh look. I believe that is Mr Repington, is it not?" Miss Diana asked.

Julianna had been trying to concentrate on the game but immediately looked across the room to the door to see who Miss Diana was referring to. She looked at the men that had just walked into the room and Julianna did not see Mr Repington among them. It took her a moment to realize that the Mr Repington Miss Diana had been referring to had been Matthew Repington, not Hugh Repington.

She turned back feeling disappointed and annoyed.

"Shall we move to another table? Perhaps try another game?" Miss Diana suggested.

"That is a wonderful idea." Lady Amelia scanned the room and pointed to an empty table in the corner. "How about that table over there? I believe it is set up to play Faro."

"I am in favour of that," Miss Diana said standing up. "I had the best luck the last time I played."

"Do you agree, Lady Julianna?" Lady Amelia asked still sitting at the table.

"Yes. Faro will be a nice change." Julianna began to follow them across the room realizing halfway across the room that they would be passing by Lord Norsely's table. As they passed the table the men looked up most of them smiling and nodding. Julianna glanced over at Lord Norsely who to her surprise made a point to smile and nod. She smiled back at him relieved that he seemed to have forgiven her after the incident at the opera.

They had barely sat down at the table when Matthew Repington and Mr Webb walked up. "May we join you?"

"Yes, of course," Miss Diana said happily.

Mr Repington sat down across from Lady Amelia. "I have not played Faro in a very long time. I am surprised that it was even offered."

"I have seen it a few times this Season. It is Lady Halswood's favorite game," Miss Diana explained.

"I do find it rather fun and I do not really care whether it is in fashion or not," Lady Amelia said.

"Neither do I," Julianna agreed with her.

Someone said something at a nearby table causing the ladies there to laugh.

"I am not surprised by that at all." Julianna recognized the person speaking to be Lady Sarah.

Miss Danielle leaned in toward the table and said, "Who would be? What I am surprised by is the fact that after her behaviour at the opera that she is still getting invited to parties and balls. I will be in high dudgeon if she is allowed vouchers to Almack's."

"I shall have my mother contact the patronesses of Almack's to enquire about it," Lady Sarah told them.

"Shall we get started?" Matthew suggested brightly reaching for the wooden box.

Julianna smiled gratefully at him. "That sounds lovely."

Matthew began setting up the game while Lady Amelia, Miss Diana, and Mr Webb conversed gaily clearly trying to lighten the conversation. Julianna was not upset as much as she was annoyed that Lady Sarah and Miss Danielle had upset everyone else at the table. She could take the rude comments about herself.

Across the room, there was an uproar at the table playing Vingt-et-un. Several of the men were talking loudly.

Miss Diana turned back to their table. "That does not sound good."

"That is why we did not join them," Mr Webb said quietly.

"Oh?" Lady Amelia said looking toward the table where they were still talking loudly.

"Yes," Matthew agreed. "Most of them are a trifle disguised, although I expect more than a couple are well into their cups."

The talk at the table got louder so much that all talk in the room stopped as people stopped to watch. Julianna could not hear what was said but Lord Norsely stood up so suddenly that his chair fell back to the floor.

"You had better watch what you say!" He yelled pointing at one of the men still sitting at the table. "I'll not have you cutting shams about me!"

"I have said nothing but the truth," the other man said,

Lord Norsely swore loudly and turned away from the table. He nearly fell over the chair he had knocked on the floor. In his anger, he picked up the chair and threw it over the table barely missing those still seated. Without another word, Lord Norsely stormed from the room.

"That was quite a display," Lady Amelia commented.

"Quite. I shall be more than surprised if he is allowed back into Almack's," Matthew said loudly.

The room erupted in laughter and while Julianna appreciated Matthew's comment she could not help but be troubled by Lord Norsely's behaviour.

CHAPTER SIXTEEN

"I am so glad that you suggested that we go riding today," Julianna said as they rode into Hyde Park.

"I'm glad as well," Lady Amelia agreed. "Timothy had mentioned that he wanted to go and I immediately thought of you. I sent a note to you straight away."

"I suppose I shall thank you, Mr Sedgwick, as well," Julianna said with a laugh.

Mr Sedgwick bowed, well, as much as he could while riding upon his horse. "I am glad to be of service."

The park was so quiet with only a few people walking about the fashionable time where most people would visit the park would not happen for several hours. Julianna was grateful not only for the quiet in the park but also to be able to ride her horse. She had not had a chance to do so since returning to London.

She was also very grateful for Lady Amelia had become a great friend. Amelia was not one of those people that felt the need to fill every moment of silence with idle chatter. Julianna had found that she did some of her best thinking while out riding her horse and she felt she needed much time to think right then.

Weighing most heavy on her mind was her concerns regarding

Lord Norsely. She had already been struggling with her feelings about whether she wanted to enter into a courtship with him. After all, this was her second Season, and while she was in no hurry to marry, it was an expectation. Her parents had not interfered before so the introduction to Lord Norsely seemed odd and sudden. Given the incident involving his brother she quite understood the reasoning and possibly a rush to settle into an arrangement.

While Julianna had always known that she would marry either a Peer or a gentleman from a respected family, she had still hoped to find someone special. She wanted to be in love, though she realized the unlikely slant to her desire.

She had been hopeful upon their introduction, but Lord Norsely's behaviour during their recent meetings had taken a toll. And then there was Mr Hugh Repington adding a wrinkle to the whole thing. In truth, her reactions to Hugh Repington had been rather telling.

"Amelia, I heard that there was some issue at Webb's card party the other night," Mr Sedgwick asked after they had ridden a short time. "You were at that party, were you not?"

Lady Amelia gave Julianna a quick glance before answering. "Yes, but Lady Julianna and I were there together."

"I heard that Davidson nearly came to blows with someone at the Vingt-et-un table." Sedgwick went on to add, "Someone said that the affronted party was upset because they had lost the game."

"I am not certain, but I believe it was Lord Norsely who argued with Mr Davidson." Julianna had spoken up so that Lady Amelia would not have to.

"We could not see who Lord Norsely was upset with, we only saw him stand up and yell at someone still seated at the table."

"Did they really almost come to blows?" Mr Sedgwick asked.

"They did not. Although I would not have been surprised if it had come to that," Lady Amelia told him.

"Nor I." Julianna kept her eyes forward and said quietly, "He threw a chair."

"He did what?"

"When he stood up to confront Davidson, Lord Norsely knocked his chair to the floor. When he turned abruptly to leave, he nearly stumbled over the chair. Apparently stumbling angered him further, so much so that he picked up the chair and threw it over the table.

"The Vingt-et-un table?"

"Indeed. Luckily no one was hit by the chair."

"What happened next?"

"Mr Repington said something humorous and everyone laughed." Lady Amelia made a silly face. "It was a very odd evening indeed."

"Repington? Which one? There are five of them you know," Mr Sedgwick quipped.

"It was Matthew Repington," Julianna supplied.

"Did I just hear my name in vain?"

To her amazement, Matthew Repington rode out from behind a stand of trees on another trail that crossed their own. Not far behind him came his sister, Lady Henrietta and even more surprising, his brother, Hugh.

"Hello!" Lady Amelia exclaimed.

Lady Henrietta lifted her hand in greeting. "Hello!"

Matthew had ridden over next to Mr Sedgwick who said, "My sister and Lady Julianna have just been telling me about the excitement that occurred at Webb's card party a few nights ago."

"Oh yes it was quite a night," Matthew agreed. "It was most likely the highlight of the Season. I am quite sure people will be talking about it for a long time."

Lady Henrietta grimaced. Falling in next to Lady Amelia the horses continued down the trail. "Lord and Lady Marsfeld will not be happy, since the scandal involving Mr Townsend had only just died down."

Julianna had come to a complete stop when the others appeared. She held back to let the others pass. Mr Repington, Hugh, this time, stopped a little ahead of her and looked back waiting for her to join him. She urged her horse to move forward and they followed the others along the trail.

"You did not want to partake in the gossip?" Hugh asked her.

Without thinking she let out a dry chuckle. "No. I do not. I was there to witness Lord Norsely's abhorrent behaviour and I've no need to speak about it now."

He looked at her for a moment and then nodded. "I believe Lord Norsely has been acting quite odd since he was ill several months ago. Whether it is due to the illness itself or his brother's murderous plot, I could not say."

"I would imagine that either happening would be cause enough to alter one's personality. Having to endure both seems a tremendous burden," Julianna said.

"The gossips will be sure to smear his name in London now."

Julianna shrugged. "At least they are no longer speaking about me."

Hugh raised his eyebrows in question.

"Certainly, you have heard about my embarrassing night at the opera?"

"Perhaps, although the account was rather amusing."

Thoroughly confused Julianna looked over at him and realized what he had said. Unable to keep from smiling she replied, "Indeed. It is no laughing matter."

Hugh grinned at her and she laughed feeling better than she had in days.

"So, Mr Repington, how are you enjoying London?"

"It has been good. I still miss riding in the country most mornings though. Sometimes I wonder if living in London is worth the trouble."

"I can understand that. Although I find merits in both living in the country and in London. I think it is best if you were able to do both. I truly enjoy the slow pace of the country and being able to go riding every day if I want. But London is so vibrant. There's so much to do. You can enjoy all of the balls and parties as well as the opera and theater. I do not think I would want to live exclusively in

London but I also would not want to live solely in the country either."

"Because you would grow tired of either with too much exposure?" Mr Repington asked.

"Perhaps, but I think it is more of that one makes me appreciate the other when I am there." Julianna thought about how she felt when she had to return to London. "When I am at Alverston I appreciate the quiet mornings, and going riding but I also miss my friends and the theater. When I am in London I appreciate seeing my friends and while I will still miss the quiet mornings it is something I look much forward to when the Season is over."

Mr Repington seemed surprised by her response and Julianna wondered if she had said something wrong.

"You would be happy living in either London or the country as long as you got to visit the other during the year?"

Julianna thought about his question for a moment as it seemed somewhat important for him to know her feelings on the matter. "Yes. If the visits were prolonged, I think I would find that agreeable. Is there a particular reason for your interest?"

"When I finished my studies at the Inns of Court I was chosen to be a barrister and as such, I can either take a position with the government or I can present cases to the bar," Hugh explained. "I am trying to decide on which I would like to do."

Julianna nodded. "And one would have you staying in London for much of the year while the other quite possibly would have you living elsewhere."

"Precisely. I know the truth of it and yet I still cannot decide."

"Perhaps if you spoke with someone who has taken a position with the government you would be able to discern what you truly want to do."

"Hmm," Hugh said.

"I would think it would be easy enough to find someone in London to speak with." Julianna watched him intently.

He had a curious look on his face when he said, "It is much easier than you think."

Julianna did not know what he meant by that but said nothing assuming he would tell her if he saw fit.

"It just so happens that my elder brother, James, has a position with the government."

It was clear that he was reluctant to talk to his brother. "Do you not get along?"

"No," he answered slowly.

"Has he maligned you in some way? Tried to block your way as a barrister?"

"No." Hugh sighed and looked away. "He has actually been quite supportive of my endeavour."

"I am quite puzzled that you are hesitant to speak with him, especially since he might have the answers that you seek."

"It is because I am a foolish young man," Hugh blurted out. "I am concerned over being compared to him and I resent that he became a barrister before I did."

Julianna had heard similar arguments from her older brothers. "Does he do a poor job as a barrister?"

"No, he is well respected by all in Parliament."

They had left the park and were nearing the mews. Julianna passed by him looking back over her shoulder. "Then I would think being compared to him would be a good thing."

Julianna continued into the stable stopping next to the mounting block to dismount. She slid off reaching her foot down but her skirt got caught and she felt her foot miss the block. With nothing to grab onto she began to fall backward until she felt two strong hands on her waist, and then she found herself face to face with Hugh.

Her heart fluttered and she felt her breathing quicken. She looked up at him and realized that his eyes were neither brown nor green, they were a hazel color that she had not seen before. A green so vibrant against the warm, deep brown that made her wonder about the man himself.

He had seemed as much of a contradiction, since they met at the stables of Eastbridge. Sensible and staid upon one meeting and then as she found out at Almack's, passionate and daring the next.

"I..." Was all she managed to say before Hugh leaned forward pressing his lips to hers.

The kiss was soft and fleeting, and she leaned into him before she could stop herself. He hesitated briefly before kissing her again, his lips gentle and strong at the same time. The sound of horses approaching the stables suddenly broke the spell and Julianna moved to push Hugh away in the same moment that he stepped back.

"All right now?" He asked her his eyes roaming her face.

"Yes, thank you," Julianna said straightening her skirts wishing she did not sound so breathless.

CHAPTER SEVENTEEN

"Why are you pacing out here?" Matthew asked coming into the hall from the drawing room.

Hugh spent most of the late afternoon and evening in the library looking over some correspondence but found that he could not concentrate. After an interminable dinner with his parents and siblings, he was restless, cursing himself for giving up the small house to move back to his family's residence.

Hugh knew why he was agitated but he did not want to share that with Matthew. "I suppose that I have been living alone for too long and I am not used to having so many people moving about the house at all hours."

Matthew raised an eyebrow and smirked. Clearly, he did not believe Hugh's excuse but to his credit said nothing about it. "I was thinking about going to White's tonight. You should come with me."

Being in the crowded gambling club did not exactly sound much better but staying home did not appeal to him either. "Perhaps a drink will assist in altering my mood."

"Hear, hear!"

Less than an hour later, they were seated at a table that Matthew had managed to procure in a quieter corner. The tables around them were filled with gentlemen playing cards and enjoying some spirited conversation.

Matthew handed him a glass of whiskey. "Drink up and then you can tell me what is bothering you."

"What makes you think there is something to tell?" Hugh asked lightly.

"You have been in a sour mood since we got home from riding in Hyde Park."

"Nonsense."

"Oh really? You snapped at Henrietta when she asked you about attending Almack's this week," Matthew reminded him.

Hugh vaguely recalled speaking to her and seeing her hurt expression when she left the library. He took a long drink and then looked up at Matthew. "I thought I had hidden my feelings."

"I am sure if you had stayed at your house you would have succeeded but there are far too many of us at Repington House." Matthew glanced at the tables around them. "Have you made a decision regarding the position with Fairburn?"

"No, I have not," Hugh said and then looked up at him suddenly. "How did you know about that?"

"Father." Matthew held up his hands when Hugh scowled. "He made mention earlier this week that you had met with Fairburn."

"I am sure that he did. I would most likely have made my decision now if it were not for Father's interference."

"Has he caused you difficulties?"

"Not directly, no."

"I do not understand." Matthew frowned. "Father seemed to think he was assisting you. He said his only interest is for you to get a good start."

Hugh sighed in exasperation. "I did not require his assistance. I have little desire to start my profession as a barrister knowing I got the position as a result of my father's interference."

"I do not believe that is the case. You should discuss the matter with Father before you make such assumptions."

"Speaking with Father has been exactly what I have been avoiding since I was chosen to be a barrister. You well know the problems he created for Philip and James," Hugh told him. "Although, at this point, Father's interference is the least of my concerns. It was made clear to me at the Eastbridge house party that it would behoove me to find a wife. I have been endeavoring to do just that but now I realize that there is much more to think about. If I took a position with Parliament then I would be living in London for most of the year."

"Yes of course."

"If I were to present cases to the bar then I would mostly likely need to find a residence outside of London." Hugh looked at Matthew.

"You think this might be a concern in regard to choosing a wife?"

"When I began to seek a wife, I was looking for someone that would like to live in London and host parties."

"Whichever lady you choose will have no choice but to live wherever you live," Matthew pointed out.

"Of that, I have no doubt." He was frustrated that Matthew was not understanding, although Hugh knew it was not his fault. "Yet I would want my wife to be contented at home."

Matthew took a moment before replying. "I thought you were simply looking for a suitable match."

"It will do me no good to have a wife who is miserable every day. It would be ideal to find a wife who would enjoy living in both London and the country." He recognized the words as the same ones Lady Julianna had spoken in Hyde Park. Their private moment in the stable came back to him and he tried to expel it from his memory, continuing to dwell on it would only lead to madness.

"This all makes me wonder if I should be asking about your courtship with Lady Priscilla."

"And I have not formally pressed my suit but as you know I have been paying some extra attention to her." Hugh picked up his glass again.

"You and Lady Priscilla would make a favourable match," Matthew said. "However, you look fairly agonized when I see you with her."

"Lady Priscilla is young and quite preoccupied with the glitter of London, fashion, and parties."

"She would probably not be happy living in the country then."

Hugh shook his head. "No, I would think not."

"And what of Lady Julianna?"

"Lady Julianna is much more sensible," Hugh answered before realizing what Matthew had done.

Matthew smiled but said nothing.

"Why are you bringing up Lady Julianna?"

"I would think it is obvious."

"Obvious? What are you talking about?"

"I think Lady Julianna would be a good match," Matthew said. "A better match for you."

"Lady Priscilla is the perfect choice." He was shaking his head again. "Lady Julianna is too opinionated and…"

"And what?" Matthew asked him.

"And I think I might be in love with her." Hugh let out a long sigh and dropped his head to the table.

Matthew let out a chuckle. "Finally. I never thought you would come to admit that."

Hugh picked up his head to peer across tabletop at his younger brother. "You knew?"

"Yes, of course. Although it was Henrietta who figured it out first."

"Henrietta? Leave it to her to tell everyone save me," Hugh said in a mocking tone.

"Once she pointed it out then it was quite easy to see," Matthew tried to reassure him.

"Thank you, dear brother," Hugh said. "But what am I to do? Lady Priscilla is as I said, the perfect choice, her family is well respected, she is well-versed in London society and she is due a fair-sized inheritance."

"She is also a vicious gossip without a care for anyone else, their reputation, or their feelings." Matthew shook his head as though Hugh was addled. "Answer me this question."

"All right."

"Tell me how you feel about the idea of being married to Lady Priscilla a year from now?"

Hugh grimaced. He could not control his reaction. The idea of being married to Lady Priscilla was wholly disheartening.

Matthew took that as an answer. "And how do you feel about the idea of being married to Lady Julianna?"

The smile was so natural that Hugh could not stop it.

Matthew leaned across the table to look at Hugh. "Brother, please listen to me. I would rather see you with someone who makes you smile like that than to see you with someone who the mere thought of makes you grimace. This should not be about being flush in the pockets."

He was more confused than ever. Pushing back from the table he stood up. "I am going to get us another drink."

As Hugh made his way through the crowd to procure more whiskey he ran nearly headlong into Lord Norsely.

Hugh took a step back and watched as Norsely wavered in front of him. Hugh very well could have stepped out of the other man's way but he was already in a sour mood and did not particularly feel like it.

"Repington," Norsely slurred.

"Well, I see you are well into your cups tonight, Norsely," Hugh commented.

"I am here celebrating my betrothal," Norsely said holding up a bottle of rum.

Alarmed Hugh asked, "Betrothal? To whom?" He had known that Norsely was paying attention to Lady Julianna but he had seen her just that afternoon. Hugh could not think that she could have already excepted Norsely's proposal.

"To Lady Julianna although she does not know yet so… shush

about it." Lord Norsely put a finger to his lips in a spirited manner, the effort in coordination nearly knocking him over.

"You are celebrating already?"

Norsely shrugged causing another stumble. "My father has decided, so there is nothing else to do but celebrate."

"Your father has decided?"

"He has stated that it is the thing to do to save the family name, so I shall ask her on the morrow."

"You do not care for her?" Hugh asked him his panic turning into anger.

"She is just another young chit at the marriage mart." Norsely shrugged and smiled. "But I am a dutiful son. So it will be."

Hugh was furious and pulled his arm back about to plant a facer when Matthew pushed his way in between them.

"Norsely, I suggest you leave as I cannot hold him back for much longer."

Norsely staggered into the crowd without a look back.

"Pompous scoundrel," Hugh muttered.

Matthew let go of him and took a step back. "And if you continue on your path to marry Lady Priscilla you are no better."

Hugh stood there a moment longer watching Matthew walk away, swore under his breath to go after him.

CHAPTER EIGHTEEN

"Excuse me, Lady Julianna. This letter arrived for you."

"Thank you, Bernard," Julianna said taking the letter from the butler.

She hoped that it was a note from Lady Amelia. Julianna so wished for a distraction. Ever since they had gone riding she had been thinking about Hugh Repington. Their unexpected kiss in the stable continued to play through her mind.

In her two Seasons, there had been a few stolen kisses and while they had been nice and a bit exciting they were nothing like the kiss with Hugh. Even before the kiss, Julianna had known that she had fallen in love with Hugh, and she had attempted to ignore it. It would be even harder for her knowing that Hugh had feelings for her as well. She was not naïve enough to think that one kiss meant that Hugh was in love with her, but she was also certain that there was more than friendship between them.

Dwelling on it would do her no good, she thought and let out a long sigh. She turned the envelope over several times and finally opened it and pulled out a folded piece of paper.

She had just finished reading the letter when her mother came into the drawing room. "Bernard said that a letter had been delivered."

"Yes, mother. I have just read it. it is from Lord Norsely."

Her mother smiled broadly. "What does it say?"

"He has invited me to accompany him on a carriage ride in Hyde Park."

"Oh, how lovely," her mother exclaimed.

Julianna knew that her mother would not like what she was about to say but she went on anyway. "I do not wish to go."

"We have spoken about this before, Julianna."

"Mother, I have tried to be understanding and cooperative, though I believe I should stop doing so at once." Julianna stood up to face her mother. "After his behaviour at Mr Webb's card party, I am surprised you even want me associating with him."

"What behaviour are you speaking of?" Her mother's face was stern but questioning.

"It was at the card party as I said. Lord Norsely was playing Vingt-et-un and got into a rather heated argument with another gentleman."

"Oh, men and their card games," her mother said dismissively. "They can get quite ruffled at times. It is nothing to be fussy about."

"I wish it had been that simple. Lord Norsely stood up suddenly and he knocked his chair back to the floor. After his heated exchange, he was so angry he threw his chair at Mr Davidson."

"Oh my."

"It went over the Vingt-et-un table," Julianna explained. "Fortunately, no one was hurt."

"I am sure that it was an alarming sight but there is no need to become ruffled about it, dear."

"What was an alarming sight?" Julianna's father asked walking into the drawing room.

"Lord Norsely throwing his chair at another gentleman at Mr Webb's card party the other night," Julianna said quickly before her mother could shush her.

Her father narrowed his eyes. "I heard something about that, but had not heard who the gentleman was. Certainly I did not know you had been there to witness it."

"Father, I do not feel comfortable spending time with Lord Norsely any longer. Between his recent behaviour and knowing the violence that his brother had perpetrated, I simply do not feel safe with him." Julianna then turned her mother to say, "If Father has already heard about the incident, then there can be no doubt that the gossips have already begun to speak about it. I will be the next subject if I spend more time with him."

Julianna's mother gasped and looked to her father who said, "Yes, I think it would be best for you to stay away from Lord Norsely. When it is possible I will speak to Lord and Lady Marsfeld."

Her mother took the letter from her hand. "I shall send a note declining the invitation."

The door to the drawing room opened as her mother turned away. Bernard glanced at Julianna before announcing, "Excuse me, there is a Mr Repington here to see Lady Julianna."

Julianna's heart leapt and she could barely breathe. Her father looked puzzled. "Please show him in."

Julianna sat down on the settee and hoped she looked presentable. A moment later Bernard appeared in the doorway again but the man with him was not Hugh Repington.

"Good afternoon," the man said.

Her father stepped forward. "Good afternoon, Mr Repington."

Recalling Mr Sedgwick's comments about there being many Repington brothers, she decided this man was one of Hugh's brothers.

"Thank you for seeing me unannounced. I have come to speak with Lady Julianna over a legal manner."

"Julianna?" Her mother asked.

"Legal matters?" Her father asked at the same time.

This Mr Repington, James, she repeated in her head, smiled and she recognized it as the same as Hugh's. He gestured towards the chairs, "Perhaps if we all sat down."

"Of course," her father said. Julianna sat down on the settee with her mother on one side of her and her father on the other.

"What is this about?" Her father looked confused, but interested in getting to the bottom of any legal matters that might be affecting his daughter.

"I suppose I shall start at the beginning." James opened the leather bag that he had placed on his lap. He looked at Julianna's mother and said, "Lady Alverston, I apologize that I am the bearer of this news but I must inform you that your uncle, Silas Mowbray has died."

Her mother still somewhat confused by what was going on managed to nod and then said, "Uncle Silas, it is a wonder he lived so long."

"Yes, he lived a long life, nearly eighty-four years to be exact. He was very fond of you and your family and that is the reason why I am here."

"But you said this had to do with Lady Julianna. I do not understand." Her father stated.

"Well as you know, Lady Alverston's Uncle Silas was also the Earl of Ryleigh, and as he did not have any living children his title would normally cease upon his death."

"Normally?" Julianna asked. She had been watching them go back and forth trying to figure out what was going on.

James smiled at her. "Yes, but this is far from a normal situation. The Earl of Ryleigh was a close friend of King George. When Silas' son died he went to the king, and similar to the Earl of Mansfield in 1776 and the Duke of Marlborough in 1792 your uncle received a special patent naming a remainder of his choice."

Her mother began to speak but her father held up a hand. "Please go on, Mr Repington."

"Silas Mowbray, the Earl of Ryleigh, chose Lady Julianna Merchant as his successor."

Julianna shook her head sure that she had heard wrong. "I do not understand."

"You are now the Countess of Ryleigh, in your own right."

"Is that even possible?" Her mother was asking looking at her father.

"I assure you that I have done all of the research into this and it is perfectly legal and binding." James looked to Julianna again. "It seems that Lady Julianna made quite an impression when she spent a summer with the earl. He wrote in his journal that he would always remember the special care you took with him."

"Special care?" Her mother shook her head and scrunched up her nose.

"Oh, I remember." Julianna had only been ten years old. "He had been injured after falling off a horse. I spent my afternoons with him, sometimes reading to him or helping him move into the garden."

"And stealing cakes from the kitchen for you to share," James added and laughed when Julianna looked surprised. "He mentioned that in his journal as well."

"I do not even know what to say," her father said.

"Nor I. I am a countess?" Julianna simply could not believe it.

"Yes, you are. You are like every other Peer with one caveat. Your husband shall execute your hereditary office, as well as sitting in the House of Lords."

"But she is not married," her mother blurted out.

"That is not an issue,' James replied. "Although I would caution you to be wary of sudden interest as there will be some that will want to take advantage of a ripe situation such as this."

"Thank you. I had not thought of that," Julianna said quietly.

CHAPTER NINETEEN

Hugh could wait no longer and he found himself paying a visit to the Merchant residence. He had spent the morning doing what he could to secure his financial future. His attempt to speak with James had been fruitless though, James was said to be in London but he could not be found at his Parliament office or his London residence.

The door opened and an older man said, "Good afternoon, how may I help you?"

"I wish to speak with Lady Julianna. I apologize for visiting unannounced."

The servant seemed to take it in stride and shrugged before stepping back. "Please come in."

Hugh entered the house and looked around the large foyer.

"Your name, sir?"

"Mr Hugh Repington,"

The man frowned briefly but nodded and left the foyer.

He heard a door open and mumbled voices and then someone saying, "Who is here now?"

His heart sank. Was he too late? Had Norsely already been there?

"Send him in, Bernard," he heard a woman's voice say.

Hugh followed Bernard down the hall and into the drawing room. Lady Julianna stood up when he entered looking shocked and surprised to see him. Her mother and father were also in the room.

He could stand it no longer and rushed to her side. "Am I too late? Has he already been here?"

Julianna looked up at him the confusion plain on her face and then her eyes widened. "He just left."

"Damn my stubbornness. Have you accepted his proposal?"

"Proposal?" Julianna frowned.

"Lady Julianna, I implore you not to marry him."

"James?"

"Who? No, Norsely."

"Lord Norsely?" Lady Julianna shook her head. "I do not know what you are talking about."

"Lady Julianna, please hear me out. I love you and I know I have only just been chosen as a barrister but I have already been offered a position within the government." He looked to Lord Alverston. "I am prepared to do whatever I need to in order to provide for us. I do not intend to rely on assistance from you or my parents in any way shape or form."

"Mr Repington," Lady Julianna said sounding exasperated. "Have you spoken with James?"

"James who?" Hugh was frantic, things were not progressing as he had expected.

"Your brother, James Repington," she replied.

Hugh realized she was asking because of their conversation in Hyde Park. "I looked for him this morning to seek his counsel but he was not in his office."

Lady Julianna glanced at her parents and then back at him. "I think…"

Worried that she had not understood his intentions, he forged on to not lose his nerve or any more time. "Please say you will marry me."

"Yes, of course," Lady Julianna said with a smile. "I was only trying—"

"You will?" Hugh asked not believing he had heard correctly.

"Yes." Lady Julianna looked to her parents. "I hope neither of you plan on objecting."

"Would I argue with the Countess of Ryleigh?"

Lady Julianna laughed.

"Who?" Hugh asked wondering if it was his turn to be confused.

"That is what I was trying to tell you. Your brother, James was here earlier, I am actually surprised you did not see him leave."

That would explain why Hugh could not find him earlier. "There was a carriage going down the street when I pulled up. What was James here about?"

"It is somewhat complicated but my great-uncle, the Earl of Ryleigh died and he had received a special patent to choose his successor." Lady Julianna sighed. "As I said, it is all very complicated but he has named me to take over his house and title."

"Title?" Hugh looked over at Lady Julianna and waited for a response.

Lord Alverston spoke up. "I have seen the paperwork. Your brother has assured us that it is all legal and binding."

"I am sure that he has." Hugh turned back to Lady Julianna.

"Apparently, I am now the Countess of Ryleigh."

"My lady," Hugh said bowing in front of her. "I am honoured to be in your presence."

"And I am more than honoured to become your wife. If the offer still stands, of course."

"Indeed it does." Hugh could not contain his smile. "I suppose my future is sealed. As a husband and a Peer. I could not be happier."

The new countess smiled brightly and went to her betrothed. "And so our life together begins."

A BRAVE NEW LIFE

MATTHEW

CHAPTER ONE

"Mother said that you received a letter from the Archbishop," Henrietta told him from across the table.

Matthew nodded as he took another drink of tea. Henrietta still looked at him expectantly, so he added, "Yes, it arrived yesterday afternoon."

After a moment Henrietta sighed in exasperation. "You are rather infuriating today. What did it say?"

"I have been assigned to a small town named Whitehall."

"Where is that?" Henrietta asked with a frown.

"It is in the north I believe, near Manchester."

"Oh, feathers! I had hoped you would be closer to London or perhaps Surrey even."

Matthew chuckled. "It is unlikely I will ever be assigned to London, but Surrey would have been nice."

"How long until you have to leave?" Henrietta asked and he could see that she was trying not to pout.

"I have a little more than two months to put my affairs in order before I have to appear in Whitehall."

"Well, I for one, am very happy about that. I wish for more time with you before you move away, too."

Matthew was glad of it the change. He had much to do before he left for Whitehall. It had been barely a month since he had taken his vows to join the clergy. He had returned to his family home at Castborough to reflect on his vows and spend time with his family before assuming his duties at the Abbey in Whitehall.

"When do you suppose Mother and Father will be returning to London?"

"I am uncertain about that but I am planning to return with Hugh and Julianna at the end of the week."

Matthew thought about that for a moment. He was not obligated to wait for his family in order to make his return to London, but he knew his mother would be much more understanding about him leaving if he was not alone.

"Are you planning on visiting London yourself?" Henrietta asked him.

"Yes, I had hoped to attend a few more social events before I left."

"It will be good to see you at Almack's."

Matthew smiled at his sister, the youngest and only girl among his siblings. "Hopefully you will not be the only one glad to see me."

Henrietta's eyes lit up. "And to whose favour are you hoping to receive?"

Matthew stop short surprised that his sister had not guessed. "Why Miss Abigail Underwood, of course."

It was Henrietta's turn to look confused. "Abigail Underwood? I did not know that the two of you were still so close."

Matthew straightened his jacket. "Why ever not?"

Henrietta looked away quickly. "Lady Abigail has garnered the attention of Lord Turnbull."

Matthew was somewhat surprised to hear this, but he knew that Lady Abigail was quite popular. "Lady Abigail has many friends in and around London. I am sure she was clearly amusing herself in my absence."

Henrietta nodded. "I am sure that is the case, I apologize if I worried you."

"Not at all dear sister. I appreciate your concern."

Henrietta stood up abruptly. "I think I shall go get ready for dinner. You know how Aunt Gertrude can be."

"Aunt Gertrude? Do not tell me she will be at dinner tonight."

"Oh yes. Indeed she will be with us."

"It will be nice to see Uncle Edmund, but Aunt Gertrude is a difficult woman." Matthew shuddered.

Uncle Edmund was their father's younger brother. Edmund lived not far from Castborough after serving a commission with the British Army. Matthew had always looked forward to seeing him. He had great memories of his uncle getting into mischief with him and his siblings when they were younger.

Gertrude, his wife was another story entirely. A younger daughter of a duke from the north, she had made it very clear from their first meeting that she was neither impressed nor intimidated by the Duke and Duchess of Castborough. It made no matter that neither of his parents had done anything to make her act in such a way.

She had at one point made a comment, implying that their father had somehow stolen the title from Edmund. Every person in the room had grown quiet not quite believing what they had just heard. It had been Henrietta who had broken the silence. Truth and logic spelled out by the innocence of a child.

"Father's the oldest son, the titles always passed on to the oldest son. The only way that Uncle Edmund could receive the title was for my father to die." Henrietta had looked at her father and the back to it Gertrude. "Aunt Gertrude, you do not want Father to die, do you?"

Aunt Gertrude had gasped swiping a hand out at Henrietta who had already taken a step back as though she had suddenly realized Gertrude's true personality. "Impudent child."

Uncle Edmund had grabbed his wife's hand. "Your comment did imply such an event."

Aunt Gertrude's eyes flashed malevolently and Uncle Edmund turned to Henrietta with a chuckle. "My dear wife simply misspoke. We all want your father to live a long and happy life, my dear Henrietta."

Henrietta had gone over to her father winding her arm around his neck. She hugged him tightly, almost making him gasp for air.

"Do not worry I am not going anywhere anytime soon." Father had laughed at her sad face, a low rumbling laugh that never failed to make them all smile.

While she had refrained from making any more comments about the Duke of Castborough, she had continued to act disdainfully about everything that she encountered. Every time Matthew saw her she had the same pinched look about her face, as though she had just smelled something ghastly.

It was a wonder that his mother continued to invite Uncle Edmund and Aunt Gertrude to come visit. Those were the moments that Matthew realized the depth of his mother's patience.

CHAPTER TWO

"Ah, how nice of you to join us." Matthew ignored his brother's jab as he entered the drawing room to stand near the window. The room looked like some sort of macabre tableau. The room was full of people but not a soul speaking, it was a sure sign that Aunt Gertrude had already said something distressing to someone.

Matthew turned to ask Henrietta a question but before he could do so, Mrs Gibbs walked into the room. "Dinner is ready if you would like to move to the dining room."

"Wonderful, thank you, Mrs Gibbs." Matthew's mother said as they got up to leave the room.

Aunt Gertrude gave her a disapproving look. They had all heard her opinion on being too friendly with the servants. It was quite ridiculous as Mrs Gibbs had been with the family for years. She had begun her employment as the governess, having been able to keep five young boys and a spirited girl in check had made her the perfect choice to be appointed the head of the house. She was very nearly a part of the family which is most likely why Aunt Gertrude disapproved so very much.

"Lord Colgrave, would you like me to take Miss Susanna?"

Matthew's eldest brother, Philip, turned to his wife. "Caroline, what would you like?"

Caroline smiled at her husband and then turned to the girl with red hair sitting on her lap. "What do you think, Susanna?"

"I want to go eat the kitchen with Mrs Gibbs."

"You do?" Philip asked, his eyes wide.

"Yes, please," Susanna pleaded. She leaned closer to her father and whispered very loudly, "Mrs Gibbs always gives me extra dessert."

Philip started to get up from his chair. "Well, then maybe I should go eat with Mrs Gibbs, as well."

"No!" Susanna put both hands on his chest and pointed to Caroline. "You have to stay with Mama."

"Oh," Philip said. "Yes, how silly of me."

Mrs Gibbs smiled and held out her hand. Susanna slipped off Caroline's lap stopping to whisper to her father. "I will make sure that Mrs Gibbs brings you an extra dessert."

"Thank you, my dear. That is very sweet of you," Philip said touching a finger to her petite nose.

"She is so charming," Elizabeth said sharing a smile with James.

"She must get that from her mother," James surmised. Just two years younger than Philip, James delighted in teasing their eldest brother.

"She does indeed, for which I am eternally grateful," Philip replied taking Caroline's hand in his.

"As we all are," Henrietta added garnering laughter from most of the room as the servants began to bring in the dishes to be served for dinner.

"I am so glad that we can all be together for this dinner." His mother looked around the table. "I only wish Charles and Beatrice had been able to join us."

"Have you heard from them lately?" Elizabeth asked.

"I received a letter from Beatrice last week," Henrietta answered.

"How are they enjoying India?" Lady Ryleigh asked.

"Beatrice says the weather is extremely warm but she is becoming accustomed to it. She has begun learning how the local people keep cool. They have only recently moved into the permanent residence and she was looking forward to finally setting up house."

"How wonderful for her," Aunt Gertrude said her voice sounding snide.

"Isn't it though?" Elizabeth asked. "What an amazing adventure she and Charles have embarked on. I think it is quite wonderful."

Matthew spoke up hoping to keep Aunt Gertrude from making another comment. "And what of Charles? How is he faring?"

Henrietta smiled knowingly at Matthew, she was quite protective of their older brother. He was lieutenant in the British Army that had turned his commission into a position with the East India Company near Bombay. "Charles has been given a battalion of his own. He and Captain Wainwright may be in command of their own outposts very soon."

"Very good," Uncle Edmund said to the annoyance of his wife. "Charles has done very well for himself. It seemed like an odd leap for him when he left London, but it was a very shrewd decision."

"He was always one of the smartest of the lot of us." James looked down the table before adding, "Second only to Hugh, of course."

"Thank you." Hugh nodded. "Charles was always the most daring though. While the rest of us would hesitate, Charles had no qualms about taking those leaps. In all that time I never ever saw him feel regret that he had taken the chance."

"So, will you be joining your brother in India?" Aunt Gertrude asked.

"No, he will not." This was from Lady Ryleigh who leaned forward to address Aunt Gertrude herself. Lady Ryleigh, who was the Countess of Ryleigh in her own right, had been married to Hugh for less than three months. "Hugh will be much too busy holding my seat in Parliament. As you well know, as my husband, Hugh will represent my interest in the House of Lords."

Aunt Gertrude sniffed, seemingly realizing her comment was not only insulting to Charles and Hugh but also Julianna, Countess of Ryleigh, herself. "Oh, yes. I had forgotten."

Hugh smiled amiably. "Quite all right, Aunt Gertrude."

"We are looking forward to Parliament coming back into session in the next month," Lady Ryleigh told them.

"I can imagine." Then apparently forgetting her manners once more, And Gertrude said, "Your marriage had quite the unexpected boon for you Charles. Did it not?"

Lady Ryleigh made to stand up but Hugh gently laid a hand on her arm calming her in an instant. Hugh tilted his head as he looked at his aunt and said, "Yes, I feel extremely blessed to have found a caring young lady who is not only beautiful and smart but also kind enough to be understanding of those around her who are not as kind and caring."

Henrietta who was seated next to Matthew had to cover her mouth to keep from laughing out loud.

James seeing that the conversation was lacking gestured across the table to Matthew. "Matthew, what are your plans between now and your appointment?"

"I am hoping to leave for London with Henrietta in the next few days."

"London?' Elizabeth asked. "I thought you would stay here until you were to leave for Whitehall."

"I am hoping I will not be long in London, but I have several social engagements that I need to attend. I will most assuredly be I returning to Castborough and eventually on to Whitehall."

"Perhaps Abigail Underwood will save a dance for you." Henrietta teased him and offered a wink.

"I should be so lucky," Matthew said in reply.

"Lady Abigail's sudden betrothal was quite the surprise, was it not?" Lady Gertrude said.

Matthew felt his heart drop. Surely Aunt Gertrude was being spiteful after the previous conversation.

"Her betrothal?" Elizabeth asked. "We were in London only a week ago and there was no news of this."

Lady Gertrude looked quite excited that she knew something with the others did not. "As I said, it was quite sudden. The news was spreading around the day that we left London."

Henrietta glanced at Matthew before asking. "Are you quite sure?"

"Yes. The story I heard was that Lord Turnbull visited Lady Abigail's father to ask for her hand. Lord Turnbull is a first son, so I cannot imagine that Lord Galloden would have any reason to refuse."

Henrietta sucked in a breath and Matthew felt his face grow hot. Clearly, he was not good enough for the likes of Abigail Underwood seeing as he was a fifth son. His mind was whirling, the conversation was continuing but he could barely hear it. He could not fathom what had happened and all he wanted to do was escape to the silence of his room.

"Perhaps we should retire to the library for some sherry," Matthew heard his father say.

"That sounds lovely, dear," his mother agreed.

Matthew stood up with the rest of them but when they had reached the hallway he turned to Hugh. "Please give everyone my apologies but I have business to tend to."

Before Hugh could respond Matthew turned on his heel and continued down the hall.

CHAPTER THREE

"I do not understand why you made me come to this," Diana said to her mother.

"Lady Rossington invited us. That is why we are here." Lady Walford peered out the window of the carriage waving a gloved hand at Diana. "Now calm yourself and I do not know what is wrong with you tonight."

"We have already discussed what is wrong with me." Diana sighed loudly and looked away. They had spoken in detail about the party before they had left the house. "I do not wish to be here. I do not think I will know anyone in attendance."

Her mother shook her head, "Do not be ridiculous, Diana. You know Lady Sarah and Miss Danielle, do you not?"

"Yes, of course, I do," Diana replied.

Her mother was quite correct, she most definitely knew Lady Sarah and Miss Danielle. She did not particularly like either young lady, as they seemed to only be happy if they were gossiping. On more than one occasion she had been witness to their often cruel behaviour towards the other young ladies. Diana kept that to herself, certain her mother would only try to explain away their bad behaviour.

"It is good for you to be seen at social events, especially at something so important like the Rossington's Ball."

Her mother had said the same thing about her attending house parties, dinner parties and going to Almack's. It was her mother's reasoning for everything. The Season, Diana knew, was the best opportunity for a young lady to find a gentleman to marry. Although Diana was not opposed to getting married, she did not worry over it the way that her mother did.

As if reading her mind, her mother suddenly turned away from the window to say, "I do not want to upset you but I am concerned about your prospects for marriage."

The carriage began to slow and Diana could not help but laugh in shock. "Why ever for?"

"Most of the young ladies this Season have entered into courtships or are betrothed." Her mother patted Diana's hand. "As far as I have seen, you have not garnered attention from any gentleman this Season."

Diana blinked at her mother. "Any gentlemen? Surely, you are making a joke. I have been going to parties, balls and Almack's all Season and I have never found myself lacking for a dance partner. You are raising a breeze about nothing."

The footman chose to open the carriage door at that moment and Diana moved to get out before her mother could say anything more.

Once inside, Diana was glad to leave her mother speaking with Lady Rossington and Lady Bellingham. The ballroom was already fairly crowded and she feared that she would find no one that she knew at the ball. Many of her friends had gone to the country, either attending house parties or returned home for one reason or another. Diana had barely walked a few steps into the ballroom when she heard someone call her name. She turned around to see Jonathan Webb standing against the wall.

"Mr Webb, good evening," she said hoping her relief was not evident on her face.

"Good evening, Miss Diana." He gave her a shallow bow. "Would you like to dance?"

Much happier seeing a friendly face, Diana smiled and said, "Thank you, Mr Webb. That sounds lovely."

Mr Webb offered her his arm and then led her into the middle of the ballroom.

"Are you enjoying the ball?" Miss Diana asked trying to make conversation.

Mr Webb looked around as if he were thinking about the answer. "I shall say I am enjoying it immensely but I only just arrived before you."

His reply made her laugh and he smiled at her. "I have not been to many social events in the last few weeks. I wonder if you have seen Lady Amelia in that time."

She was not surprised that Mr Webb was asking about Lady Amelia as she had seen the two of them together quite a bit in the weeks earlier. "No, I believe she is at a house party in Kent."

"Well, that does explain her absence as of late." Mr Webb said and moved them through the next turn.

Diana felt bad about how sad he looked. "I do believe she said that she would be returning to London this next week. "

Mr Webb glanced at her quickly, "Oh you think so?"

"Yes, most definitely. Lady Amelia made a point to ask if I would be at Almack's this next Wednesday."

Mr Webb seemed quite happy to hear that Lady Amelia would be returning to London so soon. Diana could not blame him one bit, she had missed her friend as well.

She had done her best to avoid as many social events as she could but her mother had other ideas. Diana had hoped she would see other friendly faces at the ball tonight. Seeing Mr Webb so soon after her arrival had been quite fortuitous.

It was quite a surprise to her though when they finished their dance and move to the edge of the ballroom that they ran right into Lady Henrietta and her brother, Matthew.

"Miss Diana! I am so glad to see you," Lady Henrietta said with a big smile.

Diana was surprised at Lady Henrietta's greeting, not because of anything the young lady had done. They certainly were on friendly terms, she simply had not expected Lady Henrietta to be so happy to see Diana.

"It is so nice to see you as well," Diana said. "Are you enjoying the ball?"

"I am." Lady Henrietta looked around the crowded ballroom. "Everyone looks forward to Lady Rossington's party each year."

"Yes, of course," Diana said. "I was surprised that more people were not in attendance, but I suppose the night is still young."

"Indeed," Lady Henrietta agreed and then grimaced as she surveyed the large room. "I see Lady Sarah and Miss Danielle are here. I suppose they have not had time to cause any trouble yet."

Diana shook her head. "Not yet."

"But as you said, the night is still young," Lady Henrietta quipped.

Diana smiled and said, "Indeed."

CHAPTER FOUR

Matthew watched his sister talk to Miss Diana and wondered again why he had agreed to come with her. It had been a week since he had heard the rumour about Lady Abigail Underwood's betrothal. It had taken another day to find out that it was, in fact, true and that she had indeed accepted the proposal from Lord Turnbull.

Learning the news had been a shock and he had felt hurt and embarrassed that he seemed to be the last to know. He had tried to keep busy, but his mind kept going back to Lady Abigail. He then decided he would forgo his trip to London and plan to travel to Whitehall early.

Unfortunately, Henrietta's plans had overridden his own. She had expected to travel to London but was unable to do so by herself. Hugh and Lady Ryleigh had originally planned on accompanying Henrietta to London but Hugh had business to tend to that required them to return to the Ryleigh estate. Matthew had been the only other person available to travel with Henrietta in order for her to attend the Rossington ball, as well as Almack's the following Wednesday.

Matthew looked around the ballroom hoping to see a door out

to the garden if nothing else he could retire to the library. If anyone came upon him he could claim he had a headache and sought a few moments of quiet in order to quell the pain.

"Repington," Jonathan Webb said to him.

Matthew had been so preoccupied that he had not seen the man standing behind Miss Diana. "Webb, good to see you. How are you enjoying London?"

"It has been enjoyable although somewhat quiet."

Matthew was not sure what the man was talking about but nodded anyway. "I have only come to London in the last few days."

"Attending another house party, I assume," Webb suggested good naturedly.

"No. On the contrary, I recently took my vows and had gone to Castborough to straighten my affairs before I head off to my assignment in Whitehall."

"Congratulations," Webb told him. "What brings you back to London?"

"My dear sister." Matthew waved a hand over to where she was still talking with Miss Diana. "She had social engagements but no chaperone. So here I am."

"At least, it is not Almack's," Webb said.

"You are correct there, although I expect I will be in attendance this coming Wednesday."

Webb looked resigned and nodded grimly. "As will I."

"Good evening Mr Webb." Henrietta smiled up at the taller man. "How very nice to see you this evening."

"Thank you. It is good to see you as well. Your brother was just telling me you have only just returned to London."

"Yes, our father had business to tend to back at Castborough. Thankfully, Matthew was able to accompany me on my journey to London or I would still be there."

Matthew chuckled dryly. "You make it sound as though Castborough and is a horrible place to be."

"Oh no, it is not that. It is simply that I would much rather be at a ball or a party and having fun with friends."

Matthew noticed that Miss Diana had smiled and then looked away, for some reason he wondered if she felt the same way as he did about the subject. "Yes, well, the friends part I am in agreement with. I am not so sure about the parties and events."

Henrietta seemed to take pity on him, Putting her hand on his arm. "Yes, dear brother, and I completely understand. But do not be disheartened it will not always be this bad."

Miss Diana leaning slightly towards Henrietta as though she was going to ask a question but before she could say anything she was interrupted.

"Oh, look who has come. Good evening, Mr Repington. How are you this evening?"

Matthew turned to see Miss Danielle and Lady Sarah. He could have gone a whole lifetime without seeing either of them. He was thankful, however, that he would not have to deal with Lady Judith, Lady Sarah's close friend. Lady Judith had often been involved in the same sort of malicious behaviour. In her quest to make another young lady miserable, Lady Judith had been compromised and forced to marry Mr Townsend. After their marriage, they had been exiled to family land in the north. Matthew had felt they had gotten off easy, but at least Miss Beatrice and his brother, Charles had found each other through the ordeal.

"Good evening," Matthew said with a polite nod to both ladies.

Miss Danielle smiled sweetly. "I do hope you are enjoying the party."

Lady Sarah made a show of looking around the ballroom. "I do not see Lady Abigail in attendance tonight."

Matthew smiled graciously and glancing around the ballroom himself. "Is she not? I had not noticed."

Lady Sarah leaned closer to Miss Danielle and said, "Oh, yes. I would think that she was busy preparing for her wedding to Lord Turnbull."

Miss Danielle giggled. "Well, then, I do hope you are able to enjoy the party."

Matthew gritted his teeth unable to trust the words that might pass his lips.

"Oh, we most definitely will enjoy the party." Miss Diana was at his elbow subtly linking her arm through his. "We have been looking forward to this for weeks, have we not, Mr Repington?"

Matthew looked down at Miss Diana and the genuinely sweet smile on her face. He could not help but smile. "Yes, I believe it will be quite lovely."

He heard Webb snort in laughter behind him. Matthew looked back to see the dark faces of Lady Sarah and Miss Danielle.

"I have been looking forward to it for what seems like forever," Lady Henrietta added with a giddy laugh. "Lady Sarah, have you by any chance heard from Lady Judith?"

"No, I have not," Lady Sarah replied stiffly. She made a quiet comment to Miss Danielle and the two young ladies turned and walked away without another word.

Matthew stood there with Miss Diana's arm intertwined with his for a moment, he was unsure what to think of the exchange. He had not thought Miss Diana as being a hanger on. Before he could work out something to say to her, she let go of his arm and stepped away.

She began to laugh, pausing to gasp out, "Oh, Mr Repington, I am so sorry. I did not mean to put you into a difficult situation, but I so hate their nonsense."

"Oh, Miss Diana, you were brilliant!" Henrietta gushed.

Matthew founding himself laughing as well. "No apologies are necessary. My sister is quite correct that was rather brilliant. I have never seen Lady Sarah or Miss Danielle speechless before. It was well worth the confusion on my part."

"I was more than happy to have done it. I have seen them be so very cruel to people in the past that I could not pass up the opportunity to make them pause." She laughed again, "Lady Henrietta you were magnificent, as well, asking about Lady Judith."

"How could I not?" Lady Henrietta asked. "You would think she would have learned from what happened to her friend."

"Lady Sarah would have to think of someone other than herself. She seems not capable of that feat." Miss Diana turned back to him. "Thank you for playing along."

"I was all too happy to comply. I am so very thankful that I was here to witness it," Matthew admitted.

Miss Diana giggled again. "You are quite welcome, Mr Repington."

Matthew put a hand to his chest and bowed slightly in front of her. "Would you honour me with the next dance, Miss Diana?"

"Yes of course. We would not want to disappoint Lady Sarah and Miss Danielle."

"Quite right," he agreed with a laugh.

They found their place among the other dancers just as the music began to play. He and Miss Diana were still laughing when the dance ended. As they walked back to join Henrietta and Webb, Matthew thought that maybe this party would not be so bad.

CHAPTER FIVE

"I had not thought to find you here," Henrietta said coming into the drawing room.

Matthew closed the book he had been reading. "Where did you think I would be?"

"In the library or in your room, it seems that you are always reading or studying." She shook her head. "Do you not tire of it?"

"There was much reading that I was inclined to do prior to taking my vows but I have always enjoyed reading. That should not surprise you."

"It does not really. I am excited about tonight, but it is too early for me to go upstairs to begin readying myself."

Matthew had not meant to, but he grimaced at the mention of Henrietta getting ready to go out.

"Do not look so sour," Lady Henrietta told Matthew. "We are going to Almack's, not the guillotine."

Matthew pinched the bridge of his nose before answering his sister. "I am fully aware of where you are going tonight. I simply do not wish to go with you."

He should have known better than to talk to her about not wanting to go to Almack's. He could have taken his book into the library to read but instead, he had come into the drawing room to sit on one of the upholstered chairs that was placed near the window.

While Henrietta had always enjoyed attending the balls and parties of the Season, it had never been one of Matthew's favourite activities. He did not like the crushing crowd that often attended Almack's on Wednesday nights.

Even when he was younger, Matthew had never shared the thrill of gossiping that most seemed to enjoy. It seemed to him that if someone was having difficulty already it was unfair for them to the deal with the rude hum of others. That sentiment was felt even more so after his dealings with Lady Abigail.

Henrietta and others had tried to warn him but he had not listened. Even after witnessing her callous and appalling behaviour towards others, he had not believed she was truly unkind. He had been fooled by her charm to think that he was different and he had naively thought that perhaps his attentions could change her demeanour.

A sigh came from Henrietta, clearly unaffected by his pronouncement. "Surely, you do not expect me to forego my night at Almack's?"

Matthew cringed at the thought of what their mother would say if Matthew had kept Henrietta from going to Almack's. "No, of course not."

"Oh, really. Well, then." Henrietta raised her eyebrows in surprise.

"And I'm not being sour," Matthew told her with a scowl.

Henrietta nodded and then began to laugh. "You most certainly are being sour. Whatever is wrong with you?"

Matthew frowned at her. "There is nothing wrong with me. I am allowed to have an opinion on whether I want to attend a social event."

Henrietta watched him for a moment and then asked quietly, "Is it because of what has happened regarding Lady Abigail and Lord Turnbull?"

"No, it is not because of Lady Abigail. I have no desire to be foisted on the marriage mart." He was trying not to sound frustrated, but he was having a difficult time

It was Henrietta's turn to frown "I thought you wanted to be married, at least you did before you went to take your vows. What has changed?"

Matthew simply shook his head and got up from his chair to look out the window into the small garden. His sister was quite right, he had indeed been looking for a wife before he had taken his vows. That had also been before he had heard the news that the woman he thought would be his wife had accepted a proposal from another gentleman. It had discouraged him greatly and he could not see how the situation would improve before he left for Whitehall.

"Matthew, I know what is going on." Henrietta's voice sounded exasperated. "I know full well you were going to ask for Lady Abigail's hand."

"I do not wish to talk about Lady Abigail Underwood. Ever again."

Henrietta stood up as well. "I do hope that you are not allowing Lady Abigail's vile behaviour to upset you."

Matthew shook his head. "I have just told you that I do not wish to speak about it. Or her. I have simply decided I will be better served to concentrate on the reflection of my vows both to the clergy and my upcoming appointment in Whitehall."

"You are being quite ridiculous," Henrietta told him her exasperation turning to anger. "I have told you from the beginning that Lady Abigail was selfish and spoiled. There are plenty of other young ladies in London that are pretty, sweet and sincere. If you had listened, you probably would not be this upset."

"I am not upset. You are correct, of course, that you shared your opinion about her. Now, as I will be the new curate in Whitehall I must put the abbey first. And that is that."

Henrietta stood looking at him for a moment before seeming to give up. "I do not completely agree with this course of action, but I cannot deny that it is your decision to make. No matter how wrong I believe that you may be, I cannot make you do what I want you to do. I only want you to be happy."

"I know, Henrietta." Matthew appreciated both her exasperation and her kindness. "I am truly grateful you care so much. You are indeed a good sister."

She touched his arm very briefly and then turned from the window. "I think I shall go read in my room until it is time for me to begin readying myself for tonight."

"Very well. I will be ready and await you here."

Matthew was glad to be done with the conversation, but he could not help but admit that when Henrietta had said there were plenty of young ladies that were pretty, kind, and sincere that a vision of Miss Diana's laughing face appeared unbidden into his mind. He had no idea where the thought came from.

CHAPTER SIX

"Diana, you look especially lovely tonight."

"Thank you very much, Aunt Grace," Diana replied, thankful that her aunt had come with them. She looked down at her dress and smiled. "This dress is my favourite and I always like to wear it for special occasions."

"Well, I daresay that a night at Almack's is quite special. I am sure you will get plenty attention from the gentleman in attendance."

They were waiting in line waiting to be admitted into the Hall.

"One would hope so," her mother said, scorn plain in her voice.

Diana's smile faltered. She looked away quickly embarrassed beyond words. She could not believe that her mother would say such a thing—much less in front of Aunt Grace, but also where other people in line could also overhear.

Her aunt turned to Diana's mother. "My goodness, Frances, what kind of comment is that?"

Diana's mother smiled sweetly. "Dear sister, I was just commenting on my hope that Diana would make a good impression tonight at Almack's. It is not as though she has anyone chasing after her."

Mortified Diana looked down at her hands saying a silent prayer that her mother would stop talking.

"Well that is a bunch of Fustian nonsense!" her aunt exclaimed reaching for Diana's hand. When she had her hand in her grasp, she squeezed gently. "I am most certain that the majority of the gentleman here are quite beneath your touch, Diana. I am not just turning you up sweet either."

"Thank you, Aunt Grace." Diana was so grateful for her aunt. The woman was kind and smart but did not let other people push her around. It mattered little that night, though, as her mother had turned to speak to someone else completely ignoring what Aunt Grace had said.

It was not long before they were let into Almack's and Diana was relieved that Aunt Grace was able to direct Diana's mother to a corner suggesting that they should speak with Lady Halswood.

"After all, she will be holding her party fairly soon," Diana could hear Aunt Grace say. "You will want her to see you here, I am sure."

Her mother nodded and let Aunt Grace guide her across the room.

Even though they had waited several minutes to enter, the ballroom at Almack's was not very crowded so early in the evening. Diana looked around as she made her way through the ballroom. She had crossed over to the other side of the large room when she saw Lady Henrietta smiling immediately upon seeing her friend.

"Lady Henrietta, good evening. Have you been here long?"

"We have only just arrived, the wait seemed longer this evening than usual."

"Yes, it seemed that way to me as well," Diana replied, but she found herself looking around the ballroom. She had wondered earlier that day if Lady Henrietta's brother, Matthew, would be in attendance. Now that she was at Almack's she was quite looking forward to the idea of Mr Repington being there with them.

A moment later Mr Repington joined them. "I have not seen Mr Webb, I wonder if he will be attending tonight."

Diana spoke up to say, "I believe he will be. As Lady Amelia had made it known that she will most likely be in attendance."

Lady Henrietta clapped her hands gleefully. "I had hoped those two would find each other."

Diana nodded but stopped when she noticed that Lady Sarah and Miss Danielle were standing together not far away watching them and whispering to each other.

Lady Henrietta let out an exasperated groan. "Oh, do not worry over them. In fact, ignore both of them. They are only looking for a reaction and more drama to gossip about. Let us not give it to them."

"Yes, I know. Those back biters are really frustrating, though."

Henrietta turned so her back was to them causing Diana to turn away as well. "Eventually if people ignore them there will not be anyone else for them to gossip about or anyone to listen."

Matthew seemed to not give a care about what anyone was doing. He was standing quietly by Henrietta surveying the room.

The room had begun to get more crowded and music began to play signaling the beginning of the dancing. Diana had been so preoccupied that she had not realized that Lady Sarah and Miss Danielle had moved from their previous spot.

"Well, it is Almack's. Only those with vouchers are allowed in but I must say I am often surprised about who they actually let in on Wednesday nights," Lady Sarah said to miss Danielle and another young lady that Diana had only met once before if her memory served her correctly the lady's name was Jane Lynnfield.

Jane smiled at Matthew who nodded politely in return.

Lady Sarah leaned in and said, "Oh no, he is a fifth son."

To his credit, Mr Repington's face did not change at all although Diana could see the annoyance in his eyes. Once again Diana moved next to him while Lady Sarah looked on. Diana had sought for something to say but Matthew beat her to it.

"Oh, there you are!" Matthew looked down at her with an astonishing smile. "The music has started I was worried that we would miss the dance."

"My apologies for worrying you. I was not far behind."

"Would you like to sit this dance out?"

Diana peered out to the people already taking their places in the ballroom. "I think I would like to dance. If you are agreeable to that?"

Matthew leaned forward sweeping his hand behind him in a low bow. "It would be my honour."

Matthew offered his arm and Diana slipped her arm through his, pausing to wave at the young ladies who were standing stock still staring at them. "If you'll excuse us."

Very clearly irritated, Matthew, with Diana at his side, left before either young lady could say a single word.

The music started and although his dancing was perfect, Diana could tell he was still quite upset. She could not help wondering if he was upset with her.

"My apologies, Mr Repington. I am so very sorry. I had not meant for my joke last week to inconvenience you so much."

He frowned at her for a moment and then shook his head. "Lady Sarah and her friends are an inconvenience. Speaking with you and getting to dance with you is most definitely the best part of my being at Almack's tonight."

"Thank you," she managed to say.

The music ended in the next moment and Diana was glad of it as she was sure her face was still as red as a field poppy. She was so very thankful that when they returned to the edge of the ballroom that Mr Webb and Lady Amelia had arrived and joined Lady Henrietta. Diana hoped she was acting normal and not as flustered as she felt inside.

CHAPTER SEVEN

Diana squinted and took another step back from the easel. She reached out with her paintbrush to add another brush stroke. She looked out the window and tilted her head. The sun had moved changing the shadows in front of the tree again. With a sigh, she rinsed her brush deciding to focus her attention on the flowers growing in the planters on either side of the tree.

The previous summer she had sketched the small garden at their London residence. This summer she had decided to paint it in watercolors. In her previous Season, she had not thought to bring her watercolor paints with her. Diana was determined to bring them to London this Season. It had caused quite the argument with her mother, claiming that she did not trust that the paints would not ruin their belongings. Diana had disagreed with her mother completely. Instead of arguing with her mother, she had simply pointed out that her watercolor painting was a skill that she needed to practice and order to be proficient.

She had repeated her own mother's words to her. "Every young lady should be proficient in literature, music, and the arts."

Apparently not wanting to contradict herself, her mother had finally agreed to purchase the necessary paints and brushes once they arrived in London.

Although it was very important for her to practice her painting, it would have been more truthful to have told her mother that she found it highly enjoyable. She was fascinated by the bright and vibrant colours found in nature. It made her extremely happy to bring those hues to life on the canvas. Diana knew quite well though, that her mother would care little about her joy in painting. Her mother seemed to only be concerned with those activities that would bring her a husband.

Diana glanced back and forth between the canvas and the view out the window. "Perhaps more yellow daffodils would help." She dipped her brush into the water and then ran it across the yellow watercolor block before touching her brush to the canvas in quick dotting motions.

The door opened behind her, but she ignored it thinking it was Lewis coming in to collect her afternoon tea tray. She nearly cried out in surprise when her mother spoke.

"Will you be done with that anytime soon?"

Diana nearly dropped her brush but was able to catch it without getting yellow paint on the canvas or her smock. "Goodness! Mother, you startled me."

"Nonsense. Am I not allowed to walk into my own drawing room?"

"Of course, Mother. It is just that you rarely come talk to me while I am painting."

It occurred to her it was likely one of the reasons that Diana enjoyed painting so much. Her mother had chosen to do needlework when she was young and had not the proficiency of Diana with watercolors. It seemed to annoy her mother greatly that Diana had a talent for painting.

"I thought it would benefit you more to practice in silence." Her mother stood across the room near the settee. "Are you nearly done? I have something to speak to you about."

Diana tried not to sound exasperated. "Do I need to sit down for you to speak with me? I can finish my painting and listen to you at the same time. If it pleases you, of course."

Her mother scowled for a moment and then visibly relaxed as she sat down on the settee. "It makes no matter to me where you are, as long as you are listening."

"Yes, Mother," Diana said dutifully.

"Lord and Lady Browerton are having a dinner party tomorrow evening and I have accepted an invitation on your behalf."

Diana did not look away from the canvas, continuing to dot the yellow paint onto it while endeavouring to keep herself calm. It had taken her but a moment to realize that the Browerton name was familiar to her, the parents of Jane Lynnfield. To her mother, she said, "I do not think I recognize that name. I do not wish to attend a dinner party where I know no one."

"Do not worry yourself over that. The invitation came through Lady Alderside, Lady Sarah's mother. I believe you actually know Lady Sarah's friend, Jane Lynnfield."

"Mother," Diana began, hoping her mother would understand her. "While I do know Lady Sarah and Miss Jane, they are not young ladies I speak with often."

"This will be the perfect opportunity for you to do so." Her mother stood up and turned to leave the room. She stopped and turned back around, tapping her foot lightly. "There will be several gentlemen in attendance for you to speak with as well."

Diana turned back to the canvas blinking quickly to avoid a rude response. She could not pinpoint when her mother had started becoming so querulous. Like many other young girls she had been taught to be ladylike. She was taught the importance of being clean and quiet.

As Diana had gotten older, it had seemed normal for her mother to be fussy over every detail. Her mother did not like Diana to go riding because her riding habit got dusty from being in the stable. It seemed as though this Season her mother had gotten even worse, criticizing the smallest perceived infraction.

"Your father and I are concerned about you this Season."

"Father?" Diana raised an eyebrow.

"Yes, your father has decided that you should be betrothed by the end of the Season."

Diana could hardly believe what she was hearing. "The end of the Season?"

"Yes, he is well acquainted with many of the parents of the young gentleman that shall be at this dinner party."

"So, Father is going to pick out a husband for me?"

"If it comes to that, yes."

"I see." Diana continued to paint filling much more of the canvas with daffodils than she had originally intended.

"As you well know, your father and I want you to marry well. It is important that you catch someone's eye at this dinner party."

She stood holding the brush in her hands, frozen. Finally she put the paintbrush down. She would not be able to continue painting while she felt so hopeless. Diana let out a sigh.

"I shall endeavour to do as you ask."

CHAPTER EIGHT

Matthew stood next to Henrietta and tried not to feel so agitated. It was not Henrietta's fault that he had once again been forced to accompany her to yet another event. Their parents had been delayed at Castborough and had not yet arrived in London. She could not go unescorted.

For his sister's benefit, he smiled and said, "Dinner seemed to go well. Perhaps playing cards will go as smoothly."

Her smile was tight when she said, "We shall see."

He was not sure what she meant but before he could ask she stepped forward. "Good evening, Miss Jane. What a lovely dinner. Thank you so much for having us."

Matthew looked at the young lady his sister had just addressed, recognizing her from their night at Almack's. She was one of the young ladies who had recently befriended Lady Sarah. By the sudden look of displeasure on the young lady's face, she had also remembered the exchange.

"Lady Henrietta, you are quite welcome. I thought your parents would be attending with you."

Henrietta had clearly seen Miss Jane's hesitation and Matthew saw his sister's eyes narrow before she said, "Yes, I am sure you did. I apologize for the confusion regarding your assumption. My father, the Duke of Castborough, had some important business to tend to and has not yet arrived in London. My brother, Matthew, has accompanied me tonight."

At the mention of the duke, Miss Jane's eyes lit up and she suddenly seemed to remember her manners. Miss Jane turned to Matthew with the same smile she had given him at Almack's the previous week. "Good evening, Mr Repington. I do hope you are enjoying yourself tonight." She offered her hand with enthusiasm.

Matthew took her hand and almost immediately released it. "Thank you, the evening has been most enjoyable so far."

Miss Jane's hand hung in the air for a moment as though she was unsure what to do with it when Matthew released it so quickly. "Now that dinner is over, everyone is gathering in the drawing room for tea and card games."

"Thank you, Miss Jane. You have been very helpful." Henrietta walked past her and headed to the other side of the room.

Matthew was still marveling at how his sister had summarily dismissed the other young lady in her own home when Miss Jane came into the room asking everyone to take their seats at the small tables scattered around the room.

There was some scrambling as people took their seats at one of the larger tables. Matthew moved to a smaller table and sat down, immediately standing back up when Miss Diana stopped across the table from him.

"We seem to be tablemates this evening." She laughed, but sounded somewhat nervous. Whether she was uneasy about speaking with him or because of the party he was not sure. He hoped he was not the source of her obvious anxiety.

"Yes, how fortuitous." He was truly glad of it, too. Every minute with these people reminded him of Lady Abigail, and he felt the fool for not seeing her as being the same.

She sat down and he took his seat once more. She looked around the room. "I fear that we have been seated at the other end of the table as some sort of punishment."

As if proving Miss Diana's point, Lady Sarah whispered something to Miss Danielle that caused them both to look down at the end of the table and laugh.

Tired of their malicious behaviour, Matthew smiled broadly and waved, leaning closer to Miss Diana to say, "I am happy to say that I believe that we have gotten the better part of the deal."

Matthew did not think that Miss Diana had seen the exchange between the two other young ladies but by her reaction, she must have known what he meant. "I have no doubt that we will have a much more pleasant time here. My heart goes out to your sister."

His sister had been seated in the midst of Lady Sarah and her spiteful friends. Matthew caught his sister's eye and she gave him an icy smile. "Yes, I believe you are quite right, she does not appear to be enjoying herself in the least. I will no doubt get an ear full."

"If it were anyone else I would be concerned but your sister seems to be one of the few people seemingly unaffected when they decide to direct their vitriol towards her."

Matthew watched his sister, her continued graciousness amongst the other girls was rather commendable. "Yes, I know firsthand that she is a formidable opponent. She truly does not care what they think of her."

Miss Diana sat up straight. "Being the daughter of a duke I am sure is rather helpful."

"Yes and no." Miss Diana raised an eyebrow in question. He nodded with a weak smile and went on with his thought. "You see, Henrietta is certainly aware that the only reason she was invited tonight is due to our father being the Duke of Castborough. Most of these young ladies have at one time or another attached themselves to Henrietta. She can see through their motives easily. And she has no desire to lord her station over others. So the attempts at friendship from these lot has never gone anywhere."

"Your sister is one of the nicest people I have ever met." She paused for a moment and then looked at Matthew with a grin. "I suppose I could say that for her brothers as well."

Matthew raised an eyebrow at that. "Oh?"

She seemed to realize that her statement could be construed as rather forward. "Well, yes. I just remember how nice you and your older brothers have been in dealing with Lady Sarah and her friends. I, for one, am thankful for the assistance given to Miss Beatrice and Lady Julianna."

As much as he would have liked to, he could not argue the point with her. There had been more than a few occasions where either he or his brothers had felt it necessary to step in to deal with the maliciousness of that set.

"Yes, well, it is difficult for us to stand idly by while others are being mistreated."

"Excuse me." Their conversation was interrupted by someone who stood next to their table.

Matthew looked up to see Henry Crandall standing next to the table. "Yes, Crandall?" Matthew said impatiently.

Crandall gestured back towards the larger table. "They are playing a game and we have been instructed to switch seats. I left that table and I am to replace you here."

Matthew scowled at the other man. "Oh, the devil take it!"

Without a glance behind him, Matthew stocked across the room and sat down at the other table. He played the card game but poorly as his attention kept going back to Miss Diana and her conversation with Crandall.

"If you will excuse me," Matthew said standing up. "I believe I need some fresh air." With that, he walked out of the drawing room and left the house pacing near their carriage vowing not to return until the party was over.

CHAPTER NINE

"What are you doing all by yourself in here?" Henrietta asked pausing in the doorway of the library.

Matthew held up the book in his hand. "I was reading. Trying to, at least."

"To me, it appears that you are moping." She sat down in the chair next to him.

"I am not moping." He dropped the open book onto his lap. "I was reading in preparation for my appointment in Whitehall."

"Oh, I apologize for my intrusion."

"Thank you, but it is not necessary." Matthew had barely been able to concentrate. Since the dinner party at Miss Jane's London residence, he had been able to think of little but Miss Diana. He had not changed his mind about finding a wife, but he kept thinking of Miss Diana sitting at the card table with Henry Crandall. The man had seemed quite interested in his conversation with Miss Diana. It had concerned Matthew, while Crandall was not a complete rake, he was shockingly loose in the haft.

If Crandall had been paying the same amount of attention to Henrietta, Matthew would have made sure to keep an eye on him. Matthew had nearly convinced himself that his concern for Miss

Diana was born of the same sense of responsibility to defend those that are being mistreated. However, as time went by he was starting to wonder.

Even more so, he had started to regret not going to Almack's the previous week. He had originally been quite pleased his parents had arrived in London so he no longer needed to act as Henrietta's chaperone. In recent Seasons, Almack's had lost its charm and he rarely attended unless specifically asked to attend usually by one of his siblings.

Matthew let out a huge sigh and then looked up realizing Henrietta was still sitting next to him.

"Are you planning on sitting in this stuffy library all day?" She leaned in and tilted her head.

With no plan in mind, only that he did not want to be pestered by Henrietta any longer, he closed the book with a loud clap and stood. "No, I do not."

Henrietta stayed seated and with a wry look on her face asks, "What are you going to do now?"

Matthew had not anticipated her asking more questions and cast about for an idea. After a moment, an idea came to him and he nearly shouted. "Yes! I am going to take a walk in the park."

"You seem rather excited about going to the park." She looked at him suspiciously before she stood. "Enjoy your walk. Hopefully, you will not make a cake of yourself."

Matthew chuckled. "Thank you very much, dear sister."

He set the book on the small, round topped table next to his chair, picked up his coat and left the library. The idea of taking a walk in the park had been a good one, not only had it gotten Henrietta to stop asking him questions, but some fresh air would probably do him some good.

There had been far too much on his mind as of late. Between taking his vows, receiving his appointment as the curate in Whitehall, and the news of Lady Abigail's betrothal, it was no wonder that he was a little befogged himself.

It was not long before Matthew was walking the short distance from their family residence to Hyde Park. It was a beautiful summer afternoon, warm but the slight breeze was cool and inviting. He had barely breached the entrance at Grosvenor Gate when he saw a young lady with dark curly hair. His heart leapt but then he was almost immediately disappointed when the young lady turned and revealed that she was not Miss Diana.

He continued his walk, determined to not be discouraged or in a bad mood. The only problem was that instead of a relaxing walk he had found himself searching around him. He hoped to see Miss Diana among the many people taking advantage of the pleasant weather.

Upset at his grumpy disposition, Matthew forced himself to stop walking and take a rest. He leaned against a tall oak tree in an attempt to gather himself.

Reminding himself silently that getting married was no longer something he wanted. He must stop this absurd melancholy. Perhaps in a few years when he was settled in Whitehall he could think about finding a wife. Surely there would be young ladies looking for husbands in the north.

"Repington?"

Matthew turned around to see Jonathan Webb standing on the path. "Webb. Good afternoon."

"And good afternoon to you." Webb's voice was low and his countenance was despondent.

"What brings you to Hyde Park this afternoon?"

"I was hoping some fresh air would clear my mind."

Matthew pushed away from the tree, he certainly understood how Webb was feeling. "Has it helped at all?"

Webb paused, his brow furrowed as they fell into step to continue down the path. "Not in the least. You?"

"No. I am afraid not," Matthew said with a shake of his head. "You look rather troubled though, my friend."

Webb stared down the well-worn path, large oaks on either side providing welcome shade. "It is Lady Amelia, that I am worrying over."

Matthew was surprised when the man spoke but pleased that he sought his counsel. "Is she not well?"

"No, she is well. It is just that I cannot seem to stop thinking about her."

"Ah, I see." Matthew was quite sympathetic to the other man's plight. "From what I have seen you get on well together."

"Yes, of course, quite well really." Webb's look was wistful and he smiled weakly.

"And you would like to start a formal courtship?"

"Yes," he replied. "I am hesitant though because I am unsure about her feelings. I have no idea if she would be amenable to a courtship and eventually a marriage."

Matthew frowned. "Hmm. As I said, it is quite evident that the two of you are friendly. Does that not mean that she would welcome a courtship?"

"I do not know. Your sister and I are friendly, does that mean that she welcomes a courtship with me?"

This caused Matthew to stop mid step. "Yes, I see what you are on about."

"Well, then, I suppose that is not a good measurement. I need more than that to make a decision on the matter." Webb shook his head and frowned deeply.

"I am afraid I am as ill prepared as you are on the subject," Matthew confessed. There had to be some way for Webb to find out. It took less than a minute for him to work it out. He suddenly snapped his fingers. "Henrietta!"

"What about her?"

"I will ask her about Lady Amelia," Matthew told him. Holding up a hand when the other man wanted to object. "I will not give you away and I will not implicate myself either. Henrietta has aided my brothers in the past in this area. I am sure she will be equally helpful in this case."

Webb looked doubtful. "I hope so."

"Will you be at Almack's this week?"

Matthew's mind was whirring. Perhaps he could find out more

about Miss Diana while he was asking about Lady Amelia for his friend, Jonathan Webb.

"Yes, I do plan to be there."

"With any luck, I will have some answers for you then." Matthew nodded confidently and slapped him on the back.

The other man nodded. "That would be very welcome indeed."

They continued down the path in silence as there was nothing else to say. Both men had their thoughts on their own immediate futures.

CHAPTER TEN

Matthew entered Repington House wondering how he should approach his sister. It had been a good idea on his part, but he had not thought about what he would say.

"Back already?" Henrietta stood in the doorway of the drawing room.

"Yes." Matthew looked up and nodded. He still had not decided what he was going to say but figured it would be better to act now rather than put it off. He joined her in the drawing room taking a seat in the chair next to the settee where she sat.

"Did you have a nice walk?" Henrietta asked her needlework on her lap.

"It was rather nice."

Henrietta looked up at him "Did you see anyone interesting along the way?"

"Why do you ask?" Matthew asked suspiciously.

Henrietta looked at him as though he was addled. "Because it is a lovely day and I thought perhaps there would be a good amount of people enjoying the afternoon."

Matthew felt like a fool, of course, she was right. "The park was well attended but not crowded."

"That does make sense. As I am sure most of the people will not show up and for another hour or so when it is the fashionable time to be in Hyde Park."

"I had not thought of that, but you are correct." Matthew realized this would be a good time to bring up his questions. "I have not been to the fashionable hour at Hyde Park this season. Have you gone?"

Henrietta nodded. "I have been a few times. We like to go on Tuesdays to see people before we plan to attend Almack's."

"We?" Matthew asked hoping to hear Lady Amelia's name mentioned.

"Well, I certainly do not go to the park alone." Henrietta scowled at him again. "I believe I have gone with Lettie, Beatrice, and other friends. I often happen upon Lady Amelia and her brother in the park as well."

"So, Lady Amelia visits Hyde Park with her brother, not with a suitor?"

"Not that I have seen," Henrietta answered and then quickly looked up. "Why are you asking? Should I let Lady Amelia know that you are interested?"

"No!" Matthew said with more force and volume than necessary. With no other choice, he looked sheepish and waved his hand. "My apologies. I must confess that I am not asking these questions for myself."

Henrietta thought for a moment. "By any chance did you run into Mr Webb in the park?"

Matthew smiled before he could stop himself but held up his hands in a questioning manner. "It is possible, although it is possible that I met with the Prince Regent himself."

Henrietta snorted. "I am quite sure that as lovely as Lady Amelia is, the Prince Regent cares not who strolls with her in Hyde Park."

"Quite right," Matthew replied drily.

"Not that you need to know this, but I believe Lady Amelia would be delighted to see Mr Webb at the park." Henrietta's eyes brightened as she shared information. "Or the Prince Regent, for that matter."

"She is not receiving the attention of any other gentleman?" Matthew had to get the full picture to not get Webb's hopes up unnecessarily.

"Mr Crandall has been asking her dance each week at Almack's."

"Interesting. Then he is not looking for a courtship with Miss Diana?"

He realized his mistake almost immediately as Henrietta smiled. "No, I do not believe so. Mr Crandall seems to be making the rounds. I have been lucky enough to garner enough dance partners that I need not worry about his attentions."

"Well, that is good to know. I would not want to have words with Mr Crandall."

"On my behalf, or Miss Diana's?"

Matthew opened his mouth to answer but had no idea what to say.

Henrietta laughed softly and softly clapping her hands. "Oh, I adore this. Miss Diana is one of my favourite people."

"She is quite lovely," Matthew agreed. "but…"

"Oh, not this nonsense about you not wanting to marry. I understand your reluctance after that awful Lady Abigail Underwood, but Miss Diana is quite nearly the opposite. Pretty and caring, you would be a fool to overlook her."

Frustrated Matthew blurted out. "I am not overlooking her. So much so that I cannot stop thinking about her. My only worry is that I have no idea of how she feels about me."

"Oh, is that all?"

"Yes, that is all." He was annoyed that he sounded as exasperated as he felt.

Henrietta leaned over and patted his arm. "Do not worry, my dear brother. I will help you."

Matthew sighed. "I am not so very sure that is a good thing."

Henrietta's laughter failed to allay his fears.

CHAPTER ELEVEN

"I believe that tonight will be most interesting." Diana's mother had been making similar comments since the dinner party held by Lord and Lady Browerton.

Diana had decided to stop arguing with her mother and had taken an agreeable tone of late. "I truly hope so." She smiled and turned away to hide her boredom with the topic.

They had only just arrived at Almack's and were just entering the large ballroom. While Diana wanted little to do with her mother's plans, she was glad to be at Almack's and looked forward to seeing Lady Henrietta. If she were being honest with herself, she would admit that she was hoping to see Matthew Repington as well.

Diana had made her way around to the other side of the ballroom when she saw Lady Henrietta arrive. It took only a moment for Lady Henrietta to see her across the ballroom giving Diana a little wave. Thinking to meet her halfway Diana took a few steps until she saw Mr Crandall working his way through the crowd. It did not appear he had seen Diana yet but she did not want to give him the impression that she was hoping to meet him as he came her way. Instead, she took a few steps back hoping he would not see her standing on the other side of a small group of young ladies.

Diana was relieved when he asked another young lady to dance.

She moved back to where she had been standing just as Lady Henrietta emerged from the crowd.

"There you are," Lady Henrietta fairly exclaimed. "I thought for sure I had seen you but then it seemed as though you had disappeared."

"My apologies. I stepped aside when the music started in an effort to sit this dance out."

"Yes, of course." Lady Henrietta seemed to scan the ballroom. "I see that Mr Crandall is in attendance."

"Indeed." Diana hoped her face did not give away her true feelings on the matter. "I do recall seeing him earlier."

Lady Henrietta turned back to Diana and said, "I understand Mr Crandall has been paying particular attention to you as of late."

Diana grimaced before she could stop herself. "I suppose. We danced twice last Wednesday."

"Are you not in favour of a courtship with him?"

"I realize that Mr Crandall is from a respected family and he is quite fashionable, but I fear there is not much more about him I admire."

"Oh?" Lady Henrietta raised an eyebrow and cocked her head to the side.

"He can be quite sour. He laments his position as a third son, complaining about the inadequacies of his two older brothers." Diana watched the same man cutting a fine figure in the ballroom and felt nothing but gratitude that she was not his dance partner. "He seems to find nearly everything beneath his touch."

"Well, that is rather unfortunate." Henrietta followed Diana's gaze around the room. "We seem to have enough of that in London."

Diana nodded in agreement. "He is the last in a long line of gentlemen who treat me as though I should be grateful they are giving me the time of day."

"It is completely infuriating." Lady Henrietta glared at Mr Crandall as he continued to dance.

"Although I dare say that I am glad I have seen how he truly acts now and not after a courtship had started."

"You are quite correct. I am sorry you seem to have had unfortunate luck this Season." Lady Henrietta sighed sympathetically.

Diana let out a long sigh. "It would be so very nice to find a gentleman who is stable and solid. Someone who is simply happy with the life he is living. A man who is comfortable where he is and with what he has."

Lady Henrietta nodded. "I am in agreement with you on that. Unfortunately, those gentlemen seem few and far between."

"Were your brothers like this before their marriages?"

"No, I do not believe so, although I believe Philip acted a bit high in the instep. From the stories I have heard from James and Hugh, it seems that it is possible Philip was half foxed during much of the time before he met Caroline." Lady Henrietta thought for a moment and then added, "Matthew, though, is quite another story."

Diana happened to look up to see Matthew standing across the ballroom. "How so?"

"Matthew is the most stable and responsible of all of us. He has never had a single complaint about being a fifth son. It never occurred to him to be upset or to reject the idea of joining the clergy. He has always been happy simply being Matthew. He is a remarkably good brother to us all."

"It is wonderful to know that at least one gentleman exists."

Lady Henrietta looked across the room wistfully. "Yes, I will miss seeing him at Castborough."

"Oh, will he be staying in London after the Season?"

"No," she turned back to look at Diana. "He has garnered an appointment as the curate in Whitehall."

Diana was surprised by the news. She and Matthew had talked

often but the subject of his studies and the upcoming appointment had never come up. She had not imagined that hearing about his appointment to Whitehall would upset her so much. Her throat growing tight, she swallowed and said, "I am glad for him, but I fear I shall miss him as well."

Lady Henrietta drew closer to her. "He does not leave for six weeks. There is still time."

Diana's breath caught, and she looked up meeting her friend's eyes. She dared not hope that Lady Henrietta was saying what she had initially thought "Do you really think so?"

Lady Henrietta gave her an encouraging smile. "Yes, I know for certain there is more than enough time."

She nodded at Lady Henrietta feeling her first sense of real happiness all Season. "Thank you, it is wonderful news for sure."

"Please call on me if there is any way I can be of assistance." Lady Henrietta gently placed a hand on Diana's arm.

Diana felt tears threaten to spring to her eyes. "Thank you. I could not ask for a better friend."

"Nor I," Lady Henrietta replied. "Would it not be better if you were a sister?"

It was nearly more than Diana could take. She cared so very much for Matthew, it seemed not possible for her to be so blessed. "I feel I should not even fathom it, but it would be far more wonderful than I could have ever dreamed."

CHAPTER TWELVE

Matthew stood across the room waiting anxiously while Henrietta spoke to Miss Diana. He wondered if Henrietta had remembered her offer to assist him. They were still speaking and then he began to worry that she had remembered. When Henrietta had offered her assistance, he had thought it was a good idea but now he was having second thoughts.

Did he really want to know if Miss Diana had no interest in him at all? The thought made his throat go dry. He could not help but think it would have been easier not knowing how she felt rather than the confirmation that she had no feelings for him in any way.

Waiting on the edge of the ballroom, he also had a full view of the entrance to Almack's. He watched the crowd come and go with feigned interest as he thought. He was starting wonder if he should have stayed home when he saw Webb working his way through the crowd.

"Webb," Matthew acknowledged him before glancing back over to where Henrietta and Miss Diana were still speaking.

"Repington," Webb said with a nod. He stood next to Matthew for nearly a minute shifting awkwardly in place. "I am hesitant to ask this, as I worry over what I might learn. Yet, I am unable to stop myself from asking. Did you by any chance have the opportunity to speak with your sister on the matter that we discussed the other day in Hyde Park?"

Matthew wanted to chuckle at the poor sod but the fact that his situation was not very much different than his own sobered him up quickly. He turned to Webb grateful to do something other than watching and waiting to hear from his sister.

"Yes, I went home straight away from the Park and spoke to her at once."

Webb stared at him for what seemed like several minutes before saying, "And?"

"Oh!" Matthew feigned surprise. The other man looked as though he might faint. Matthew might have felt bad but since he had good news for Webb he let it pass. "Henrietta was very helpful."

"She was?" Webb

"Yes, indeed." Matthew clapped the other man on the shoulder. "Henrietta was quite confident that you will have no objections were you to suggest a courtship with Lady Amelia."

"Oh," was all that the man uttered.

Matthew expected his friend to be relieved, but he looked even more stricken than before. "Webb, are you well?"

He shook his head quickly as though trying to shake off a stupor. "I had prepared myself for the worst. I had not thought that I would need to prepare myself for good news as well."

"It is understandable. Now you know how Lady Amelia feels you can begin to look forward. You will need to plan what you will do next."

Matthew was happy for his friend but it once again reminded him of Lady Abigail Underwood's abhorrent behaviour. While he knew that Diana was quite different, in almost every way, he still worried that he would be fooled again. Matthew barely finished the thought when his sister, caught his eye and nodded. He had almost missed her nod it was so quick but there was no denying what it meant.

Matthew took a moment to compose himself. "Perhaps we should go speak with the young ladies before someone else asks them to dance." It was clear from Webb's face that he had only just noticed that Lady Amelia had joined Henrietta and Miss Diana. "Yes, I think that would be best."

Matthew and Webb crossed the room easily skirting the edge of the ballroom. Matthew nodded back at Henrietta in a silent thank you for her assistance.

"Good evening, Mr Repington." Miss Diana lowered her eyelashes, then looked up at him again. "Are you enjoying Almack's tonight?"

Matthew could not stop himself from smiling at her. "I am finding it quite agreeable. Thank you. And how is your evening?"

Miss Diana glanced at Henrietta before saying, "It has been quite interesting thus far, and I am quite looking forward to the rest of the night."

The music began to play and Matthew found himself saying, "Would you like to dance?"

"Yes, that would be lovely."

Matthew led her to the center of the ballroom, feeling as though he and Miss Diana had started something extremely special. He tried not to think about it as he felt as though it was all too new and fragile. As they glided around the room they did not speak very much but he did not mind as he was enjoying their quiet moment together.

After the dance was over they returned to where Webb and Lady Amelia were still standing with Henrietta

"I cannot believe the crowd tonight," Lady Amelia was saying as they joined them once more.

"It is quite the crush tonight," Webb agreed with her.

Matthew looked around surprised by the number of people.

"Goodness!" Miss Diana remarked, looking up at him. "I had no idea."

Matthew had been so intent on Miss Diana that he had not noticed the growing crowd around them.

"It is no wonder that you did not notice," Henrietta said, causing Matthew to send her a warning look.

Neither he nor Miss Diana needed to be reminded of their preoccupation during their dance. He did not wish her to feel as though either of them had done anything improper.

Henrietta gave him a funny look as Webb spoke up. "There was some sort of hullabaloo outside preventing many from entering earlier."

"Oh! I wonder what happened?" Miss Diana asked.

"I believe I heard someone say that a carriage was involved. Whether it lost a wheel or had a runaway horse, I am not sure," Lady Amelia explained.

Matthew was about to comment when he saw Miss Diana's mother, Lady Penhaven coming over to them looking rather cross.

"Diana, please come with me."

Miss Diana looked concerned as she glanced at Matthew and then followed her mother. Her mother took her aside and although Matthew did not want to intrude he was extremely concerned about Miss Diana. Her mother seemed to be quite upset with her, and Diana did not look happy either. Her mother took Miss Diana by the hand and led her through the ballroom. With the ballroom of Almack's so crowded, Matthew could not see where they had gone but a short time later he saw Miss Diana dancing with Mr Crandall.

Henrietta had accepted an offer to dance with Timothy Sedgwick, Lady Amelia's brother upon her return she immediately glanced around for Miss Diana. Matthew was able to discern the moment his sister saw her friend was dancing with Mr Crandall. Henrietta's smile disappeared and she sent a worried look to Matthew. Finding himself hurt, discouraged and thoroughly disheartened, once again, Matthew left Almack's not sure what he was to do next.

CHAPTER THIRTEEN

Diana walked down the stairs, the house so quiet that she worried her footfalls would be heard along the upstairs hall. For nearly a week, she had gotten up early in the morning sneaking down to the kitchen in the dark hours before dawn for her morning meal. Once she was finished eating she would return to her room to read or sketch.

Diana could not even retrieve her watercolor paints from the drawing room as she had claimed a headache for the last two days. She had laid back against her pillows with her eyes closed when her mother had come to talk to her.

Her mother had been intolerable since she had caused the horrible scene at Almack's. Diana had been completely caught off guard by her mother's insistence that she stop speaking with Mr Repington. It had upset Diana but even more so when her mother had gone on to point out that Matthew was a fifth son, not at all what Diana's father expected for her. Diana had tried to reason with her mother but there was nothing for it. She had gone so far as to lead Diana across the ballroom to where Mr Crandall had been standing with several friends.

Mr Crandall had been extremely solicitous to Diana and her

mother. It was clear, at least to Diana, that Mr Crandall knew exactly what was to happen. Diana found his arrogance and general demeanour to be loathsome. She found it more and more difficult to spend time with him and remain civil.

There was a knock at Diana's door and she fell back to her pillows her eyes closed hoping her mother would go away if she appeared to be asleep. It was only a moment later that Diana heard her aunt say, "I know you are not sleeping. I just want to talk."

Diana opened her eyes and gave her aunt a sheepish look. "My apologies. I thought you were Mother."

Aunt Grace grimaced at Diana. "Well, that is quite distressing. I shall need to check my image in a mirror more often."

Diana giggled and shook her head. "No, of course not. Mother always comes in to see me although she never really asks as to how I am feeling. Yet the only thing she ever speaks about is how she is feeling and her thoughts on the matter. Any matter, really."

"Yes well, your mother is very good at thinking about only herself."

"I used to think that she meant well but I do not think that any longer." It made Diana sad but would not help her or the situation.

"I do not know. Perhaps she does mean well. I think it is quite possible that she does not know any other way. I seem to remember that her mother was fairly awful."

"She was?"

Aunt Grace nodded. "Oh, yes. There was a time we were not sure whether your mother and my brother would actually be able to marry."

DIANA OPENED her mouth to reply but sat there for a moment. "I have never heard that. That must have been troubling for them."

"It was very troubling for them. My brother was quite upset for a long period of time," Aunt Grace told her. "That is what is so surprising about how they are treating you now. I would have thought your father would remember what he went through."

Diana shifted on the bed a little. "I had not thought you would know about that."

"It is the reason for my visit. I wanted to find out, for myself, what is going on." Aunt Grace shook her head in disapproval. "It was quite the gossip this week as well as your mother's behaviour at Almack's. I am afraid it did not go unnoticed."

"That is my fault, of course, according to Mother." Diana stood up, moving across the room to stand at the window. "She was angry with me for dancing with Matthew Remington. He is the youngest son of the Duke of Castborough."

"And she was upset because he is a younger son?"

"Yes, apparently Father has decided that I should marry better than that."

"And how do you feel?"

"I care not when someone was born or in what order compared to their siblings. I care about their heart. Mr Repington is a good man. He is responsible and happy with his life. He respects and is close to his family."

"And what of this Mr Crandall?"

Diana frowned thinking about Mr Crandall. "I do not like speaking ill of people but there is not about much about Mr Crandall I like."

"How so?"

"It is hard to explain but he is not happy with anything. He complains constantly about anything and everything. Most of all, he holds great resentment about being a third son. For some reason he believes it is sort of an injustice that has befallen him. He has made it quite clear he feels that almost everything he encounters is rather beneath his touch, including me."

"Surely not." Aunt Grace grimaced and then frowned deeply.

"Indeed. He has made it more than obvious on each of our interactions that I should be grateful that he has even given me the time of day."

"I do not like that at all."

"You can imagine that I am not fond of it either."

"Yes, I imagine not." Her aunt looked out the window as if in thought. Then she turned and looked directly into Diana's eyes. "You said that Mr Crandall is not happy about being a third son, yes?"

"It is quite true. He acts as though his older brothers wronged him in some way. So, the simple fact that they were born is an insult to him."

"What a bunch of nonsense!" Aunt Grace shook her head and pursed her lips. "Mr Crandall grouses about something that is normal to the rest of us, while your father wants to force you into marriage with someone because of their status."

"I believe Father is friends with his father, Lord Dunwold." Diana sighed. "So, it seems it has turned into something rather complicated."

"It makes no sense to me. What is the difference between a third son and a fifth son?"

"Nothing, as far as I am concerned."

"It is not as though it is really any closer to the title in any practical manner… unless there are several deaths in the family which is not terribly likely. Perhaps your Father is planning on eliminating Mr Crandall's elder brothers."

Even though she knew that Aunt Grace was being humorous, Diana was still upset and let out her breath loudly. "That thought has occurred to me as well. Although, not in regards to Father, but perhaps Mr Crandall. It was not so long ago that Mr Townsend attempted to kill his own brother so he could be the heir."

"It would not be the first time that sort of thing has happened." Aunt Grace bit her bottom lip. Then she shrugged. "Well, there's little we can do about any of that or what anyone may be planning. You have explained all of this to your mother?"

"Mother will not listen to anything I have to say about Mr Crandall. He is from a respectable family and above reproach in her eyes. I have also explained that it does not matter to me whether a gentleman is a third son or a fifth son, or a fiftieth son for that matter," she finished her voice rising in exasperation.

"Clearly your father and mother have decided that it matters to them."

"I suppose that is what is all that matters at this point." Diana felt more hopeless than she had ever felt.

"Well, that is what is important to them." Her aunt sighed. "Your father would not approve of me speaking about this but with the way he is behaving I cannot say that I worry much over what he thinks."

"What do you mean?"

"Just that you should have some say in a decision that will affect the rest of your life. Diana, you are smart and caring, and even with all the mistreatment from your mother you are quite strong."

Diana let out a harsh brittle laugh.

"You are. You have endured years of your mother's corrections and criticism and yet still have a mind of your own. Much more so than any other young ladies that I have seen at Almack's this season or any before."

Diana did not know if she agreed with her aunt about being strong, but she was more mindful about most things than many of the other ladies. "I suppose, not that it helps me much now."

"It will serve you well. As I said your father will not be happy with me but I must tell you I feel that you should follow your heart."

"That seems a highly impossible feat just now."

"Your parents found a way to get what they wanted." Aunt Grace smiled mysteriously and reached out to take her hand.

Diana wanted to argue that she cared not what her parents had done but decided that Aunt Grace was telling her this for a reason. She let a long sigh and settled in to hear the message her aunt was trying to send.

CHAPTER FOURTEEN

"Matthew, I thought you were going to the Farringham's dinner party tonight," his mother asked when he came down the stairs. She was most obviously dressed for the dinner party, he recognized the robin's egg blue gown as one of her favourites.

"You look beautiful, Mother." He kissed her cheek and continued to walk into the drawing room. "No, I have decided to stay home."

"Thank you, dear." His mother followed him into the drawing room with a concerned look on her face. "Is there something amiss?"

"No." He sighed. "At least, nothing I cannot deal with on my own."

His mother stood quietly, the passive look on her face not changing as she tried to find out what was wrong. "I know you are perfectly capable of dealing with your own problems. I was merely wondering why you looked so Friday-faced."

"My apologies, Mother. I believe I may go back to Castborough to prepare for my appointment in Whitehall."

"You want to return to Castborough now?"

Matthew nodded, hoping she would not press him further. "Yes. I have grown tired of London."

His mother raised an eyebrow, seemingly unconvinced. "I believe you should think about your decision for a few days before doing anything rash."

Matthew nodded. "That is certainly sound advice, Mother. I shall do as you ask." He did not actually agree with his mother's advice, but he did not want to alarm her. A few extra days would not kill him, anyway.

"Perhaps you need to get out of the house. I understand you not wanting to go to the Farringham's dinner party, it is going to be a bit of a mull. Far too many people have been invited for it to be a proper dinner party, truthfully. I am quite sure most of the gentlemen will be half-foxed before dinner is even served." She said with a laugh and a shake of her head. "Do not stay here wandering the empty house."

Before Matthew could reply she added, "Dear, as long as you are here you should take heed of the advantages London has to offer."

"Thank you, Mother. Have a good evening."

After his family had left for the dinner party, Matthew paced in the library regretting his agreement to remain in London. He wished he had left for Whitehall already.

There were still several weeks before he could go but he had not lied when speaking to his mother, he could not stand being in London any longer. His disappointment over the news of Lady Abigail's betrothal to Lord Turnbull had been nothing compared to how he was now feeling about Miss Diana and her unexpected interest in Crandall.

Restless and with no idea of what to do, Matthew grabbed his coat and left the house following his mother's advice. He had walked a fair amount before turning back, with a firm destination in mind. A drink at Whites would be the assistance needed to ease the torment. Matthew walked into the exclusive club and almost immediately ran into Webb who was standing just inside the doorway peering hesitantly into the crowded room.

"Hello, Webb. I did not expect to see you here tonight."

Webb looked just as surprised to see Matthew. "Likewise. I thought you would be at the Farringham's dinner party."

"I was thinking the same about you."

Webb glanced back toward the door. "I was headed there just now, but decided to stop in here first."

"And I decided at the last minute not to attend, sending my apologies along with my family."

Webb frowned. "I am wishing I had done the same."

"Will Lady Amelia not be in attendance?" Matthew asked him after a few moments of silence.

"No, she will not. She was also invited to the piano recital held by Lord Colborne, I believe Miss Helena is her cousin. She had accepted the invitation several weeks ago."

"My mother stated that the dinner party will be rather large perhaps your absence would go unnoticed," Matthew suggested.

"I should not like to be rude though." Webb sounded resigned as he looked longingly into the club.

"Perhaps one of the servants could have a message delivered. You could send your apologies and claim that you fell ill at the last moment."

Webb looked positively overjoyed at the thought. "That is a great idea indeed." He moved swiftly into the club calling to the first member of service he came upon.

Matthew surveyed the room while Webb dictated his note and directions for delivery.

Webb joined him. "Well that is taken care of. Shall we get a table?"

"I believe I see an empty table in the back. Just over there." Matthew gestured toward the back of the room. "If you want to go sit I will get us our drinks. Whiskey?"

"Yes, please," Webb agreed and began making his way to the back.

Matthew turned to get their drinks and was almost immediately set upon by Nigel Coombs. Stifling a groan, Matthew turned to the other man.

"Coombs."

"Repington, I do not think I have seen you in Whites this Season."

"That is not surprising in the least. I have not frequented the club much this Season." Matthew shrugged. "I suppose I have had too many other social engagements to attend."

Coombs nodded. "I would imagine so."

"Not that it has done you much good."

This came from behind Matthew and he turned to see Henry Milling leaning against the wall.

"Milling, I see you are already jug bitten."

The other man laughed and moved to stand next to Coombs. "Is it not why you are here as well? To drink your sorrows away?"

"My sorrows?" Matthew chuckled. "Surely not."

"No? It should not be so surprising." He turned to Coombs and said in a quiet voice, although clearly loud enough for Matthew to hear. "He certainly got over Lady Abigail quickly. It is just a shame he has had the same luck with Lord Penhaven's daughter."

Matthew shook his head, "I have no time for this nonsense."

He took a step to move around the man, but Milling moved into his way. "Have you not heard?"

"I have no idea what you are talking about, nor do I care." Matthew again stepped aside.

Milling followed him. "So, you do not know? That is quite interesting."

Matthew was getting irritated and he turned around and finally said, "Fine! What is so blasted important that you feel it necessary to speak to me about it now?"

"Only that Miss Diana Windham and Mr Crandall should be announcing their betrothal quite soon."

That stopped Matthew short. "What are you talking about? They have not even begun to court."

"Her father approves the match and therefore a betrothal is due any day now."

Matthew did not know what to believe. It was quite well known that Milling was the sort of man who liked to stir up trouble. Anything Matthew did or said would surely be spread around the club and most of London before the sun rose the next morning.

Matthew nodded. "It is good that they have received her father's blessing. I wish them every happiness."

Milling sneered at him. "Oh, I am sure you do. Come along, Coombs."

The man turned away nearly stumbling over his own feet, Coombs looked back apologetically but followed anyway.

Matthew was about to head for the door, having had enough of Whites for one night. He ran almost directly into Webb.

He held up two glasses of whiskey. "I just came to find you." He saw Matthew's face and blinked. "Something amiss?"

"Quite."

Webb looked down the way Milling and Coombs had gone. "What has happened?"

"I have just found out that Miss Diana will be accepting a proposal from Mr Crandall. It s expected any day now."

Webb scowled. "Are you sure?"

"That is what Milling said."

Webb shook his head. "I should not believe him if I were you. He only wishes to upset you. He is a bigger gossip than any bored housemaid could ever hope to be."

"But…" Matthew sighed and looked away

"Come, let us go have our drinks."

Matthew followed his friend to the table too dejected to argue.

"Sit down," Webb told him.

Once they were seated Webb set a glass of whiskey in front of him. "I have heard the same rumour about Miss Diana but according to Lady Amelia, it is not the case. Her father is in favour of a match but Miss Diana is not. She is actually quite upset about her father's plans and is not happy that these tales are going about."

Matthew sat up straighter. "Miss Diana is not in favour of the match?"

"She is not." Webb sat back in his chair. "Perhaps you should find a way to speak with her before you decide what to believe."

Matthew took a long drink and set his glass on the table. "That is probably wise."

CHAPTER FIFTEEN

"How are you this morning?" Henrietta looked up at Matthew when he entered the room.

Matthew sighed not sure what to tell her. It had been more than a week since he had talked to Miss Diana and several days since he had the encounter with Milling and Coombs at Whites. He was still hopeful that Webb was correct, but it was becoming more difficult for him to believe as time passed without him being able to speak with Miss Diana.

If only he had a chance to speak with her, he might be able to find out how she really felt. After Henrietta had spoken to Miss Diana there had not been time for Matthew to speak with her himself. All he knew was that he needed to do something before he left for Whitehall.

"I seem to have a dilemma." He had no idea what to do and Henrietta had been very helpful before. He decided it was time to trust his sister again.

"Oh? What has happened?" She tilted her head and waited quietly for his response.

"I was at Whites the other night with Jonathan Webb when we encountered Nigel Coombs and Henry Milling."

Henrietta grimaced before saying, "I am sorry for that. Mr Coombs is quite the gossip and that Mr Milling is just awful."

"You are quite right on both counts." Matthew was surprised that Henrietta had heard about them before. He knew that his older brothers had some dealings with the two men but had not known Henrietta was privy to those conversations. Getting back to his dilemma, he said, "I was told that there is a rumour going around that Miss Diana is to be betrothed to Mr Crandall."

Henrietta looked up sharply. "Yes, Miss Diana is quite upset about the rumours. She has no wish to marry Mr Crandall, in fact, she does not even like him. Spending time with him is a chore she quite despises."

Henrietta's words made him feel better but there was still the problem that he had been unable to see Miss Diana. Her mother had blocked his every attempt.

"Webb said the same thing on advice from Lady Amelia. My concern now though is that I am unable to speak with Miss Diana. Her mother has kept her from being available to accept visitors."

Henrietta hummed to herself. "That is a dilemma. I think we shall need to create a situation designed to allow you to talk to her. Perhaps I could invite her on a ride in Hyde Park."

Matthew was skeptical. "That might work but I worry that her mother would be suspicious since you are my sister."

"Of course, that makes sense. If her mother came along as a chaperone that would defeat our purpose and if caught it would cause more distrust."

Matthew blew out a long breath. "So, what are we to do?"

Henrietta was staring at the table and then suddenly snapped her fingers. "I shall hold a card party."

"How would that be any different from going to Hyde Park?" Matthew asked.

"Because it will not be just the three of us, I will invite Mr Webb, Lady Amelia, Mr Sedgwick and several others. Miss Diana's mother will be here and there would be no reason for her to object."

Matthew was skeptical. "I do not know if this will work."

"And as we know, Lady Penhaven would not decline an invitation from the Duke and Duchess of Castborough. She is too conscious of standing to reject such an offer."

Matthew realized that Henrietta was quite right. It was the perfect opportunity to speak with Diana if not completely alone then during a quiet card game. Hopefully, it would be enough. He would have to make the most of what time he did manage to steal.

"What do you think?" Henrietta asked him, waiting anxiously for his response.

Matthew could not help smiling at his younger sister. "I think you are rather brilliant and quite dear to go to so much trouble to help me."

Henrietta waved his comment away looking a trifle embarrassed. "It is beneficial to all of us. I will get to have a card party, you and Miss Diana will have a chance to speak. I am quite sure that Lady Amelia and Mr Webb will be happy about it as well."

"Well, for whatever reason I will still be thankful for your help in the matter." Matthew beamed at her.

He was extremely grateful for her help but he was still somewhat skeptical. He hoped Lord and Lady Penhaven would be occupied long enough for him to say what was needed to Miss Diana. And from there, he hoped what he had to say would matter to her.

CHAPTER SIXTEEN

Matthew walked down the stairs feeling apprehensive and hopeful at the same time. Not surprisingly Henrietta had thought of a perfect solution. Their parents had been thrilled to hold a card party at her request and Lord and Lady Penhaven were more than happy to accept the invitation.

The card party was due to start within the hour. Several small tables had been set up in the drawing room. Card games had been set up at each table.

"Are you ready?" Henrietta came up next to him in the hallway and reached out to take his hand.

Matthew looked down at himself. Squeezing her hand, he stepped back and straightened his coat. "Yes, I believe so."

"That is good. I am quite sure that we are going to have a very enjoyable evening."

"I, for one, am thrilled about that." While Matthew trusted that Henrietta had a plan to get everyone together, he was not sure that the ulterior purpose would be able to be met.

As if reading his mind, Henrietta shook her head slightly. "You must stop fretting about it. I have it all planned out and it will work, too. As long as you do not make a mull of it."

"A mull of it? I do not even know what is to happen. How could I make a mull of it?" His voice was indignant at his sister's accusation.

"Oh, stop." Henrietta laughed. "As I told you, do not be worried, I know what I am about."

Matthew's scowl at his sister gave way to a smile. He held up his hands in surrender and said, "I appreciate your assistance and I bow to your expertise in this matter."

"As well you should." Henrietta lifted her chin in support of her confidence.

Matthew simply shook his head and walked away.

It was not long before people began arriving for the party. Matthew stood off by himself in the corner of the drawing room, so as to not be the first person Lord and Lady Penhaven saw when they arrived.

It was then he realized that everyone Henrietta had invited was someone who was very close to her. If there were any questions asked, they would all happily cooperate with Lady Henrietta and no one would think there had been anything to worry over.

Webb had arrived early, no doubt hoping to spend more time with Lady Amelia. Matthew was happy to have an ally to speak with and even more so when Miss Diana arrived with Lord and Lady Penhaven.

Matthew tried his best to continue speaking nonchalantly with Webb. He happened to look over just as Miss Diana was scanning the room and their eyes locked he was overjoyed at the quick smile that came to her lips confirming his hope that she would be happy to see him.

Whatever happened for the rest of the night Matthew would hold on to that one smile because it had meant so much to him. He chose to take it as a sign of good things that may be coming.

CHAPTER SEVENTEEN

Diana looked away quickly when she saw Mr Repington. She glanced at her mother thoroughly relieved to see that she was fully engrossed with speaking with the Duke and Duchess of Castborough. Her mother had completely missed the swift smile that she displayed upon seeing Mr Repington across the room.

She had been very fairly certain when Lady Henrietta had invited her to the card party that he would be in attendance. She was not sure if he would be angry about the rumours that have been going around about her and Mr Crandall, but she was hoping to find out for sure.

The whole bit of gossip had been her mother's doing, Diana knew, which had made it all the more upsetting. Dealing with the chatter of London's social elite was hard enough to endure but to learn that your mother was the one starting the hearsay was even more disheartening.

"Oh, Miss Diana, I am so glad you were able to attend." Lady Henrietta rushed up to her with a broad and sincere smile.

"I am so thankful you invited me. It promises to be a wonderful night," Diana said smiling at Lady Henrietta.

"Yes, indeed, that is just what I was hoping for." Henrietta beamed and looped her arm through Diana's warmly.

Lady Amelia joined them. "I have been looking forward to this all week. Thank you so much for inviting me. What a wonderful idea to get us all together!"

Diana let Lady Henrietta lead them across the drawing room and away from her parents. She was not sure what her mother would do when she realized Mr Crandall would not be in attendance. Although Diana did not know for sure that he would be absent, she was fairly confident that Lady Henrietta had not invited him. It had not been that long since they had spoken at Almack's, and Lady Henrietta certainly would have remembered their conversation.

"You two sit here. I want to make sure you are in the right place when we get started later." Lady Henrietta pointed to a table near the window. "I will return in a moment once I greet everyone."

Diana watched as Lady Henrietta greeted each person and then casually directed them to sit according to some pattern that only she recognized. Smiling to herself, she was looking forward to what was in store for the evening more and more.

Once everyone had been seated Lady Henrietta announced, "I am so glad everyone is here. I plan on making things interesting throughout the evening."

"I am intrigued. What is to happen?" Miss Hannah was sitting at the Whist table and tilted her head in query.

"It would not be any fun if I told you before it all happens." Lady Henrietta looked stern and smug at the same time. Then she giggled and shrugged. "You will just have to wait to see."

Miss Hannah sat back in her seat clearly pouting but smiled when Mr Roberts began to tease her about her impatience. There was some murmuring and laughter as people began to guess at Lady Henrietta's plan.

Lady Henrietta had just sat down with Diana and Lady Amelia when Mr Repington and Mr Webb joined them.

"I am surprised you are not over playing Whist," Lady Amelia remarked to Mr Webb who sat down across from her at the table.

Mr Webb looked across the room at the table she mentioned. "It appears that I had no choice in that. Lady Henrietta showed everyone to their seats. There are only a few left, Matthew and I decided we should sit before she forgets about us."

Diana laughed. "She does seem to have planned everything out down to the last detail." Since Lady Henrietta had taken the time to do so, Diana was sure she had a purpose for the evening. Though Diana could not guess what that special purpose might be.

"Not that I am complaining, mind you," Mr Webb said swiftly before glancing at Lady Amelia who blushed and looked away shyly.

"Of course not," Mr Repington said. "My sister would certainly ring a fine peal over us if we did complain."

Lady Henrietta gasped in indignation. "I would not. That is complete nonsense."

"Would you not?" Mr Repington asked pushing his chair back from the table. "If I were to move to that table say over there you would have no complaint?"

"Matthew, sit down," Lady Henrietta said sharply causing everyone to laugh.

"Nonsense, indeed," Diana agreed with another laugh.

"Oh, the devil take you all." Lady Henrietta feigned a pout and then frowned. "I am going to go visit with my guests Perhaps they will appreciate me."

"Do you think she's really upset?" Diana could not help but ask Mr Repington as Mr Webb set up the game.

Mr Repington shook his head, watching his sister move from table to table talking and laughing as she went. "I highly doubt it. She would be walking around talking to everyone regardless. though. That makes it difficult to be sure."

Diana was content to assume that Lady Henrietta was not annoyed as she looked to be enjoying herself. They finished their game and Lady Amelia stood up followed by Mr Webb.

"Are you leaving us?" Diana asked.

"Lady Henrietta has waved us over," Lady Amelia explained with a shrug before following Mr Webb.

"Oh, so she has begun her intrigues." Diana looked around wondering if someone from another table would be joining them.

Mr Repington looked around. "It looks like we might be on our own."

"Oh?" Diana asked, not minding it in the least. "Your sister seems to have spent a great deal of time and effort planning this card party."

Mr Repington began setting up the next game. "Yes, she spent an entire afternoon deciding whom to invite."

"Goodness," Diana replied looking around the room at the people gathered there.

She was not surprised by the ladies and gentlemen she had invited. They were all fun and happy, not a gossip among them. Diana appreciated the fact that she could enjoy herself without the worry of being insulted or having something twisted into rumours to be spread around town the next week.

"Have you been enjoying the Season? It seems as though I have not seen you in some time." Matthew looked at her and raised an eyebrow in question.

"Yes, it has been some time." Diana had not expected him to have noticed the time as acutely as she had. "I was feeling ill this last week and skipped many of my social engagements."

"I am most sorry to hear you were feeling unwell. It is a relief to see that you were feeling well enough to attend tonight." He laid out his cards.

"Yes, thank you." She played her cards as well. "I have to admit that Lady Henrietta's invitation hastened my recovery."

He turned to look at her. "Something to look forward to?"

Mr Repington had no idea how right he was. "In a way it was, I had been upset about some rumours that had been floating about regarding myself and Mr Crandall. Your sister's invitation was a great distraction from that."

"I imagine so." He stared intently at his cards. "I found the rumour to be distressing as well."

Diana hoped she understood his meaning. "It is my hope that if I stay far away from Mr Crandall for the remainder of the Season the idle gossip will cease to be interesting."

"Just the Season?" Matthew placed a card on the table.

Diana shuddered. "I would rather not see him ever again but that seemed overly rude to point out at the start. I would hate to seem unkind about another human being."

Mr Repington looked over and smiled. "Some truths can be difficult to speak."

"I believe that, too." Diana could barely look away from him. She had not noticed how green his eyes were, she supposed that his green coat made it more pronounced. She looked down at her cards realizing it was her turn. "Is that something you learned in your studies?"

"Yes, although it was something I have understood for a long time When you have five siblings you learn quite a bit just from being in the same household." He seemed to hesitate, so she waited. "It did indeed assist me in my path to the clergy though."

Diana wondered if he hesitated because of his calling or because of his remark about his siblings. "Your sister said that you had taken your vows. That is quite commendable."

"Thank you. I have been appointed to a position in Whitehall."

Diana placed another card on the table. "I understand Whitehall is in the north, is that correct?"

"Quite right, near Manchester."

"It sounds quite lovely. I grow tired of London rather quickly each Season." Diana stared across the room. "I should like to live somewhere quiet. Whitehall must be wonderful in the spring."

"More than beautiful, I would say." Diana looked back to see that he had been looking at her when he spoke. "Are you quite sure?"

Diana did not look away. "Oh yes, Mr Repington, I am quite sure."

"Matthew." He smiled and blinked slowly. "Please call me, Matthew."

"Matthew," she said and stopped, she liked how it sounded. "Matthew, I have never been so sure of anything in my life."

"I understand. I am feeling the same certainty."

A moment later the drawing room door opened the Duke and Duchess of Castborough appeared followed by the parents of many of the card players including Miss Diana's.

Her mother's face had barely registered her disapproval before Lady Henrietta had stood up and announced, "All right, everyone! It is time to switch tables. Players to whom I gave an extra card please switch tables."

Matthew stood up and nodded at Miss Diana. "It was a pleasure, Miss Diana."

"Yes, thank you." He walked away before she even finished speaking.

He and several others changed tables as though Lady Henrietta's instructions had been a planned part of the evening. Of course, Diana realized that they had been but just not in the way her mother would think. Lady Henrietta smiled from the Whist table as Lady Amelia and Miss Hannah came to sit down with Diana.

CHAPTER EIGHTEEN

Matthew had enjoyed speaking with Miss Diana at the card party and Henrietta had been more than helpful even after their first encounter making sure that he and Miss Diana were able to, at least be at the same table while playing cards. He had never been happier knowing that Miss Diana felt the same way he did.

The best part had been seeing her laughing and enjoying herself at his sister's card party. There had only been one moment where she had not looked happy and that was when her parents had walked into the room. Lady Penhaven had looked very upset but as soon as Henrietta had moved people about, Miss Diana had gone back enjoying herself again.

It was in that moment though, that everything had changed for him. Matthew made a promise to himself and silently to Miss Diana that he would do everything he could to make her happy. He never wanted to see her look that upset again.

He knew more than ever that he cared deeply for Miss Diana and he must do something soon. If he could have, he would have already asked her to be his wife but he was determined to do what was proper. He knew how he felt about Miss Diana and he had spent a considerable time reflecting on his vows. There would be no way around it, Matthew would have to speak with Miss Diana's father, Baron Penhaven, to ask for her hand in marriage.

It would be difficult as it was clear that Lord and Lady Penhaven did not favour a match between him and Miss Diana. As he had told Miss Diana, some truths were hard to speak and this was a truth he could not deny. Because honesty and dedication mattered so much, he could not accept his post in Whitehall without speaking this truth before he left.

His decision made, Matthew pulled on his coat and left the drawing room. Calling out to Fletcher, "Notify the footman that I am to leave at once."

"Yes, sir," Fletcher replied turning down the hall to the kitchen.

Matthew went into the library and wrote a quick note, handing it to Fletcher. "Please see that Lady Henrietta receives this upon her return to Repington House."

"Yes, sir," Fletcher said tucking the note into his pocket. "Will you be waiting for the carriage in the drawing room?"

"No," Matthew shook his head. "I shall wait for it on the sidewalk."

"Very well, sir." Fletcher nodded and walked over to open the door.

Matthew walked through the door and then stopped. He turned back and said, "Thank you, Fletcher."

Normally stoic, the man smiled slightly before nodding again. "Good day, sir."

"Good day, Fletcher."

The ride in the carriage did not take long. The London residence of Lord Penhaven was located just outside Mayfair as well. The carriage stopped in front of a large house and Matthew could not help but wonder if he should have walked the distance so he would have had time to prepare himself for the conversation ahead. Of course, Matthew also knew that would have only been more time for him to delay the inevitable.

Blowing out a long breath, Matthew got out of the carriage and swiftly walked up the steps. He knocked on the door and half a minute later a white-haired man greeted him. "Good afternoon, sir. May I help you?"

"Yes, I am here to see Lord Penhaven."

"Is he expecting you, sir?"

"No, he is not. I had no time to make an appointment."

"Please do come in." The man stepped back and opened the door wide. "May I get your name?"

"Yes, of course. Matthew Repington." Matthew's heart was beating so fast he felt as though he had run all the way from Repington House.

"Please wait here while I notify Lord Penhaven."

"Thank you." Matthew waited anxiously in the entry hall. The Penhaven residence was very nice, not as opulent as Repington house but it was certainly kept up and well furnished. The house seemed rather quiet and Matthew wondered if anyone was actually in the residence. That was until he heard Lady Penhaven shriek from somewhere down the hall. "No, he can wait forever on the front steps."

Matthew was unable to hear the servant's response as he was clearly speaking in a more respectable manner.

"You let him in? Perkins, what were you thinking?"

"The man in question is clearly a gentleman. How am I to discern between someone who is to see Lord Penhaven for business reasons versus someone else? Perhaps I should leave everyone on the front steps until my lady can meet them at the door."

Even though Matthew was the subject of scorn he could not help but smirk at the older man's brash comment. Lady Penhaven was not as amused by the man's comments snapping, "No, of course not. And watch your tone, Perkins."

The door Matthew presumed to be to the drawing room opened and Perkins emerged once more. "Mr Repington, if you will follow me, Lord Penhaven will meet with you in the library in just a moment."

"Thank you."

Matthew waited in the library not sure if he should sit down to wait or stand. He was still debating his options when the door opened and Lord Penhaven came into the room. The man was nearly as old as Matthew's own father. His hair had begun to creep back from his forehead, but he kept the back longer revealing some of the waves that were quite evident in Miss Diana's hair. Certainly not as curly as hers but still similar.

"Mr Repington, to what do I owe the pleasure of your visit?"

Matthew had expected a greeting and some small talk before he got to the meaning of his visit, but he would proceed if necessary. "Good afternoon, Lord Penhaven."

"Good afternoon, Mr Repington," Lord Penhaven replied, his annoyance clear in his voice. "Why are you here?"

Matthew took a deep breath and straightened his shoulders. He did not look forward to the conversation, but he would do it for the woman he loved. "It is about Miss Diana."

"I expected as much," the older man said walking around to stand behind the large desk.

"I care for her very much and only wish for her the best." Matthew began his speech trying to appeal to the older man's sense of fatherly protection.

"As do I."

"I could go on and on, but I will spare you that and get to the point of my visit. I wish to marry your daughter and I am asking for your blessing." Matthew held his breath as he waited for the man's response.

Lord Penhaven nodded several times and then began to laugh.

CHAPTER NINETEEN

Diana knelt next to the fireplace straining to hear what was happening downstairs. Her bedroom was above the library and she could often hear what was going on there through her fireplace as the two rooms shared a chimney.

She knew that Matthew was there to see her father. Her mother's shrieks had been heard all through the house. It made her even angrier to know Matthew had heard them as well. She leaned forward and then she heard it, laughter, coming from the library.

She sat back on her heels wondering what could have made her father laugh. Surely Matthew had not said anything humorous. It took her only a moment to discern that her father's laugh was one of condescension and derision.

Diana let out a frustrated groan. She had always thought her father respectable and honourable, but she no longer felt that way. If he would treat Matthew, who had shown responsibility and respect by coming to speak to her father, so horribly he was certainly not the man she had once thought he was.

Angry and disheartened Diana pushed up from the floor to pace in front of the two windows that looked out onto the street in front of the house. She had known her parents did not approve of a match with Matthew, but she had not thought they would be so callous as to disregard her feelings on a matter that would affect the rest of her life.

How they could think that awful Mr Crandall was a better choice for a husband than someone as responsible and caring as Matthew Repington, she would never know. She refused to think about what would happen if she could not marry Matthew. She could barely stand dancing with Mr Crandall, much less living in the same house with him. The thought of a life with him made her shudder.

"There has to be another way," she muttered to herself as she paced. She stopped and looked out the window, the vast area of Hyde Park was visible in the distance. If only she and Matthew could leave all of this madness and live in Whitehall where no one could bother them.

Her aunt's words came back to her. "Your parents found a way."

Diana had never found out what her parents had done to get around the wishes of their parents, but she knew what she and Matthew could do if they had the courage. She stared out the window again and let herself imagine being married to Mr Crandall. She was sure that a day would not go by where he would fail to remind her how lucky she was that he had married her.

She did not even have to imagine the joy of being married to Matthew. She would need no such reminders of her good fortune as she would wake up each day feeling blessed and thankful that she was married to him.

She rushed to her desk and wrote out two quick notes. She folded one in half and addressed the front. The second letter she folded twice and then rolled it as tightly as she could. Praying that her mother would stay in the drawing room, Diana hurried down the stairs. To her relief, Perkins was standing in the entry.

"Perkins, can you please send this letter out right away?"

"Yes, of course, Miss Diana," he replied.

"Thank you very much. And, if you please, do not mention it to

Lord or Lady Penhaven." Her eyes pleaded for him to do as she asked.

He glanced at the library door and shook his head. "Certainly not, Miss Diana. I will keep this between us."

She nodded and blew out a breath readying herself for what was to come next.

"Miss Diana, if there is anything else that you need assistance with please do not hesitate to ask."

"Thank you, Perkins." Diana gave him a grateful smile before turning toward the library.

Not bothering to knock Diana opened the library door and walked in to see her father sitting behind his desk with a nasty look upon his face while Matthew stood looking rather dejected.

"Diana, you should not be in here. Go directly to the drawing room and wait for me to come talk to you." Her father's anger was thick, but she did not care.

"No, Father, I will not." She did not back down even as her words garnered a look of shock from him. "This has much more to do with me, than with you. Do you not think I should have some say into what is being discussed here?"

"No, I do not. You are not capable of making a sound decision." Her father stood up. "You will marry Mr Crandall and you will thank me for it."

"I will do no such thing. I will not marry Mr Crandall, nor thank you for the honour. He is a vile man who treats me with disdain."

"It is no wonder if you talk to him the way you have talked to me," her father retorted. "No daughter of mine will marry a fifth son."

Diana gasped at her father's words.

Matthew stepped in front of Diana. "Lord Penhaven, I realize you are upset but you must not take your anger out on Miss Diana."

"I will do anything that I bloody please. You will leave my house and never return," he bellowed at Matthew before turning to

Diana. "And you will go to the drawing room and wait for me to join you."

Matthew looked as though he was going to say something else and Diana stepped forward to face him. "It is no use, Matthew. He will not listen."

He looked down at her and the look of anguish on his face nearly broke her. She shook her head as she pushed the rolled note into his hand her own body shielding the action from her father's eyes. "I am so very sorry. You should leave before anything untoward can happen to you."

Matthew nodded and left the library.

Her father looked smug and proud of himself.

"You are as vile as Mr Crandall," she told him. "I will never forget the words you have said today, nor will I forgive you."

"Diana, you must—"

She did not wait to hear what he was to say as she spun on her heel and left the library. She flew up the stairs to prepare for what was to come next.

CHAPTER TWENTY

Matthew walked into Repington House having little memory of his journey back there. He was stunned and heartbroken that Lord Penhaven had been filled so completely with disdain that he had dismissed all of Matthew's efforts to speak with him. It was Diana's capitulation though, that had shocked and hurt him far more than any of the insults and threats that Lord Penhaven had hurled at him. Her quiet acquiescence had felt like a knife piercing his heart. It felt as though there was a gaping hole in his chest from which he would never recover.

Numbly, he walked up the stairs not seeing anything around him in his miserable state. He heard voices downstairs but did not turn to look to see who it might be, wanting only to be alone in his room. He had thought he had been devastated by Lady Abigail's distant rejection of him, but he had been so very mistaken.

He would spend a few more days in London to get his affairs in order before returning to Castborough. It would not be soon enough before he could travel to Whitehall to begin as the curate at the parish there.

It was not until Matthew walked into his room and began to pull off his coat that he remembered that Diana had pushed something into his hand in her father's library. He had been so focused on stopping her father from speaking the contemptible words to and in the presence of Miss Diana that he had altogether forgotten that she had done so.

He stared at the roll in his hand, surely a note. Unsure if he should read it or not, he dropped heavily onto the end of his bed. Matthew did not think he could bear to read Diana's dismissal of him in her own hand. It had been more than troublesome to hear her speak the words to his face.

He was about to toss the rolled paper across the room when he remembered that she had entered the room defiant and ready to contend with her father. Hoping that what he was about to read would be better than the words she had spoken to him, he unrolled the note.

He read the note over several times to assure himself that he had read it correctly. If she was suggesting what he thought she was, their lives would be changed forever. It would be wonderful and frightening, daring and joyous. No matter what they encountered, he did not care. If they could be together forever, he would do anything and everything he could to make it happen.

CHAPTER TWENTY-ONE

The following evening, Matthew waited at the Grosvenor Gate of Hyde Park, his carriage parked nearby. He had been waiting for some time and was anxious about the meeting. He had arrived early not quite certain when the sun would be going down. Not missing the sunset was of the utmost importance.

Of course, he was not even sure what he should be looking out for. Someone on foot? Or perhaps a carriage? He did not know. With as much circumspect that he could manage, he had examined each person and every carriage that had passed near the gate.

His worry rising, he pulled the note from his pocket and unrolled it to read once more.

My dearest Matthew,

I fear that my father will all never agree to our marriage. If you still wish it and have faith in me, I know we can find a way for us to have the blessed and wonderful life we both dream of.

Please meet me tomorrow evening at sundown near the Grosvenor Gate at Hyde Park.

Until tomorrow,

Diana

EVEN KNOWING the logic of it, he still worried that Miss Diana had changed her mind or even worse, had been found out and prevented from coming. The thought made his heart stop and his stomach to churn.

The past two days had been so tumultuous, Matthew could not imagine what he would do should she not be there to meet him. He supposed that he would simply be forced to do what he had planned to do before—go back to Castborough and then on to Whitehall. Alone.

He had barely rolled the note up again when a carriage pulled up and stopped at the gate. The door opened and a woman got out wearing a dark blue hooded cloak. She looked around cautiously her eyes stopping at him and she pushed back the hood. Although he had been thoroughly convinced it was Diana he was utterly relieved to see her face smiling at him. She hurried to him and he was amazed by her beauty and overwhelmed by his feelings for her.

"Matthew! You came. I was so afraid you would not want to see me."

"Why would you say that?"

"My father was so awful to you. I worried you would be put off permanently by his deplorable behaviour." She looked down and frowned. "I would not have blamed you."

Matthew shook his head. "All is well. At least I hope it is."

She nodded. "I said horrible things to you. It broke my heart to speak in that manner, but I knew my father would not falter nor concede. I feared talking to him further would have only caused the circumstance to be more troublesome."

"I am glad you know him well enough to see that. I still had hope I could convince your father otherwise," Matthew confided.

"So you forgive me for telling you to go?"

"They were the most painful words I have ever heard. Though once I read your note I understood completely."

"I cannot apologize enough. I was so very worried that you would throw the note away in anger without even reading it."

"I very nearly did," he admitted with a grin.

She gasped and covered her mouth, "Oh goodness."

"Yes, I returned to Remington house and I was quite upset. I had not even looked at what you had put into my hand. When I discovered it still in my hand I was afraid it would say the same things that you had said to me in your father's library. I was about to throw it across the room when I remembered you had come into the room upset at your father and wanting to speak your mind. I trusted that you had been defiant when you wrote the note and that you would not be saying goodbye to me."

"I cannot tell you how happy that makes me to hear these words."

"Your note brought me a lot of joy as well. But Diana, as much as I want to marry you, I do not want you to regret your decision. It will likely be a decision that will sever ties with your family. I think you should be certain before we move forward."

Diana smiled up at him and took a deep breath. "If you are still wanting to marry, I would be so very happy to travel to Gretna Green with you to do so."

CHAPTER TWENTY-TWO

Diana held her breath waiting for his answer.

"Are you really sure?" He winced as he watched her smile falter.

"Matthew, of course. Yes, I am sure."

"Please do not misunderstand me. I only ask because I do not wish to make you choose between myself and your family." He frowned. "I would hate myself forever if I made you unhappy and then you lost your family, too."

She smiled again. "That is precisely why I could not be more sure. It is because of my mother and father I have been forced to choose. They care only about what they want with no regard for my wishes. But you, Matthew, you are altogether concerned about my feelings without a care for your own. That is how I know for certain what I want right now."

Matthew took both of her hands in his. "Diana, will you make me so very happy and marry me?"

"Yes! Yes, of course, I will." Diana was so overjoyed, she could barely breathe.

Behind them, the door to the carriage opened and Diana felt

Matthew stiffen. She squeezed his hands. "It is all right. It is only my Aunt Grace."

"She is assisting you?"

"Yes. She was the one that helped me see I had to follow my heart. She also showed me that I could be creative to find a way to do that." Diana watched his face go from surprise to complete shock to understanding in such a brief amount of time. "Did you not tell anyone of your plans to meet me?"

"I left a note for Henrietta. I should think she will receive it when she returns from Almack's." He squeezed her hand and then rushed over to help Aunt Grace out of the carriage.

"Thank you, Mr Repington," Aunt Grace said straightening her skirt.

"It appears that I should be thanking you." Matthew smiled and nodded. "Diana says that you have been a great help to her—and ultimately to me."

The older woman waved him away with a laugh. "I only reminded Diana that it is her life, not her father's."

"Still, it was something I needed to hear." Diana stepped over to her aunt and hugged her warmly.

Aunt Grace pointed into the carriage. "Diana's valise is in front of the seat, there."

Matthew leaned forward and brought out Diana's travel bag.

"You two need to leave soon. Diana, I can hide your absence until tomorrow night or perhaps the next morning but after that, I cannot guarantee your parents will not have found out that you have gone."

Diana looked at Matthew who spoke up to say, "At that point, it will not matter. We will be far enough ahead of them that they will not be able to catch up with us."

Night had fallen and she was delighted to know that they would soon be on their way. She was happy to hear that Matthew was confident that they would reach Gretna Green without interference from her parents. She knew the journey would not be easy and that it would take several days but she knew it would be well worth any discomfort. After all, it was the beginning of her new life with Matthew and that was worth it all.

"I am glad of that." Aunt Grace turned to Diana. "I will go collect your watercolors and canvases in the morning while your mother is out. I have the rest of your belongings at my residence and I will keep them safe until you can return to London or I get the opportunity to come visit in Whitehall."

"Aunt Grace, we cannot thank you enough." Diana hugged her aunt tightly and wiped away a sentimental tear.

"Diana is quite right. You have done so much for us. I cannot thank you enough. I do hope to see you in Whitehall often." Matthew took Grace's hand and squeezed it gently.

"Oh, hush, both of you," Aunt Grace said dabbing at her eyes. "The biggest thanks you can give me is to make it to Gretna Green safely. Be happy together." She hugged Diana again and then pulled Matthew in as well. " Now go quickly!"

Matthew picked up Diana's valise in one hand and took her hand in his other and they ran across the street to his waiting carriage. He opened the carriage door and then turned to Diana. He looked into her sweet face with a sparkle in his eyes. "My love, are you ready to start our lives together?"

"Yes, I certainly am. I love you, Matthew Repington. So very much."

"And I love you, Diana." He dropped a kiss onto her cheek before helping her into the carriage and they rode off into the night. To their future and their life together.

A LADY'S FAVOUR

HENRIETTA

CHAPTER ONE

"Have you attended many recitals so far this Season?"

Henrietta Repington shook her head and turned to her friend, Lady Amelia Sedgwick. "I have not. Although I did decline two such invitations. I had other engagements to attend but I must admit that I was rather relieved as it was quite probable that it would not be an enjoyable time."

"Yes, that seems to be the case, more often than not. Although I do believe Miss Hannah will prove that wrong today."

"Oh yes, I believe she has a very lovely voice. Quite refreshing, indeed."

Henrietta had attended many recitals in previous Seasons. Most of them were not too terribly awful but there were some that had been somewhat torturous to sit through. She had gone to one recital that the singing was so shrill that the hunting dogs had begun barking and the footmen had to be sent out to quiet them.

Henrietta had been happy to attend this recital, however. It was well known that her friend, Miss Hannah, had a lovely voice and her younger sister played the piano forte quite beautifully. It promised to be an enjoyable event.

"I see Mr St. Clair is in attendance this afternoon," Lady Amelia pointed out.

Henrietta could not help but smile, Mr St. Clair had been paying quite a bit of attention to her in the last several weeks. Henrietta had been rather happy about it as he was one of the most fashionable gentlemen of the Season.

He had attended nearly all the most important balls and parties. Henrietta looked forward to seeing him at any social event. He was quite entertaining and seemed to always be kicking up larks. She thoroughly enjoyed that he never seemed to be serious about anything.

"Oh, is he here?" Henrietta asked innocently.

Lady Amelia laughed. "As if you did not notice him the moment that he arrived. You do not fool me at all."

Henrietta laughed along with her friend. "It is quite difficult to not notice him. He seems to always be smiling or laughing."

"And surrounded by people," Lady Amelia added.

"Yes, he does seem to be quite popular. I must say that I am pleased that while he always seems to be up to something, he does not seem to thrive on gossip so many others seem to partake in."

"That is quite true," Lady Amelia agreed. "It is most unusual, but a good thing indeed."

Henrietta watched Mr St. Clair. as he moved through the drawing room greeting the other ladies and gentlemen who had already arrived. He was fairly tall and impeccably dressed in the latest fashion. His light brown hair was long enough to curl near the collar of the dark green coat that had been tailored to fit his fashionably thin frame. Henrietta was still watching him when he looked across the room. His eyes swept over her and he smiled. Henrietta smiled back and then swiftly turned away.

"Are you suddenly feeling shy, Lady Henrietta?" Lady Amelia asked her.

"Certainly not." Henrietta opened her fan and covered her face as she giggled. "But Mr St. Clair does not need to know that now does he?

"Certainly not," Lady Amelia repeated and laughed as well.

"Good afternoon, Lady Amelia," Jonathan Webb said walking over to join them. "Lady Henrietta."

Henrietta was neither surprised nor annoyed at having Mr Webb join them. He and Lady Amelia had been entirely enamored with each other for quite a while, only having just started an official courtship in recent weeks. Henrietta had seen him arrive shortly after Lady Amelia had asked about Mr St. Clair. "Good afternoon, Mr Webb. How are you this afternoon?"

"I am well. Thank you for asking." He turned to her friend and asked, "Lady Amelia, are you enjoying yourself?"

Lady Amelia's cheeks reddened slightly but, but smiled demurely. "Yes, it has been quite a lovely afternoon."

Mr Webb glanced around the room. "I have rather glad that I was able to attend."

"I am, as well," Lady Amelia agreed.

Henrietta hid her smile behind her fan. It was truly a joy watching her two friends begin their courtship. It had been more than obvious to everyone around them that they were perfect for each other, even their awkward moments and seemingly uncomfortable silences seemed right for them. Propriety dictated that the two of them could not be alone, but Henrietta was sure that if they had gotten the chance to talk longer than two minutes by themselves that they would have been betrothed already, quite possibly last Season.

After having a hand in her brother's recent marriage, she was beginning to think that she might have to do something to aid in Lady Amelia and Mr Webb's path to the altar. She was still thinking about that when she heard someone behind her.

"Hallo, Lady Henrietta," Jeffrey St. Clair said sweeping a magnificent leg. "I am so very elated to see that you are in attendance."

"Good afternoon, Mr St. Clair." Henrietta stifled a giggle as he bowed dramatically in front of her. He was always doing or saying something amusing.

"I am pondering whether I shall get up and dance during the recital. Perhaps a jaunty jig," he suggested hopping on one foot.

In response, she fluttered her fan for a moment and then snapped it shut giving him her haughtiest look. "I will not listen to your fustian nonsense today."

She turned away from him as though she were intent on what Lady Amelia was saying to her brother, Timothy Sedgwick. Henrietta was trying to keep her face solemn but the corners of her mouth were threatening to give her away. Not that Mr St. Clair would think she was serious, since he never thought anything was serious.

"Today?" He asked turning his head as though he had not heard her. "Only today?"

"Mr St. Clair, I…" She started to speak but did not finish as the door to the drawing room opened and Miss Hannah entered followed by her sister, Clara and their mother.

"I suppose we shall take our seats," Lady Amelia suggested. "It appears the recital shall start rather soon."

"Quite right," Henrietta said an agreement.

Several rows of chairs had been set up on the far end of the drawing room and Lady Henrietta followed Lady Amelia and Mr Webb as they took their seats.

Henrietta tried to ignore where Mr St. Clair had gone to, fighting the urge to scan the room to see where he had taken his seat. They had only been seated a moment when she heard him say from a chair behind her, "At least I can enjoy the view, if not the music."

Henrietta stole a glance at Lady Amelia to see if she had heard the comment. Her friend's smile was proof that she had indeed heard what had been said by Mr St. Clair.

Miss Clara had sat down at the piano forte definitely a sign that the recital would be starting soon. Lady Amelia gave Henrietta's hand a quick squeeze before returning her attention to the two sisters getting ready to perform. Henrietta looked forward to speaking with her friend when they had a chance to be alone.

CHAPTER TWO

Patrick Wainwright stood up from the large desk and walked to the window. Shaking his head as he looked out the window at the street below. It felt odd to be back in London. Only a year had passed since he had left the shores of England to travel to India but it seemed so much longer than that. When he had started his journey home, he believed he would be happy to be back in London but he felt like a stranger now.

Perhaps he had been gone from England too long. Between his commission on the Peninsula and his service in India with the East India Company, he had been away more in the last few years than he had been home. If England meant home, of course.

It was more likely that he had not been looking forward to facing his father, the Earl of Ellesmont. They had not often gotten along and that tension between them had worsened as he had gotten older. It had been odd that obtaining his commission and going off to fight on the Peninsula had been a relief if only to get away from his father.

Unfortunately, his relationship with his older brother, Frederick Wainwright, the Viscount of Denholme, was not much better. While Patrick had never really cared that he was not the heir to the title,

Frederick had done everything he could to remind him at every turn.

Patrick had learned quickly that if he complained it only looked as though he was grousing about his brother being the heir. It had seemed easier at the time to simply stop speaking with his brother. This had gone on so long that they hardly spoke at all. Patrick had not missed the uncomfortable interactions in the least, but their mother had been highly distressed by the distance that had fallen between the two brothers.

"Thunder an' turf!" Patrick exclaimed, realizing that he was pacing back and forth in front of the windows of the library. He hated being in the empty house, it was unsettling, the silence served only to cause him to recall events that he would rather forget.

Denholme Hall had long been the family London residence and Patrick had spent much time there since he was a child. He had been surprised upon his arrival to find that everyone had left for a house party in the country and would not return for several days. His passage back to India had already been booked as he had only returned to England to deal with a few business matters and to visit his mother.

He turned back to go to the desk when he noticed the leather satchel sitting on the chair near the door. Inside were letters that had been written by Charles Repington and his new bride, Beatrice, that Patrick had carried over the long journey from Bombay to London. Charles was the third son of the Duke of Castborough, and while Charles and his father had been at odds at times, they had remained close overall.

Patrick had agreed to deliver the letters to his family upon his arrival in London. Thankful he had something to do, Patrick put on his coat, collected the satchel and nearly ran out the front door.

Repington House, the London residence of the Duke of Castborough was not far from his family's home. Patrick had only started up the steps when the front door opened.

"Major Wainwright, good afternoon," an older man with white

hair greeted him.

"Good afternoon, Fletcher," he replied. "Are the duke and duchess in residence today?"

"Yes, sir. Do you have news from Lieutenant Repington?" Fletcher asked, his face passive only a slight tremor in his voice gave a sense that he was worried.

"I do. He and Beatrice both send their best wishes." He held up the satchel with a smile for the man. "And a bundle of letters for everyone here in London."

"Very well, Major," Fletcher said, a slight smile on his lips. "Please follow me."

Patrick followed him into the drawing room. "If you will please wait here, sir."

"Thank you," Patrick said with a nod.

Patrick had barely walked across the room when the door reopened.

"Major Wainwright!" A booming voice greeted him.

"Your grace," Patrick said to the imposing man who was the Duke of Castborough. "Thank you for seeing me."

"Of course," The duke said pausing as the duchess entered the room.

"Major Wainwright, how lovely to see you. Come sit down." The duchess gestured to the settee and the surrounding chairs. "Fletcher will be bringing tea in shortly."

"Thank you," Patrick said sitting down in a chair across from the duke the leather satchel still in his hands.

"I had not heard that you were returning to London. I would think Ellesmont would have mentioned it," the duke remarked.

"I am afraid my decision to travel was somewhat last minute. It is possible that my letters had not arrived before my mother and father left for Kent."

"Of course, it is a wonder they arrive at all after traveling so far." The duchess seemed to understand as she gave her husband an admonishing look. "How was your journey? You look very well."

"Thank you. It was better than expected. I feel very fortunate that the East India Company is so very efficient." Patrick held up the satchel. "I was commissioned by Charles and Beatrice to bring you some letters and other gifts from India."

"Oh, Major Wainwright, thank you," the duchess said. "I am so glad that they are enjoying their time there."

"It has taken some time to get settled in but they are very happy," Patrick assured her as he opened the satchel. "I have several letters and…"

The door to the drawing room opened and Lady Henrietta entered.

"Major Wainwright! I did not know you had returned to London!"

"Good afternoon, Lady Henrietta," he said standing up swiftly. "I only just arrived two days ago."

She saw the open satchel sitting on the chair where he had left it. Her eyes were wide when she asked, "Did you bring something back from India?"

He smiled at her. "Yes. I brought letters and some gifts from Charles and Beatrice." He pulled a bundle of letters from the leather satchel. "In fact, there are several from Beatrice addressed to you."

Lady Henrietta clapped her hands. "Oh, how wonderful!"

He held out the letters to her. "I believe there is one from Lieutenant Repington, as well."

She took the letters that he offered stopping to lay a hand on his arm. "Major Wainwright, I am so very grateful that you took the time to do this. Thank you."

"I was happy to do so," he told her.

She went to sit on the couch looking at each letter before opening it. He was surprised how much she had changed since the last time he had seen her. He had never thought her young but somehow she had grown up in the year that he had been gone. Trying to ignore the warmth he still felt on his arm from Lady Henrietta's touch, Patrick turned back to the duke and duchess.

CHAPTER THREE

"Excuse me, Duncan," Patrick asked knocking on the side of the carriage. "Why have we stopped?"

Patrick had left the house rather early to visit his solicitor, he had been reluctant to take the carriage, but he had hoped to return to Denholme Hall before the city grew too busy. The carriage had slowed down for a bit and now it was completely stopped.

"My apologies, sir," Duncan said leaning down from the driver's seat to speak with him. "The building on the corner is being repaired and there is debris in the street. It is a busy day and there are carriages passing by in both directions. There is great confusion as the carriages try to make their way around. I expect we will be able to get through very soon, though, sir."

"It is fine, Duncan," Patrick told him before sitting back in his seat. He drew his pocket watch out and sighed. "Half past eleven." If he had been back in Bombay, he would have just finished a training session with the soldiers and be walking to the main outpost building to eat the mid-day meal. It was hard work, but he appreciated being able to use his training to further his profession. It seemed even more clear now that he was in London. He liked to be busy, and he appreciated a challenge, which seemed the complete opposite of the lives led in London.

The carriage started moving again albeit very slowly. As they moved around the building on the corner, Patrick could see a structure built up around the corner, a monstrosity of wood and rope. It was a wonder anyone was able to get around the corner at all.

It was not long after that the carriage pulled up in front Denholme Hall. Patrick had just entered through the front door when voices could be heard in the house. It took him a minute to understand what was happening.

"Sir," a short man with wavy reddish hair hurried into the entry. "I am sorry. I had no time to prepare."

"I am not put out, Harcourt."

Harcourt looked behind him and very quietly said, "Neither your father nor mother know that you arrived home from the solicitor."

Patrick paused contemplating leaving as Harcourt was clearly suggesting. After a moment, he shook his head, it was past time for someone to take a step toward making amends. "No, I will stay."

Harcourt looked dubious but simply said, "Lord and Lady Ellesmont are in the drawing room. I have instructed Irene to prepare a tray for tea."

"Thank you, Harcourt."

Patrick walked to the drawing room door and hear the end. He waited at the door reminding himself that this was his family, not some unknown enemy. It seemed odd that traveling to India seemed perfectly normal while spending an afternoon with this family seemed rather daunting.

Finally, he blew out a long breath and stepped into the drawing room. Neither of his parents seemed to notice him at first as they were both reading letters that must have been received while they had been away. Without a word, Patrick crossed the room and sat down in one of the chairs that had been placed next to the settee.

"When you go back to Ellesmont, be sure to speak to Harold," his father instructed still not looking up from the letter that he was still reading.

"I had not been planning on visiting Ellesmont but I can do so if you require it," Patrick told him.

It was his mother not his father who looked up first. "Patrick! What are you doing here? I was not expecting you until much later." His mother seemed particularly put off by his arrival.

It was not the greeting he expected, after all, he had returned to visit her as much as to see his solicitor. He stood up. "Perhaps I shall go out. I can come back later."

"Goodness, no." his mother exclaimed. Although it seemed more out of exasperation than concern. "You are here now. You should stay and be with us."

"Yes, do sit down," his father blustered.

Patrick fought the urge to tell his father he would rather stand and returned to the chair.

"Hello Father, Mother. How was Kent?"

His father narrowed his eyes at him but his mother said blithely, "It was lovely. Lady Bradfield threw a lovely party."

"I am glad you enjoyed it," Patrick said with a smile. While his mother often sided with his father on most things she really was a sweet and gentle person.

"It's too bad you could not join us," his mother added.

"Do not try to make him feel guilty," his father said and waved his hand toward Patrick. "Training the poor people in India is extremely important."

"I am training Englishmen to guard the outposts in India, Father."

His father nodded and returned his eyes to his correspondence. "Quite right, I would think you would be glad to be back in England, the weather in India is bloody hot."

As his father had never traveled to India, Patrick could not be sure what he was basing his opinion on, Patrick suspected the hearsay of others.

"It is their cooler season right now, so it is actually much nicer in India currently."

Once again his father narrowed his eyes at Patrick. "So you are saying that you would rather be in India?"

Although Patrick would rather have agreed with his father just to be obstinate, he replied, "No, of course not, Father. I was simply replying to your comment about the weather in India. As you have not been there, ah… recently I thought only to explain."

His father went on as though Patrick had not spoken. "I trust you are making arrangements to return to England permanently. Are you not?"

"I have no plans at the moment to do so."

"I cannot believe how glad I am to be back in London.," His brother Frederick said coming into the room. "I like Kent but if I am not at Ellesmont. I prefer to be in London."

"Of course, Frederick," his mother replied immediately.

"Speaking of Ellesmont be sure that you speak to Harold the next time you are there," his father said holding up the letter he had been reading. "There are several issues with the tenants that need to be dealt with."

Patrick sat there wondering how long he should wait. All they spoke about was business matters at Ellesmont. His father had asked Patrick a question, and he had tried to answer it. Although it seemed rather clear that his father did not care for an actual answer.

"Patrick, hello," Frederick said as though he had just noticed his brother sitting there. I had not realized you had arrived."

"Clearly," Patrick said.

"I am often so busy that I do not notice small things like that. Father has had me taking care of many aspects at Ellesmont to help him while Parliament is in session."

Patrick nodded not too much in agreement as much as realizing that it had taken his brother less than five minutes to remind him that he was the heir to the title. "It is quite understandable."

"Forgive me, I do not quite remember the reason for your visit. Have you finally given up on India and have returned to London?"

"No, not at this time. I needed to meet with my new solicitor as the old one had become ill and is no longer practicing."

"So you are planning on staying in India?" His brother grimaced and did not bother to cover it up.

"Yes, I—" Patrick began to say.

His father interrupted looked at his brother. "Your brother seems to enjoy marching about in the heat of Bombay. That will not last though. Mark my words, he will be back in London permanently by year's end."

His father and brother shared a smirk and his mother just shook her head.

"Perhaps if you would actually listen when you ask a question you might actually learn the answer."

Frederick shrugged. "Father is right. I believe you wish to be home but you are too stubborn to admit it."

Patrick stood up. "I care not what either of you thinks. Perhaps I prefer Bombay over London because of the likes of you."

"You are ungrateful and jealous," his brother retorted. "I hope you go back to India and never return!"

His mother gasped and Patrick spun on his heel and left the room the sounds of his father sputtering in the background as he left the house.

As soon as he was out on the street, he admonished himself for letting his father and brother's comments get to him. He had known that they would act that way, and he had been foolish having tried at all.

CHAPTER FOUR

Henrietta stood in her room staring at two of her favourite dresses. One was a butter yellow gown adorned with white ruffles on the sleeves and the neckline. The other was a pear green gown with ribbons that decorated the sleeves and the skirt. She loved each dress equally but she could not help but wonder which dress Mr St. Clair would like the most.

She stared at both dresses for a few more minutes and finally decided on the yellow dress. The ruffles appealed to her and she thought that the colour would look the best with her hair. Henrietta had dark curls that looked lovely with her creamy complexion.

The night promised to be quite enjoyable as she would be attending Almack's with Lady Amelia and her brother, Mr Sedgwick. The duke and duchess had been invited to a dinner party at the Duke of Collingsworth's London residence. It did not take her long to finish her preparations for Almack's that night and she hurried down the stairs to wait in the drawing room.

Henrietta was still waiting in the drawing room when she heard voices in the hall. At first, she could not make out what they were saying and then her father's voice could clearly be heard saying, "Good evening, Lord Ellesmont."

Henrietta frowned thinking about what Major Wainwright had said when he had brought the letters from Charles and Beatrice. She had read her letters quietly while Major Wainwright conversed with her parents. It had been her understanding that Major Wainwright parents, Lord and Lady Ellesmont were not presently in London, having traveled to Kent to attend a house party. Henrietta went to the door to peek out and saw that indeed, Lord Ellesmont was following her father into the library.

She could no longer hear what Lord Ellesmont was saying, but she clearly heard her father when he turned around and said, "And what of Major Wainwright?"

Henrietta went back into the drawing room and sat down on the settee. She had been so looking forward to going to Almack's and she was sure that she would see Mr St. Clair again. As much as she tried to focus on her upcoming evening and seeing her friends again, Henrietta could not stop thinking about Lord Ellesmont's answer to her father's question.

"And what of Major Wainwright indeed?" Henrietta repeated. She went to the door again and could see down the hall that her father had not closed the library door behind them. It was quite understandable though as the library windows caught the afternoon sun and the room could get stifling hot in the evening. Mother often opened that door open to keep it from overheating.

Henrietta spotted the chair that sat at the end of the hall and knew what she wanted to do. It was a dilemma as she knew it was not any of her business but the idea of not knowing was something she could not stand. She left the drawing room and walked calmly down the hall deciding it would be best if she acted as though she was simply walking to the stairs. Intent on the large staircase, she walked past the base of the stairs to the chair knowing that she would be able to hear most anything to happen in the library from that corner of the hall.

"Every single time we speak, we end up arguing it by the end of it," Lord Ellesmont.

"There must be something that is happening that you are

simply not aware of. If it happens every single time," her father replied.

"Yes, one would think so," Lord Ellesmont replied. "You have five sons and a daughter, and you seem to have no problems with any of them. I have but two sons and we seem to be at each other's throats all the time."

"We get along now, but it has not always been so." Her father paused for a moment and cleared his throat. "Both sons?"

"Yes, both sons. Frederick is lazy and more concerned about being fashionable than learning all that needs to be done as the Earl of Ellesmont. And every conversation with Patrick begins with him being defensive and ready to fight."

"Is Frederick often part of these conversations?" the duke asked.

Lord Ellesmont looked up for a moment and said, "More often than not, Frederick is present during the conversations with Patrick."

Her father coughed lightly. "It was not that long ago that Philip and my second eldest, James, were constantly at each other's throats as well. Philip was not taking his duties as the heir to Castborough seriously. During that time James stepped in to assist with the tenants and other business when Parliament was in session and I was unable to deal with it."

"James did not want to help?" Lord Ellesmont suggested.

"No, James was all too happy to help. The issue was that Philip felt the compunction to remind James that even though he was putting in the work, it did not matter. He made sure James was reminded that he was still the heir to the title. James was not happy that not only was he the one doing the work while his brother attended parties and played cards at White's but then was mocked for his trouble."

"I see. Yes, I can see how that would be upsetting."

"Major Wainwright seems responsible and astute, I cannot see him reacting poorly for no reason." Her father told the other man.

"Patrick is all that you say but also obstinate and sullen. I admit that it seems likely that Frederick is part of the problem." There was a pause and then a scraping sound that Henrietta soon realized was Lord Ellesmont standing up. "I had not thought of it before, but Frederick is often bringing up his duties at Ellesmont when Patrick is around."

"Surely as a reminder of who is first born," The duke said. "How do you react when Frederick does this?"

There was a loud sigh. "I tend to talk to Frederick about what needs to be done. It is rare for him to show an interest his duties at Ellesmont, so I make sure to discuss what he wants to know. And apparently, in doing so, I further upset Patrick."

"It appears so."

"Patrick makes it most difficult as he is always ready for an argument."

"Perhaps it is because he knows what will happen." There was a pause and Henrietta could almost see her father lifting his hand in the pointing gesture he often made when talking. "You and he start talking, then Frederick interrupts to speak with you about Ellesmont business. No wonder he is acting sullen. I would be too if I were constantly treated as though I was less important. Would you not?"

"That is not..." Lord Ellesmont blustered a bit. Henrietta not catching all that he was saying. "I am very proud of Patrick. He is immensely responsible, trustworthy and knowledgeable in so many ways."

"Have you told him that?"

"Well, no,"

"Perhaps you should."

Henrietta leaned forward straining to hear Lord Ellesmont's reply when the distinct sounds of a carriage reminded her that she should be in the drawing room. She hurried down the hall, slowing down as she passed the open library door.

"And your sons, they are on speaking terms now?"

"Yes, they are quite close," was the last she heard as she entered the drawing room. She had barely sat upon the settee when Fletcher came through the door.

"Lady Henrietta," he said the barest trace of a smile upon his face. "Lord Eastbridge's carriage has arrived to take you to Almack's."

"Thank you, Fletcher." Standing up slowly, she smiled at him and said, "I have been so bored sitting in here for so long."

Fletcher nodded. "Yes, of course. Have a lovely evening."

CHAPTER FIVE

Henrietta walked down the steps slowly trying to fight the urge to run out to the waiting carriage. A footman waited to assist her through the already open door. She stepped up into the carriage, Lady Amelia was sitting on the seat in the back while Mr Sedgwick sat across from her.

"Good evening, Lady Henrietta," Lady Amelia said. "Come sit here with me."

"Thank you, Lady Amelia. Good evening," Henrietta replied sitting next to her friend. "Hello, Mr Sedgwick. Are you playing chaperone this evening?"

"Yes and no," he told her with a smile.

Lady Amelia spoke up. "He was going to be my chaperone but Mother thought it best to have Aunt Agatha come with us. She is following behind in her own carriage."

Henrietta turned to Lady Amelia. "How wonderful. I love Lady Agatha."

"You do?" Mr Sedgwick asked.

"Oh, yes. I quite adore your great aunt."

Mr Sedgwick looked somewhat horrified. "Why ever for?"

"I think I know the answer," Lady Amelia said with a knowing smile. "It is because Aunt Agatha spoke up when Lady Judith tried to aid Mr Townsend in ruining Miss Beatrice."

"Yes, you are quite right." Henrietta clasped her hands in front of her. "Lady Agatha was magnificent. I will never forget it."

"If she had not spoken up poor Miss Beatrice would have been forced to marry that awful Mr Townsend, instead of your brother, Charles.

Henrietta grimaced remembering the terrible scene. Henrietta's brother Charles had stepped forward to defend Beatrice, but it had been Lady Agatha that had made the connection that it had been Lady Judith that could not explain where she had been. "I will always be thankful not only for her helping Beatrice but that she had figured out Lady Judith's part in Mr Townsend's scheme."

"Judith and Mr Townsend deserve each other." Mr Sedgwick shook his head. "As far as I know, they have been forced to live at one of Lord Marsfeld's properties in the north."

"Charles had known that Mr Townsend was acting strangely around Beatrice. But it was Lady Agatha who really had the most to do with catching Lady Judith and Mr Townsend in their lies and deceit." Henrietta was thinking about the scene at Lord and Lady Westerton's ball. She was reminded that Major Wainwright had been there as well. She began thinking again about hearing Lord Ellesmont talking about his relationship with his two sons. Henrietta had only met Lord Ellesmont on a few occasions but after several comments, her brother, Charles, had made she had begun to suspect that Major Wainwright and his father did not get along.

"Aunt Agatha does not suffer fools gladly," Lady Amelia said. "She very much likes Charles and Beatrice."

"Speaking of Charles and Beatrice, Major Wainwright is back in London. He came over to Repington House to bring us several letters and some gifts Charles and Beatrice had sent to us from India."

"Oh, how exciting!" Lady Amelia exclaimed. "How are they? I wonder how Beatrice is faring in such a strange and fascinating land."

"They both seem to be doing quite well. Charles has adapted so well to his position with the East India Company that he may be assigned his own outpost to command," Henrietta waved her hand unsure of the exact details. "Beatrice is excited to have recently just set up house and has garnered the advice and assistance of some locals from Bombay. She is already learning how to adapt to the weather."

Lady Amelia opened her fan and waved it was a sigh. "Poor Beatrice must be tremendously miserable. If it is this hot here, I could only imagine how hot it is in the jungles of India."

"Actually it is in the midst of their cold season there. So she is probably rather enjoying the weather right now." Henrietta was both surprised and proud of herself that she had remembered that fact she had only just been reminded of it by Major Wainwright when he had come to visit.

"And how is Major Wainwright doing?" Mr Sedgwick asked.

"As expected, Major Wainwright has already been put in charge of several East India Company outposts in the region including the one that Charles would be commanding It has something to do with their chain of command."

"Is he coming back to London permanently?" Lady Amelia asked as they stepped out of the carriage.

"I do not believe so." Henrietta turned to Mr Sedgwick and asked, "I may be talking out of turn but may I ask if you know about Major Wainwright's brother, Frederick?" Mr Sedgwick grimaced upon hearing the name. "Frederick Wainwright, or Lord Denholme, is not what you would expect after meeting Major Wainwright. Most everyone would describe Major Wainwright as responsible, caring, and trustworthy. Unfortunately, Frederick is the complete opposite. He is lazy, manipulative and thinks only of himself."

"That is too bad," Henrietta said. "And he has always been this way? It is not something that he became when he finished school or for some other reason?"

Mr Sedgwick shook his head. "I went to school with both Lord

Denholme and Major Wainwright. Lord Denholme was always complaining and demanding people treat him with respect and Major Wainwright was a good friend and earned respect through his actions." Henrietta was not surprised Major Wainwright had been on the peninsula with Charles. Henrietta's brother had thought highly of him and while she trusted all of her brothers, it was Charles that would trust the most in matters of judging someone's personality.

"It is maddening to know that there are people out there that only care about themselves. They only serve to make everyone around them miserable," Henrietta said.

Lady Amelia nodded glancing around the ballroom. "That is only too true and seems more so during the Season."

"Yes, it really does." Henrietta was about to say more but they were interrupted.

"Good evening, Lady Henrietta." Mr St. Clair said having joined their group.

"Good evening, Mr St. Clair," Henrietta said smiling at the man.

"Would you like to dance?" He wore a silly smile and Henrietta smiled back.

"Yes, of course. Thank you." Henrietta took his arm. She glanced back at Lady Amelia and waved.

CHAPTER SIX

Patrick had walked for quite a while before he found himself on the doorstep of White's. He did not drink often after his time on the Peninsula he learned it was quite easy for a lost soul to try to find solace at the bottom of the whiskey bottle. He had helped many former soldiers find their way home after a night of drinking and he never wanted to suffer the same plight. As he stood there, but he reasoned that one evening at White's would not turn him into a drunkard.

He had just stepped toward the door when he heard someone call his name. "Major Wainwright, I did not know that you were back in London."

He turned to see James Repington, Lieutenant Charles Repington's older brother.

"Repington, hello. I have been in London for only a few days."

James opened the door to White's. "Come in and have a drink with me. You can tell me about how Charles is doing."

Patrick nodded and followed Repington into the club. It was fortuitous as it was not likely that James would be in White's long and therefore Patrick would be less likely to drink himself into a stupor.

They found a table and soon had a glass of whiskey each in front of them. "Before I ask about my brother, tell me about how you have enjoyed India. It sounds quite fascinating but I am quite sure that Elizabeth would not be in favour of the trip or the climate."

Patrick smiled. "Neither the journey nor the weather is very enjoyable, but I have found the work quite rewarding."

"I am not at all surprised. Charles had always said that you excelled as a soldier and he felt that his own success on the Peninsula was directly related to your training."

Patrick and Lieutenant Repington had known each other for sometime before obtaining their commission but had become friends while serving. He had not known, however, that Lieutenant Repington had been so affected. In his state of annoyance, it seemed that much more significant, and he took another sip of his whiskey to tamp down his feelings of emotion. In an attempt to change the subject he asked, "And how is Elizabeth? Is she enjoying the new house in Surrey?"

James began to speak about the new house that had been built at Castborough near Surrey and Patrick enjoyed the opportunity to hear about a family that was not constantly arguing with each other. He had always hoped that one day that he would be able to forge a new sort of relationship with his father and brother but after their conversation earlier that day he was beginning to think that it would never happen.

"Excuse me, sirs," a young man asked having stopped at their table. "Are you James Repington?"

Repington gave Patrick an odd look and nodded. "Yes, I am."

"I apologize, sir, but I have been sent to retrieve you. There has been an accident and his grace, the Duke of Castborough has been injured."

James stood up quickly his chair falling to the ground with a loud crack. "What happened? Where is he?"

Patrick stood up as well. "Is there anything that I can do?"

"Thank you, Major Wainwright, but…"

The young man turned to Patrick. "Are you Major Patrick Wainwright?"

"Yes, I am." Patrick was unsure of what was to come next.

"My apologies, sir. Your father was also injured in the accident if you will both come with me I can take you to them." The men hurried from the club. The young man leading them towards an awaiting carriage. Then Repington stopped turning to Patrick. "It is Wednesday, is it not?"

Not knowing why it mattered Patrick answered, "Yes, it is Wednesday."

"Henrietta. She will be at Almack's tonight. I do not wish her to hear about this from the gossips."

"Yes, of course. I will go retrieve her for you." Patrick nodded and made a quarter turn to go.

"Wait, though, Major Wainwright. Are you quite sure? What about your father?"

Patrick shook his head. "You will have much better luck getting things done and quickly as you are living here in London and people will listen to you."

"I see. All right, then. Let me be off." James turned his head and took a step to head out.

Patrick came to a sudden stop, realizing he had walked there having left his carriage at home after the argument. "Oh, I will need to borrow a carriage. I walked here."

"Yes, of course. You can take mine." Repington turned to call to one of the young men to have his carriage retrieved.

Once in the carriage, Patrick hurried to Almack's trying not to think about his father and how badly he may be injured. He had a fleeting thought about having to deal with his brother but pushed it aside more concerned about reaching Lady Henrietta before she heard the news from someone else.

Almack's was as crowded as he had remembered from his last visit. He moved through the crowd looking for Lady Henrietta, hoping to find her quickly and equally dreading speaking to her once he had.

He had completed a circle of the ballroom and was nearly ready to look in the refreshment room when he spotted her across the ballroom. She was wearing a yellow dress, the curls of her dark coloured hair just touching her shoulders. She was standing with Lady Amelia, Jonathan Webb and another gentleman Patrick recognized but whose name escaped him.

As he approached the small group, Lady Henrietta turned and saw him. The immediate smile that came to her lips would have normally made him quite happy. "Major Wainwright, I am so happy to see you. I did not realize you would be in attendance tonight."

"Lady Henrietta," he said and nodded at the others. "I must speak with you."

"Oh?" She tilted her head curiously.

He felt horrible knowing he was about to deliver bad news and realized he would have done anything to avoid upsetting her. Shaking his head, he said, "I was sent to retrieve you. There's been an accident, James…"

"An accident? James! Is he all right?" She exclaimed rushing up to him.

Patrick looked down at Lady Henrietta feeling a rush of feelings he had not expected, caring, protectiveness and most of all, regret. "Lady Henrietta, I am so sorry. It is not James who has been in the accident. It is your father. I was with James when we received the news. He was worried about you and I offered to come to Almack's with the intention of taking you back to Repington House while he went to check on the situation.

Her eyes filled with worry she nodded, "Yes, of course. I need to inform Lady Agatha as she is my true chaperone tonight."

"I will be happy to accompany you through the ballroom," Patrick offered, knowing that Lady Agatha could be quite difficult when she wanted to be.

"Thank you." Patrick led her across the ballroom where the older dowager sat with the other chaperones talking and keeping a close eye on the younger people in the ballroom.

"Lady Henrietta," the older woman said as they approached. Lady Agatha seemed surprised to see him but that was not unexpected as not many people had known that he had returned to London. "I just heard the news. Major Wainwright, I am so sorry. Please let us know if there is anything we can do."

"Yes, of course," he said without thinking. As they walked away, he could not help but wonder if the older woman knew something he did not.

CHAPTER SEVEN

Patrick walked into Denholme Hall later that night. He was not sure how long he stood in the entry hall, not knowing where he should go or what he should be doing.

Harcourt rushed in from the hallway. "Sir, you are home. Is there anything I can do for you?"

Patrick turned his head as though looking for something that he could not find. Finally, he said, "I will be in the library."

"Yes, sir."

Patrick moved slowly from the entry he took two steps into the library and stopped. He stared at his father's desk for a moment and then turned back to the hall, calling out, "Harcourt, I will be in the drawing room instead."

If Harcourt answered Patrick did not hear it. He opened the door to the drawing room, not bothering to close the door behind him as he staggered past the chairs to collapse onto the settee. He was not sure how long he laid there sprawled out across the bench. The words of the physician repeating over and over again and his mind.

"I am sorry, Major. The Earl of Ellesmont has died. I had hoped for better news but his injuries were far too great for him to overcome. My deepest condolences to you and your family."

His mother had been sent for and he was thankful the physician had taken the burden from Patrick to tell her the awful news.

After speaking with Lady Agatha at Almack's, Patrick had begun to prepare himself for what was sure to be bad news, but he had not been prepared for the news he had finally received. His father was dead. He would never get used to hearing that. As devastating as that news was, Patrick also had to deal with learning that his brother had been injured as well.

"Sir," Harcourt said from the door. "There is someone here to see you."

Patrick started to shake his head no when he saw Timothy Sedgwick standing behind Harcourt. He did not have the energy to tell him to go away and simply said, "Fine."

Sedgwick walked into the room and sat down in one of the upholstered chairs next to the settee. Patrick sat up but said nothing.

"I heard about the accident and came by to express my condolences and offer my assistance."

Patrick shook his head slowly and opened his hands in a questioning gesture. "I am truly grateful. I have only been in London for a few days. I never imagined anything like this could happen."

"I had not known that you were in London until I saw you in the ballroom of Almack's."

"It was necessary to return to London to deal with business matters. I had hoped to renew some friendships and then be on my way back." Patrick stopped and sighed. "I am at a loss."

"I am sure that your mother is comforted by your presence. Without you, she would be dealing with this tragedy by herself," Sedgwick pointed out gently.

"I had not thought of that, and I am glad to be here to aid her."

"How is she?"

"She is doing well, given the circumstances. Mother is quite strong. She is staying with my aunt tonight as her residence is very close to Lord Alderside."

Sedgwick frowned. "Lord Alderside?"

"Yes," Patrick said. "Lord Alderside's residence is quite close to where the accident happened and directed his footmen to bring the injured men into his house and sent directly for the physician."

"I heard that scaffolds collapsed. But I did not hear any more than that."

"They were going to into Mayfair for the dinner party at the Duke of Collingworth's. My mother had been feeling ill and stayed home to rest."

"A blessing as she may have been injured as well," the other man remarked. "What happened?"

"They were turning the corner on to St. James Street when another carriage driven by a drunkard came around the corner too fast. The building there is under repair and risers have been set up into the street. Debris is all around. The other carriage went through and in the darkness drove too close to the building. The carriage collided with the scaffolding causing the structures and much of the building to come down."

"Horrible. Just horrible." Sedgewick stood patiently, shaking his head.

"From what I have heard, my father's carriage had stopped when the other carriage appeared attempting to allow for it to pass. When the scaffolding fell, it hit directly onto my father's carriage. Nothing remains but splintered wood and some twisted iron. My brother and the horses were the only ones to survive. Mother would have been lost had she accompanied my father."

Sedgwick nodded. "And what of the Duke of Castborough?"

"His carriage was following behind my father's. The duke got out of the carriage to try to help and was hit with debris falling off of the building. He has several broken bones but is likely to recover fully."

"I am sure that is a relief to the duchess and his family," Sedgwick replied somberly.

Henrietta's worried face came to Patrick's mind. "Yes, that is certainly good news. Something for us to hold on to after a day that was far worse than I ever imagined."

CHAPTER EIGHT

"Has there been any change?" Henrietta asked as she descended the stairs.

"No," James answered. "The physician was here earlier to administer more medication. Father has broken many bones and is in a great deal of pain. The medication will keep him quiet while he begins to heal."

"How will the physician know that he is healed if he is to be kept quiet?" Henrietta was frustrated. She did not like to see her father appear so helpless. It was something she truly thought could not happen. Her father was a tall and strong man that never seemed to retreat from any challenge. It was difficult seeing him lying nearly lifeless in the bed.

She had tried to keep her feelings to herself to stay strong for her mother. It was not until after they had come home and Henrietta had gone up to her room that she had broken down into the tears she had been holding back ever since she and Major Wainwright had left Almack's.

He had been so calm and comforting on their carriage ride from Almack's that Henrietta had been completely shocked to find out that his father and brother had been involved in the accident as well.

James sat with their father while the physician had done what he could to make him feel more comfortable. It was while she and her mother were waiting that Henrietta had learned that Major Wainwright's father had perished in the accident, his brother was badly injured and it was unknown when or if he would recover.

Lord Alderside had heard the commotion and had arrived shortly after ordering his footmen anyone who would listen to move the injured men to his residence.

In the few days since the accident, Henrietta had started each day checking on her father hoping and praying that she would come in to see him awake and hear his deep voice. She had spent the afternoon reading to him in the small room they had set up to care for him near the kitchen.

"Oh, Henrietta, here you are," her mother said.

"Good evening, Henrietta. You look lovely tonight." Her mother said coming into the room. "I have been looking for you. You need to go ready yourself for the party."

"Oh. Mother. Must I go to the party tonight?" Henrietta asked. "I would rather stay home."

"And do what? Mope around?" Her mother pursed her lips and then frowned. "No, you need to go to the party. Your father has been injured, yes, but he will be fine. You need to go to the party and show everyone the strength of the Repingtons."

Henrietta nodded. "Yes, Mother, it will be difficult, but I will do my best."

Her mother put an arm around her shoulders. "I know that you will feel better after you see your friends and you are out of the house. Your father would not want you here worrying yourself."

"I hope so." Henrietta was doubtful that she would feel that much better but the thought of seeing Lady Amelia and Miss Hannah made her feel like there was at least something to look forward to.

A LADY'S FAVOUR

"I have called upon Lady Agatha to chaperone you again tonight."

Henrietta smiled. Her reaction was not as enthusiastic as it had been days before but she was still looking forward to seeing the older woman. "I will endeavour to behave under her scrutiny."

Her mother laughed. "I will surely hear about it if you do not. Not that I am worried in the least. Now go upstairs to ready yourself before Lady Agatha's carriage arrives.

"Yes, mother." Sitting with her father had made her feel better to spend time with him and she had hoped that she would not have to attend the party that night.

Less than an hour later Henrietta was sitting across from Lady Agatha in the carriage line waiting to go into the party.

"Lady Agatha, thank you for acting as my chaperone again tonight."

"I'm quite happy to do so," the older woman smiled. "How are you, dear?"

Henrietta started to say that she was well but instead blurted out, "I am upset. Everyone keeps telling me not to worry. How could I not?"

Lady Agatha patted Henrietta's hand. "Do not let others tell you how you should feel. Of course, you are worried. I would be surprised if you were not. Remember though that your father is a strong and stubborn man. He will be back to himself before you know it, I am sure of that."

"Thank you." Henrietta felt a bit better with the advice.

That did not last though as once inside she had to endure the stares and whispers from the others waiting in the entry hall. She wanted to tell them all to go away and wishing even more so that she had stayed home.

"Lady Henrietta," Lady Amelia said rushing up to her. "I am so glad to see you. I have been so worried and wondered if you would be here at all."

Henrietta gave her a grateful smile. "I must admit that I did not want to come but my mother said it would be better for me to keep my engagements rather than just linger around the house."

"I can certainly understand you not wanting to come out but I also agree with your mother." Lady Amelia squeeze Lady Henrietta's hand for a moment and let go. "We will endeavour to have fun tonight. Perhaps we can annoy Lady Sarah in some way."

"It is a possibility. There is so much to choose from what where shall we start." Henrietta looked around the room. "Is that your brother she is speaking with?"

"Yes," Lady Amelia said with a grimace. "She has been talking to him quite a bit as of late."

"Egads. That must be disconcerting for you."

"Oh no," Lady Amelia said with a quick shake of her head. "Timothy is only being polite. He well knows what a spiteful cow she can be."

Henrietta straightened her skirt and said, "Well that is good to know. I rather like your brother, I should not like to have to give him a talking to."

"Neither would he." Lady Amelia paused and held up a finger. "Although I think I should like watching you have a word with him."

Both girls laughed and Henrietta was suddenly struck with guilt for having a good time while her father lies injured and Major Wainwright's father was dead.

Her face must have shown her thoughts because Lady Amelia squeezed her hand again and said, "Do not worry over your father. He is a strong and formidable man. He will surely make a full recovery."

Henrietta nodded not trusting herself not to burst into tears.

"Why is everyone so Friday faced here?" Mr St. Clair suddenly said from beside her.

"And who do you think is Friday faced, Mr St. Clair?" Lady Amelia asked a bit sharply.

Henrietta thought perhaps that Lady Amelia was upset that Mr St. Clair' would ask such a question. Henrietta did not mind it as she was sure that he was trying to simply make Henrietta smile.

"I realize that you are rather used to everyone laughing and smiling around you but..."

"But now I am here so now it's time for everyone to laugh and smile." Mr St. Clair laughed heartily and looked around the room.

Lady Amelia frowned. "I think I shall like a drink."

"That sounds lovely." Henrietta followed Lady Amelia to the dining room. Lady Sarah and Miss Danielle were just leaving and Henrietta heard Lady Sarah's spiteful voice. "I am not so sure that Major Wainwright would be all that upset about his father's death."

Miss Danielle turned to her quickly. "No?"

"Oh, I see you did not know," Lady Sarah said looking around rather gleeful that she could gossip a little bit more. The Earl of Ellesmont and Major Wainwright did not get along. It is quite well-known that Lord Ellesmont preferred his older brother, Frederick over his younger son."

"No, I did not know that, although I am not surprised." Miss Danielle did not attempt to hid the look of distaste on her face.

Henrietta frowned wishing she could say something to make the two young ladies stop speaking so ill of Major Wainwright. Neither of the two ladies new Major Wainwright very well, in fact, the only interaction that they had probably had was the day that Lady Judith was caught in her deceit with Mr Townsend. It actually made quite a bit of sense that they would be acting maliciously towards Major Wainwright since he had assisted Charles that day.

As Henrietta fumed at their comments, Lady Amelia leaned closer and said, "Do not pay them any attention. They are horrible and petty there is no truth in anything that they say."

"I know. They just anger me so," Henrietta nodded turning away from the other young ladies.

"From what I understand not many listen to them anymore as they are quite well-known for their lies and prevarication."

When they returned to the drawing room Mr Webb was standing with Mr St. Clair looking rather uncomfortable. Henrietta had often noted that Mr St. Clair could be rather boisterous and she could understand why someone as staid as Mr Webb could find him exhausting.

"I suppose we should go rescue Mr Webb," Henrietta suggested.

Lady Amelia nodded. "Yes, I think that would be a very good idea."

"...and from what I understand, Major Wainwright hated his father terribly. He was just waiting for the moment when the earl would die." Mr St. Clair was finishing his thought on the accident when the ladies joined them.

For the first time since becoming friends with Mr St. Clair, Henrietta was not happy to see him.

CHAPTER NINE

"Excuse me, Sir," Duncan said standing at the door. "Dr Lambert is here. He would like to talk to before he leaves."

"Of course," Patrick answered. He is almost grateful for the interruption. He had been standing next to his father's desk for some time. He had gone around the desk to sit down but memories of his father sitting behind the desk as he conducted business or met with friends made him pause. It was an odd feeling to think about his father never sitting at that desk again.

Patrick had come into the library to write several letters. One of which was to the East India Company letting them know that his return to India would be delayed, his original plan had been to visit England for no more than a month. His passage back to India was to leave in two week's time it was quite clear to him that he would need to stay in London until his brother made a full recovery.

In the meantime, his mother would need all the help she could get. She was understandably devastated by his father's death and quite worried about Frederick. Even when his father was well, his mother was not very independent and somewhat fragile. With his father gone Patrick feared that she would be even more frail and infirmed.

Duncan cleared his throat reminding Patrick that he and Dr Lambert were waiting. "Please show him in." A moment later Duncan had returned with Dr Lambert. He was a young man not that much older than Patrick himself and yet he was the physician who was looking in on his brother, the new Earl of Ellesmont.

"Good morning, Dr Lambert." Patrick gestured toward the upholstered chairs that sat near the fireplace. "Please sit down."

"Thank you, Major Wainwright." Dr Lambert said before sitting down in one of the chairs.

"Have you been able to look in on Frederick yet this morning?"

"Yes, I just came from seeing him." The doctor nodded solemnly.

"Has there been any improvement at all?" Patrick asked him.

"Not at this time. It is the injuries to his head that are the most concerning. He was either struck by falling debris or hit his head when he was thrown from the carriage. It is that injury that is causing him to sleep. There is no way of knowing when he may awake again."

Patrick shook his head. "Is there anything else we can do for him?"

"One of the young maids, Mary, I believe, is making sure someone is always with him. She has water and broth for him in case he wakes. If he does, she will be able to get something in him."

"And that is all we can do? Wait?" Patrick sighed heavily as he watched the doctor's face.

"Unfortunately, yes. We will simply have to wait to see what will happen." The man looked regretful. "I do wish there was more."

"Thank you for letting me know. If there is anything that I can do or anything that you need, please do not hesitate to ask."

"Thank you. I would like to speak with your mother if possible." He paused as though picking his words carefully. "I want to make sure she is well. I worry that in her state of mourning she may fall ill herself."

Patrick stood up. "Thank you. I understand. I have been

worried about the same. I would be most grateful if you would look in on her as well."

Dr Lambert nodded. "I will be here to check on your brother tomorrow morning. Please send for me if anything changes."

"Thank you," Patrick said as the physician left the library.

Patrick moved to the desk ignoring his earlier apprehension. He was needed here, and he sat down and quickly wrote the letter to the East India Company explaining that he would be delayed in his return.

He took up another piece of paper and began to write a letter to Lieutenant Repington but paused, his pen hanging over the paper. Although he was fairly sure that his family had already sent word of his father's accident he had no way of knowing what he had actually been told.

Patrick sat back in the chair debating what he should do next. With a sigh he stood up again and left the library, calling to Duncan to have his carriage brought up

Repington House was not far from Denholme Hall but Patrick had learned that being without a carriage at hand could be very inconvenient. Fletcher answered the door and directed him once again to the drawing room.

He was staring out the window when James Repington came to greet him.

"Major Wainwright, good morning."

"Good morning, please excuse my intrusion," Patrick said.

"Do not apologize. It is no intrusion at all," Repington told him. "Let us sit."

"I had been planning to call on you but it was a last-minute decision to visit this morning." Patrick followed him over to sit in the same chair that he had sat several days before talking to the duke and duchess.

Repington seemed to sense his hesitation. "How is Lord Denholme?"

"His condition has not changed. The doctor came to check on

him this morning and although there has been no improvement he is still of a mind that my brother may recover."

"That is good news indeed. I hope he is correct." Repington nodded curtly, but looked sincere in his words.

Remembering what spurred him into coming to Repington House, Patrick cleared his throat and looked at Repington. "I wrote a letter to the East India Company earlier today informing them that I would not be returning to India as I had planned. I also wanted to write to Lieutenant Repington and yet I knew not what to say."

Repington nodded. "I was forced to do the same the night of the accident. Several letters were sent off, one to Charles in India, as well as one to Whitehall to notify Matthew, among others. Philip is at Castborough and will be traveling to London as soon as he can."

"I was spared that, mostly as my father's solicitor has taken over informing most everyone."

"I am glad of that, for you." Repington leaned forward. "Please accept condolences on the loss of your father, on behalf of myself and my entire family. If there is anything that can be done to help you or Lord Denholme please do not hesitate to ask for assistance."

"Thank you," Patrick replied, thankful for the good thoughts but unused to the tightness in his chest that accompanied them. "I am truly sorry your father was injured in an attempt to help my father and brother."

"Thank you. He is quite known for his impulsive actions. Rushing headlong into danger to aid a friend who was injured is not all that surprising," Repington said with a smile that spoke of a fondness for the often over bearing Duke of Castborough.

"Has there been any change in his condition?"

"The physician seems to think that he is improving. He is still being given medication to keep him quiet while his injuries heal." Repington said. "My brother, Hugh, and Henrietta have been sitting with him in the mornings and afternoons and say that he does seem to hear them. We are hoping for the best."

"Excuse me, sir," Fletcher said coming into the drawing room. "Dr Lambert is here to examine your father."

Repington stood up and turned to Patrick. "If you will excuse me, Major Wainwright."

"Yes, of course," Patrick said as the other man left the room.

Patrick sat for another moment thinking about what Repington had said about his siblings and he could not help but wonder what it would have been like to grow up close to his brother and his father.

CHAPTER TEN

"What are you reading to him?" Henrietta's mother asked coming into the room.

Henrietta held up the open book. "*One Thousand and One Nights.*"

"*One Thousand and One Nights?*" her mother asked sounding shocked. "I do not think that is very appropriate for you to be reading."

"Perhaps not," Henrietta said with a shrug. "Father had only acquired it a week or so before the accident. I know it is something he wanted to read so I am reading it to him now."

Her mother looked as though she was going to scold her that finally just nodded. "Dr Lambert is here to see your father. Hopefully, he will have good news for us today."

Henrietta stood up and set the book on the chair. For the most part, her father looked as though he was simply sleeping except for the bandage that covered his shoulder. She also knew that underneath the blankets bandages covered his legs as well, but it was a comfort to her that he at least appeared well.

When she looked up, she found her mother looking down at the bed with concern. "I believe he is improving. I know he can hear me when I am reading. One of the characters had made a decision to do something rather nonsensical and as I was reading Father frowned and shook his head slightly."

Her mother smiled looking fondly at her father. "I can see him doing that, too. If he were awake, he would set the book down and explain to us all why the character was making such an absurd decision."

"That is what I thought," Henrietta agreed, sharing a smile with her mother.

"Come with me to the drawing room we shall sit and have some tea while Dr Lambert sees to your father."

"Yes, of course," Henrietta followed her mother down the hall stopping to watch James walk by with the physician.

Her mother had already entered the drawing room, and she heard her say, "Major Wainwright, good morning, I did not know you were here."

Henrietta found herself hurrying down the hallway to join her mother.

"Good morning, Your Grace." Major Wainwright saw Henrietta enter and added, "Good morning, Lady Henrietta."

"Good morning, Major Wainwright," she greeted him and sat down on the settee.

He was standing next to one of the chairs looking as though he might leave.

"Please join us for tea. I believe Fletcher will be bringing it in quite soon," Henrietta said before she could stop herself.

Her mother had not sat down yet and said, "Yes, please do. I will be right back."

Her mother left the room presumably to go find Fletcher to bring them the tea. Henrietta sent a silent thank you to her mother. She turned to him.

"How are you? I was so sorry to hear the news about your father."

"Thank you," he said quietly. She knew that he had not gotten along with his father, but it was clear that he had cared for him, anyway. No matter the relationship, the death of a parent could not be easy.

"How is your brother recovering?"

He did not say anything for a moment and Henrietta feared that she had upset him further. She was just about to apologize when he said, "Dr Lambert has said that we will have to watch Frederick closely, but he is hoping for a full recovery."

"I am happy to hear that there is some hope."

"Yes, I agree. I was glad to hear that your father is expected to recover fully as well."

"It is a relief, for sure." Henrietta did not know if she should say anything more. While she was extremely relieved that her father would most likely recover she felt guilty speaking about it after Lord Ellesmont's death.

Captain Wainwright seemed to understand as he said, "How have you enjoyed your Season, thus far?"

She knew she must have looked surprised. "I have not been to Almack's in some time. You looked quite lovely when I was there to bring you home. I felt horrible having to tell you such awful news and take you away from a lovely evening."

"I am so thankful that you came to find me at Almack's. James told me that you volunteered to come find me that you were worried about me hearing about the accident from one of the gossips in attendance."

"I did not want you to worry. And that would have been a most horrible way to hear bitter news."

"I am very thankful, especially knowing how worried you must have been about your father and brother. I cannot thank you enough."

"I was…"

"Here we go," Fletcher said setting a tray down on the table next to the settee. He poured tea for both of them. "There is a tray of biscuits Nancy baked earlier this morning."

"Thank you, Fletcher," Henrietta said.

Henrietta was not sure what to say to Major Wainwright she only knew that she wanted him to stay and speak with her longer.

"Will you be staying in London for very long?"

"I was due to go back in two week's time, but I have canceled my plans to return to India for the time being. I must remain here until my brother recovers. If that does indeed happen." His voice trailed off though he was able to finish his thought.

She knew he was wondering if his brother would recover at all. It made her heart break thinking about how awful it would be if she lost her father and worried over losing one of her brothers. Even simply thinking about it was unbearable.

Having overheard Lord Ellesmont's feelings about Captain Wainwright she knew it must be even harder for him. She hoped that Lord Ellesmont had gotten a chance to speak with Captain Wainwright before the accident.

CHAPTER ELEVEN

"I am so pleased to hear that your brother is improving," Patrick's mother said to him.

They had just finished speaking with the physician who had made his usual visit as he had each morning since the accident. "Of course," Patrick said.

He understood her happiness, but the physician had not actually said that Frederick was improving. He had only said that the fact that Frederick's eyelids were fluttering at times was possibly a sign that he could wake soon. Patrick debated over discussing it further with his mother but came to the conclusion that she was much in need of hearing good news. It would do neither of them any good for him to disabuse her from her hopeful thoughts.

"Frederick would be rather perturbed if he were awake," his mother said and then laughed. "Of course, if he were awake he would have no reason to be perturbed."

"Mother, I hate to interrupt but what is it that Frederick would be perturbed about?" Patrick asked concerned that her grief may be causing her to be confused.

"Frederick was invited to a dinner party at Lord and Lady Haverfield's. He would be upset he had missed it." His mother smiled. "Frederick was quite involved with the events of the Season."

Patrick frowned. His father and brother had made it sound as though Frederick had been hard at work traveling between Ellesmont and London helping their father with family business. Clearly, that was not the case. "Yes, how perturbing."

"Oh!" His mother exclaimed. "I have a great idea that I am sure Frederick would be quite happy about."

"What is that?" Patrick asked.

"You should go to the dinner party in his place," she replied.

"No, I could not do that," Patrick said immediately.

"Why ever not?" His mother looked at him with wide eyes.

"It would be improper for me to attend a frivolous dinner party while in mourning."

"I do not think that it would be improper." She looked at him apparently waiting for him to argue with her. When he said nothing she added, "You would be doing it for me and Frederick."

"I do not wish to go but if it pleases you, I will do so." Patrick sighed and looked away.

"Thank you. I think it will be good for people to see you there representing the family."

Patrick did not agree with her but he would do what she asked. "When is this dinner party?"

"Tonight. I have already sent a note to Lady Haverfield that you would be attending in Frederick's place."

Patrick tried not to show his anger at her actions, simply standing up. "If I am to attend tonight, I should go prepare to be out for the evening.

Later that evening, Patrick was standing in the entry hall at Lord Haverfield's London residence wishing he had skipped the dinner party and had gone to White's instead. If he did not think that his mother would hear of his absence from Lady Haverfield he would have done so without hesitance.

He turned nodding to Jonathan Webb where he stood across the room, thankful that he had seen a friendly face. Normally, he would not care and would keep to himself as he had learned with his training as a soldier. He had never been overly fond of social functions such as these and even less so given the circumstances. Even the hot months in India seemed more enjoyable to him.

"Major Wainwright, so good to see you," Webb said crossing the room to meet him. "I feared I would not know anyone in attendance."

"I must admit that I feared the same. It was a last-minute decision that I should attend in my brother's place," Patrick explained. "At my mother's behest, of course."

"Of course," Webb said with a nod. "With any luck, the night will go by swiftly."

"That is my hope as well," Patrick agreed, ignoring the looks he was receiving from several young ladies. He was quite sure that the night would not pass swiftly enough.

"I cannot believe he is in attendance," he heard one of them say. "His father only just buried and his brother on his deathbed. It is a disgrace."

"Do not listen to them."

Patrick turned to see Timothy Sedgwick had joined he and Webb. "It seems that if Lady Sarah is speaking it is only to gossip about others in a most disparaging manner. No one else agrees with her except her small inner circle."

"It seems somewhat exhausting to keep up such talk." Webb looked across the room and suddenly smiled.

Patrick followed his gaze seeing that Lady Amelia and Lady Henrietta had just arrived and were being greeted by Lady Haverfield. As relieved as he had been to see Webb and Sedgwick, it was nothing compared to how happy he was to see Lady Henrietta. His reaction to Lady Henrietta's presence was a great surprise to him. As she was Lieutenant Repington's younger sister, he had seen her quite often the previous Season and his fondness for her was surely due to her relation to his close friend.

He watched Lady Henrietta as she spoke with Lady Haverfield, listening intently and smiling. Lady Henrietta moved away as more people arrived. She saw him and smiled before he could respond she was joined by St. Clair, looking very fashionable, if not half foxed by the way he seemed to waver next to Lady Henrietta. It seemed odd to him that he and Lady Henrietta appeared to be friends but then again Patrick did not know St. Clair well at all.

Patrick tried to ignore the spark of irritation that flared through him when St. Clair leaned in to speak to Lady Henrietta. All he knew was that he did not like him very much. It suddenly occurred to him that perhaps his dislike was borne of jealousy.

CHAPTER TWELVE

All through dinner Henrietta looked over frequently at Major Wainwright who had been seated at the other end of the long table. She had been seated with Mr St. Clair on one side and Mr Sedgwick on the other, Mr Webb and Lady Amelia sat across from her.

Under normal circumstances, she would have been more than happy with the arrangement but lately, she had found herself tiring of Mr St. Clair's constant nonsense. He seemed quite unable to carry on a normal conversation without trying to be humourous or make everyone laugh.

It made it worse for her to think that she had always known he was like that, even liking that about him. It was only lately that she had realized how important it was to be able to have an honest and sincere conversation. It was fine that he enjoyed kicking up larks, but she had learned there were times to be serious as well.

Finally, after what seemed an interminable amount of time had passed, the dinner was finished. Henrietta looked forward to moving to the drawing room where she could move about and speak to others without being bound to her dinner companions.

As expected several tables had been set up for various games to be played. Henrietta sat down at the table already occupied by Lady Amelia and Miss Hannah. They were soon joined by Mr Webb and Mr Sedgwick.

"Lady Henrietta," Miss Hannah started and then paused seeming to think about what she wanted to say. "I had not gotten a chance to ask, but how is your father faring?"

Henrietta returned her smile. "He is improving. The physician—"

"I am glad that he is improving. I will be glad when he is back on his feet," Mr St. Clair said dropping down into the remaining chair.

"Thank you, so will I. I have been so worried." Henrietta blinked quickly, not understanding why he cut her off.

"Yes, we all know. You seem to speak of nothing else." Mr St. Clair looked across the table at Mr Sedgwick and Mr Webb. "I had been so looking forward to this evening but now I just look forward to it being over so that I can go to White's and truly enjoy myself."

Lady Amelia and Miss Hannah gasped while the other gentlemen seem surprised by Mr St. Clair's words.

"Why not go now? No one is stopping you. Certainly not I." Henrietta replied a smile fixed upon her face.

Mr St. Clair seemed to understand that he had taken a wrong step and smiled apologetically. "I do not mean to sound unfeeling, but you used to be witty and jovial most of the time now you seem to always be serious and sad."

"Yes, of course. You are so right. What in Heaven is wrong with me?" Henrietta tried not to scowl as she stood up. "If you will forgive me, I seem to have developed a headache." She spun on her heel and left the drawing room.

It was not until Henrietta was in the hall that she realized there really was not any place for her to go. She nodded at the footman that stood in the entry and walked past him to the stairs. She was pacing in front of the staircase a few moments later when Major Wainwright walked out of the drawing room.

"Lady Henrietta, are you well?"

"Yes, perfectly fine." Her reply was sharp and she instantly regretted snapping at him.

"Lady Amelia was worried about you. She said that you had a headache."

Henrietta had forgotten about that. "Oh, right. Yes, and its name is Jeffrey St. Clair."

"Ah," Major Wainwright said with a nod. "I cannot say that I am much surprised."

"No?" Henrietta looked back toward the drawing room. "I suppose I must admit that I am not all that surprised myself. Mr St. Clair can be immensely amusing at times but I am learning that he is equally hoggish. He is always in need of attention and adulation, without it he becomes truculent."

"That certainly makes him less amusing," Major Wainwright agreed. "I have to admit I was surprised that you are closely acquainted with him."

Henrietta's heart sank and she turned away walking up several steps on the staircase before turning around to sit down. She suddenly felt bereft and was not certain as to why, although she suspected that it had to do with Major Wainwright. She hated that he might be disappointed in her or that he thought of her as a silly school girl. Not that she could really blame him, she most likely would have thought the same about anyone else given Mr St. Clair's behaviour as of late.

"It was a surprise to me as well. I was at a party several weeks ago and had been doing my best to avoid Lady Sarah and her vile friends. Mr St. Clair had apparently noticed my movements and had asked me what I was doing. When I explained he thought it was a grand game and joined me." She smiled and shrugged. "He made me laugh and I suppose that was enough at the time."

Major Wainwright had moved to the side of the stairs to talk to her through the balustrade. "I did not mean to imply that you needed to explain yourself. You are of age and allowed to choose the people with which you would like to spend your time. You owe me nothing in that regard."

"Thank you, I appreciate that," Henrietta said. She was being more than truthful being the youngest of six siblings and the only sister meant that she received a lot of advice about nearly every subject known to her. She could only imagine what Matthew would have said to her regarding the subject of Mr St. Clair. She suddenly sat up a little straighter and turned to look at Major Wainwright. "It is all Matthew's fault."

"Matthew? Your brother?" Major Wainwright asked, justifiably confused.

"I am afraid so. He married Diana and they left for his appointment in Whitehall soon after their wedding," she explained.

"I had heard of his appointment but not that he had married."

"It is because he is gone that I am in this mess now." Major Wainwright frowned and she went on. "I have been accustomed to Matthew accompanying me to the events of the Season. He was always making amusing comments and I suppose I missed that."

Major Wainwright stared at her for a long moment. "You think of Mr St. Clair as you would one of your brothers?"

"An annoying brother," she said with a nod. It was a disconcerting revelation as she had rather liked Mr St. Clair for a time. With a sigh she stood up, "I suppose I should be gracious and return to the drawing room."

"If you are ready, I shall accompany you."

When she met him at the bottom of the stairs, he looked pleased. The question that came to mind was whether it was because she was rejoining the party or that her feelings for Mr St. Clair were not romantic she was not sure. It did make her quite curious about Major Wainwright.

CHAPTER THIRTEEN

"Has Dr Lambert come out yet?" Patrick's mother asked him. "No," Patrick said glancing back at the door where the physician had gone. "He said it may take a little while."

"I am so worried, Patrick."

"I know, as am I." Patrick sighed.

It had been less than an hour since and the young woman caring for Frederick had come running in saying there was something wrong with Frederick. Patrick had instructed her to send for the physician while he had gone in to check on Frederick. His brother was having a fit of tremors, his limbs stiff and his entire body shaking. Patrick held his brother down so he would not hurt himself. The tremors had passed quickly only to return as Dr Lambert arrived.

Patrick had seen similar reactions to soldiers that have been injured when he served on the Peninsula but even if he had not he would have known it meant his condition had worsened by the look on Dr Lambert's face. It was not something that he could share with his mother and he was worried about her well-being and how she would take even more bad news.

"Mother, I think you should go lie down and take a rest,"

Patrick suggested. "I can come talk to you when Dr Lambert is finished."

His mother was wringing her hands. "No, I want to stay here. I want to speak with Dr Lambert about Frederick."

Patrick tried again. "I understand, but you do need to rest. If you go lie down, I will summon one of the servants to get you when the physician comes out."

"I am not leaving this chair until I speak with Dr Lambert, so save your breath."

"It is understandable," Patrick said. "I am worried about your health as well. I do not want you to grow weary and become ill."

He did not know if she had a response to that because the door opened and Dr Lambert emerged from Frederick's room.

"How is he, Dr Lambert?" Patrick's mother asked as she stood.

Dr Lambert said nothing for a few moments crossing the room to sit in the chair next to Patrick's mother. "Lady Ellesmont, Major Wainwright, I am sorry that I do not have better news for you."

"What is it?" His mother asked.

"I am afraid that Lord Denholm's condition is worsening. The tremors he is experiencing are due to the injuries to his head."

"Is there anything that can be done to ease them?" Patrick asked already knowing the answer.

"I can give him medication to ease the tremors." Dr Lambert shook his head. "But I am afraid that there is nothing that can be done beyond that."

"What does that mean?" Patrick's mother asked her eyes frantic.

"There is nothing to be done. Lord Denholm will not likely recover."

"Not likely recover?" She repeated looking to Patrick. "What on Earth does that mean?"

Dr Lambert looked apologetically to Patrick who said, "Mother, Frederick will most likely continue on the way that he is until he slips away in his sleep."

"Die?" She whispered. "You are saying that he will die, too."

It was not a question, but Patrick responded anyway. "Yes, Mother, he will die."

As his mother began to weep quietly Patrick turned to Dr Lambert. "Please do whatever you need to keep Frederick as comfortable as possible."

"I will give him more medication." He glanced at Patrick's mother and frowned. "However, more medicine may hasten his decline, I am afraid."

"Extending his time would be a purely selfish exercise on our part. His comfort is far more important."

Dr Lambert nodded his approval. "I will do as you ask."

"Thank you," Patrick said.

"Of course, my apologies. I can understand it is quite a shock."

Patrick shook his head. "I witnessed such injuries during my time on the Peninsula. I was not as surprised by your findings after seeing the tremors."

The physician went back in with Frederick and Patrick moved to sit next to his mother.

"Mother, you should go lie down. You have had a terrible shock. And there are likely to be more troubling days ahead."

"Is it not a shock for you as well?" His mother looked at him with clear disappointment.

"Yes, of course, it is. I suppose my experiences on the Peninsula have affected the way that I react to death."

She looked at him and nodded slowly. "I pray that it is has prepared you as well."

"Yes, Mother," he said and stood with the intention of helping her to her room.

She looked up at him and laid a hand on his arm. "Patrick, for all intents and purposes, you are now the Earl of Ellesmont."

Patrick opened his mouth to argue but the realization of what she said slammed into him like a kick to the chest. If Frederick died, Patrick would inherit the title and the responsibilities.

Never once had he wished this could be his. It had seemed an awful burden and had felt poorly for Frederick when they were younger for having to endure the constant reminder that someday he would inherit the title. In all of his years, he had never even imagined that something would happen that would make him the Earl of Ellesmont.

After finally convincing his mother to go lie down, Patrick paced the house. He had been so disconcerted by the death of his father and his brother's injuries that he had not thought what it would mean losing them both. Patrick walked down the hall and turned into the library and then stopped suddenly, the sight of his father's desk made him turn around and leave the room. He began to walk into the drawing room and stopped again, assailed by memories of the last argument with Frederick and his father.

With an exasperated groan, Patrick spun on his heel and headed straight for the front door. He needed to clear his mind and he would not be able to do so with every piece of furniture in the house reminding him how much he did not fit into this world.

Patrick started off in one direction and then almost immediately turned around. Going to White's or another club would do him no good. He refused to end up like others who had drowned their sorrows sitting at a table with an unending glass of whiskey. He knew he would be much better off taking a walk through Hyde Park. It was early afternoon and not likely to be too crowded.

Patrick reached the gate to the park and sat off on the first path he came across not caring where he went only wanting peace and some time to think. He had not planned on returning to London and had only done so because of the pending business matters. It had seemed a waste to travel so far simply to sign some papers. He supposed deep down that he had hopes that he could spend work toward mending the relationship between him and his father.

Being truly honest he had hoped that his father would in some way be proud of him and the accomplishments that he had made in his travels to India and employment with the East India Company. Instead all Patrick had was the knowledge that there are last words to each other were words spoken in anger.

Although given more time or another opportunity to speak with his father, Patrick had to admit that he could not foresee a different outcome. He and his father had not ever truly gotten along and Patrick could not remember a time that their meeting did not end in an argument. Somehow that made him even more despondent than missing the chance to reconcile. He continued down the path wishing he had never left India.

CHAPTER FOURTEEN

"Lady Henrietta, this was a splendid idea," Miss Hannah announced.

"I must agree," Lady Amelia said. "If my mother asked me one more question, I would have given her a less than a ladylike answer."

"I am glad that you both were able to join me," Henrietta replied as they walked along.

Henrietta's mother had suggested that she get out of the house as she had done little but sit by her father's bedside. Henrietta had declined several social events in the past week due to her continuing worry over her father. She hated to admit it but Mr St. Clair's words at the dinner party had upset her. It had not been her intention to upset or sadden her friends.

In the past, Henrietta had visited Hyde Park most often with her brother, Matthew, and she had not gone since before he had left for Whitehall. She had not realized how much she had missed Matthew until she had spoken to Major Wainwright. Being the youngest and the only sister of the six siblings had its blessings and burdens. Matthew was the closest in age to her, being only two years older, they had always been quite close. Whether they had been laughing or arguing she had always relied on him.

With Matthew gone and her father injured she had felt lost and alone. Her mother was already distressed looking after her father, Henrietta could not bear to upset her further. She had not wanted to leave the house but to please her mother Henrietta had sent notes to both Lady Amelia and Miss Hannah asking them if they would like to visit Hyde Park with her that afternoon.

"I was very pleased to have received your note," Lady Amelia assured her.

"Shall we talk of only happy things?" Henrietta turned to face Lady Amelia with a pointed look. "Perhaps of you and Mr Webb?"

Lady Amelia's cheeks reddened. "How is it that you already know? He spoke with my father only two days ago."

"It is so very wonderful," Miss Hannah said clapping her hands.

"I think we shall all celebrate, as the rest of us all knew that it would happen. We simply had no idea when the two of you would figure it out," Henrietta said with a smirk.

Lady Amelia laughed. "There is nothing wrong with taking your time to get to know someone."

"You sound like your mother," Henrietta blurted out.

Lady Amelia gasped. "I do not."

Henrietta laughed and Miss Hannah said, "Are you quite sure, that you do not?"

"Oh, not you, too?" Lady Amelia laughed. Then she turned back to Henrietta and said, "Now that Mr Webb and I are to be married, perhaps you and Mr St. Clair would be next."

Henrietta felt the smile fade, and she continued down the path. "No, I do not think that will ever happen." Henrietta could not abide the actions of Mr St. Clair as of late. She could hardly believe that she had thought him entertaining.

"Surely you are not rebuffing him simply because of his behaviour at Lord and Lady Haverfield's dinner party, he was likely jug-bitten by the time dinner started."

Henrietta did not want to argue with her friend but the fact that he had arrived at the dinner party in his cups—or that he had gotten that way soon after he arrived—did factor into her judgment of his behaviour. Clearly, though, it was not simply his behaviour at the dinner party, even though that had been abhorrent. It was the aggregation of so many nights spent doing the same exact thing. The fact that he was critical of her sadness and concern over her father's condition was truly surprising and upsetting.

"It is not only that. There are many reasons for me to think twice about a courtship with Mr St. Clair. He thinks only about finding mischief and anything else that amuses him. He has no consideration for anyone else around him."

"I thought you liked that he was always so amusing, is that not right?" Miss Hannah asked seeming genuinely confused.

"I did. At first." Henrietta nodded. "He was amusing to be around, he made me laugh and I liked that, of course. The error was mine and I am aware. I assumed that Mr St. Clair was caring and felt some affection for me."

Lady Amelia glanced over at Miss Hannah. "I am sure he does, perhaps he has never had to deal with sickness or death."

"That may be true," Henrietta acknowledged. "I suppose I should be happy for him that he has been so blessed. I am afraid, though, that any affectionate feelings I had for him perished after hearing so many thoughtless comments from him over the last few weeks."

Henrietta continued walking stopping only when she heard Lady Amelia say, "Timothy, what are you doing here?"

"Good afternoon, to you too, dear sister," Mr Sedgwick said. He looked back down the path where Mr Webb was still walking. "I encountered Webb on my way back from Bond Street. I thought perhaps you would like to see him."

Henrietta saw that Lady Amelia immediately glanced back at her. Henrietta smiled and said, "The more the merrier." Even though she did not really feel that way, not that she was in any way upset to see Mr Webb or Mr Sedgwick, she had looked forward to speaking with her friends and taking her mind off her worries. She had not thought her mother would be so correct, it was not evident until she had gotten to the park with her friends.

Lady Amelia nodded her thanks clearly not wanting to upset her friend. "Thank you, Timothy. That was rather nice of you."

Mr Sedgwick smiled at Miss Hannah and said, "I have my moments."

Henrietta tilted her head, even as preoccupied as she was she could see that Mr Sedgwick had not come to the park solely to deliver Mr Webb. He had also clearly wanted to see Miss Hannah.

"Shall we walk?" Mr Sedgwick asked after Mr Webb had joined them.

"Of course," Miss Hannah said looking up at him.

As they fell into step on the path, Henrietta found herself following behind them alone. She thought about turning around and going back home, but she knew that would be a childish response that would only serve to upset the people that she cared about.

She followed along for a few minutes and happened to glance off to the side and then suddenly took another look thinking that her mind was playing tricks on her.

"Major Wainwright?"

He looked up surprised and then his face softened. "Lady Henrietta, I had not expected to see you here."

"To be honest, I had not expected to be here," Henrietta replied stepping off the path. "But it is a beautiful day and I cannot waste it by being miserable."

Major Wainwright looked around as though he was just noticing the nice weather. He seemed upset almost lost, Henrietta wanted to ask him how he was doing but after having so many people ask her the same thing over the last few weeks she could not get herself to ask him.

Instead, she asked, "Tell me about your time in India?"

He seemed surprised. "You really want to know? You did not seem too interested when Charles and I spoke of it last Season."

"Of course, I like to tease Charles, he is always so serious. When I noticed Beatrice spoke up in his defense, I kept doing it."

"Until Charles noticed?" Major Wainwright joined her on the path.

"Yes," Henrietta smiled. "Beatrice too. She seemed not to realize how much she cared for him. Of course, her mother's constant complaints did not help either."

"I remember. It was what convinced Charles that he should take the position in India."

Henrietta had been shocked when Charles had announced that not only were he and Beatrice getting married but that they would also be traveling to live in India after their wedding.

When she failed to respond Major Wainwright went on. "As you can imagine, India is much different from England in most every way. Britain and the East India Company has had a strong presence there for quite a while though so there are some comforts of home that we are also able to enjoy."

Henrietta walked with him down the path and felt much better letting his deep voice soothe her.

CHAPTER FIFTEEN

"Did Dr Lambert talk to you today?" Hugh asked.
"Yes, he is quite happy with Father's progress," Phillip explained. "He believes that it is time to start reducing the medication."

Henrietta had been approaching the door to her father's room. Nearly every afternoon she had gone in and sat with him. The first week or so she had sat and read to him out of the latest book he had been reading, *One Thousand and One Nights*. After several days of that though, she had grown tired of the stories and had simply begun to talk to her father while she sat next to his bed.

She was sure that he could hear her while she was speaking. Sometimes mumbling something as though it was a response to something she had said. Hearing that he might be more coherent or able to respond made her quite happy.

Henrietta stopped in the doorway and said, "I am here to sit with Father. How has he been today?"

"He is most definitely improving. Dr Lambert was in earlier and is very pleased with how he is doing."

"That is so wonderful to hear." Henrietta sat down in the chair next to their father straightening the sheets around him.

She glanced over to find that her brothers were looking at her. "Is everything all right?" She asked suddenly worried that she had misheard what had been said about their father's recovery.

"I believe so," Hugh replied. "Today is Wednesday, is it not?"

"Yes, it is," Henrietta answered. "Why do you ask?"

Hugh and Philip exchanged a look. Philip stepping forward to say, "It is just that it is Wednesday and under normal circumstances, you would be getting ready to go to Almack's this evening."

"Yes, I will be attending this evening. Mother's maid will be helping me get ready later this afternoon." Henrietta waved her arms in a shooing motion. "Now you two go on so I can read to Father."

Philip held his hands up in surrender. "Yes, madam. I will be in the library if I am needed."

Henrietta smiled at her eldest brother. "Thank you, Philip."

Her two brothers left, and she turned to her father. "Good afternoon, Father. I hope you are feeling better and looking forward to coming back to us soon."

Most afternoons she told her father about what she had done the night before and that morning. Today though she surprised herself by saying, "I saw Major Wainwright in Hyde Park the other day. I have always known that he is a good man, responsible and trustworthy. But I do not think people realize how truly strong he is."

Henrietta took a deep breath and smiled.

"He has endured the loss of his father and now I fear his brother will perish as well. He is being strong for his mother's sake, I am sure. I worry though, Father. Who shall be strong for him?" Henrietta sat forward in the chair. "I believe it to be true that he did not get along with his father and brother, but their loss still must be a tremendous shock. How is he to deal with it all alone?"

Her father made a sighing noise. She nodded absent mindedly. "Yes, I know. Gentlemen are brought up to be staid and independent and never show feelings, but I cannot help but think he is in need of a family like anyone else. Is he so different from my brothers? Each of them needs each other, and me, I suppose."

She sat back in the chair again thinking about Major Wainwright, her heart aching at his plight. "I daresay that they are all the better for their adoring wives as well. Charles and Beatrice would not have been able to marry and travel to India without the counsel and assistance of Major Wainwright. I have never met a more responsible, trustworthy and caring man. Aside from my brothers and, of course, you, Father."

She reached out to take his hand in hers and squeezed it gently.

"I am distressed over Major Wainwright, Father." Her father made another noise. "No, I do not think that I am worrying over nothing. He is a good man, he deserves to be happy."

Henrietta spent the rest of the afternoon speaking to her father and also reading more out of his book. Although she did not feel much like going to Almack's that night, Henrietta left her father and hurried to prepare for her evening out. She was glad to have the extra help of her mother's maid, otherwise, she would have been late for sure.

Once again Lady Amelia's Aunt Agatha served as her chaperone. Henrietta riding in Philip's carriage with Lady Amelia while Mr Sedgwick accompanied Lady Agatha in a second carriage. They were forced to wait in a large carriage line as people waited to enter the ballroom at Almack's. When they finally entered the ballroom Lady Amelia sighed with relief. "I did not think I could stay in that carriage a moment longer."

"It did feel like we waited much longer than we have before." It had been a long wait that Henrietta found herself wishing that she could have stayed home. She enjoyed her time with Lady Amelia and she looked forward to seeing Miss Hannah and Mr Webb as well. She supposed it was because she had overheard Hugh and Philip speaking that morning about her father possibly waking up soon. She had missed him so that she wanted to be by his side when he awoke from his prolonged sleep.

"Oh, thank goodness, I am so glad you are here," Miss Hannah said rushing over to them. "Goodness, Miss Hannah, are you all right? Is there anything amiss?" Lady Amelia asked.

"It is Lady Sarah and Miss Jane," Miss Hannah shook her head. "They are being simply awful tonight."

Henrietta grimaced. "Moreso than usual? Have they been bothering you?"

Miss Hannah suddenly looked to the corner of the room where Henrietta could see Miss Hannah's sister, Clara sitting with Lady Matilda. "No, it is Clara that they have been harassing. Mr Kendall asked her to dance and then stopped and said that he changed his mind."

"He did not! How rude!" Lady Amelia exclaimed.

Miss Hannah nodded. "Clara was quite confused until she heard Lady Sarah and Miss Jane laughing."

"I am surprised Miss Danielle was not also part of it," Henrietta remarked.

"She has not arrived yet," Miss Hannah told them and then visibly cringed. "They are coming this way now."

Henrietta rolled her eyes at Miss Hannah knowing that Lady Sarah could not see it from where she stood. Miss Hannah covered the sudden smile with the quick movement of her fan. Henrietta gave her a quick nod before turning back to face Lady Sarah.

"Good evening, Lady Sarah, Miss Jane," Henrietta greeted them. If nothing else she would show that she could be gracious.

Lady Sarah rolled her eyes at Miss Jane. "I am surprised that you are here tonight, Lady Henrietta."

Henrietta tilted her head. "Why is that?"

"I was sure, Lady Henrietta, that you must be so very devastated that you have fallen out of favour with the lovely Mr St. Clair." Lady Sarah stood there with a delighted look on her face waiting for Henrietta's reaction.

"I can understand your confusion, but it is Mr St. Clair who has fallen out of favour with me." Henrietta motioned with her fan. "He was amusing for a time, but I have grown tired of him."

Lady Sarah turned to Miss Jane and made a quiet comment

causing Miss Jane to snort. "Yes, of course, how silly of me. Perhaps you can marry Major Wainwright and move to India and be a savage."

"That sounds lovely. I thank you for your good wishes." Henrietta smiled sweetly at her. "Lady Sarah, tell me again and to whom you are betrothed?

"I? I am not betrothed," Lady Sarah said confused and angry.

"No?" Henrietta took a step forward towards the other young lady. "Perhaps if you spent more time being pleasant than acting as a gossiping cow, you would have the luxury of dismissing gentlemen who no longer amuse you."

Lady Sarah's face grew red and Miss Jane gasped.

Henrietta turned toward Lady Amelia and Miss Hannah and said, "If you will excuse me, I think I have had enough for tonight."

With that, she stormed out of Almack's stopping on the sidewalk long enough to ask for her carriage to be brought around.

CHAPTER SIXTEEN

Patrick walked into White's hoping to find a table in the corner in which he could drink whiskey until he no longer cared about anything. His brother had succumbed in the early hours of the morning. He had spent most of the morning comforting his mother, which he had not minded except for the fact that he would not have to do it if his brother had survived.

He had then spent the rest of the day speaking with his father's solicitors assuring that all business affairs were in order so that Patrick could step in and keep everything running as smoothly as possible.

White's was more crowded than he had anticipated and he contemplated leaving but the thought of returning to the dreary house was not something he could even think about doing right then. His mother had decided that his brother should be returned to Ellesmont immediately. He was sure that she could not bear having him laid out in the house.

They had been able to avoid that practice with his father as he had been injured so severely that viewing was not possible. His mother and her brother had taken his father's body to Ellesmont to be laid to rest as soon as possible. Patrick had stayed in London to keep watch over Frederick's recovery.

It now felt like a waste. He had not been present at his father's service and his brother had died, anyway. It should not have been a surprise to him as he felt that it was somewhat symbolic of his relationship with both his father and his brother. Patrick had spent his life trying to spend time with his father while Frederick had constantly run in to interrupt with something he wanted to do or speak about. Missing his father's service seemed a last stab from his brother.

He heard someone call his name, and he scanned the room noticing Sedgwick waving from a table in a back corner. He had not wanted to see anyone he knew, but it was probably wise that he did not drink alone that night.

He made his way through the room joining Sedgwick at the table. "Wainwright, sit down," Sedgwick said by way of greeting.

Patrick sat and while the other man procured a new glass that he promptly filled generously from the bottle of whiskey that had already been sitting on the table.

"Thank you," Patrick said taking the glass.

"Drink up, Major. You deserve it." Sedgwick nodded once and looked at him sagely.

He took a long drink and set the glass on the table.

"Are you fit for company?"

Patrick shrugged not sure how to answer.

Sedgwick's voice softened. "I heard the news about Frederick. I am sorry."

Patrick had not thought that the news would get out so fast. He supposed that since people had known Frederick had been badly injured they were had likely been waiting to hear about his recovery. He nodded. "Thank you."

"How are you faring?"

Patrick shrugged again before taking another large drink from the glass. "I do not really know. It is as though I can feel nothing. It is like I am empty."

Sedgwick tipped the bottle and Patrick began to protest. "Quiet. One night of drinking will not take on the cut nor make you bosky for all time."

Patrick knew he was right and stopped arguing. "I have been very careful to not drink away my problems. I have seen so many others hide in the bottom of the bottle."

"I doubt that will be an issue for you," Sedgwick told him. "The fact that you are worried about it at all is probably the first indicator that you would not succumb to the temptation so easily."

Patrick was about to reply when someone stopped at the table. He looked up to see Mr St. Clair and Mr Kendall standing there. They were the last two people Patrick wanted to see, but he was determined to stay civil for Lady Henrietta's sake.

"St. Clair, Kendall," Sedgwick said somewhat curtly.

The two men barely acknowledge Sedgwick completely focusing on Patrick.

"I am surprised you are here," St. Clair said somewhat accusingly.

"Why is that?"

"You are so good and proper. So far above us all, I am surprised that you would deem to grace us with your presence."

Patrick chuckled. "I am the second son of the Earl of Ellesmont, who purchased a commission in the British Army, that is all. Nothing more nothing less."

"That is what you say but we see you for what you really are." St. Clair seemed to stagger a bit.

"I am sure you do," Patrick replied hoping to two pathetic sots would go away.

"Let me be the first to congratulate you on becoming the next Earl of Ellesmont."

Patrick stiffened. "You are talking rubbish."

"The news of your brother's passing has moved about London rather quickly." St. Clair gestured behind him. "I am surprised White's has not had some sort of betting with regard to it."

Patrick shrugged. "I doubt that anyone truly cares."

St. Clair waved his arm and nearly fell down, he was so jug bitten. "The Season was going so well before you came to London."

"I am quite sure. Please enlighten me," Patrick invited him.

"Now that you are here Lady Henrietta is barely speaking to me and it is all your fault."

Patrick glanced at Sedgwick wondering if St. Clair was speaking the truth about Henrietta. Sedgwick nodded confirming what the other man had said.

"How is it my fault that you have fallen out of favour with a young lady?" Patrick paused. "Perhaps you have shown her this side of you too many times. As you said, I have only been in London for a short amount of time and yet nearly every time I have seen you, you have been more than a trifle into your cups."

Mr Kendall made a comment under his breath that Patrick did not hear. St. Clair growled at him. "I am sure that I can change Lady Henrietta's mind. I only need a moment or two with her alone to coax her into a courtship."

Patrick stood up so quickly his chair clattered to the ground behind him. He stared down St. Clair who took a step back. Patrick advanced on him, his voice low but steady. "If Lady Henrietta wants nothing to do with you, then you very bloody well listen to her. If I hear even a whisper that you have upset her in any way you will have to deal with me, her five brothers and the Duke of Castborough himself."

Kendall snorted. "The duke is not fit enough to do anything at the moment, let alone defend his daughter."

Patrick turned on him so quickly that the man stumbled backward. "Do you know that for sure? Are you willing to be implicated in the wrongdoings of your friend here? Are you willing to take the same punishment?"

Kendall opened his mouth as though he would respond but finally closed his mouth and shook his head. Patrick pointed out the door and Kendall scurried away so fast that he nearly knocked down Lord Ramsbury in his haste to leave the club.

"Why are you still here?" Patrick growled at St. Clair who took one last look at Patrick before he too scuttled out the door.

CHAPTER SEVENTEEN

"Good evening, sir."

"Good evening, Harcourt."

Patrick had barely climbed the steps of Denholme Hall when the front door had opened. It had been a relief when they had finally pulled up in front of the large house. He waited by the door for his mother to join him.

She seemed apprehensive about entering and he gave her an encouraging smile. "You will feel better once you are inside and have something to eat."

She nodded, her smile grateful. "Yes, I think that would be nice."

Before Patrick could say anything, Harcourt stepped forward to take his mother's small bag. "I will have Dinah bring in a tray of tea and biscuits to the drawing room."

His mother had been staring at the door to the library finally looking away to say softly, "Thank you."

He and his mother had returned to London after the long trip from Ellesmont. He had attempted to convince his mother to stay behind at the country home but she had been quite adamant about returning with him to London. Not wanting to upset her, he had acquiesced quickly, he could not blame her for not wanting to be alone in the large house. It had been his intention to speak with his aunt about accompanying her for an extended stay once the Season was over.

It was not until they had left Ellesmont that he had learned his mother's true intent on accompanying him back to London.

He had not wanted to sit in silence for the trip. "When we arrive back in London, I will be sure to contact Mr Bolton regarding the issue with the tenants."

"That is a good idea," she said quietly turning from the window. "You will also need to petition the Lord Chancellor."

Patrick was caught off guard by her suggestion but was able to steer her away from the conversation quickly. "Yes, of course. I think I shall call on Aunt Nora and have her come stay with you for a time."

She had nodded and had not brought up the Lord Chancellor subject for the rest of the trip.

He had spent the last several days avoiding the conversation as there had been enough for him to deal with being back at Ellesmont. It had been necessary to visit all the tenants on the entailed land around Ellesmont. Each of the tenants had spoken so fondly of his father and Frederick, it had been both comforting to hear while also making him feel even worse. How could it be that the tenants of his father's land seemed closer to both his father and brother than he had himself?

They had barely sat down in the drawing room when she turned to him. "You need to petition the Lord Chancellor for a writ of summons."

"You mentioned that in the carriage."

She continued on as though he had not spoken. "So that you can be seen during the next session of Parliament."

"Of course, Mother, in due time." Patrick did not want to think about all that now.

"You must do so right away. Not only are you the rightful heir to the title, you are now the Earl of Ellesmont. I intended to speak with you about this some time ago but I had not wanted to think about the idea that your brother would not recover." Her voice wavered with emotion and she paused to gather herself.

"Mother, we can speak about this later, when you are—"

"No. I have put this off for far too long. Even if Frederick had lived, it is likely that he would have been unable to perform the duties of the title." She shook her head. "It pains me to say it, but it was better to say farewell to our dear Frederick now rather than watch him suffer."

"It seems useless to discuss what could or could not have been at this point. We can only go on from where we are." Patrick greatly hoped to steer the conversation away from where it had ended up.

"That is the truth, indeed, but promise me that you will petition the Lord Chancellor upon our arrival in London."

"Mother, please."

"No, Patrick you must promise me. I need this from you."

Anger suddenly erupted inside him. "No, I will not promise you!"

She drew back as though she had been slapped. "Why ever not?"

"Because I do not want the blasted title!" He shouted at her and jumped up from his chair to pace the room. "It will only serve to remind me that neither Father nor Frederick gave two shillings about me."

"Patrick, that is not true. Not in the least."

"Do not dare to tell me that they cared one bit about me." He shot her a warning look. "I was gone to India for a year. It took mere minutes when I came back before they were both making disdainful comments about me or my position with the East India Company."

"Your father was very proud of you."

Patrick let out a barking laugh. "So proud that he told everyone all I could do was train savages how to march."

"But he did not mean those things."

"Perhaps the title should go to Stephen, at least Father liked him."

"Your cousin?" His mother frowned. "You are being ridiculous. How could you not want the title? Your father would have wanted this for you."

"Enough!" Patrick said. "I cannot listen to any more of this."

Once more leaving the house in anger, he had no intention of a destination but soon found himself in front of Repington House. He was not sure what brought him there, but he went to the door hoping to find James in residence. Patrick had sought his counsel once before and perhaps it would benefit him again. He had calmed down considerably since leaving Denholme Hall.

"Major Wainwright, good evening."

"Thank you, Fletcher. Is Mr Repington in residence this evening?"

Philip Repington walked down the hall into the entry. "Major Wainwright."

"Lord Holgrave, good evening. I am sorry for intruding."

"James has gone back to Surrey. Is there anything I can help you with?"

Patrick hesitated.

Holgrave gestured toward the hall. "Come with me to the library we can talk there."

"Of course," Patrick followed behind. He had already disturbed the household he did not want to be rude on top of that.

"I was sorry to hear about Lord Denholme," Holgrave said before handing him a glass of whiskey. "I know this has been difficult for you."

"Thank you. It has," Patrick admitted. "My relationship with both my father and brother had not often been good but I still feel their loss acutely."

The other man nodded. "There was a time that I did not speak to my father nor my brother, James. Ridiculous behaviour borne of youth and conceit and I nearly died before I came to my senses."

"It is fortunate that you were given the opportunity to make amends." Patrick looked at the floor, clearly wishing he did not feel such regret.

"Believe me I know I am extremely lucky. It was only later that I realized everything that had happened needed to be left in the past. It did no one any good to drag that behind me." Holgrave leaned toward Patrick. "Half of what I had believed turned out to be false assumptions on my part, anyway."

Patrick nodded. "It seems too much energy wasted focusing on things that cannot be changed."

"Quite right," Holgrave agreed. He held up the whiskey bottle. "More."

"No, thank you." Patrick sat absentmindedly thinking about what he had said.

"What are you to do about your position in India?"

Patrick looked up surprised. Holgrave was the first to not automatically assume he was going to give up everything he loved in order to assume the title of Earl of Ellesmont.

"I have not decided," he said truthfully. "I suppose I will have to weigh my options."

"Always smart."

Patrick leaned back in the chair. "There is much to consider."

"So, you liked living in India?"

The question was so like the one that Henrietta asked that Patrick immediately wondered if she might be at home. "I enjoyed the challenge and being able to use my training to further my profession."

Holgrave nodded. "I have heard from more than one advisor that it was a very shrewd venture. I can only imagine how successful you would be as the Earl of Ellesmont."

"I do not know about that," Patrick told him.

"Only one way to find out," Holgrave said his eyebrows raised. "Now tell me about my brother, Charles."

CHAPTER EIGHTEEN

Henrietta set the book down on the table next to her father's bed. "I think I hear voices again. I am going to go check."

She moved to the door and peered down the hall. Earlier she had done the same thing, listening until she had indeed heard voices in the entry hall. A moment later she saw Philip come out of the library presumably to see who had arrived.

It had been a complete surprise when she heard him call out Major Wainwright's name and then lead him into the library. She had not known that they were very well acquainted. It was that question that had kept her in the doorway as she had wanted to run down the hall to greet him but did not think it would be proper.

She had gone back in to sit with her father reading quietly so she would be able to hear when her brother and Major Wainwright came back out into the hallway.

Henrietta stood at the open door watching as her brother shook hands with Major Wainwright and walked away. She hurried down the hall slowing to a natural pace when she reached the stairs.

"Oh, Major Wainwright, good evening." She spoke as calmly as possible though her heart was beating wildly.

"Good evening, Lady Henrietta." He smiled and nodded, seemingly happy to see her.

She had not seen him since before he had left London to lay his brother to rest at Ellesmont. About to extend her condolences when she stopped, he looked weary, and she was sure that he had tired of hearing the somber thoughts of others.

"I had not realized you had returned to London. I am glad you will be here a bit longer."

"Thank you. I am, as well." He almost seemed relieved she had gone on as though nothing terrible had occurred.

"Lady Henrietta, would you like me to bring you and the major some tea in the drawing room?"

She turned and smiled at the man, feeling deep gratitude at the opportunity. "That sounds lovely, Fletcher. Thank you." She replied quickly before Major Wainwright could protest. "Perhaps Nancy would like to sit and work on her knitting."

"Yes, madam," Fletcher said with a smile.

Counting on Major Wainwright's social graces Henrietta turned and walked down the hall. As expected, he followed her into the drawing room. She sat down on the settee and tried not to laugh as he stood awkwardly near the door. It would be unseemly for them to be caught in the drawing room alone. The door was open though, and she did not foresee her own family accusing her of any improprieties.

Before she could say anything to him, Nancy came in with a basket in her hands. She saw Major Wainwright and smiled at Henrietta moving to the far corner the window. "I will just sit over here. Thank you, Lady Henrietta."

Henrietta smiled back. "I know you wanted to finish the blanket for your sister."

"I do want to get it done," Nancy said with a laugh. "Her wee one will need it very soon."

Major Wainwright relaxed, finally sitting down in the chair she had started to think of as his. "What brought you to Repington House this evening?"

He seemed surprised at her question and she worried that she had offended him. "I came to talk to your brother, James, but I ended up speaking with Lord Holgrave since James was not in residence."

"Yes, James returned to Surrey two days ago." It made sense to her now that he had been speaking with Philip. "He will return to London in a few weeks when Parliament is back in session."

He nodded, his jaw tightening.

"Was Philip not helpful?"

"No, he was more helpful than I had originally thought."

"I am glad of that," Henrietta said wishing she could say more.

"He told me how he had once been at odds with your father and brother."

"Oh yes, it is quite true. He and James did not get along at all for several years. They do not always agree with each other, but they certainly get along better now."

"I had hoped for the same sort of resolution but that was not to be."

"I am quite possibly speaking out of turn, but I do not feel I should keep this to myself any longer."

"What is it?" He asked and then paused as Fletcher came in with a large tray of tea and biscuits.

Henrietta took her cup of tea looking over the rim. "Your father was at Repington House the day of the accident."

"I did not know that."

"I did not think you did. He came seeking my father's counsel regarding his relationship with you. He did not like that every time that he saw you that you were fighting."

Major Wainwright seemed surprised. "I did not know he even noticed it happened so often."

"He did. He was very upset and told my father that he was very proud of you and what you have accomplished."

Major Wainwright's head snapped up. "He did?"

Henrietta nodded. "Mind you, I did not hear the full conversation as they were speaking to each other in my father's library, but I did hear that much.

Henrietta did not want him to think she had been eavesdropping though that was exactly what she had been doing.

"I am not sure if I am completely ready to believe that," Major Wainwright told her. "He never spoke those words to me, but I somehow can understand him speaking them to someone else."

"He sounded quite sincere," Henrietta told him. Hoping he would believe her. "He asked my father what he should do differently."

"I am not sure what to think. I have spent years not getting along with my father or brother. It is difficult to just set all of that aside now." He shook his head in frustration. "It has even caused me to have words with my mother."

Henrietta felt heartbroken for him. "Major Wainwright, I am sure that your mother will understand a momentary lapse in composure. She is not the only one that has been through much these last few weeks."

"That is true. I have argued with her often enough in the last few days."

"Over what?" Henrietta asked and then immediately realize that she had overstepped her bounds and raised a hand. "Forgive me, Major Wainwright, I did not mean to obtrusive."

"You are not being obtrusive. Your assistance is greatly appreciated." He looked over at her. "You are being quite kind to me. I have not felt that in some time."

Henrietta suddenly understood what may have been troubling him. "Please know that I am always happy to speak with you, as are my brothers. I know Charles trusted you implicitly and I know you will make the right decision, whatever that may be."

CHAPTER NINETEEN

Patrick got up from the desk to look out the window. To his great surprise, he saw that there was light on the horizon. He had stayed up all night thinking about what Lady Henrietta had told him about his father. He did not want to believe, but he did not think that Lady Henrietta would lie to him even to make him feel better. She had nothing to gain by telling him such a story and he could not ignore what she had said.

Once he began to think about the possibility of his father confiding in the Duke of Castborough, Patrick could understand it however slightly. After years of them not getting along, Patrick had quite given up on ever being able to speak with his father civilly. It seems that his father had fallen into the same sort of habit. He was sure that Frederick had only helped to perpetuate the same behaviours that had caused so many of the arguments.

Perhaps if he had not taken the position with the East India Company. He might have been able to… he stopped himself mid thought. It was clear that part of what he enjoyed about his time in India was that no matter what he did, he would do so without the harsh scrutiny of his father and brother. The fact that he enjoyed his work and did it well made it an easy choice when the position was offered to him. He realized that he could do the same as the earl, now sadly.

He had no desire to be the Earl of Ellesmont but he was honour and duty bound to do so. He was proud of his family name and while he cared little for the title, he would do his best to uphold it. Returning to London did not please him although the thought of seeing Lady Henrietta more often cheered him immediately. He suddenly saw an image of he and Henrietta at Ellesmont and he realized that he would be happy to give up his freedom if he could have Lady Henrietta by his side.

Patrick paced the room and then shook his head. "I shall not come to a solution until I sleep."

He left the library and fairly staggered up the stairs, hoping he would have a solution in mind when he awoke later in the morning.

CHAPTER TWENTY

Patrick woke up several hours later feeling refreshed. He dressed as soon as he got up and once again left Denholme Hall to pay a visit to Repington House.

Fletcher had let Patrick in but before he could even be announced, James Repington came into the entry hall smiling.

"Major Wainwright, I am so glad you are here. I was just about to send for you."

Patrick felt himself frown in confusion. "Send for me? Why?"

"Come with me." Repington turned down the hall towards the drawing room.

He was surprised when Repington took him past the closed door and stopped to open a door at the end of the hall. Patrick was even more surprised when he entered the room to the Duke of Castborough awake and sitting up the bed there.

"Your grace, I am so glad to see that you are awake and look so well."

"Thank you, Major." The duke nodded with a brief smile. Then his face turned serious. "I was very sorry to hear about the fate of your father and brother."

"Thank you, Your grace." Patrick had been expecting to speak with Lord Holgrave or possibly with Repington. Speaking with the duke had not even entered his thoughts, and he was suddenly incredibly nervous.

"I am sorry your father did not get to speak with you before the accident. He was very proud of you and was very thankful you were so responsible and independent. It was his opinion that Frederick was lazy and lacked motivation, your father had grown tired of trying to make him take responsibility due him as heir to the title."

Patrick nodded. "I am grateful to hear this from you. Lady Henrietta had said the same, but I was reluctant to believe it. I should have trusted that she would not lie to me for any reason."

The duke nodded at him. "Your father would be immensely proud that you would be the next Earl of Ellesmont. I know you will do a fine job as well."

"Thank you," Patrick told him trying to tamp down the emotion that was welling up.

"If I may, I believe you will be much more happy and successful if you were to have an ally on your side. You need someone strong and caring, someone, that you can trust to always tell you the truth no matter what."

It took Patrick a moment to work out what the duke was trying to say. "Yes, I agree. That is actually the purpose of my visit. I had expected to speak with Lord Holgrave or Repington in order to ask for your blessing. It is complicated I realize and I expect a long courtship first but…"

"You have my blessing," Repington interrupted him. "With no reservations."

"And you have mine as well," the Duke of Castborough told him.

"Again, thank you." Patrick grimaced with nervousness. "I hope Lady Henrietta is as receptive to the idea as you have been."

"I do not believe you need to worry about that," the duke said with an oddly confidant smile.

CHAPTER TWENTY-ONE

Henrietta had been waiting in the drawing room. She heard Major Wainwright arrive, and she was trying to wait patiently while listening intently so that she might talk to him before he left. He had seemed so distraught when she had spoken to him last, she had thought of him often and hoped he had come to believe what she had told him about his father.

She was just starting to contemplate getting up and going to the door when James came into the drawing room.

"Henrietta, please come with me." His words were abrupt, but she did not see his face long enough to see if he was bothered. He went back into the hall almost as quickly as he had entered the room.

Worried she got up and followed him. "Has something happened to Father?"

She was so upset upon entering the room that she almost missed the fact that her father was awake. He was sitting up against several pillows smiling at her.

"Father!" She cried out and rushed to his side. "I am so happy that you are awake. How are you feeling?"

Her father reached out with his left hand, his right still

bandaged. "I am tired and I ache, to be sure. But I am happy to be alive and able to recover."

"I was starting to worry that you would never awake," she confessed to him.

"I know." He winked. "I remember you saying it many times."

"You could hear me? I knew it!" she exclaimed and then realized everything that she had said while she sat next to his bed. She wondered if he remembered all of her conversations.

"I will speak with you later but now I must rest, and you need to go find Major Wainwright."

"What?" She looked at him and then to James who was smiling. "He is still here?"

"Yes, I sent him to the garden to wait for you," her father told her.

"Thank you," she leaned over and kissed him on the cheek. "Rest now. I will come visit you later in the day."

She left the small room and went back down the hall to the library. The door to the garden was still open.

Major Wainwright was standing close by and before she could say anything he turned around.

She gestured back toward the house. "My father has awakened, did you know?"

"I did. I just spoke with him," he said and then seemed to make a decision. "Lady Henrietta, I would like to speak with you."

"Yes, of course." Henrietta could sense he was nervous and wanted to make him feel more comfortable. "Is it all right if we sit?"

Major Wainwright offered her his arm. "I believe I saw a bench under the tree."

"Yes," she answered taking his arm. "Were you able to come to a decision?"

"It is why I am here," he said once they had sat down. "I was very apprehensive accepting the title given the relationship between my father and myself. I know I must take the title and the responsibility though."

"Your father would be quite proud of you." Henrietta nodded with a bit of reverence.

He shifted on the bench to face her. "I realized that I can only imagine staying in London if you agree to be by my side. You are the only person in my life who believed in me, just me. Not as the son of the Earl of Ellesmont, not as a soldier on the Peninsula."

Henrietta could hardly believe what she was hearing. She was so overjoyed. "Of course, I believe in you. Certainly, I do."

"I would like to court you, before any announcement is made. I am not expecting you to feel the same as I do, but you need to know that I care for you very much."

"I…" she started, wanting to tell him so much about how she felt and yet he would not seem to let her.

"I know this is sudden but…"

"Yes!" she blurted out.

"What? Yes? Yes to what?" He was so confused.

"Yes, I will marry you! I have cared for you for such a very long time. I did not think you would ever see for me, Henrietta instead of Lady Henrietta or Charles' younger sister."

"Yes?" he repeated his look of shock turning into a smile.

She nodded at him, she could not stop smiling. "I am in agreement that we shall court for a certain amount of time while you are still in mourning."

He stood up and in his jubilation, he picked her up and twirled her around before setting her gently down once more. "We shall be so very happy."

"Shall be? I am so very happy right now, Patrick." Her joy spilled over and she was unable to contain herself.

"Say it again. Please?"

"I am so very happy?"

"No, my name," he said softly leaning towards her.

She looked up at him. "Patrick."

He had the sweetest smile on his face when he said, "I love hearing my name on your lips."

"I love you, Patrick." Henrietta could not stop herself from telling him.

He surprised her by saying, "And I love you, Henrietta. It means the world to hear you say it to me. I never thought I would be in your favour."

"Oh, Patrick. You are most definitely in my favour. Indeed." She laughed quietly and shook her head, not believing where the day had taken her.

She leaned into him and he dropped a kiss onto her cheek. "Shall we go tell your father?"

Henrietta laughed. "If I know my father, he already knows."

JOIN KELLY ANNE BRUCE'S READERS GROUP

If you want to stay up to date on new releases and get notifications about sales and other fun stuff, join Kelly Anne's Readers Group. You might even get a freebie or two!

http://kellyannebruce.com/join-the-readers-group/

ALSO BY KELLY ANNE BRUCE

Want to find more sweet and clean Regency romance stories from Kelly Anne?

The Jilted Earl

The Duke's Heart

Their Second Chance

The Duke's Big Surprise

Find all Kelly Anne's books on her Amazon Author Page!

http://amzn.to/2daUf2L

ABOUT KELLY ANNE BRUCE

Kelly Anne Bruce has loved the Regency era of English culture since her teenage years. The country estates, London city happenings, and lovely wardrobes are part of the allure.

But the people of that time are what draws Kelly in. The hierarchy in society is fascinating. A sense of pride in who they are and where they come from matters even if the person isn't from nobility. Their concern over propriety while behaving less than properly gives plenty of opportunities to tell a tale.

Kelly Anne is an American, married to an Englishman. They live in Cambridge, which happens to be her favourite city in England. Their two cats and a dog run the household remarkably well!

Facebook
   https://www.facebook.com/AuthorKellyAnneBruce/

Amazon
   http://amzn.to/2ozVNs7

Website
   http://www.KellyAnneBruce.com

SWEET RIVER PUBLISHING

Sweet River Publishing is dedicated to sweet and clean stories. Our authors write wholesome and inspiring stories to make our readers feel good, encouraged, and happy. They strive to write entertaining stories you'll enjoy immensely.

These stories are suitable for all ages!

If you'd like to hear about new releases, special prices, and other good news about our authors, you can join the group to be part of the fun.

http://www.subscribepage.com/fromfb

www.sweetriverpublishing.com

Printed in Great Britain
by Amazon